THE TWO-SPACE WAR

BAEN BOOKS by LEO FRANKOWSKI

A Boy and His Tank
The War with Earth (with Dave Grossman)
Kren of the Mitchegai (with Dave Grossman, forthcoming)

The Two-Space War (with Dave Grossman)

The Fata Morgana

Conrad's Time Machine

[redacted]

THE TWO-SPACE WAR

DAVE GROSSMAN
LEO FRANKOWSKI

[redacted]

THE TWO-SPACE WAR

A Baen Books Original

Baen Publishing Enterprises
P.O. Box 1403
Riverdale, NY 10471
www.baen.com

ISBN: 0-7434-7188-1

Cover art by Tom Kidd
Interior illustrations by Elyse A. Ruskey (designed by Dave Grossman)

First printing, February 2004

Library of Congress Cataloging-in-Publication Data

Grossman, Dave.
The Two-Space war / by Dave Grossman & Leo Frankowski.
p. cm.
ISBN 0-7434-7188-1
1. Interplanetary voyages—Fiction. 2. Space warfare—Fiction. 3. Space ships—Fiction. I. Frankowski, Leo, 1943- II. Title.

PS3557.R6717T88 2004
813'.54—dc22

2003022163

Distributed by Simon & Schuster
1230 Avenue of the Americas
New York, NY 10020

Production by Windhaven Press, Auburn, NH
Printed in the United States of America

10 9 8 7 6 5 4 3 2 1

CALIPH: Ah, if there shall ever arise a nation whose people have forgotten poetry or whose poets have forgotten the people, though they send their ships round Taprobane and their armies across the hills of Hindustan, though their city be greater than Babylon of old, though they mine a league into earth or mount to the stars on wings—what of them?

HASSAN: They will be a dark patch upon the world.

Quoted in *Other Men's Flowers*
by Field Marshall Earl A.P. Wavell

On Warriors and Warrior Scientists

My "day job" is to be on the road, almost 300 days a year, training soldiers (the Green Berets, the Rangers, the USMC, etc.) and cops (the FBI, the ATF, the CHP, the RCMP, etc.) about the psychology and physiology of combat. It's a *great* job. I teach them and then they teach me, in an endless, ever refining feedback loop. I can never thank them enough for putting it on the line for us, every day, and for sharing their experiences with me. You can get a better feel for what I do, and take a look at some of my scholarly writings on these topics, on my web site: www.killology.com, or my books, *On Killing* and *On Combat.*

I need to thank my fellow "warrior scientists." The concept of *science* fiction has usually involved the integration of *science*, or projected science, into fiction. This is the first book to integrate the new field of "warrior science" into fiction. The characters in my book cite real "twenty-first century" researchers such as Alexis Artwohl, coauthor of *Deadly Force Encounters*, and Bruce Siddle, the man who coined the term "warrior science" and the author of *Sharpening the Warrior's Edge*. I sincerely believe that hundreds of years from now these pioneer friends of mine will be remembered and cited.

The combat experiences of my characters are based upon the latest research, on what I'm teaching, *and* on what those who have been there have taught me. Any errors are my own!

On Poetry and Science Fiction

If not otherwise indicated, the titles and authors of the poetry used throughout the book are listed at the end. Lord Wavell and his book, *Other Men's Flowers*, deserve special mention. Wavell was the commander of the British Empire's armed forces in World War II. After the war he put all the poems that he had committed to memory (that's right, *to memory*) in a book. Wavell, perhaps the last of the great "warrior poets," is one of the models for my hero, Lieutenant Melville.

I've tried to craft a world in which deep respect, even veneration for poetry could exist, but in reality there's no need to make up such a world. Throughout history, from Homer through Lord Wavell, warriors existed in that world. In an environment such as two-space, where technology can't exist, the power of well crafted words would again be the key to men's hearts. The leader who masters such words would have a powerful edge in mastering his men.

I also wanted to construct a world in which science fiction would be the primary literature to survive from our era. The creators of SF are "pure poetry" to my soul, giants on whose shoulders I stand.

On Poets

But most of all I thank the poets who have gone before me. The poets of words and the poets of bullets, blows and swords. They wrote down their poems, or their narratives of combat, or they allowed me to interview them. They made it possible for me (as Lord Wavell puts it, quoting Montaigne) to build a garden "of other men's flowers."

When you read these poems, I encourage you to read them aloud. Or, if you're in a public place, at least mumble them quietly! For poetry was meant to be spoken, not read, and you lose half the joy if you don't let these words, these ancient, powerful words, roll off your tongue and o'er your lips.

Hopefully the words in between the poetry will give you some small measure of pleasure as well.

And Finally

To Leo Frankowski, a great partner and true gentleman, friend, and scholar of the old school. To our publisher, Jim Baen, who has proven himself to be a good friend and a man of vision. To my faithful and true friends and proofreaders: Rocky Warren, Steel Parsons, John Lang, Elantu, CC, and many others.

Most of all, to my princess and favorite proofreader, my Jeanne. In Beethoven's words, "From the heart it has come, to the heart it shall go."

Hooah!

Dave Grossman

The Crew
of Her Majesty, the Queen of Westerness'
24-Pounder Frigate, *Fang*

Lt. Thomas Melville, Captain
McAndrews, his steward
Ulrich, his coxswain, "cox'in"
Archibald Hargis, his clerk

Lt. Daniel Fielder, First Officer

Lady Elphinstone, Ship's surgeon, a Sylvan
Mrs. Vodi, her "lob-lolly girl"
Pete Etzen, a corpsman (medic), "Doc"
Thadeaus Brun, a corpsman (medic), "Doc"

Brother Theo Petreckski, Ship's purser, a monk

Mr. Caleb Tibbits, Ship's carpenter, "Chips"

Mr. Darren Barlet, Ship's master gunner, "Guns"
Sgt. Don Von Rito, Ship's gunnery sergeant, "Gunny"

Chief Petty Officer Bronson Hans, "Chief." Later "Mr."
and Ship's sailing master

Marines
Sgt. Broadax, a Dwarrowdelf. Later "Lt."
Cpl. Kobbsven
Private Harold Jarvis

Rangers
Josiah Westminster
Aubrey Valandil, a Sylvan

Midshipmen
Jarad Crater. Later "Lt."
Buckley Archer. Later "Lt."
Garth Aquinar
Faisal, Chang, Hezikiah Jubal, Lao Tung, Kande Ngobe, and Ellis Palmer

Ship's Dogs
Ship's Cats
The Monkeys

"FANG"
24-Pounder Frigate

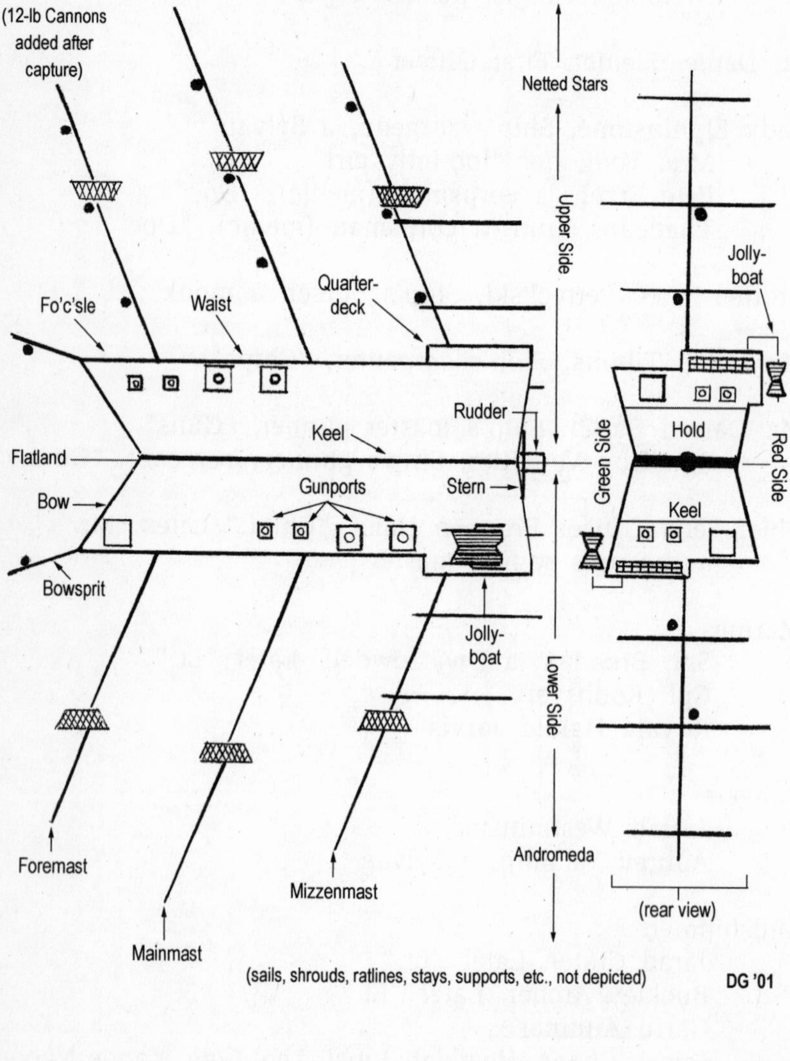

(12-lb Cannons added after capture)
Netted Stars
Upper Side
Jolly-boat
Quarter-deck
Fo'c'sle
Waist
Rudder
Hold
Keel
Red Side
Green Side
Flatland
Gunports
Stern
Bow
Keel
Bowsprit
Jolly-boat
Lower Side
Andromeda
Foremast
Mizzenmast
Mainmast
(rear view)
(sails, shrouds, ratlines, stays, supports, etc., not depicted)
DG '01

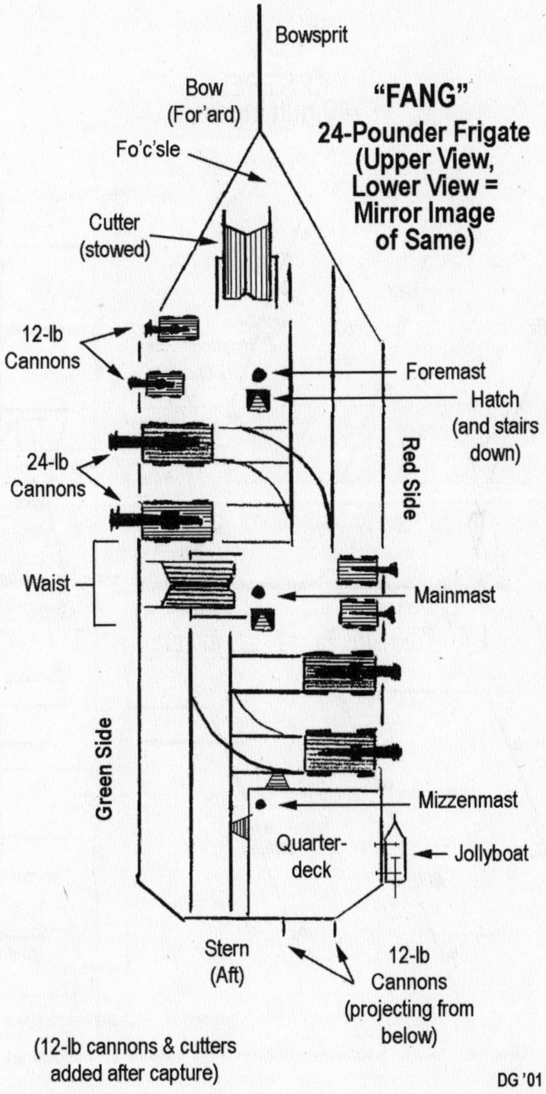
Bowsprit
"FANG"
24-Pounder Frigate
(Upper View,
Lower View =
Mirror Image
of Same)
Bow
(For'ard)
Fo'c'sle
Cutter
(stowed)
12-lb
Cannons
Foremast
Hatch
(and stairs
down)
24-lb
Cannons
Red Side
Waist
Mainmast
Green Side
Mizzenmast
Quarter-
deck
Jollyboat
Stern
(Aft)
12-lb
Cannons
(projecting from
below)
(12-lb cannons & cutters
added after capture)
DG '01

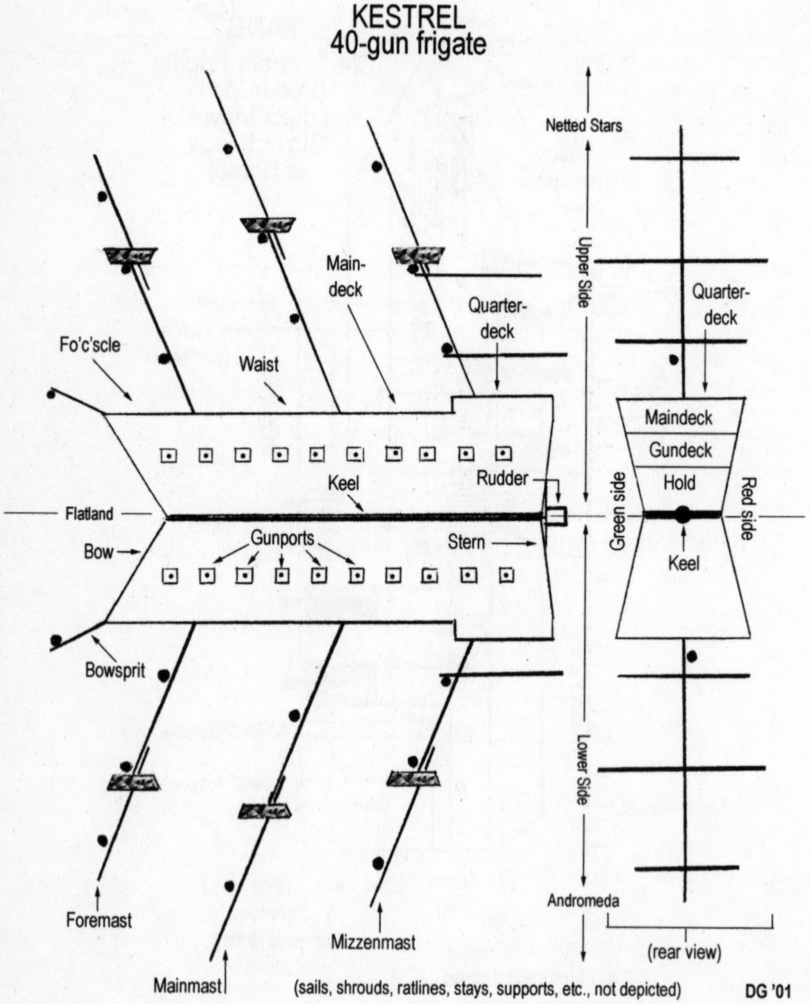

KESTREL
40-gun frigate
Netted Stars
Upper Side
Main-
deck
Quarter-
deck
Quarter-
deck
Fo'c'scle
Waist
Maindeck
Gundeck
Hold
Keel
Rudder
Flatland
Green side
Red side
Bow
Gunports
Stern
Keel
Bowsprit
Lower Side
Foremast
Mizzenmast
Andromeda
(rear view)
Mainmast
(sails, shrouds, ratlines, stays, supports, etc., not depicted)
DG '01

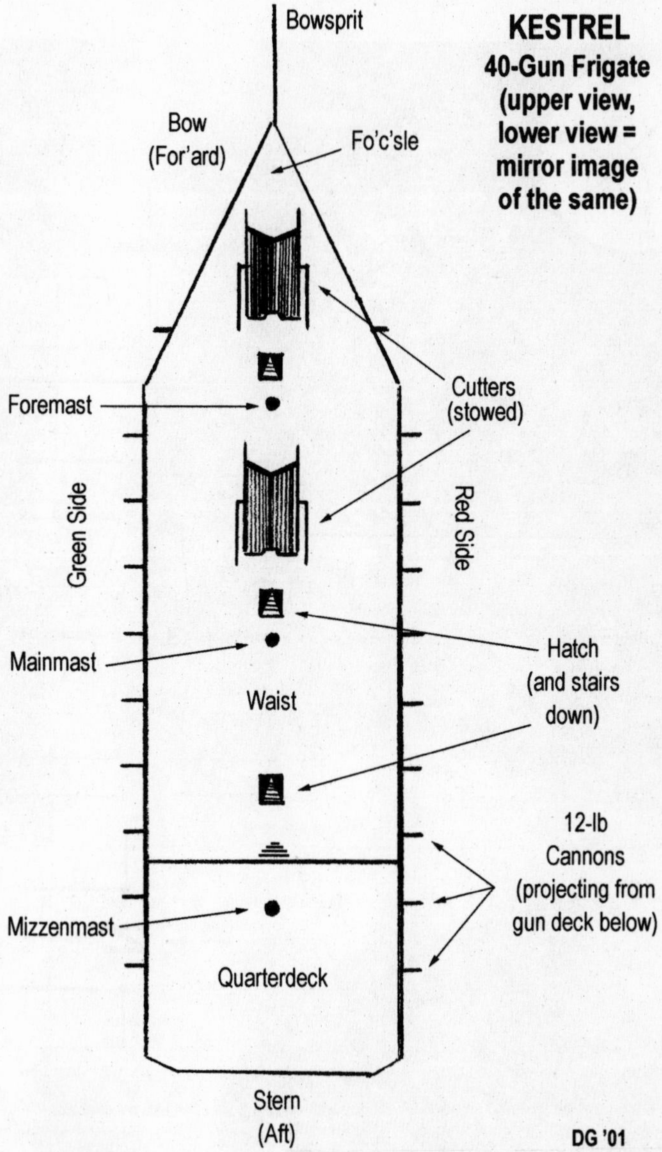

KESTREL
40-Gun Frigate
(upper view,
lower view =
mirror image
of the same)
Bowsprit
Bow
(For'ard)
Fo'c'sle
Cutters
(stowed)
Foremast
Green Side
Red Side
Mainmast
Hatch
(and stairs
down)
Waist
12-lb
Cannons
(projecting from
gun deck below)
Mizzenmast
Quarterdeck
Stern
(Aft)
DG '01

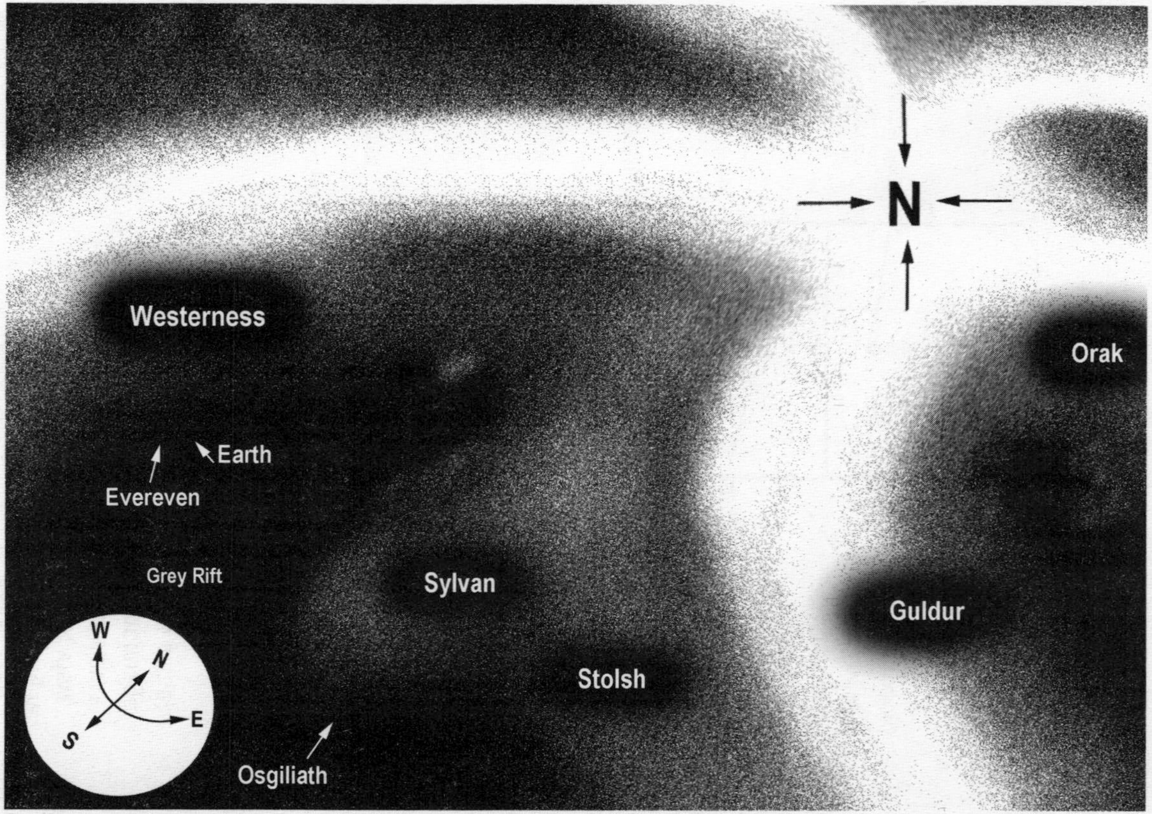
N
Westerness
Orak
Earth
Evereven
Grey Rift
Sylvan
Guldur
Stolsh
W
N
E
S
Osgiliath

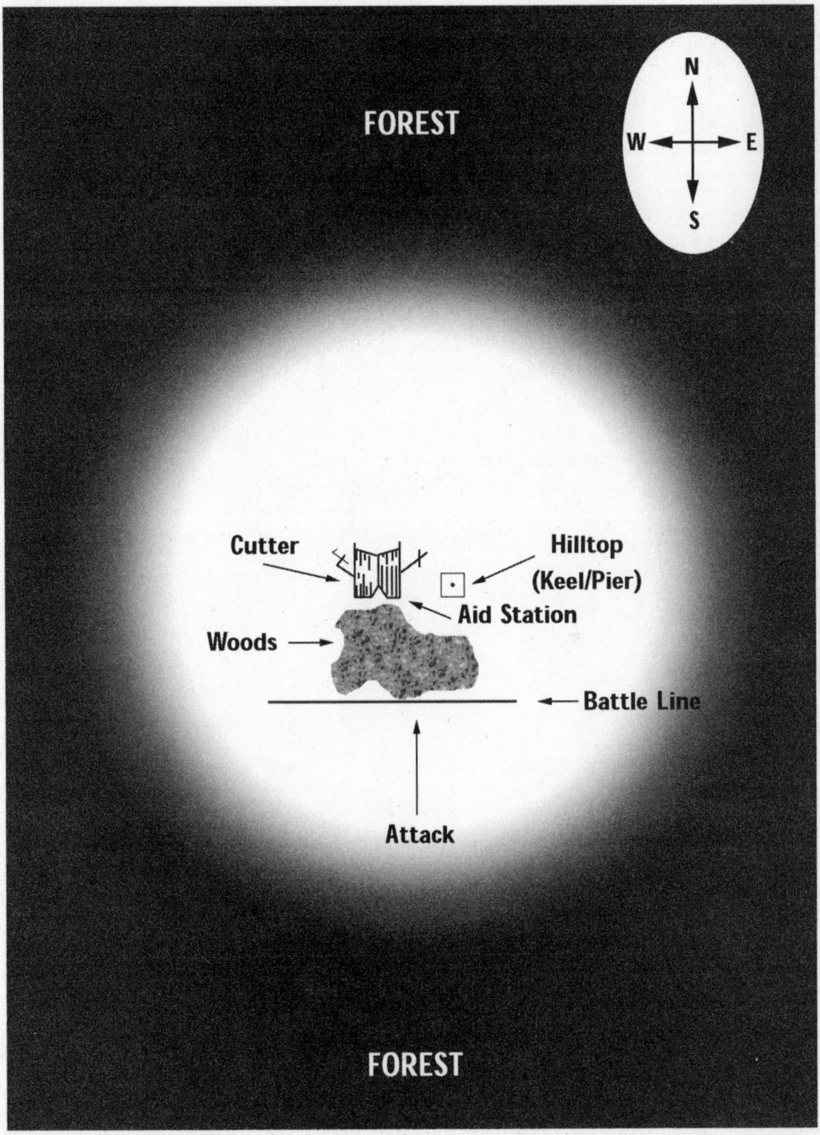
FOREST
N
W
E
S
Cutter
Hilltop
(Keel/Pier)
Aid Station
Woods
Battle Line
Attack
FOREST

Chapter the 1st

A Race of Rangers

They were the glory of the race of rangers,
Matchless with horse, rifle, song, supper, courtship,
Large, turbulent, generous, handsome, proud, and
affectionate,
Bearded, sunburnt, drest in the free costume of
hunters . . .

Retreating they form'd in a hollow square with
their baggage for breastworks,
Nine hundred lives out of the surrounding enemy's,
nine times
Their number, was the price they took in
advance . . .

"Song of Myself"
Walt Whitman

"What *does* that boy think he's doing?" muttered Lieutenant Thomas Melville. He sat on the Pier in the oppressive heat of mid-afternoon. He'd received only one wound in their recent battle, an ignominious clawing of his right buttock. Not too deep, but sufficient to make him sit carefully. Spread before him was the emerald shade of the copse of huge trees they'd fought so hard to defend. Exhausted and spent from desperate battle, he watched little Midshipman Aquinar as he crawled into the white bones of their beached cutter.

He looked out on the vast expanse of forest that encompassed their hill. Reaching up and behind him he put a hand on the Keel of his Ship, which now formed the Pier. <<Funny, we know nothing about this world, except what we can see from here, or what our scouts tell us. We're like some old sailors. Like Columbus, making first landfall on a new continent. All we could tell from two-space was that it was a green world, and would probably support life. Then we had to crash, like some sailing ship smashing itself on a reef to enter into a new land. Now you, my friend, my old Ship, are the link, the Pier across that reef.>>

<<Yep, yep.>> Answered *Swish-tail*, <<I'm there, and I'm here!>>

Through this strange, telepathic link with his faithful Ship, Melville "heard" these words, but they came with a great weight of context and additional information that was subtly communicated, so that Melville knew exactly what *Swish-tail* meant. The Keel of his little ship now disappeared up into two-space, into Flatland, forming a link between the two realms. It was here, and there.

<<Funny, in the old, classic science fiction novels they were always talking about going into the fourth or fifth dimensions to go between planets. Ha! Things just get further apart when you add dimensions. I wonder why none of them thought about going the other way, into the second dimension. Into Flatland. A book called *Flatland* was one of the very earliest science fiction novels, dating all the way back to the nineteenth century. It seems so simple, really. Just pop into two-space where things are so much closer together, sail to where you want to go, and pop back out. The problem is that instead of orbiting around a world, looking at it from outer space, in Flatland all you see is this big green and blue blob that you sail into. Just like seeing green shores on the other side of the reef. Unfortunately, you have to crash your ship to get across the reef, and you have no idea what's waiting for you.>>

<<Yep, yep. Came down with a crash!>>

Melville thought back, <<This world could work you know. We were supposed to find an unclaimed world on the frontier between the Guldur and Stolsh empires. This was a historical first, a cooperative effort with the prominent Sylvan world of Osgil. A trading base right between Guldur and Stolsh would have really paid off for us and the Sylvans. Still might, if only *Kestrel* would come back for us. Do you really think she's still out there?>>

<<Think so . . . Feel her there . . . >>

<<But we had to wreck you to get here.>> Melville added, looking sadly at his old command, his little cutter, lying on its side next to the copse of trees that topped this hill. <<Do you regret it?>>

<<Nope. Is good world.>>

Still, it was sad. Was there anything in the universe quite so sad as a beached sailing ship? Especially a Ship of two-space, looking like two old-time wooden sailing ships joined at the waterline, with masts protruding out from both top and bottom. They were majestic and grand, with their sails spread as they sped from star to star, across the shoreless seas of Flatland. But even a one-masted cutter like his lively little *Swish-tail* was pathetic and sad the instant you cut the contacts to the Keel and beached it in three-space.

Immediately after their crash landing, Melville and his small crew pulled out the precious Keel and lovingly planted it in the living earth like a mast, or a flagpole at the top of the hill. The rest of Melville's company came down the Keel from the *Kestrel* and their mothership left them, never to return. Or at least not yet.

Many of the pure white Nimbrell timbers were stripped from *Swish-tail*'s hull to form a platform around the Keel, which now became a Pier. Melville was here to "talk" with *Swish-tail* after their battle. She was his friend, and a commander needed someone outside the chain of command to visit with. She seemed to be happy there, planted in the living earth. A Ship died and a world was born. Soon, she would merge with this world, becoming its gateway to Two-Space.

They paused in companionable silence as Melville leaned back against the Keel and watched little Midshipman Aquinar make another trip from the bowels of the old cutter. Again he reached lovingly up and put a hand on the white Moss coating the Keel and asked, <<What *does* that boy think he's doing? Usually our

midshipmen and ship's boys are only interested in food and sleep. "Nasty, brutish, and short," that's them. So what's *this* all about?>>

Early in their forays into Flatland, humans had discovered the remarkable white fungus they'd named Lady Elbereth's Gift or Elbereth Moss. Like everything in Two-Space, Elbereth Moss existed only in two dimensions. But it was also capable of growing on the portion of a Pier that extended into normal, three-dimensional space, like the encrusted sea creatures on the pilings of a dock at low tide.

In two-space it just appeared, like a fungus, adhering to and eventually coating Nimbrell wood and Keels in two-space. It was white and impossibly thin. It also provided oxygen and light. Most of all, across time, it became sentient, giving life to the white Ships of two-space. The men of Westerness communicated their awe and respect by making proper nouns out of terms like Keel, Pier, and Ship, when referring to a sentient life-form.

Melville *felt* the Ship respond to his idle question. <<Good boy. Trust him.>>

But he wasn't really thinking about the boy. Melville was thinking about *Kestrel,* their mothership. Wondering if it would ever return to take them home to Westerness and Evereven, where "softly silver fountains fall." Most of all, at this moment, Melville wondered if he would ever again take a long cold drink of water. To distract himself from his thirst and exhaustion, he watched the boy's trips with detached bemusement. The little barefoot midshipman had taken off his blue jacket, and was dressed now in a dirty white shirt and sailcloth trousers, like some crawling worm or moth flitting back and forth.

This was the boy's fourth journey. He couldn't be after the water barrel; the tap to the barrel was on the other end, and the area where the little midshipman was crawling was considerably lower than that.

Each time, Aquinar crawled over the bodies of the creatures they had just killed, cut down in windrows, with rifled musket, pistol and sword, as their little company defended the tiny perimeter. This was Melville's miniature world. A grove of trees with their precious shade atop a grassy hill, the bones of their cutter with its precious water barrel, and the Pier where he sat.

Within the bowels of the cutter, and spread out on the west side, the far side from the little midshipman's approach, was the aid station. Here, under the shade of sailcloth tarps, were many marines and sailors, and one dog, all seriously wounded in their recent battle. They were tended by Lady Elphinstone, their Sylvan surgeon. She'd been attached to their ship as a part of this cooperative effort between Westerness and Osgil. She was fair of face, with her golden hair pulled back behind her head in a bun. She wore a buttercup yellow gown, with a grass green sash about her waist. Both were now stained and smeared with the leaking lifeblood of many men. The surgeon was assisted by Petreckski, their monkish purser, his brown robe well concealing the blood of their wounded. Their two buckskin-clad rangers, bone weary after their long chase and fierce battle, were also contributing their extensive healing skills.

Deep in the shade of the trees were their dead. Six men, two ship's dogs, and one cat were lovingly laid out under careful guard, lest their bodies be defiled by local creatures. They rested amidst the trees they'd died to defend. Soon they would be buried there.

Melville had no idea what the boy thought he was doing, going back and forth from the bowels of their cutter to the depths of the woods. But he knew just exactly what these dead aliens were doing here.

Several of the strange, six-legged, dingy white "apes" had died up here on the Pier as they tried to work their way around the left flank. There was one close to him. Close enough to prod with his foot.

In books, the writers often talk of people voiding their bowels when they die. You could get the impression from these gritty, realistic writers that this always happened. But the truth was that it only happened if you had a "load" in the lower intestines. Thus, Melville could tell which creatures had fed well last night, and which hadn't. This fellow, with the local equivalent of flies crawling in and out of his mouth and across the facets of his compound eyes, had eaten very well last night.

The mouth was located at the top of the creature's skull, the vertical nose slits below that, and the compound eyes were low in the skull. Except for when the head launched forward on its accordion neck (mouth first, teeth first, in violent attack), it remained nestled back into the creature's . . . chest? . . . thorax? The end result was that the mouth (a very respectable mouth, full of very nasty and creditable teeth) was at the top of the skull, with the compound eyes protected, barely peeking out from where they crouched in the chest cavity. Now, relaxed in death, the head protruded from the body and the ape's eyes seemed to look reproachfully up at him, ignoring the intruding flies.

> An orphan's curse would drag to hell
> A spirit from on high;
> But oh! more horrible than that
> Is the curse in a dead man's eye!

Well, this was no "man" thought Melville, it probably wasn't even sentient, but it was a living creature that he'd helped to kill. "Your fault," he muttered, looking his accuser in the eye. "Don't blame me. You were the ones that had to go and attack *us*, with all that howling and screeching. What did you expect?"

<<Bad monkey!>> added *Swish-tail,* <<Bad!>>

<<It's a dead monkey! That makes it a good monkey!>> replied Melville, jokingly, prodding it again with his foot.

<<Ha! Yup!>> replied the little Ship, getting into the spirit of their grim little jest. <<Good monkey. Goood Monkey.>>

The thing that the "realistic, gritty" genre of writers generally *didn't* write about was the fact that, in the intensity of battle, many of the *living* combatants *also* voided their bowels. Again, it generally happened to those with a "load" in the lower intestines.

All energy was redirected toward survival. "We need more power, Captain! Bladder control? I don't *think* so. Sphincter control? *We don't need no stinking sphincter control!* Ye laddies get that energy down in the legs where we *need* it!"

And, as usual after battle, when the normal postcombat nausea set in, several of the young ones lost their breakfast as well.

It was going to be hard to clean up the mess, living and dead, with barely enough water to keep them alive for another few weeks. There was plenty of ships biscuit, salt pork and dried peas, but precious, precious little water.

They had been digging a well into the hill ever since their arrival. After all, if the trees were alive, they must be getting water from somewhere. They were down a hundred feet and still going through dry dirt, the walls shored up with logs.

Melville smelled the reek from his own troops and looked out at the stinking heaps of their dead attackers. How *were* they going to clean up this filth, and return things to shipshape navy fashion? Somehow the books never talked about *this. Did I miss a class at the academy?*

Actually, on his first day at the academy they told him this might happen. "Adventure," they called it. "A rendezvous with destiny."

Captain (retired) Ben James, Dean of the Department of History had lectured them on their first day. Five foot, eight inches tall, well over two hundred pounds, he looked like he would tire just combing his hair, deadly only with a red pencil . . . until you got a look at the ribbons on his dress uniform, and then you learned to pay attention to him. He was indeed a history professor full of surprises.

"Cadets," he began, looking at them with steely intensity, "you are on the first day of an adventure that, if you stick with it, will ultimately see you in command of ships sailing the shoreless seas of two-space. When you enter into two-space, you'll truly understand why our culture and society is the way it is.

"Most of you are from here on Westerness, and have never even traveled in two-space, or 'Flatland' as it's often called." Young cadet Melville puffed up his chest and felt very superior upon hearing this. *He* had served for several years as a ship's boy before being selected for the academy. On his first day at the academy he was happy to embrace any comforting source of superiority.

"In this strange environment any complex or advanced technology can't exist. What builds and prospers our empire are wooden ships . . . and iron men. We depend on the relatively crude technology of our ships, similar to eighteenth-century Napoleonic-era sailing ships. Even simple block-and-tackle pulleys tend to decay quickly, and there is no need for jibs or stay sails, so the rigging is very simple.

"Even simple weapons technology, such as muzzle-loading muskets, require daily maintenance in this environment. Thus we are back to Napoleonic-era weapons. Namely cannons, swords, rifled muskets, and bayonets.

"But never forget that you are warriors, and the most formidable weapon in two-space lies between one's ears! 'This is the law: The purpose of fighting is to win. There is no possible victory in defense. The sword is more important than the shield and skill is more important than either. The final weapon is the brain. All else is supplemental.' So says Steinbeck, and *so . . . say . . . I.*"

Melville was sitting, reflecting on all the advantages his prior service would give him here at the academy. Visions of academic glory were unfolding before him when Captain James brought him crashing back down to earth.

He was just envisioning himself as the Brigade Captain in his fourth year when Captain James singled him out, "Mr. Melville . . ." Boom. His heart began to pound in his chest and all eyes were suddenly on him. The cunning old sea dog knew when someone wasn't paying attention, and he wasn't about to tolerate it. "When did our ancestors make the first landing on Westerness?"

Okay, this was easy. This was the year 422, and the years were tracked from the founding of Westerness. "Four hundred and twenty-two years ago, sir!"

A disappointed sigh and condescending look came from his tormenter. "Wrong, Mr. Melville. I thought you had some prior experience with the Navy. Didn't you ever get around to learning that in the Navy we track all dates by Earth years? You, of all people should have known that. Gig yourself. Ten demerits."

Oh good. Just great. The very first demerits handed out, and they were to him, "mister prior service." For a few seconds there was a roaring in his ears and tunnel vision shut out everything but his tormentor's face. But he never again made the mistake of not paying attention to Captain James, and he vividly remembered every word the crusty old sailor said that day.

"I want you never to forget that mankind made it into two-space on its own, without the aid of any foreign planet and with our own science and technology, in 2104. However, we were a while learning how to survive in that strange environment.

"When that great innovator and researcher, Kenny Muraray, created the first Pier, he was amazed to see it disappear up into nothing. Like Aladdin's rope or Jacob's ladder. Perhaps it had happened before, perhaps this is the source of these legends. Soon, Moss grew on the Keel and they went up and studied two-space.

"Westerness was colonized by the men of Old Earth, four hundred eighteen Earth years ago, in the year 2210. This was almost a century after mankind's first, disastrous entry into Flatland, when the computers came back from the two-space with the Elder King's Gift. This was a devastating virus that brought about the Crash, a complete and irrecoverable collapse of their worldwide Info-Net.

But still the Pier was there, and those early pioneers went from the equivalent of the dugout canoe to the mighty frigates of today in just a few centuries.

"Over the following centuries the vast majority of human colonies emanated from Westerness, with our vast, ancient forests of Nimbrell trees. Earth's high technology couldn't be exported across two-space. Since no technology can exist in Flatland, technology can't be transported between worlds. A computer program, printed out on paper, can be a full cargo for a ship—and that's the only way such a program can be moved between worlds! Indeed, any bio-technology, nano-technology, gene manipulation, or artificial organs in a body will result in a rapid, horrible death if brought into Flatland. On major, starfaring worlds there is little need for technology beyond Victorian levels, so we simply don't bother with it.

"On a few high-tech worlds, like Earth, the citizens have decided to embrace nano- and bio-technology, which gives them long lives. But the price they pay is that they can't travel beyond their world! The poor, poor bastards are trapped on their world. They gained a few extra decades of life in their old age, but they lost the universe." He said that with such sincere sadness, disgust and disdain that the cadets couldn't help but be influenced.

"On Earth, only the very young, at great risk, will dare to travel off-world. The result is that within two hundred years of our colonization they lost control of their empire. Westerness, supported by other low-tech, retroculture worlds, took over. Gentlemen, we . . . are . . . determined *not* to let that happen to us," he said with a pointed finger and intense fierceness.

"Since the demands of maintaining a two-space empire drives our train, and since the allure of high tech can destroy our empire, as happened to Earth, we *chose* to stay at a basic technological level. 'Retroculture' is the name for what we've done, a term first coined by a man named Bill Lind in the late twentieth century, when the backlash against their toxic modern culture began to spontaneously spawn organizations like the Society for Creative Anachronism, the 'Victorian' craze in women's culture, the antiques craze, old house renovations, and Renaissance festivals. The result is that today we live in a hodgepodge of Georgian, Victorian, and Edwardian technology. That is, generally the eighteenth, nineteenth, and early twentieth centuries.

The homes and communities of sailors, those ultimate conservatives, are some of the most dogmatic about keeping low tech."

Then the old sailor's face smiled gently and lovingly. "In the Navy this is reinforced by our veneration of Tolkien's *Lord of the Rings*, and the extensive biographies of great sailors such as Horatio Hornblower and Jack Aubrey."

Suddenly glowering out at them from beneath his bushy eyebrows he added, "And, I will say *right* now, that I won't tolerate any young wiseacre who wants to espouse the errant belief that the narratives of these great sailors, who have been such an inspiration to us, were actually fiction."

Having made his point, he relaxed and continued. "Thus we live in a world of intentional, creative anachronism. We've established a true retroculture, reaching back into our past to build the best community we can. The people of Earth, when they deign to come off their planet, sometimes refer to us as 'Hokas.' It's quite appropriate to challenge them to a duel and to kill them without mercy or pity for such an insult." Suddenly the steel in this seemingly roly-poly old navy officer was coming through in his voice. "As though any earthworm would risk his sad, dull, centuries-long life by participating in a duel. Thus social ostracism is the only acceptable response if no duel or abject apology is forthcoming." The cadets in the classroom found themselves leaning back in their seats as they looked into the feral eyes of a man who had meted out death in duels and combat.

"Because, you see gentlemen, we are not 'Hokas,' we are the Kingdom of Westerness. Our culture and our values now rule one of the greatest empires in the galaxy, while their values and their decaying culture sit festering and rotting on one lonely, sick old world.

"But, do you see? It is the nature and demands of two-space, which most citizens will never see, that makes our culture the way it is. And keeps it there across the centuries. *Most* citizens will never see two-space, but *you*, you gentlemen, will travel in that mystical realm.

"And the most amazing thing of all about that realm is what we found when we finally got there." Here the old sea captain's voice grew low. He leaned forward and rested his hands on the front desk. His eyes, his voice, his whole body communicated wonder and reverence. "Others had already been there. Somewhere in the primordial past some ancient, Ur-civilization appears to have seeded much of the galaxy with genetically similar stock. Other races were there before us for centuries, even millennia. Sailing the seas of Flatland, moving from world to world in wooden Ships, we found the fair elves who live high up in the vast trees of low gravity worlds, and the doughty, stouthearted dwarfs who mine deep into high gravity worlds.

"There are even orcs and ogres! And wolves, complete with goblin riders. All can be found out in the vast galaxy. There are even legends of a silicon-based troll-like life-form! And so gentlemen, *today you begin your rendezvous with destiny*, in a universe filled with exotic creatures, wooden sailing ships, elves, dwarfs, and *adventure*! What was for centuries, nay millennia, our wildest fantasies will become your reality!

"Now, polite folk speak of Sylvan and Dwarrowdelf rather than elves and dwarfs, because, quite frankly, we are uncomfortable talking about it. Our feeling toward this whole matter has, as one writer put it, 'almost a religious nature, like the favor of some god . . . to be treated with great respect, rarely named, referred to by allusion or alias, never explained.'

"Even the Sylvan and Dwarrowdelf themselves have embraced Tolkien as a fascinating form of semi-prophecy. Tolkien always did insist that the power of his work was in its "applicability" not its allegory, and now the applicability of his writing has come to have a form of widespread cultural influence very much like the Bible, but more secular and perhaps even broader in its impact. Yet they too are uncomfortable talking about it. Just as the Greek culture and language was embraced by the conquering Romans, so has our culture and language become the *lingua franca* for the elder races, and our literature, especially Tolkien, was key to that.

"Gentlemen, we may actually be looking at literal telepathic quality possessed by some of the most 'prophetic' earthworm authors. It's truly remarkable to observe how many modern-day, high-tech marvels have their antecedents in fable. Scrying glasses, flying carpets, telephones, they're all there. Almost makes you wonder. Though personally I believe we are looking at a case of parallel evolution. Fantasy makes our dreams and nightmares real. So does technology."

Huh? thought Melville. *Is this old geezer completely nuts?*

Well, Melville had thought so at the time, but now here he was, stranded on a distant planet with a mad dwarven marine sergeant, a monkish purser, a beautiful elven surgeon, and a crew of stranded sailors, surrounded by dead aliens. *And* a pair of rangers who seemed to think they were Strider and Legolas, bringing the hosts of Mordor along behind them. "Ha!" he muttered, "'rendezvous with destiny,' my bleeding arse."

<<Yep, yep!>>

Their attackers had first appeared in close pursuit of his two rangers, Josiah Westminster and Aubrey Valandil, as they returned, posthaste, from an extended foray downslope. They were looking for water. Instead they found company and brought them home for lunch.

Their gunshots, louder and louder as they drew near, heralded their return and marked their running battle through the woods for nearly a full turn of the glass. The entire company stood ready as the two buckskin-clad rangers burst from the emerald green tree line and began to race up the slope, their two dogs loping along at their heels, framed by the mouse gray trunks of two huge trees.

From his position on the military crest of the hill, Melville could look south at an endless sea of forest. How it stayed green in this arid land was a subject of discussion. Probably deep roots that reached into the water table. The thickly wooded forest ended abruptly around the hill, to form a bald knob covered with golden stubble, with a little clump of trees just below the crest on this south slope.

The exits from Flatland into living worlds usually came up on high ground. High ground which they now must defend or die.

Valandil was a Sylvan, and along with their surgeon he represented his species' contribution to this first cooperative endeavor between the Sylvans and the Kingdom of Westerness. He was from Osgil itself, the oldest and greatest of the low-gee, heavily forested worlds that they loved. This world felt close to a standard Earth gravity, but even in a full gee the Sylvan ranger's long strides carried him with the effortless grace of his race. He was slender and fair of face with his blond hair flowing behind him.

Josiah was Westerness born and bred. "Large, turbulent, generous, handsome, proud, and affectionate," indeed. He was also broad shouldered, dark haired with a thick black mustache, and deeply tanned by a lifetime of experience under distant suns. His strides almost matched Valandil's as they loped up the slope.

Few men can load a musket on the move, but this pair can load their double-barreled, rifled muskets at a dead run. At present, anything other than a run and they'd surely be *dead.*

The paper cartridges in their ammo pouches are actually two cartridges, held loosely together, side-by-side, by bits of waxed paper, with two percussion caps on top. There is a flash of their hands that is too fast to see even at close range. The rangers slap a paper tube of powder and minié ball into each barrel. At the same time the percussion caps are bitten off and held in their teeth. A flash of the double-barrel ramrod, the butt of the weapon bounces once on the ground as the ramrod seems to flick in and out. Another blur of hands as both hammers come back and the percussion caps are spit into place. They both spin and fire. Their dogs turn with them, looking on with doggy glee, adding their bark to their masters' deadly bite.

"Ch-BANG!" The sound of percussion cap and black powder explosion blends into one sound as both rangers fire their first barrel. Their targets are still concealed behind the mouse gray boles of the emerald trees, but there can be little doubt that the two leading foes have suddenly been distracted by recent difficulties in normal biological processes . . . like breathing. Melville had never seen Josiah miss a man-sized target at 250 yards, and Valandil simply refused to waste the powder to prove that he could.

"Ch-BANG!," again, as they both fire their second barrels. The instant the second shot is fired, the two rangers and two dogs spin and trot uphill. Four loads a minute is a good rate of fire for a veteran marine standing still. At a dead run these two rangers have their weapons loaded again before Melville can count to fifteen. Nothing less is expected from a ranger.

This time as they spin and fire, Melville can see their targets. A wave of dirty white apes surge out of the wood line, approximately a hundred yards behind them. "Ch-BANG! Ch-BANG!" Four gaps appear in the wave, only to be immediately filled.

In a running retreat such as this there are two possible strategies. Against cautious enemies who value their lives you can spread out your fire, and keep their heads down. The brave and foolish die first, and the rest will hopefully stay honest and cautious, keeping a respectful distance.

Against a truly determined and fearless enemy, the best you can do is pick off the ones in the lead. In a sort of enforced natural selection, the fastest die first. If you do this long enough and hard enough, and if you're fast enough and lucky enough, maybe you can outrun the rest.

The furry white wave coming at Melville's little company appeared to be singularly determined and fearless. *What* did *they do to irk this lot?* thought Melville as he watched them swarm out of the wood line. Probably the eternal story. Boy sees alien, alien sees food. Boy objects, alien takes offense. Whatever the reason for the alien attack, Melville's force clearly wasn't going to outrun *this* bunch. The only option was to stand and fight somewhere, and *this* was the spot.

Chapter the 2nd

Battle: He Is Dead Who Will Not Fight

. . . And life is colour and warmth and light,
And a striving evermore for these;
And he is dead who will not fight;
And who dies fighting has increase.

"Into Battle"
Julian Grenfell

Melville's troops were in a line, facing downhill. The grassy stubble made the slope a golden brown, ending abruptly when it hit the gray boles and emerald leaves of the forest. Many habitable worlds in the galaxy had been seeded by a mysterious ancient civilization, but this was a world with its own, independently evolved ecology. Flitting across the slope were splendid, beautiful, red and blue things that looked a bit like dragonflies that glistened in the sun like rubies and sapphires, unlike anything they'd ever seen before.

Every warrior in that thin line had a clean shot at the approaching foe. When speed was required their muskets were loaded with paper cartridges and minié balls, but now every double-barreled musket in the line was carefully and lovingly prepared with precise loads of powder, and carefully selected minié balls and percussion caps. The first shot would be at 250 yards. Precision and care was required at this range. As the enemy drew closer, less care and more speed would become the order of the day.

The center of the line was anchored in the southern, downslope edge of the little copse of trees. The wings extended straight out to the left and right, prepared to wheel back and defend the trees and the bones of their cutter, which was immediately adjacent and upslope of the trees. Twenty-four redcoated marines formed the center of the line. Six bluejacketed sailors were on each wing.

Lieutenant Melville and Sergeant Broadax stood in front of the line.

Melville was a man of Westerness. He was tall and slender in a blue jacket and sailcloth trousers, with nut brown hair tussled by the light breeze.

Broadax was a Dwarrowdelf in sworn service to the Crown of Westerness. She was short, squat and wide, dressed in marine red, with long dark hair jutting out from under a round iron helmet. She looked like the stump of a mighty tree, painted red. Except this stump had the stub of a cigar clenched in her teeth, and a thin little beard on the point of her chin.

Other than Broadax, and a few sailors with a kerchief tied to protect a bald head from the sun, the rest of the company were bare headed. Everything about them was a product of their endless years sailing the seas of Flatland. Their hair was generally short, since water was a scarce and precious commodity in two-space and long hair was almost impossible to keep free of fleas and other exotic vermin. They were also barefooted, having built up thick calluses from a lifetime aboard ships where the floorboards and spars were coated with Elbereth Moss. When their bare feet were in contact with the smooth white Moss they were in contact with their Ship, and they didn't want to scar or scuff the precious Moss with rough boots or shoes.

Both Melville and Broadax knew that anything they had to say to their men was best said in front. Throughout history military leaders knew that they needed to get out in front if they wanted to influence the behavior of their troops. They also knew that the one in front usually died first. They weren't out front because they *wanted* to. They were in front of their men because they *had* to.

Over the centuries military leaders had succeeded in convincing themselves that it was bad for morale for leaders to die. A little blood was okay, even good for the troops' morale, but death was definitely out. So they tried hard to find a balance between necessity and stupidity. In this case Broadax and Melville had worked out a plan. A tried and tested plan. One leader led from the front to direct and exhort, and one stayed behind to direct, push and prod.

Private Jarvis' heart was pounding in his chest. He'd been taught the breathing exercise to prevent this from happening, but his training failed him. He was already experiencing a loss of peripheral vision, like looking through a "toilet paper tube." And he was experiencing "auditory exclusion," in which his sense of hearing "tuned out" as his brain focused all attention toward his vision, the primary sense bringing in survival data.

The marines here on the left flank were commanded by the huge Corporal Kobbsven. Sergeant Broadax was striding down the front of the line just as Kobbsven was passing on some of his old soldier wisdom. "Yah, yew betcha," said Kobbsven, "I svare it's true. If ya put a coat of olife oil on yar bayonet blade unter a full moon, then the blade von't schtick in the enemy. Olifes represent peace, and under the full moon there's power to resist stickin' to the enemy. 'Course, it vouldn't vork on an ordinary vorld, but once that blade comes out into Flatland the Elder King makes it so."

"Really, Corp'rl?" squeaked Jarvis.

"Kobbsven," said Broadax, stopping abruptly and scowling up at the towering corporal, rolling her glowing stub of a cigar to the corner of her mouth. Red veins in her eyes, set between a repeatedly broken nose, made the map of two small neighboring villages separated by a vast mountain chain. "We ain't got no olerv earl, an' this wurld ain't got no moon. So it looks like we's scruwd, blued and tattooed. So how 'bout if ye jist remember to twist the blade as ye pull it out! Ye *think* 'at might wurk too?!"

There was only one thing in all the world that Kobbsven feared, and she was standing in front of him, looking him squarely in the belt buckle. "Uhh, yeah, Sarge, I reckon that'd wurk. . . ." Kobbsven was a giant of a man with a huge, scraggly, handlebar mustache. He was standing at rigid attention, but despite all efforts his belly was at ease. If Broadax's eyes were the maps of two mountain villages, then the pink lines in Kobbs' two cheeks were the map of a thriving metropolis being savagely mauled by a ferret.

"All right yew lot, listen up! Look at me! Look at *me,* Jarvis!" roared Broadax, glaring at him as she strode in front of the marine private and caught his eye. Her glare was particularly effective. A veritable concentrated essence of NCO glare flowed out from the small space between her helmet and beard, and her voice echoed in the hot stillness as she clenched her cigar in the corner of her mouth. "Don't let yer mind wander, son. It's too small to be out on its own!" A ripple of nervous laughter went through the ranks, easing the tension.

"By the Lord, all of ye'd better pay attention to *me.* I'll make yer life a hell of a lot more miserable than they will if ye don't listen up!" She scanned the line and made sure every set of eyes was on her. As they looked at her they began to listen. As they looked and listened they were able to shake off the spell of tunnel vision and auditory exclusion. Jarvis' training began to kick in and he started taking slow, deep breaths.

Broadax stood with her stubby legs planted as if the 1.5 gees of her homeworld's gravity held her down. Her twenty pound, double-bladed battle-ax hung lightly in her left fist, carried at the balance point, right up near the business end. "Lads, in this heat yer powder is gonna perform extra well an' ye'll shoot flatter, so ye can aim a little lower than usual. The heat shimmer is also gonna distort their image an' make it look a little higher than it really is. *And* some of ye sorry bastards will tend to overshoot when ye shoot downhill."

Everyone nodded as she continued. "We're gonna get a lot of cheap shots at 'em as they come up this hill. By God I almost feel sorry for 'em. By God I do! But it's no damn good if ye waste it! We will fire our first volley when they pass the two-hundred-and-fifty-yard stake, but I want ye to treat it like two hundred yards. Then we'll adjust from there. When we've loaded our last volley we'll fix bayonets an' see if the bastards can digest cold steel!"

There was a lot of drop in the trajectory of black powder projectiles at 250 yards. You had to aim well above your target. But Broadax's marines trained extensively for this kind of combat. The key was using the ramrod with great precision, so that you "seated" the bullet down with consistent pressure, every time.

The weird twisting of Flatland wouldn't tolerate anything more complex than a rifled musket, and that only with daily maintenance, so their sights were a crude but effective set of posts that weren't even placed on the sailors' muskets. "Ye damned blueboys," she added, looking first left and then right to catch the eye of the two groups of sailors on the wings. "Jist fire right at 'em, like they was on a ship right next ta ye. By the time all the factors balance out, that's as good as ye'll ever do. If ye undershoot, yer bullets will likely hit this dry ground and bounce up into 'em."

Then she concluded, reversing her ax by twirling it in her fingers like a baton and waving the wooden haft in the air with the steel in her big palm, "An' if I sees any of ye firing too high ye'll feel the smack o' me ax hilt on ye, damn me if ye don't! The lieutenant will be walking the line, an' he'll be doing the same with the flat o' his sword. So don't shame me boys, put them minié balls right where they'll do the most good." Here her voice dropped, but it still carried clearly in the hot air. "Make me proud boys, do like I trained ye." Melville could almost swear he saw a tear well up in her eye. But it was hard to be sure, what with all the gristle and hair.

Melville stood beside Broadax, anxiously anticipating his first major battle, and his first command of troops in combat. He thought he was ready, and now found himself frustrated and bemused by the way his mind kept slipping off into inconsequential distractions.

Right now he couldn't help himself from asking, not for the first time, just why *did* they call it a mini ball? There was nothing "mini" about the .50 caliber "ball," which was bullet-shaped and not ball-shaped at all. The bullet was smaller than the bore, which made it easy to ram down the barrel. A cavity in the back of the soft lead bullet expanded when it was fired, digging in to the rifling of the barrel and giving the bullet a spin that made the muskets deadly accurate. So why a mini ball? Oh well, just another mystery lost in antiquity and the Crash.

The two rangers continued to fire, "Ch-BANG! Ch-BANG!, Ch-BANG! Ch-BANG!" roughly every fifteen seconds, as they trotted across the golden stubble, bringing their newfound friends along behind them. The foe *had* to be tired by the long chase but they plodded along doggedly, not able to close the distance and obviously not willing to stop.

Broadax had said her piece and now Melville had a few seconds to say his bit before the foe hit the 250 yard aiming stake. The troops expected him to say something appropriate, and he reached deep into their heritage for Words that would lift their hearts. Something that could reach down through a frightened man's brain, and pull him up by the short-and-curlies.

"Stout servants of Westerness!" he started, as he drew his sword with a flourish. The flash of the sword caught the attention of eyes that were primed and alert to detect motion and danger. Since he was standing beside Broadax, they were already looking that way, and were psychologically primed to shift their attention to the young lieutenant and listen to his words.

He was pleased that his voice was calm and steady. Unlike his traitorous heart, pounding in his chest. He reached out for his training and breathed deeply. Just as his weapons master, old Lieutenant Ed Stack, taught him back at the academy. He could hear that gravelly voice. "In through the nose, two, three, four. Hold, two, three, four. Out through the lips, two, three, four. Hold, two, three, four."

Elite warriors have known for centuries that the autonomic nervous system, or ANS, controls your heart rate, perspiration, and adrenal flow. Your ANS can't be consciously controlled. But your breathing is one ANS mechanism that *can* be brought under conscious control. As you pull your breathing down, your whole autonomic nervous system, including your heart rate and adrenal flow, come with it.

There's a tendency in humans to place their breathing in sync with the person they're watching. As Melville took his deep breath, consciously and unconsciously many of his men did too. His calm was contagious.

Now the words, those words, those ancient, sacred words began to flow like old wine. "Warriors of Westerness. Foes are before you, and your homes far behind. Yet though you fight on an alien field, the glory that you reap here shall be your own forever. Oaths ye have taken, now fulfill them all. To lord and land and league of friendship!"

Now Melville was sure he could see a tear escape the gristle and hair around the old Dwarrowdelf's eye. She looked with pride on her young lieutenant. So far, so good. The men nodded their heads calmly and smiled fell, fey smiles. Many of them were chewing tobacco, or smoking hand-rolled cigarettes. No great cheers came from these men. They radiated an icy calm that would keep their heart rates low and their trigger fingers steady.

Melville fell back behind the line now. His purser, Theo Petreckski, stood immediately behind the line, in command of their three midshipmen, Crater, Archer, and little Aquinar. Together they formed his reserve. Farther behind them, in the cutter, was their Sylvan surgeon, Lady Elphinstone, with the ship's cat and their one wounded sailor. Three ship's dogs sat in various relaxed positions in the shade of the trees, along the center of the firing line.

> The fighting man shall take from the sun
>   Take warmth, and life from the glowing earth;
> Speed with the light-foot winds to run,
>   And with the trees to newer birth;
> And find, when fighting shall be done,
>   Great rest, and fullness after dearth.

Broadax was a master at controlling an infantry firing line. She stood in front of the line, dead center, two paces out. She held her twenty pound ax out horizontally before her in one hand, parallel to the firing line, in the same way that Melville would hold his sword out in front of him, and with no more difficulty. Her best marksmen were here in the center. Her oldest and truest marines. She paced the line while they loaded, but she would stand in the center when she gave the command to fire. That way she'd be as safe as any leader could ever be, standing in front of the firing line in battle.

Melville was stunned by the alien beauty of it all. A vast sea of emerald forest, as far as the eye could see, beneath a pure, powder blue sky. From the green forest came a dirty white wave of exotic beasts, flowing up a golden hillside, dotted with the flashing rubies and sapphires of insects glistening in the sun. Add in the scarlet tunics and royal blue jackets of the firing line. At this moment there was a flavor, a spice to his life that he'd never known. For a few seconds he savored it, and felt more . . . alive than ever before in his life.

The white tide finally showed its full measure. They weren't endless. There was a limit to their number. The enemy was now a discernible mob, roughly 150 yards long, 25 yards wide at the front, and 50 yards wide at the rear.

The rangers were still 100 yards in front of the apes, spinning and firing like clockwork, four times a minute. Ch-BANG!Ch-BANG!, Ch-BANG!Ch-BANG! Every time they each fired both barrels, turned, and loaded on the run.

Broadax was making one last, calm inspection of the line. She turned to old Chief Hans, in charge of the sailors on the right wing as he spit a stream of tobacco at a blue dragonfly. The hapless creature was picked cleanly out of the air and glued to the ground. Thinking it was raining, the bewildered insect began to burrow into the ground. "Well Chief, 'ave ye inspected yer boys?" she asked.

Chief Petty Officer Bronson Hans was a grizzled, bearded old salt who was the senior NCO in charge of their detachment of sailors. "Aye. Next y'll be teaching me 'ow to suck eggs?" he replied with a nicotine-stained grin and a stream of tobacco juice.

"Well, ye know Chief," she said, blowing a stream of cigar smoke into the general region south of his belt buckle. "They say yer memory is the *second* thing to go." The warriors around them laughed and old Hans smiled admiringly as she moved back to the center.

Broadax's ax lifted slowly and gently into the sky, moving from the vertical, as the lead element reached the 250 yard mark. These stakes were tree branches with bits of cloth tied to them. The distance had been carefully paced off and marked in all directions, as the first step in the defensive plan. They couldn't defend the entire perimeter, so breastworks or trenches would work against them if occupied by the enemy. Besides, there were no trees of manageable size to build fortifications with, and what deadwood was available was needed for cooking fires. Nor did the dry, powdery earth lend itself to entrenchments. With their small force they were counting on mobility and firepower against any attacker, and range stakes carefully placed out from all the planned defensive lines were key to the accurate and effective marksmanship.

"Remember, treat it like two hundred yards. Ready boys, readyyyy! Wait for it." They'd loaded from a standing position, but now most of the line was kneeling, some even sitting to get a more stable position as they fired. "Squeeeeze it off on my command!"

Broadax inhaled deeply on her cigar. The coal glowed deep red as she gently, almost lovingly let her ax head fall, soft as a floating leaf. Her calm voice carried clearly, as she gave the command, "Firrre."

The falling ax was the signal for the rangers to hit the dirt, pulling their dogs down with them. With a thunderous ch-BANG!, thirty-six muskets spoke and a cloud of smoke appeared. Ch-BANG! and the second barrels roared, adding to the smoke at the top of the hill. Adding even more to the carnage at the bottom. The rangers leaped up and continued their trot uphill.

The furry, white mass of aliens obstinately followed the rangers. They scuttled along on all six legs like insects. When the volley rang out they seemed to stagger, stunned by the noise as much as the bullets. A full score of the foe in the front ranks fell to the first volley, perhaps less at the second, since the smoke of the first shot partially obscured the view. Several aliens in the rear ranks also dropped from sight, caught by shots aimed too high.

The men of the firing line avoided firing at the center, where the rangers were in the line of fire. They could be relatively sure of their accuracy to the left and right, but not up and down, and none of them wanted to risk a shot directly over the rangers' heads. After a brief, stunned pause the attackers continued uphill. There was no stumbling or hesitating as they crawled over the dead and dying.

The creatures of this world seemed to have a sensitive nervous system. Happily, one hit seemed to drop their opponents most of the time, but Melville was saddened to see that the concussion of their volley dropped most of the glistening ruby and sapphire fireflies between the firing line and their opponents. If the insects weren't already dead, they were certain to be trampled by the approaching mob. In the midst of battle he was a little embarrassed to feel a twinge of sorrow at the deaths of these innocent, beautiful creatures.

Broadax walked across the front of the line, moving to the left. Melville worked his way along the back, moving right. The marine sergeant talked quietly as she moved in front of each man. The young lieutenant did the same, placing a hand on their shoulders and calling each man by name, just as he'd done many times on the firing line in training. By the time the second volley was loaded, Broadax had worked her way back to the center.

The light breeze was blowing in their faces, clearing the smoke of their first volley. It also began to bring with it the stench of their approaching foe, like a vast, rolling manure pile, replacing the warm, dusty scent of the dried grass. "All right lads, set yer sights for a hundred and fifty yards this time." Again her voice carried clearly. There was no need to shout yet. "Readddy, fire."

In the fifteen seconds since the last volley, the foe had swarmed over the two hundred yard stake. Running uphill, tired, over broken ground, they were covering about fifty yards every fifteen seconds. The rangers were now at the hundred-yard mark, still maintaining a hundred-yard lead. As Broadax's ax fell, the rangers dropped, and an instant later roughly twenty-five of the foe staggered and fell. A second later the second barrels fired and claimed another twenty or more.

The rangers were no longer firing themselves. Their goal was to get to the firing line as quickly as possible. It was likely they were very low on ammo. "Aquinar!" shouted Melville to the young midshipman behind him. "Have ammo ready for the rangers as soon as they hit the firing line."

"Aye, sir!"

One hundred fifty yards. "All right lads, treat this one like a hundred yards. Watch fer the rangers now. Yer making yer old sarge proud lads, yer shooting good. Readyyy, fire!" Fifty yards out the rangers hit the dirt again as her ax fell and the third volley swept the enemy ranks. Well over thirty fell, and at least another twenty-five were claimed by the second barrel. Still they came on clambering over their dead without hesitation.

This close they could see the foe's six legs splay out as their bellies thumped the ground, raising a puff of dust. Their heads, with the mouths on top, slammed teeth-first into the ground with a small explosion of dirt. Legs (splay!), belly (thump! dust), mouth (slam! dirt).

"Ha!" shouted old Chief Hans from the right wing. "At's the way ta make 'em eat dirt!" A roar of laughter ran down the line and an appreciative grin split Broadax's face.

"All right, lads," Broadax said, with an admiring, gap-toothed, cigar-filled grin at her fellow NCO, "silence in the line now. Concentrate on yer loading and listen fer yer commands."

. . . The thundering line of battle stands,
And in the air death moans and sings;
But Day shall clasp him with strong hands,
And Night shall fold him in soft wings.

The rangers put on a burst of speed and come into the line with grins on their faces. The firing line cheers. Their two dogs, grinning with doggy glee, are greeted by the three smaller ship's dogs with eager barks and rump sniffing. Aquinar hands fistfuls of paper cartridges to the rangers.

Josiah drops to one knee, patting his dog and panting as he puts the cartridges into his ammo pouch. He looks up at the lieutenant with a feral grin strikingly similar to his dog's. "They followed me home, sir. Can ah keep 'em?" Another cheer broke from the raw throats of the firing line.

One hundred yards. "Treat it like seventy-five yards, lads. Readyyyyyy, fire." Again, over thirty apes dropped. Legs, belly, teeth. Splay, thump, thump. Then another thirty with the second shot. Splay, thump, thump.

These were the warriors of Westerness. They'd drilled for a lifetime for this day. In their training on high-tech worlds, they'd done this in virtual reality simulators hundreds of times. By his count their company had dropped almost two hundred of the aliens by now. By God, Melville almost did feel sorry for the poor bastards. Almost.

At this range their attackers look like big, dingy white, six-legged versions of the little brown, eight-legged spider monkeys they'd seen high up in the branches of their own little grove of trees. Broadax bellows, "All right boys, load fast now, we're gonna get two more volleys in before we feed the bastards our bayonets!"

Valandil calls out in his clear, ringing voice. He too is down on one knee, one arm around his dog, checking the load in his musket. From now on the two rangers will add their fire to the battle line. "Up close they will stand up on their back two legs. They are as tall as a man then. The top half of their head is all mouth, a bullet there is wasted. A bullet in the lower part of the head or the center of the chest will drop them instantly." Many in the line nod in understanding as they load their weapons.

Sixty yards. The howling and roaring of the foe is now loud enough that Broadax has to shout to be heard out at the far ends of the line. The troops in the line are intentionally using their breathing exercises to remain calm, just as they'd been trained. They need their fine motor skill to load their weapons this last time. It took calm, steady nerves to ensure that the ramrod hit true, and to be certain they didn't fumble the little percussion caps.

The enemy's stench would be overwhelming if sensory gating didn't shut out everything but the vital input needed to survive. The only sensory input that comes in is the sight of their enemy and, if they concentrate, the sounds of their leader's commands. Previously many took time to drop to a knee or sit as they fired. Now everyone stands. "Readyyyy, lads! Fire!" Ch-BLAM! Ch-BLAM! The foe is visibly rocked this time. Well over thirty fall to the first barrel, nearly as many to the second. Legs, belly, teeth. Splay, thump, thump. Still they came obstinately on.

"All right now! Load quickly, lads!" The apes rear up on their back two legs, their front four legs reaching out. Three claws as long as a man's finger extend out from the end of each limb. Four equally long fangs protrude from each mouth, two top and two bottom, with lots of little teeth in between.

A bayonet on the end of the barrel interferes with rapid loading, so Broadax had intentionally waited until now to command, "FIX BAYONETS!" She has to bellow to be heard over the foe's eerie roars, her cigar in one hand and her ax in the other. Earlier the line had concentrated their fire at the enemy formation's flanks in order to avoid the rangers. This gave the center slightly less attention. Now the enemy formation, if you could grant that term to this mob, is in a loose wedge shape, aimed straight at the center of the line. Melville and his tiny reserve stand behind the line, ready to reinforce the center.

> The blackbirds sing to him, "Brother, brother,
>   If this be the last song you shall sing,
> Sing well, for you may not sing another;
>   Brother, sing."

Melville felt a surge of joy and elation. He knew in his heart that this could well be his "last song," and he was determined to sing well indeed.

The leading wave was barely five yards out. Melville saw that they stood approximately man high as they reared up like this. Broadax now slipped in behind the line, joining the reserve. This was the point where bravery turned into stupidity if you stayed out front, to be caught between a seemingly irresistible force and a hopefully immovable object.

"FIRE!!!"

"Ch-BLAM! Ch-BLAM!" At point-blank range seventy-six minié balls cut through the enemy mass. Some of those in the lead were each hit several times, but that wasteful redundancy was balanced out by the fact that many bullets punched straight through the upraised chest of the first target and dropped yet another immediately behind.

Now that they were reared up on their hind legs, the apes died differently. In death all six legs still splayed out, but their torso, head and gaping mouth lunged up and out in an arc that landed many of them, teeth first, with a thump at the marines' feet, gouging out a divot of parched sod with their mouths. In two cases they sunk their teeth into trees marines were using for cover. The carcasses hung there in death, imbedded into the thick gray bark by their fangs. In many cases they landed close enough that men had to scramble out of their way, creating breaks and disruptions in what should have been a solid fence of gleaming bayonets.

The roaring, raging foe paused for a split second in response to the noise and shock of the final volley, and then they lunged into the center of the line. Suddenly they were in the line, swirling and twisting in flashes of white fur, red jackets, lunging yellow teeth and gleaming bayonets.

Here a marine's mouth and jaw disappears in a smear of white bone and red blood as an ape's claw connects. There another marine is disemboweled by a blow, viscera and blood coming out and up in an arc of gray, brown and red.

Now it's the reserve's turn to contribute to the battle. Melville held a double-barreled pistol in each hand. So did his purser, Petreckski, and the three midshipmen.

An ape loomed before him. Melville snapped into "slow-motion time" and hunter vision. Every event happened slowly and with incredible clarity. It seemed to take forever to swing the weapon up to eye level. "____!" He fired the pistol in his right hand. It flashed and created a puff of smoke, but he didn't hear a sound or feel the recoil. The ape spasmed forward in its death dive, but it seemed like there was all the time in the world to step aside.

As early as the twenty-first century, Dr. Alexis Artwohl's research found that eight out of ten of all law enforcement officers in gunfights experienced this diminished sound effect. Seven out of ten had heightened visual clarity, and six out of ten experienced slow-motion time. In the five centuries since, every warrior has been taught about this, and these powerful survival responses have been nurtured and encouraged. Melville had wondered if it would happen to him, and now here it was.

On his left a marine went down and a dog placed itself over the body. Again it seemed to take forever to swing and aim. "____!," Melville fired the second barrel of his right pistol, dropping the ape and giving the marine a split second gap to recover. Again, he saw the flash and smoke, but didn't hear the sound or feel the gun buck in his hand.

Like a predator in nature, he didn't hear his own "roar," he tuned out the distracting sounds of the "herd," and saw everything his "prey" and his "pack" did with vivid clarity.

Directly in front a marine went down with an ape on his back. "____!," "____!," Melville fired both barrels of his left pistol. In the turmoil he missed the first time, but the other ball went true. The beast on the marine's back suddenly went limp, giving the man a few seconds to scramble out of the melee and then stagger back into the line.

His midshipmen were still boys in every sense of the word, but they were *very* well trained boys. They were products of state-of-the-art training and the finest combat simulators that high-tech worlds could provide. In this melee they were definitely holding their own. Melville caught a flash of little Aquinar standing on tiptoes to shove his pistol into the mouth of an ape that had all four upper limbs wrapped around a marine. The thrust of the pistol was all that stopped the ape from biting off the marine's face. "Ch-blam!, ch-blam!" The sound was muffled by the ape's mouth as a spray of gray brains and red blood fountained out the back of the beast's head.

Funny, he'd heard these shots. He knew that the diminished sound or "auditory exclusion" worked like that sometimes. You shut out your own "roar" but not others'.

In a few seconds the reserve fired twenty shots. But the real bulwark, the seawall on which the filthy white tide raged futilely, was Sergeant Broadax and her twenty pounds of double-bladed battle-ax, and the two rangers with their dogs. *She's singing,* thought Melville in wonder as he watched the Dwarrowdelf. *She is actually singing.* Lo! She sang as she slew, for the joy of battle was on her, and the sound of her singing was fair and terrible. *I wonder how she does it with that cigar in her mouth?*

Her ax flashed in arcs of red, fountains of red, as she planted her mighty thews and hacked the heads from lunging apes, as a master swordsman might flick the buds from a rosebush in idle practice in his garden. She scorned to even notice the arms and claws of her foes, striking every time for the head. Her iron helm and splaying locks were splashed with red. Her red jacket was soon torn to shreds, displaying her lingerie of finest Dwarrowdelf mail underneath.

Hers was a race of delvers, mining deep into the hearts of high-gee worlds for heavy metals. Even after long years of service to the Crown of Westerness her face wasn't well suited to endure direct sunlight. She was already red with sunburn and now her face glowed as bright as her cigar tip with exertion as the battle fury of her forefathers ran like fire in her veins.

This is what she'd hoped for when she abandoned her people to be the first Dwarrowdelf to enlist in the Marine Corps of Westerness. As a female, her own society wouldn't allow her to be a warrior. They wanted to deny her the glory of battle, but *now* she was in her element. There was no regret for turning her back on her people and her culture to fight as a mercenary for some distant kingdom. *This* is what she was born for.

The two rangers and their dogs worked as a team, like the four fingers of a hand, reinforcing, supporting, assisting, and always, always attacking. These fell-handed warriors were indeed the "glory of the race of rangers." Truly "matchless" in every endeavor.

Valandil worked high, his height and reach giving the Sylvan an unmatched ability to deflect all blows from the beasts' upper limbs. He thrust his blade into the necks and open mouths of the approaching beasts with uncanny accuracy. Josiah took the center, deflecting blows from the middle limbs, and thrusting with great strength and power to the chest and gut. The dogs went low, biting and snapping at feet and knees. These dogs were larger and stronger than the ship's dogs and with one chomp they could hamstring any ape they caught from the rear, to bring them crashing down with limbs flailing.

For one brief moment Melville had a chance to observe this masterful team at work. Three apes came at them simultaneously. Valandil blocked an ape's overhand blow with his sword edge. The ape's "hand" flew off. The ranger's sword swept forward and down in a red blur, cleaving the head off at the neck. Josiah blocked a reaching claw with the flat of his blade. He used the impact to bounce his sword point over and in, to punch into the beast's chest. One dog feigned at an ape's knee. The beast turned to face this danger and exposed the hamstring at the back of its opposite leg to the rangers' other dog. With an audible "Crunch!" of jaws the hamstring was ripped out in a mass of white tendons and red blood. The ape plunged to the ground. In the blink of an eye, three foes were down.

The team of Dwarrowdelf, rangers and dogs held the center, forming a living barricade, a reef of steel, flesh and fang that the stinking white wave of apes smashed into in futile fury. Around them, others also helped to stem the tide.

> . . . And when the burning moment breaks,
> And all things else are out of mind,
> And only joy of battle takes
> Him by the throat, and makes him blind.

Melville held his sword in his right hand. The swords of those who sail in Flatland were all straight, since the corrosive influence of that strange realm played the devil with curved surfaces. The influence of two-space also helped to keep their weapons deadly sharp. Melville didn't remember drawing his sword. He'd tossed his pistols to the midshipmen for reloading, but he didn't remember doing that either.

He was in the thick of battle now. Countless years of practice made every thrust and stroke go true without thought. Pistolcraft is a conscious skill, even at close range. Selecting, aiming and dropping a target takes careful control. But swordcraft is an unconscious skill. The hand has to move before the mind even thinks. Here again slow motion time and visual clarity kick in at odd moments.

Danger! Parry, thrust! His sword blade magically appears in a beast's mouth. Without conscious thought it flicks back. With exquisite clarity he watches the sword tip slowly draw back a viscous strand of red. Danger! Parry, thrust. Again his blade magically impales an ape's exposed chest and flicks back. Stimulus, response. Stimulus, response.

Here Petreckski, the purser, also made his mark. In the ordinary course of duty his job was to find whatever was of value as potential cargo at every stop. He was expected to be a master of many fields. Passengers, gems, creatures (and parts thereof), plants (and parts thereof), technology, writings, music, exotic food and spices, artwork, alien archeology and many others were all his responsibility.

His job was to survive and thrive anywhere, in the markets or wilds of any world. He was seminary trained, a monk, complete with brown robe and bad haircut. He was virtually useless with a rifle, but for personal defense he'd been trained extensively in mid- and high-tech close-range weapons, to include pistol- and sword-craft.

Petreckski wasn't a strong man. Most of his development was in his mind, and he carried a few too many pounds on him. His sword slashes held little power, but his thrusts were precise and deadly. He was surprisingly nimble on his feet, and he danced in and out on the edge of the fray, placing a fusillade, a blur of sword thrusts into exactly the right spot while others held their opponents' attention. Like a huge sewing machine needle, his sword flicked out, deep into an ape's eye, and then back so quickly it seemed to pull back a strand of red with it. The red sword tip flashed back out again while the old strand still hung in the air, seeming to form a red cobweb of death.

The three ship's dogs also served with distinction. Distracting, snarling, ripping, biting. In and out with lightning speed, they were as good as any man in the melee. Several marines went down in the midst of the swirling fight in the center. All three ship's dogs went repeatedly into their primary combat mode, standing over a fallen warrior and defending him with their lives.

Their efforts made it possible for several marines to get on their feet and back into battle. Still others limped or crawled back to medical support after a dog's assistance. The price they paid was two dogs who died instantly with tragic yelps of pain. One of the rangers' dogs also went down with a heart piercing yelp, battling at his master's side, his teeth clamped deep into the fish-belly white limb that pierced his lung.

~ ~ ~

The strangest event in the battle for the center was when unexpected allies appeared from above. The apes seemed naturally inclined to climb up the tree trunks and attack their opponents from above. They could launch themselves down with devastating fury upon the opponents below. This appeared to be their natural and preferred method of fighting.

One ape succeeded in reaching a tree and climbing with amazing speed five yards up the trunk to where the branches began. He leaped out on a limb and hurled himself down. The marine he landed on died instantly as all six limbs and a mouth simultaneously pierced and assailed his abused body. Several other marines were wounded before the ape could be dispatched with a bayonet thrust.

It's possible that the little company would have died to a man except that, after the first one, every ape who climbed a tree was instantly beset by a throng of little, brown, eight-legged "spider monkeys." From the very beginning of their stay in this world they'd seen these tiny creatures up in the trees of this little grove. They didn't seem to dwell anywhere else.

The servants of Westerness tried to treat them with dignity and respect, as they treated all living creatures. They gained a newfound respect for their upstairs neighbors when the little brown monkeys literally tore the large white invaders into tiny, bloody shreds. Shreds which showered down from above. Nearly a score of the apes died in this grisly manner. Many of the little spider monkeys also came down, hitting the ground with a crunch and a thump of dust.

In the center, where the final volley caused dying opponents to lunge into the line, there were gaps in the hedge of bayonets. Gaps which the enemy exploited. With deployment of the small reserve, at great cost of life and limb, and with a little help from above, the center of the line was stabilized.

Throughout history a hedge of spears or bayonets could generally be counted on to stop a cavalry charge. It's widely believed that no horse *ever* intentionally charged into a hedge of sharp objects, no matter *how* badly their riders might desire otherwise. Upon occasion a wounded or dying horse might crash into a line, creating a gap that could be exploited, but it is likely that no healthy horse ever willingly flung itself on a bayonet. The warriors of Westerness hoped the attacking apes would react the same, and they did.

Other than the fluke of creating a gap in the line with a dying horse, the primary way cavalry can defeat infantry is to use their superior mobility to swing around the line. This is what happened on the left flank.

The wings swung back according to plan, precisely as they'd rehearsed it. *All* battle movements were best rehearsed ahead of time. Even if you had only a short time to prepare, the one thing you always tried to find time for was rehearsing "actions on the objective." And Broadax had days to prepare the defense of this hill.

A navy petty officer and a marine corporal fell back behind each wing to control the movement. On the right, the west wing, Chief Hans kept everything perfectly under control. However, on the left end the line of warriors hesitated for an instant as it pulled back, and a swarm of reeking white apes poured around them. The apes swirled around the flank and over the Pier, like a flurry of snow around the end of a fence.

Private Jarvis was the last marine on the left flank. After him, the line was held by sailors. He had rehearsed this in simulators, but *this* was no simulation. Simulations could do a *lot*, but if he lived through this he'd be a *real* veteran.

His training failed him as the apes began to swirl around the left wing. He forgot to control his breathing. His heart pounded in his chest. He was "ham fisted" and clumsy as he tried to load his musket. Then the battle became a swirling maelstrom of white fur, and red and blue jackets.

Jarvis' tunnel vision was focused down to a "soda straw" as he thrust his bayonet at the ape in front of him. He didn't hear a sound. Cut off, he and the sailors to his left fought back-to-back. He didn't feel the ape's claws rake his shoulder, and he wasn't even aware of it when he wet himself and messed himself.

The only thing that saved Jarvis, and most of his comrades, was the fact that fewer apes were out on the flanks. Once a gap was created most of them ignored the warriors of Westerness and charged straight into the center of the perimeter. Some climbed the trees, where they died at the hands of their tiny cousins. A large group swung all the way around and reached the Pier, where the cutter, Lady Elphinstone and her helpless patient waited.

In the bowels of the beached cutter was Lady Elphinstone, their aid station, and their remaining water. Petreckski became aware of the threat when he heard Elphinstone's two small, single-barreled pistols fire to their rear. In a flash Petreckski turned, sheathed his blade, and picked up two freshly loaded pistols. The midshipmen had just finished ramming a paper cartridge down each barrel, cocking the two hammers and putting two percussion caps in place. He shouted to the middies, "Grab all the pistols! Follow me!"

Cutting through the woods he quickly got a line of fire to the cutter. From here it was still a fairly long pistol shot, perhaps twenty yards. At the east entrance to the cutter two apes had already been dropped by Elphinstone, but at least one other was inside the cutter where Petreckski couldn't get a clear shot at it.

Inside the cutter Lady Elphinstone knelt beside her only patient. He was Glyn Ramano, an unlucky sailor whose chest was crushed in their initial crash landing into this world. Fortunately, none of the wounded on the battle line had been brought back to the aid station yet. Elphinstone's two small pistols dropped the first two apes as they approached the eastern entrance, but now she held only a dagger as yet another came at her.

The ship's cat, perched on a beam above the intruder, launched himself at the ape. Landing on the beast's back, the cat scrambled around the neck to the left, beneath the slavering jaws on top of the head, sinking claws and fangs into the left eye as it peered out from behind the breast bone. Each facet of the compound eye burst wherever claw or fang pierced it, spraying a milky white fluid.

With a howl of rage the beast reached up with its two topmost arms and one additional left arm to impale the cat. "Mwrrarw!!" The cat squalled in pain and death.

Elphinstone lunged. Quick as lightning her right hand sunk the dagger under the creature's lower left armpit and she felt fetid air escape from its lung. "That should let some of the wind out of ye!" she shouted. She was slammed backward by the impact as the beast came forward to stand over her helpless patient. Almost casually, each of the two limbs on the ground pierced Ramano as he lay helpless.

Two legs were imbedded in the dying sailor, three were impaled in the cat. The beast's remaining arm slashed at her, but the Sylvan healer ducked under the blow and crouched back. There was escape available out the other side but she wouldn't take it, not while there was any hope that her patient might be saved.

She held her bloody dagger as the beast swayed, then the head lunged forward in a last, spasmodic death dive, jaws open wide. She leapt to the side and the ape's teeth sank into the cutter's timber. Outside a mass of other apes fought to enter the narrow way.

Petreckski stands holding a pistol in a two-handed grip. The monk's left foot and left shoulder are slightly forward. The enemy is clustered around the narrow east entry to the cutter, literally fighting to get in. He permits tunnel vision to set in. All that matters in all the world is the entrance to the cutter, the ape closest to it, and the sights of his pistol.

"____*!,*" "____*!,*" *both barrels fire, the lead two apes drop, but he hears nothing. Vision is the only sense required here, and his mind tunes out all other sensory input. Without forward momentum the apes die with a sudden splay of all six limbs, then collapse into a heap of stinking white fur.*

Both of Petreckski's hands reach back. He drops the empty pistol from the left hand. A clever middy slaps a fresh pistol into his empty right hand.

Roughly twenty yards range. Each shot has to be carefully aimed from this distance. At very close ranges most modern warriors were taught to use "point" shooting. Look *through* the weapon, point and shoot. The physiological arousal of close combat often makes the eye incapable of focusing on any close-in objects, like pistol sights. This loss of near vision makes point shooting a viable alternative at very close ranges, *if* it is practiced long and hard enough.

But bullets are not magic. They don't hit their targets by themselves. The inverse square law applies, and the odds of missing your opponent increase exponentially as you move away from the target. At twenty yards the chance of making a kill with a hasty, unaimed shot is tiny. Remote. Miniscule. At this range it was vital that he take his time and . . . aiiimmm.

The key is to focus the eye on the *front sight.* Whatever the eye focuses on, consciously and unconsciously *that* is what your fine motor muscles will work to stabilize. Everyone has baited hooks, threaded needles, and cut with steak knives. Each time we focused our eyes on the end of the tool, and *that* was what we held steady. On a pistol the vital thing is to hold the front sight steady and on the target. If you do that, everything else will follow.

Petreckski was firing a SIG pistol, which was standard issue for the Westerness Navy. He'd been lucky enough to actually train at the SIGArms Monastery, under the supervision of Father "Bang" Miller and Brother Johan Pederson. Petreckski was a faithful servant of his God. As faithful as any flawed, fallen human can be. But Father Miller taught him that God would forgive him if, just for a moment, he worshipped at the Holy Church of the Front Sight. The alternative was the Discount House of Worship: pull, point, and pray. Petreckski was certain that God could do anything He chooses, but He most often chooses to bless those who practice and prepare.

The other part of the combat marksmanship equation was even older than the Church of the Front Sight. It was, "aim small, miss small." You must pick the smallest aim point you can discern. You don't aim for the ape, you aim for a specific spot on the ape, like the yellowish patch of fur under his armpit. That way even if you miss your mark by a little, you'll still hit your foe.

The front sight, a simple blade placed on the end of the barrel, comes into focus, superimposed over the white ape's armpit, which is out of focus. Every scratch, every mark on the little sight is in perfect focus. Two-handed grip. Breathe . . . front sight . . . squeeeeze . . . "____!" Don't wait for the target to drop, don't look at the falling foe, go on to the next. Pick your mark, front sight . . . squeeze . . . "____!" The middies look on in wonder as two more apes splay and drop.

Hand the empty pistol back with the left hand where it is snatched away to reload. Breathe. Simultaneously reach back with the right and a middy slaps a new pistol, cocked and ready, into his hand. Front sight . . . "____!" Front sight . . . "____!" Each time the lead ape falls. And again. And again. "Front sight, front sight," is his mantra. If he loses concentration and focuses on his target, he'll miss, and Elphinstone surely will die. The middies reload feverishly. Finally there are no loaded pistols left to slap into his hand.

Petreckski has fired twenty-four shots in as many seconds, and twenty-four apes join the two already outside the cutter. A swirl of red and blue jackets swarm over white fur. A flash of bayonets and swords, and the few remaining apes fall. Petreckski stands confused and dazed. He has been concentrating with superhuman intensity and when all his targets are gone he isn't sure what to do.

Suddenly, there is silence. No foe is left alive. The battle is over.

Lieutenant Melville looked out at the carnage. Heaps of reeking white fur were everywhere. He was stunned to realize that the battle didn't end until the last ape died. In real life no enemy *ever* fought to the end. A few always turned and ran, or surrendered, or committed mass suicide when defeat was imminent. Here was something truly different.

In the silence, Private Jarvis stood, dazed and staggering, clutching a bleeding shoulder with his hand. He looked with wide-eyed wonder at Sergeant Broadax and said, "Dear God, Sarge, they was brave."

"Aye, maybe they was, lad," answered Broadax. "Maybe. But as the great Dwarrowdelf general, Gzagk Pazton once said, 'Untutored courage is useless in the face of educated bullets.'"

Their victory was bitter bought. Six dead, eleven seriously wounded. He'd begun the battle with forty warriors, forty-four counting Elphinstone and the midshipmen. Now over a third of his men were dead or disabled. Not to mention over half his dogs and his one cat! And it had been so close, so very close.

Uninvited, a little ditty came to mind:

> I never shall forget the way
> That Blood upon this awful day
> Preserved us all from death.
> He stood upon a little mound,
> Cast his lethargic eyes around,
> And said beneath his breath:
> "Whatever happens we have got
> The Maxim Gun, and they have not."

Well, they didn't have Mr. Maxim's machine gun of yore. Its complex mechanisms wouldn't last an hour in two-space. But they did have "educated bullets," Westerness' finest double-barreled rifled muskets, and a company of stalwart hearts with steady hands that could load and fire four volleys a minute as they "stood upon *their* little mound." And *that* was sufficient unto the day.

Chapter the 3rd

Monkeys: Kindness in Another's Trouble

Question not, but live and labour
    Till yon goal be won,
Helping every feeble neighbour,
    Seeking help from none;
Life is mostly froth and bubble,
    Two things stand like stone,
Kindness in another's trouble,
    Courage in your own.

"Man's Testament"
Adam Lindsay Gordon

<<What *is* that boy doing?>> thought Lieutenant Melville as he rested in the stifling heat and reeking stench. It was midafternoon, barely three hours after their battle. He was on the Pier, leaning back against the Keel. From here he could observe the east side of their beached cutter, and the odd behavior of Midshipman Aquinar.

<<Told you,>> replied *Swish-tail*, <<he's good boy.>>

The tap to their water barrel was above and slightly to the other side of where Aquinar was crawling. So the little middy couldn't be after their precious supply of water, which was barely enough to last another few weeks with careful rationing.

After the punishment Melville had administered to him for wasting water, and the boy's sincere repentance and remorse, Melville felt certain that young Midshipman Garth Aquinar would never again waste a drop of water. The day that the boy had spent without water was hard, but in the end it taught him a lesson that every sailor must learn. In the end it would be good for him. That is, *if* they lived through this. *If* their long overdue mothership ever came to rescue them.

Four times now Aquinar had made his little trip. His sailcloth pants and white cotton shirt made Melville think of the little middy as a dirty white moth, flitting quickly from the woods to the bones of the cutter. Then he moved slowly, ever so slowly back to the trees, like a grubby white inchworm.

Except for his one embarrassing slash on the buttock, Melville hadn't been hit in the battle, even though he was in the thick of it throughout. Yet his body ached from exertion, as though he'd been used as a punching bag by a whole family of six-legged apes. As though papa, mama, and little baby ape had all given him six licks each.

What does it matter what some little boy is doing? thought Melville. *We are going to die here. Our linkup with* Kestrel *is over a week late. We're almost out of water. Over a third of my company is dead or wounded.*

<<No! Not die!>> replied *Swish-tail*, indignantly. Melville hadn't meant to communicate that thought to his Ship, but when they were in physical contact like this he couldn't help but share his thoughts. <<*Kestrel* come!>> she added, with the pure, strong faith of a child in its parent. He felt the simple confidence of his Ship flowing through him, strengthening him

Like the boy he was watching, Melville had an irrepressible, cheerful spirit. He possessed a few gifts that were unfolding in a satisfying manner. The voice of command and authority, something that many leaders never develop, was coming early for him. He had a knack for poetry that often provided the right Words at the moment of truth, and he had the ability to communicate them well. He was a natural at tactics and military history, and he was very good with a sword and a pistol. But perhaps his most important gift was his ability to live intensely in the present.

Most people live their lives in anticipation and dread of the future. Or they desperately cling to the past. They spend most of their energy thinking and worrying about what happens next or what just happened. The only time they really deal with what is happening *now,* is when they look back on it. And because of this, most people learn how to fear, dreading the future instead of living in the present.

Perhaps it was because he *wasn't* like this, because he lived so intensely in the present, that Melville was generally fearless. It was really nothing special. Most dogs can do it. That's why they're usually happy, and often so full of joy and glee. They never had to deal with the whole human *angst* business. Melville felt that people could learn a lot from dogs. They seemed to have things better worked out, dogs.

So it was that Melville didn't need hope, as long as despair could be postponed. Like little Aquinar he was ever curious, and usually able to find the energy to satisfy that curiosity. *Swish-tail*'s encouragement was all he needed to indulge his curiosity and postpone his despair. And so he resolved to solve this mystery. In doing so he was to witness something near unto a miracle, and open a door that would save their lives and turn the tide of future events, both great and small.

The little company slept, as best they could, through the stifling dry heat of midafternoon. The boy was in the bowels of the cutter. Melville knew from past observation that he would stay there for quite a long time, so he took this opportunity to move to a better position to observe the boy's movement. The slender young lieutenant was sitting cross-legged and he rose straight up, scissoring his legs up with the unthinking ease of youth. Then he moved into the trees to get a better view. Except for the pickets and the medical personnel, Melville and Aquinar were the only ones who moved amidst the gray boles of the emerald green trees.

From here Melville could only see the boy's back, as he returned from the cutter. He appeared to be walking with great care, and then he disappeared into the woods. Minutes later he came running out to the cutter again, scrambling over the heap of apes that Petreckski had shot, oblivious to the stench and heat, to enter into the narrow gap on the east side.

Again Melville moved to another tree, where he could see the little middy's destination. Again, with a slow, careful stride, the boy returned to the woods. This time Melville could see that he held his cupped right hand tight against his belly, apparently to stabilize it. Finally it dawned upon him that the boy had *water* in his hand. A few, a precious few drops of water.

Melville understood where the water must have come from. There's always a little natural seepage from between the slats of a ship's wooden water barrel. Their crash landing on this world probably had sprung the joints of the barrel even further. The boy crawled under the back end of the barrel, and carefully, patiently caught the slow drops as they fell.

Precious few drops, but enough, perhaps, to moisten the lips of an injured man. Melville thought of their wounded, sweltering in the heat, and he felt a slow anger begin to burn within. But he didn't interfere just yet. He wanted to see what this young miscreant, this insect, this worm was doing with the water.

As he leaned around the tree to observe the middy's final destination, Melville was suddenly stunned by what he saw. A small opening, a gray bowl formed by the great trunks of several trees was now exposed to his view. Within that bowl were dozens, no, scores of little fawn-colored, eight-legged spider monkeys. They clung from the trees, they rested on the ground, and they observed from the branches above. Now that he looked more closely, Melville saw that there were hundreds, perhaps thousands more watching from the branches high above.

He remembered how those spider monkeys had dealt with the apes that trespassed into their territory. He remembered the apes' body parts raining down from the trees and he suddenly felt fear for the little midshipman, for Aquinar now knelt in the midst of this furry brown throng.

But the little monkeys didn't threaten him. They didn't even move as the boy knelt down beside a tiny, dappled brown spider monkey. They simply watched, with rapt attention.

Melville moved closer. Mesmerized, he stumbled to the edge of the bowl. He could see that the baby monkey, little bigger than the palm of his hand, lay helpless on the ground, panting with dehydration. With a great effort the little head, no bigger than a baby's fist, raised up to slowly lap the precious drops cupped in the boy's hand. When every drop of moisture was licked from his hand the boy stood carefully up, and came face to face with the lieutenant.

His little eyes began to fill with tears. "I . . . I wasn't wasting it, sir. Honest, I wasn't. They," here he gestured at the many monkeys who solemnly watched from within arm's reach, " . . . they're our friends. They helped us. Lots of them died to help us. I know how it feels to be thirsty, sir, and now . . . now *he's* dying . . . an' . . . and he needs our help."

The lieutenant had trouble finding words and his throat grew tight. "Very well," he croaked, nodding. "Carry on." He stepped carefully back to let the boy pass.

The boy began to walk back to the cutter. As he went, Melville walked beside him wrapping an arm around his shoulders. The boy's shoulders still shuddered with sobs. Melville guided him around to the west side of the cutter, through the wounded, to the front of the water barrel. There the young lieutenant drew a cup of water.

Beside him the other midshipmen, perpetually hungry, were gnawing on ship's biscuits and discussing the advisability and practicality of cooking "monkey meat." "Them apes clearly aren't sentient," Archer was saying, "and there's nothing wrong with eating something that tries to eat *you*. 'S only fair . . ."

"Mister Archer," said Melville.

"Aye, sir?"

"Mister Aquinar has discovered that there is a very slow leak coming from the underside of the water cask. Get something down there to catch any water, and be sure it's put to good use."

"Aye, sir."

"Lieutenant Melville?" Lady Elphinstone asked softly as she walked over.

Melville turned to the Sylvan healer. Her green sash on her yellow gown emphasized her likeness to a lovely flower, but now she was a yellow flower that had stood upon the field of battle. A flower much splattered with blood. "Yes my lady?"

"Josiah's dog is dead. We could not save him."

Melville felt crushed by the loss. He felt so foolish. Six men had died, yet somehow the loss of this noble dog was almost too much to bear. He felt shamed and confused by the tears that welled in his eyes. He didn't want his men to see him weep but there was no choice. He must do his duty and offer his condolences, even if his tears shamed him. *Not* to do his duty would be a far greater shame.

"Thank you, my lady." He turned to where the two rangers knelt upon the ground. Josiah was stroking the gray fur of his dog's corpse. Valandil's dog lay next to the Sylvan ranger. Her black fur was streaked with gold, her ears large and erect. She looked up at Melville with intelligent brown eyes, head cocked slightly to the side. He walked to them and dropped to one knee. Great pain and loss could be seen in their weary faces.

"I'm truly sorry for your loss," he said, looking at Josiah.

Josiah turned to him with a sad smile. "Well, he knew the job was dangerous when he took it."

It was the ranger's way to make jest of grave events. Melville grinned appreciatively through his tears. He placed a hand on the shoulder of Josiah's dog, and said his benediction. Like Josiah's jest it was his way, and it was all he had to give.

"... The burning sun no more shall heat,
    Nor rainy storms on him shall beat;
The bryars and thornes no more shall scratch,
    Nor hungry wolves at him shall catch;
His erring pathes no more shall tread,
    Nor wild fruits eate instead of bread;
For waters cold he doth not long,
    For thirst no more shall parch his tongue;
No rugged stones his feet shall gaule,
    nor stumps nor rocks cause him to fall;
All cares and fears he bids farewell,
    and meanes in safity now to dwell ..."

"Thank you, sir," said Josiah. Melville saw that there were tears welling up in the rangers' weathered, leathery eyes. Little midshipman Aquinar was sobbing openly. There had been so very much death in the boy's life, so very suddenly.

Josiah stared off into the distance and spoke musingly, in his slow drawl. "Ah can't properly communicate to you, sir, the joy of exploring a virgin world. Together, just me and mah dog, we would strike out into the great unknown. The *true* unknown. Nothing can be known about any place until a man has actually put his foot upon it. No satellite imagery, no previous explorers, nothing, absolutely *nothing* to tell you what might be around the next corner. Ancient civilizations and vast, living cities.

Strange creatures and alien races. Flowers and trees, rivers and mountains, like no man has ever seen before."

He looked at Melville and asked, "Have you ever played any of the computer games on high-tech worlds?"

"Yes," said Melville, "an extensive trip to Old Earth was part of our academy training."

"Well, sir, ah think the thing that makes many of them so addictive is the fact that you start with a blank screen." Usually quite laconic, the ranger was saying more now than Melville had ever heard him say before. "As you take each step, it's truly into the unknown, with no idea what might be waiting for you. Monsters, rivers, treasure, mountains, lost civilizations, alien species, *anything* can be in that next 'hex.' When you're done you have, in a way, almost *created* a world, a world where no man has gone before. *That* is what our life together has been like, except it was real. *That* is what it's like to be a ranger in the wilderness. Now mah partner of lo these many years is gone, and ah shall miss him. And ah do thank you for your benediction, it's most apt and befitting." The ranger looked off into the distance again, seeing the distant echoes of wonders and past glories such as few men will ever know.

Valandil looked at the midshipman and the cup of water in the Lieutenant's hand. "What errantry art thou and the young gentleman upon?"

"There's been too much death today," replied Melville, "we go to save one small life."

"'Tis well," replied Valandil. "An apt benediction upon the day. And, Lieutenant?"

"Yes?"

"Thou hast done well today. I know that 'tis hard to tell, of one's own accord. So I tell thee. Well done, Lieutenant."

"Aye," echoed Josiah.

"Thank you. 'Praise from the praiseworthy is above all rewards.'"

Then Melville put an arm around the boy's shoulder, and walked with him back into the trees. The young lieutenant stood back from the place where the little monkey lay, holding the cup of water. He poured a dollop into Aquinar's little hand and let him tend the monkey. Periodically the boy came back out, and the lieutenant solemnly poured another handful of water for the little midshipman.

Melville watched the boy's grubby, tear-streaked, sunburned face, and he had a sudden memory of the brave little midshipman standing on tiptoes to shove a pistol in a ravaging ape's mouth. He looked down in wonder at the boy. Where before he had seen a grubby white worm, suddenly he saw a butterfly, an angel. Tears began to fill the lieutenant's eyes, and he wept with pride.

It was foolish. Six of his men lay dead. Three noble dogs and a cat, too! Eleven men lay wounded. And here they were, expending precious water to tend a little cousin of the creatures who had attacked them. It was foolishness. It was madness. But Melville wouldn't have it any other way.

Tears welled up in his eyes. A teardrop escaped, ran down his cheek and hit the ground. A tear of pride. Water for the dead . . . and water for the living. Water for the gentle, water for the kind and compassionate, water for the values that his men had died for. Water for Westerness and all that it represented.

Suddenly another drop hit the ground. And another. And then more. Melville looked up through the tree branches at the sky. While he had been mesmerized by the scene unfolding before him, above him clouds had crept in from the south and a gentle rain began to fall.

Perhaps, thought Melville, just maybe, someone . . . someone Else was also weeping with pride.

The rain that fell that day saved their lives. First the tarps and sailcloths were set to collect water. The precious fluid was lovingly funneled into the water barrel and into every other available container. After that, as the water continued to flow from the heavens, they drank. The healthy helped the wounded to drink. They all drank their fill, and then they drank some more. Finally they bathed.

Pickets still stood, looking downslope, fully dressed with rifles in hand. The healthy helped their wounded mates to bathe first. The rest stood naked in the rain, passing around bars of soap, while the warm water flowed down their bodies.

Lady Elphinstone and Sergeant Broadax bathed out of sight in the center of the woods. It occurred to Melville that under different circumstances a sailor or marine might have tried to catch a glimpse of the fair Elphinstone as she bathed. But the presence of the Dwarrowdelf NCO seemed to bring any such thoughts to a sudden halt. Because of her wrath, and because . . . well, because no one wanted to see just exactly what there was . . . to see . . . there.

The aid station had expanded out to the west side of the cutter and this became the male bathing area. Petreckski and the rangers took shifts looking after the wounded, so that they could bathe.

The rain was like a warm shower. Like one great communal shower, and the men began to sing.

> "Sing hey! for the bath at close of day
> That washes the weary mud away! . . ."

After they'd sung all the traditional verses, Chief Hans added a few new verses to roars of laughter.

> "Sing hey! fer our skipper at close of day,
> Nothing or a double helping issss . . . . ever 'is way!"

"Aye!" added one old salt. "First we was bored to tears, and then a thousand hairy monkeys comes to lunch!"

"And," chimed in a marine, "first it's dry as dust and now we 'ave t'swim fir our supper! Life with our lieutenant will never be dull!"

"Aye," concluded old Hans quietly, " 'e was a right Heinleiner fer us today."

Melville knew that this was high praise, this acceptance from his men. He also knew that he didn't deserve it. He'd done little more than any other man, but in the richness of their hearts they were willing to give the victory to their leader. He was lucky, and they rejoiced to serve a lucky man.

Prior to the battle it hadn't occurred to him to worry about his ability as a combat leader, since he didn't know that a pocket Armageddon was headed his way. During the battle he was too busy to worry. But now his gut churned with emotions.

He found himself preoccupied with the battle, reliving it over and over in his mind. He second guessed himself, and thought of things that he *could* have done, that he *should* have done. He found himself doubting his ability to face such an event in the future.

He mourned his dead. Yet he was glad, no he *rejoiced* at having survived! And then he felt guilty that so many others should die and he was happy! He'd been taught in the academy that all these things would happen. The writings of the old masters, the founders of warrior science like Alexis Artwohl and Bruce Siddle had survived the Crash. For centuries they'd been required reading for all military leaders. So, intellectually he knew all about these things.

It was good to be warned. The effect would have been devastating without the warning. Still, there was all the difference in the world between knowing about these things and experiencing them. Like the difference between being warned that the adrenaline rush would happen in combat, and actually experiencing it.

In the midst of these emotions, the praise and approval of his men was a balm to his soul. It was what he wanted, what he craved more than anything else in life, even though he didn't deserve it. He knew that such support wouldn't always be there. Sometimes leaders needed to make hard, unpopular decisions. But it was good to have their support now, and he'd revel in it while he could. Even if it was coming from a bunch of naked old salts.

Prior to this, the little spider monkeys had seemed aloof, barely glimpsed as brown flashes in the upper branches. Now they hung from the lower branches, gibbering and jumping as they watched the antics of the little company below.

Melville noticed that the monkey Aquinar had saved was now hanging around the young middy's neck. The little creature clung with all eight limbs, its strange upside-down face, with mouth on top and eyes below, peering forward beside the boy's neck. All the other members of the company gathered round and gently stroked its dappled brown fur. The tiny creature seemed to accept the attention as its due.

After they cleansed their bodies, while the water continued to flow down, the company began to wash and wring out their clothing. They soaked and soaped their garments in basins created by placing sailcloth over low spots in the ground. Then they wrung them out onto the ground. The monkeys seemed to think this was a grand game. The men watched them carefully, worried that the little creatures would try to steal something, but they seemed content to be spectators at this show.

Finally, all the bathing was done, their laundry was clean and every available container was full. His men were renewed and invigorated by the rain, but he knew that it was just temporary. Melville estimated that there was about an hour of daylight left, and he was determined to put it to good use.

"Gentlemen!" he began. "We've won a mighty victory, but this hill isn't truly ours until we've removed all of our uninvited guests! Let us use the remaining daylight to send them home again. Sergeant Broadax, Chief Petty Officer Hans, if you'd see to it I'd be obliged. I suggest that we begin with the ones closest in, and I think we can make good use of the rain to float them back to where they came from."

The pouring rain was being channeled down the hill in streams, and it proved to be a relatively simple matter to half drag and half float the bodies down to the nearest stream and send them on their way. This was the kind of work best left to the supervision of their sergeants and petty officers, but the young lieutenant couldn't permit himself to slack off, and he didn't let his midshipmen do so either. Wherever the work was the hardest, Melville tried to be there, in the thick of it, assisting and guiding. His middies had no option but to follow his example.

As they worked, Melville talked with the men and with his midshipmen. He sounded them out to see how they felt. "Mr. Archer," he asked, "how did you find combat?"

"Well, sir," replied the boy with apparent sincerity, "nobody's ever tried to kill me before. It kind of made me feel important. I think it's good for a fellow's self-esteem"

"Aye, sir," added Crater with a frown of concentration, "surviving combat's sort of comforting. Only not very."

In the midst of their labor, they found themselves again with allies from above. First one little brown monkey appeared to help them, comically teaming up with two stalwart men to drag a corpse across the ground. Then another and yet another joined in. Soon there were hundreds, then thousands of the spider monkeys, all delighting in sending the invaders floating downhill. If they'd all come plunging out of the trees together they'd probably have frightened the little company, but in this gradual manner they slowly earned the trust of the men of Westerness.

The slit latrines that had been dug on the downslope sides of their position were flooded. Sergeant Broadax put her most junior troops to work digging drainage ditches downslope from the latrines. The nasty stuff always did flow downhill, and rank did have its privileges.

With the help of gravity, the deluge, and thousands of spider monkeys, all the ape corpses were soon removed. Only two were held back, along with a few dead spider monkeys, for Petreckski and their surgeon to dissect later.

Melville's food-obsessed midshipmen were hunched around a cooking fire, roasting bits of some mystery meat skewered on sticks. Aquinar was handing up a tasty bit to his monkey, who chewed it eagerly. Not really wanting to know what they were cooking, he called the "young gentlemen" to him, and walked up to Broadax and Hans.

The two NCOs were watching the removal of the last of the enemy corpses. "Sergeant Broadax, Chief Hans."

"Aye, sir," they replied together, Hans spitting a stream of tobacco juice, and Broadax still clenching her seemingly indestructible cigar in her teeth.

"I'm not too concerned about hypothermia; this rain still feels like a warm shower. But if it cools off tonight we may be in trouble. So I want a good fire going soon. Be sure it's tended all night. The men will need to debrief themselves after battle, and sitting around a fire will help. Tomorrow night will be even more important for debriefing, so be sure we have one then, too."

"Aye, sir," they replied, again in unison. They knew exactly what he was talking about. For untold thousands of years, warriors almost *always* took the nights off. Across the millennia they "debriefed" themselves every night after combat, around the campfire.

Then, in the twentieth century, starting with World War I, combat became a twenty-four-hour-a-day endeavor. From that point on, armies fought day and night for months on end, and the age-old process of nightly debriefings disappeared. Throughout that tragic century the price warriors paid for this, in psychiatric casualties and in post-traumatic stress, was profound. In the twenty-first century this process was reintroduced, using labels like "critical incident stress debriefings" and "after action reviews," but it was really something age-old made new again. It was a simple, universal human equation, first introduced by a classic science fiction author, E.E. "Doc" Smith: "pain shared equals pain divided, and joy shared equals joy multiplied." Sometimes it was even written as a formula:

(pain shared = pain ÷) + (joy shared = joy x)

As the warriors of Westerness talked that night, and on each subsequent night, they would divide their pain, and multiply their joy, making battle something that they could live with and could do again if they had to.

"What I *am* concerned about is another attack. If they come at us again, or if this meat downhill draws carnivores or carrion eaters, we need to be on guard. The men will be tired, but I think it's necessary to keep double pickets tonight. Do you agree?"

"Aye, sir," replied Hans.

"Aye, *indeed*," rumbled Broadax, sucking deep on her cigar as rain pattered off of her helmet and ran down her beard.

My God, thought Melville, *how does she keep it going, even in this rain? It's not a cigar, it's a damned nuclear fusion reactor.*

"Good," said Melville. "Sergeant Broadax, your marines will do picket duty by themselves tonight. I have another task for our sailors. Can your men handle the duty by themselves?"

The marine sergeant's eyes grew wide and she rocked back on her heels. "Sir! None o' *my* marines is solar powered *or* water soluble!" Then, with a scowl, "We'll handle it."

Melville tried to hide a grin. "Crater," he continued, looking at young Jarad Crater, his senior midshipman, "You'll be the officer in charge of the pickets tonight. I suggest you listen very carefully to any suggestions the sergeant gives you."

"Yessir!" gulped the midshipman, swallowing in wide-eyed horror at the thought of disregarding any of the Dwarrowdelf's "suggestions."

"Hans," he continued, turning to the grizzled old sailor, "I don't want to impose upon the hospitality of our newfound friends, but if another group like this attacks us, a retreat up into the trees may be our only hope. Young Aquinar seems to have won their trust. I want you to work carefully with him to get some ropes up into the lower branches." The old sailor's eyes lost their focus and he began to scowl with deep thought. You could almost see ratlines and rigging dancing in his head.

"Ultimately the goal is to prepare a method for everyone to move up into the trees quickly, but we've got to go about this gradually, earning their trust a bit at a time. If possible, I want Aquinar to spend the night in a hammock in the trees. Have the proper ropes, tackle, and supports ready to go for a larger operation on short notice. Tonight we'll get Aquinar in the trees, tomorrow night hopefully a few more can sleep there.

"Aquinar will be in charge of all aspects involving interaction with the monkeys. He'll have final say in all such matters." Everyone nodded their heads soberly. Word of Aquinar's "miracle" had spread quickly. Aquinar nodded his head. He appeared to be completely untroubled by this profound new responsibility. The little spider monkey wrapped around his neck looked on sleepily.

"Mister Archer." Here he turned and looked young Midshipman Buckley Archer in the eyes.

"Aye sir?"

"You'll be the officer in charge of the rigging and prep for movement into the trees. Remember, Mister Aquinar calls the shots on anything involving the monkeys, and I trust you to listen closely to Chief Petty Officer Hans' advice in all technical aspects of rigging." Like Crater, the young man's eyes went wide at the mere thought of disregarding such "advice." Chief Hans' grizzled face grinned appreciatively.

"Think about how to get the wounded up, and how to get our supplies up if we have to. You have full authority to strip anything you need from *Swish-tail*'s hulk. Understood?"

"Aye sir," the young man replied, gulping at the responsibility and trying to think how he'd balance it all out. He was an unusually clever lad and Melville felt confident he could work it out, especial with Chief Hans' "advice."

"All of you be sure you get some sleep tonight, and be sure your men get a chance to sleep. There are enough leaders and men assigned to each task to go turn-and-turn-about."

Suddenly, Chief Hans interrupted. "Gawd a'mighty sir. Do ya see that?"

By the last light of day they turned and watched, open-mouthed, as spider monkeys rode the corpses downstream, cheering and gibbering with high-pitched peeping noises, like baby chicks, while their macabre boats careened downstream to the far wood line. Some of them found sticks to serve as poles, and they used these to push and fend their ghastly rafts. As the corpses hit the wood line at the bottom of the hill, the tiny monkeys all leapt off, scampered up the slope, and found yet another "boat" that was about to embark downstream.

When Melville saw the monkeys using poles to assist in their bizarre rafting, he realized that they were a tool-using species. They were tool users, possibly even sentient. And they were friends.

As the last light of day ebbed away, Melville knew he'd achieved something. Just *what* they'd achieved this day wasn't clear yet, but it was more than mere survival. It was . . . significant. What more could a young man ask, than to do great deeds and be significant upon the stage of life?

Chapter the 4th
The Ship Returns: One Nameless, Tattered, Broken Man

Though giant rains put out the sun,
    Here stand I for a sign,
Though Earth be filled with waters dark,
    My cup is filled with wine.
Tell to the trembling priests that here
    Under the deluge rod,
One nameless, tattered, broken man
    Stood up and drank to God.

"The Deluge"
G.K. Chesterton

The next morning the wet, rainy world slowly, sullenly dawned, and the men of Westerness began to stir. Every man in their little company was exhausted to the bone. The rain was still warm, but it was beginning to outlast its welcome.

The wounded lay in the few dry spaces that could still be found within the hold of their little cutter. Beneath the branches of the mighty trees were more dry patches where the rest of the company slept.

As they began to move around, some of them found that they had company. Somewhere in the night, soft little spider monkeys had joined them. Melville had his. Petreckski had one. Chief Hans and even Sergeant Broadax literally had monkeys on their backs.

For Melville it was an eerie feeling. He'd turn his head, and there'd be an upside-down face staring solemnly back at him. Broadax seemed slightly embarrassed by hers, but she opted to ignore it, acting as though it wasn't there.

Little Aquinar still slept in his hammock, a full five yards off the ground, warm and dry next to the bole of a great tree. His little fawn-colored monkey still clung tightly to his neck. Dozens of other monkeys also shared his hammock, sleeping contentedly.

Melville didn't have the heart to awaken the little midshipman, but he did climb up to be sure the boy was still alive, that the monkeys hadn't killed him in his sleep. Melville was horrified at the boy's peril, but he was their best ambassador to the little monkeys. Aquinar *was* a boy, but he was also a warrior and the right man for this job. Like a loving father checking on his young child in the middle of the night, Melville watched to see that the boy still breathed. Reassured, and observed by sleepy monkeys who seemed completely unbothered by his presence, he slid back down.

At this point the huge Corporal Kobbsven strode up to Melville. He was clearly a man with a mission. "Sir! I am happy to report that there is now vater in the vell that vee bin diggin'!"

Blink. " . . . Yes. Good. Thank you, Corporal."

Their first duty that day was to bury their dead. Everyone took turns digging the graves of their comrades. Melville took his turn and made sure that each of his young midshipmen did as well. Little Aquinar awoke and descended from above in time to help dig one of the dogs' graves.

Six large holes and four smaller ones were dug. The bodies of their comrades were lovingly wrapped in sailcloth shrouds and lowered one-by-one into the graves. They'd traveled far across the shoreless seas of Flatland to reach this world, and now they'd be planted here. They would gain immortality in this land that they had discovered and died to defend. Immortality such as every sailor dreamed of. Future settlers would remember their names. Cities and mountains would be named after them. It would be a fit and proper ending for one who traveled the hidden land forlorn. Provided their mother ship returned and their sacrifice was not in vain.

Now it was Melville's time to say Words. He'd never felt so inadequate. All he could do was reach back into their heritage and set forth the Words, those ancient Words. Ten thousand applications to the griefs of a thousand years had carved these Words into their cultural consciousness. Thereby giving them the power to heal and strengthen lives in times of sorrow and loss.

Melville's personal hero, the warrior poet Lord Wavell, once wrote that, "Long funeral pieces . . . become tedious . . . by their length. Heavy mourning, deep black edges, long widowhood, unrestrained grief are out of fashion, as they must be to a generation which has indulged in . . . war." The key was "economy of words."

And so Melville chose simply to say this, as his company looked on. Above them countless thousands of monkeys, like a heavenly chorus of fawn-colored, eight-legged angels, also gazed solemnly from the trees.

"Here dead lie we because we did not choose
To live and shame the land from which we sprung.
Life to be sure is nothing much to lose;
But young men think it is, and we were young."

He turned to Petreckski. "Brother Theo," he asked, "could you say a few words?" The crew wasn't a particularly religious bunch. Yet, like the sailors of Old Earth, most of the men who sail in two-space have some spiritual aspect to them They came from many and diverse faiths, but when the mystery of life and death was upon them, the Words of a cleric, even an unordained monk like Petreckski, could be comforting.

Like Melville, Petreckski reached back to the old, strong Words that resonated in the heritage and souls of these lonely men on this distant, alien shore. In his clear, pure tenor voice he began to sing a song that was a particular favorite to sailors, and the company joined in.

"There's a land that is fairer than day,
And by faith we can see it afar;
For the Father waits over the way

To prepare us a dwelling place there.
In the sweet by and by,
We shall meet on that beautiful shore.
In the sweet by and by,
We shall sing on that beautiful shore,
And our spirits shall sorrow no more,

" . . . on that beautiful shore. Amen."

Then the dead were left to their own affairs, and the living got on with theirs. Or, as Old Hans put it, "Those who git ta live, should."

Only a few more days passed before their Ship returned, not with joy, but with more sorrow and tribulations. With yet more challenges for young lieutenant Melville.

"Sir! Sir!" called Midshipman Archer. "*Kestrel* has returned! Lieutenant Fielder has come down!"

Lieutenant Daniel Fielder and two sailors had descended from two-space, and were striding down the hill. The rain had finally stopped but clouds still hung low in the sky. The wounded were laid out to take the air.

Fielder was dark haired, thick set, with a florid face and bushy sideburns. He was junior in rank to Melville, but he'd spent many more years as a midshipman and was the older man. Melville always considered him to be a bit of a bully, and now Fielder tried to assert the authority of his years. "My God, Melville, everything has gone straight to hell, and now you've made a hash of it here!" he said, looking at the wounded. "Your company has been torn to hell!"

Perhaps Fielder would have succeeded in turning the men from Melville, but every heart was turned against him the moment this mean-spirited insult left his lips. He severed all chance of winning them over with one further thoughtless comment, as he looked at the little eight-legged monkey peering over Melville's shoulder with its comical upside-down face. "And what is that clinging to your necks? We've been in a running battle, the Ship is shot to hell and here you are playing with the local critters? Have you all gone native?" The monkey and Melville turned their heads to look at each other, and it seemed as though they were sharing the same thoughts as they nodded to each other reflectively.

Lieutenant Fielder continued his rant, "We were attacked without warning by an overwhelming force of Guldur. We gave them the slip, but they will be upon us in a few hours. The *Kestrel* is dying. Everyone senior to us is dead. A third of the crew is dead or wounded. I'm in charge. We have to abandon ship. We'll flee down to this world and scuttle the Ship. Then we'll uproot the Pier. That's the only way we can be safe. We have to hurry!"

Melville was stunned but he quickly rallied. In the end it was protocol, procedures and principle that empowered him. He replied softly, "Aye, we can evacuate the seriously wounded. But if Captain Crosby and the first officer are dead then I am senior to you, Mr. Fielder, and *I* will make the decisions here. I will inspect the Ship and the crew while you begin movement of the wounded."

Fielder screamed, "You're insane! We can't fight! I told you, the enemy force is overwhelming, our Ship is dying!"

Melville became even more calm. "I'll judge that for myself. If we are capable of inflicting damage upon our foe, then we are duty bound to do so."

"Now I know you're mad! You're filled with your poetry and it has twisted your brain!"

Melville took a deep breath and tried to reply calmly. He raised his voice so that he could be heard clearly by the sailors and marines around them, "If anything has influenced me, I hope it's duty and honor. Aye, as befits a warrior of Westerness. Duty and honor haven't 'twisted' me, they have *shaped* me so that I cannot and *will* not turn from a fight while we have the means to hurt our foe. *I* am the senior man here Mr. Fielder, and you *will* by God obey my orders!" Then Melville turned his back and walked away. Like all bullies, Fielder backed down when the odds were against him.

"Lady Elphinstone?" Melville asked their surgeon as he walked into the aid station.

"Yes?" she responded, stepping forward.

"Decide who among your charges can be released immediately for light duty, and have them sent up to *Kestrel*. Then join us on the *Kestrel* and evacuate anyone who is too injured to assist in battle." She calmly nodded her assent.

"Mr. Crater?"

"Sir!"

"Work with Sergeant Broadax and the marine detail. You'll be responsible for the movement of all wounded from the *Kestrel*. Draft the marines on the Ship if you need assistance. Evacuate only the individuals the surgeon designates." He looked briefly at Midshipman Crater, but mostly he watched for the marine sergeant to nod her understanding.

"Yes, sir!"

"Mr. Archer?"

"Yes, sir?"

"You work with our sailors to set up the rigging to lower the wounded down onto the Pier. Work with Chief Petty Officer Hans, but release him to me as soon as you're sure that you can complete the task on your own. I will be inspecting the Ship. Don't draft any assistance from the Ship for this duty. Complete this duty as quickly as you can and then return all sailors to their sections aboard the Ship." Again, Melville was addressing and looking at Archer, but he was also watching for Hans' nod.

"Mr. Aquinar, you stay with me."

"Aye, sir!"

"Does everyone understand?" There was a chorus of assent. He thought briefly about what to do with Fielder. The man seemed out of his mind with panic and dread. Best to keep him here while Melville assumed command of the *Kestrel*.

"Lieutenant Fielder?" Melville asked. Fielder had been following Melville around, keeping a slight distance. Now his only response was to glare at Melville. "I'd value your appraisal of our situation here. Please speak with Brother Petreckski and the rangers, they will give you their account of all edible plants and creatures. Their input will be vital as to whether we can stay here indefinitely. I hope to make a fresh assessment of the situation on our Ship, and certainly your outside assessment of the situation here will be of value."

This indication that Melville was keeping an open mind to the possibility of evacuating to this world seemed to mollify Fielder. "Very well," he replied, "but you'll see, the situation on the Ship is hopeless." Melville looked at the purser and the rangers, and felt confident that they'd keep the lieutenant occupied. He strode up the hill accompanied by Broadax, Hans, and the middies. Elphinstone joined them, having already designated three of her patients for light duty.

They approached the Keel of the old *Swish-tail*, now standing like a flagpole, or a mast, surrounded by a platform of white Nimbrell timbers. Melville scrambled up the ladder to the top of the platform, dropped to one knee, placed a hand upon the Keel and concentrated.

<<*Swish-tail*?>> he asked.

<<Captain!>> Melville "felt" pleasure at his presence and concern at the turn of events. <<*Kestrel* is above. She is hurt. Evil comes.>>

<<Can she fight?>> Melville asked.

<<She wants to!>>

<<Good,>> he thought. Then he tried to send his emotions to the little Ship, his first independent command. He tried to speak of his love and appreciation, and his sorrow upon departing. Soon she would transition into a world's Keel, and she would no longer speak directly to humans. Before that happened he wanted her to know of human love for her and her kind. He thought he felt it back in return.

<<Captain, what is my name?>> Suddenly Melville realized that he'd left a duty undone. It was his right and his duty to name this world, and his *Swish-tail* would take on that name. He could name the world after himself. But that was unacceptable when so many of his men had done so much more, *paid* so much more to make this possible. He could name it after his dead captain, but Captain Crosby already had a world named after him from past voyages. No, he knew who to name it after. Speaking aloud *and* to the Ship, he named this world after the person he believed had done the most to win their survival.

"<<I name thee: Broadax's World!>>" He turned and saw Sergeant Broadax beam with pride and joy, inhaling deeply on her cigar. He saw the others nod their heads in agreement.

Even *Swish-tail,* now Broadax's World, agreed completely. <<Good!>> she replied, <<I like her.>> Thus it was done.

The Keel was made of a mysterious material carefully guarded by the secretive Celebrimbor shipwrights. This class of shipwrights existed in every race that sailed the seas of Flatland, and the men of Old Earth had joined that club. *Ah, but at such a price,* thought Melville. *The "Crash" was the admission fee the Elder King claimed for Earth to join that club.*

One end of the Keel was planted in the living earth. The other end disappeared up into two-space. Nothing of the *Kestrel* or Flatland could be seen from here, except for a rope ladder that hung down from the Ship above, seeming to be suspended in thin air.

It occurred to Melville that before he climbed up the ladder he should send his monkey on its way. He'd be sad to see the soft, gentle creature go, but it would be cruel to snatch it from its green home into impending battle. Broadax, Hans, and the three middies also moved to set down the baby monkeys that had adopted them. Prior to this the monkeys always permitted themselves to be set aside whenever their presence was unwelcome. Now the result was a comical, ludicrous dance as each of the sailors tried to grab a monkey that didn't want to be grabbed.

The monkeys scampered round and about, up the Pier and back onto a shoulder. They were now in front, now down between legs, then they scrambled under jackets to hang just out of reach between shoulder blades. Melville braced himself against the Keel to grab his monkey and he felt *Swish-tail* say, <<Trust them. Good Monkeys.>>

That was good enough for him. While climbing up the Pier the monkeys were in direct contact with the Ship, and they couldn't hide their true nature from this telepathic contact. "Enough!" said Melville. "We don't have time for this. Let them come if they insist, and let us share our fates."

"Aye," said Hans, "'Of'n the unbidden guest proves the best company.'"

Melville grabbed the rope ladder and scrambled up, followed by old Hans. His head popped into two-space and lo!, "the gray rain-curtain turned all to silver glass and was rolled back." And he beheld once again the stunning beauty of the "hidden land forlorn." His ears were caressed again by that strange music, the celestial sounds of Flatland, and his eyes were bathed anew in the endless, vivid blue expanse of the "shoreless seas."

Maxfield Parrish had known these blues. To the east was light, sunrise blue where this solar system's star was influencing the vast plain of Flatland. Immediately around him was a small patch of blue-green that indicated a living world. To the south, west, and north Flatland began to darken into deep blue. In the distance he could see the midnight blue between solar systems. In the far distance he could see the sunrise blue of distant suns, blending together into a brightness that stretched all the way round the far horizon.

He looked once more upon all this beauty, and he knew again where "Kilmeny" had been.

> . . . Kilmeny had been where the cock never crew,
> Where the rain never fell, and the wind never blew.
> But it seem'd as the harp of the sky had rung,
> And the airs of heaven played round her tongue,
> When she spake of the lovely forms she had seen,
> And a land where sin had never been;
> A land of love and a land of light,
> Withouten sun, or moon, or night;
> Where the river swa'd a living stream,
> And the land a pure celestial beam;
> The land of vision it would seem,
> A still, and everlasting dream.

Flatland, or two-space (or the Calacirian, to call it by its Sylvan name), was what the sailors called the universe, the environment, the realm that they sailed in. Flatland was also what they called that blue, two dimensional barrier: the plane, the "sea" that the sailors sailed upon, which contains the whole galaxy.

In two-space the whole galaxy was squashed flat as a disc. Flatter than the flattest disc you can think of. Impossibly flat, since there *was no third dimension*. Except where they carried it around with them. This was Flatland. On a Ship you could view it from above or below, but the only way to get into real space is to go *into* Flatland, *into* the "real" galaxy.

The Keel, and the Elbereth Moss that grew in it and around it, created a field in which a piece of three-space could exist in two-space, in Flatland. Flatland wanted to squeeze you flat. It constantly compressed your little piece of three-space from top and bottom, and that downward, compacting pressure created a "wind" that pushed against their sails. The field of three-space concentrated the gravitational forces of flatland the way a sharp point will concentrate the electrical forces on a charged piece of metal, the way a lightning rod attracts the electrical forces above it. These stronger gravitational forces "above" the ship, on both sides of the plain, caused a downward flow of pressure on the ship that could be "caught" by the sails. The pressure was constant, a steady downward "wind." By using forward-leaning masts and sails they could partially capture the force of this wind, making it possible to truly sail the shoreless seas.

Their galaxy was squashed flat, but other galaxies could be seen above and below them, as stars might hang above a flat earth. Above him hung old friends, spread thickly and densely across the black "sky" of two-space. Hanging directly above was Remmirath, a stunningly beautiful group of galaxies known also as the Netted Stars. All he had to do was look up at the Netted Stars to know that he was on the "upper" side of the galaxy, as convention and tradition agreed to call it. With one glance at this constellation, or any other patch of the Flatland sky, he could immediately orient himself to the cardinal directions.

To the "north" was red Borgil, and directly to the south was the constellation known as the Swordsman. One galaxy, its disc seen from the side so that it made a linear formation, formed the Swordsman's shining belt. Two similar galaxies joined end-to-end to form his gleaming sword, thrusting to the west. The Swordsman was also known as Menelvagor to the Sylvan. Westerness had embraced it as a symbol of their kingdom, their vigorous young empire expanding to the galactic west from their beginning on Old Earth.

Direction of travel across the galaxy was designated as north toward the galactic center, and south toward the galactic rim, also sometimes called Hubward and Rimwards. Viewed from an arbitrarily agreed upon "above," west was to the left, or Turnwise, when facing north. And east was designated to the right or Widdershins.

They had only been able to loosely relate what they found in two-space to what astronomers saw in three-space. The galaxies that hung above and below them in two-space, and the destinations they arrived at, often could not be made to match any "known" location in three-space. It drove astronomers mad trying to relate the sights and destinations of Flatland to what they "knew" existed in the "real" world.

A sailor popped into two-space. He sailed across the endless seas of Flatland. He navigated by the "stars" to a new world. He popped back into three-space, and the stars were different. Who cared about some astronomer's reckoning? *He* knew where he was, and he knew how to navigate home again. What more could any sailor ask?

Many high-tech worlds flourished in the galaxy, but none of them had ever developed interstellar travel through three-space. Why should they, when the mystery, the beauty and the vast expanse of two-space and its "hither shores" awaited them? Why would any planet expend the vast resources needed to develop and conduct interstellar travel? Any civilization could sail to a virtually infinite number of worlds with no more difficulty than the sailors of eighteenth-century Earth traveled to distant continents. *If* they learned the secrets of the Celebrimbor shipwrights, and *if* they were willing to play by the rules of the Elder King.

This, *this!* was the gift of the Elder King, thought Melville, as he rejoiced in the far flung galaxies that hung so close above him. Flatland compressed distances, so that travel between worlds was practical. It also compacted distances so that the galaxies hanging above him looked as near as the Moon from Old Earth. Like most sailors he never got tired of looking at them. On the world below him he'd almost given up hope of ever seeing them again and now, for a brief moment, he rejoiced in it.

After a sailor's brief, orienting glance at the sea and the sky he turned his head and looked at the *Kestrel*, dreading what he'd see. The rope ladder hung from the Ship's bowsprit, and from here he could see no damage. All he could see was the bow of the Ship, and only the portion of the bow that was "above" the plain of Flatland, that vast, two-dimensional plain in which the three-dimensional form of the Ship floated. There might well be great damage to her flanks, stern, or below the plain of Flatland, where he couldn't see.

The *Kestrel* was of the *Falcon* class, constructed over 100 years prior with her sister Ships, *Falcon, Sparrow Hawk*, *Pigeon Hawk*, *Peregrine*, *Meriadoc*, and *Gyrfalcon*. She was what the Westerness Navy was pleased to call a frigate, with three masts extending above and below Flatland.

She was constructed of white Nimbrell timbers, which were coated with the Elbereth Moss, making her a beautiful, pure white. Except where she was painted with red trim on the "red" side, and green trim on her "green" side. She was like a great swan resting in pure blue water.

The old concepts of port and starboard, left and right didn't work when there were essentially two ships, slapped together keel to keel. So convention established that all of one side was the "green-side," while the other side was the "red-side."

Flying from her mainmast, both above and below, she flew the Westerness flag, a four-armed, pinwheel galaxy on a royal blue background.

She carried forty 12-pounder cannon, twenty above and twenty below the plain of Flatland. She was intended as much for cargo, transport and exploration as for war, with a large hold, a large complement, and six cutters. *Swish-tail*, *Sharp-ears*, and *Wise-nose* were on the deck "above" Flatland. *Bumpkin*, *White-socks*, and the captain's barge, *Fatty Lumpkin,* were lashed to the reverse deck, arbitrarily and universally referred to as "below" the vast plain formed by Flatland.

She was down to four cutters now. *Swish-tail* had been intentionally beached on the world below, her Keel used to form the Pier.

Bumpkin was lost, along with their second mate and a small crew, in an earlier exploration of a nearby world. She'd been beached on a shore and her Keel didn't raise back up into two-space. After several weeks of waiting they had no choice but to bid their comrades a sad farewell. If they hadn't raised a Pier yet, they never would. They marked this spot on their charts as a "reef," warning others away from what treacherously and deceptively looked to be a habitable world.

Melville leaned to look as far as he could down the red-side of the Ship, which was her starboard or right side from above the plain of Flatland. He saw their carpenter, Mister Tibbits in *Wise-nose*, lashed alongside the *Kestrel*, where a repair crew was working on a portion of her flank.

"Ahoy Chips!" he shouted.

The carpenter looked up from his work. "Mr. Melville! I'm so very glad to see you, sir!"

The carpenter held a warrant officer's position. He seemed to be the senior officer present, so Melville called out to him, "Permission to come aboard!"

"Aye, sir! Come and join us here, if you will, sir!"

Melville was already scrambling the rest of the way up the ladder to where he could flip up onto the deck. Hans, Broadax, the middies, and finally Lady Elphinstone followed to begin their assigned tasks.

From here he could see that the upper deck had been savaged by the most severe blast of grapeshot imaginable. The white Nimbrell timber of the mainmast was chewed almost all the way through. Great chunks of railing and decking had been blown out of existence. Much of the rigging was recently repaired, with pieces of shrouds and ratline still hanging in shambles.

The Ship's crew all wore work clothing made of old, off-white sailcloth. Sailors hung in the rigging like a flock of dirty white birds, chattering and toiling efficiently. Throughout the Ship, seamen were working under the carpenter's guidance. Several were in the cutter working beside him.

Melville went to his left, toward the red-side, moving around the cutter lashed to the deck on the Ship's bow. He hurried over to the waist and looked down at Chips in the cutter below. He grabbed a bit of railing and hopped carefully down to land beside the carpenter.

Elphinstone went straight to the dispensary to tend to the wounded. Hans, Broadax and the middies went about their tasks, but the two NCOs made a point of staying where they could hear the conversation in the cutter below. Little Aquinar stood immediately above in the Ship, awaiting Melville's orders. Throughout this part of the Ship the sailors continued to work, but they shifted subtly so that they also could see and hear the conversation on the cutter.

"Dear Lord, Chips, what happened?" Melville asked. "What could have done this kind of damage?"

"Aye, sir. But this is nothin' compared to what the bastards did with their damned huge round shot below. May the Elder King curse them to vacuum!"

"Tell me about it," said Melville, putting a hand on the old warrant officer's shoulder.

"Well sir, after we dropped you and your company off in the world below we left and went on a short explorin' trip eastward of here. It was all slow easy sailin'. All Asimov days you might say. Lots of plot and character development but precious little action. The kind of adventure *I'd* write for myself if I was doin' the writin', if you take my meanin'." The old carpenter leaned up against the cutter's mast and continued with his story, while Melville sat on the railing.

"We was about ready to turn around to come back to link up with you, when we runned into a Guldur ship comin' from the east. It was a mite smaller than ours, and she only had four guns to a side, two above and below. They was *big* guns, but we reckoned they could only be low velocity carronades. So we wasn't too worried. They signaled to pull up for a talk, and what with Westerness tryin' so hard to stay neutral and keepin' out of the Elder Races' squabbles and all, it never occurred to us that they'd sucker-punch us!" At this point Tibbits began gesturing in accompaniment to his tale.

"But old Captain Crosby was always a savvy one, he was. Our gun ports all had their hatch covers closed, nice and peaceful like, but behind the hatch covers we was loaded with double shot in every gun, manned and ready. But so did the enemy! Lootenant, those guns was no carronades! It shouldn't be possible to build cannon that big. Everyone knows that the Keel charges can't be designed to give that much energy. For hundreds of years it's been so. But they fired at us, right through their closed hatch covers, and did us more damage with one volley than we could with a dozen. I tell you, sir, it ain't natural to have guns that big and powerful.

"They let rip with grapeshot in the two upper guns, and ball in the lower. The captain, Lord bless him, the first mate, and the marine lootenant all met down on the red-side in the upper waist to come over to that Guldur bastard. The grapeshot ripped our red-side like nothin' you ever seen before! The whole boardin' party, an honor guard of six marines, and the bosun pipin' them, all disappeared! We've only got bloody bits and pieces left to bury! Four guns were destroyed, and the crew killed or wounded on two others, leavin' only four guns on the upper red-side. You see what it looks like here, but that's after weeks of fixin' and patchin' while we was on the run, with that bastard right on our tail all the way.

"The real damage was done with the cannonballs that hit us below. They punched through the hull, shattered the mainmast housin' for the lower *and* upper sides. Then they punched *right* on through and out the green-side! On the red-side they destroyed three guns, leavin' only seven below." Now the old carpenter began to pace the deck of the little cutter.

"But sir," said the old sailor as tears began to flow down his cheeks. "Sir, the vacuum-cursed dogs cut our Keel! The Keel's only holdin' together with splinters. Lady Elbereth's Gift, the Moss on the Keel, is all that seems to be holdin' the charge. And sir, the Ship is dyin'! Only the Ship, old *Kestrel* herself is holdin' us in two-space. If not for her, we would'a popped into vacuum days ago, and she can't keep it up much longer. She's dyin' sir!" The old carpenter sat and began to sob.

"Sir," he said, looking up through his tears, "you know that besides the captain, the other person the Ship talks to, just a little, sometimes, is her carpenter? With the captain dead she's talkin' to me. She's mad for vengeance. She wants at that bastard of a Guldur, but she can't, sir. She can't. I've done all I can, but she can't keep hangin' on. Any second now she's gonna pop into vacuum and we'll all die. We gotta get outa here!"

"Chips! Mister Tibbits!"

"Yessir?" he asked, looking up through tear blurred eyes at the young lieutenant.

Quietly Melville continued. "It's time to act like an officer of the Westerness Navy. *Kestrel* needs us now, more than ever, to do our duty. Our *full* duty. Whatever that may be. Whatever cup is set before us, we must take it. Now, tell me the rest of what happened."

"Aye, sir. Sorry, sir."

On the Ship above them all pretense of work stopped and everyone watched. This was the cue for Broadax and Hans to go into action.

"Ye damned blueboys!" shouted Broadax, turning her cigar stub and withering, concentrated, bloodshot Dwarrowdelf glare on them. "Git yer tails to *yer* business while yer betters tends to theirs!" She randomly selected a poor soul to torment. "'At means *you*, Andrest! If ye was any denser, I swear light'd bend 'round ye!"

Not to be outdone, Broadax's fellow NCO added his two bits. "An jist wat do ya think *yer* doin' Jonesy!" said Hans, spitting a stream of tobacco juice overboard as he selected another random victim. "You pay attention ta yer work. Nothin' is foolproof fer a truly talented fool like you!"

Then the two NCOs went about the age-old task of glowering at subordinates, but they stayed close, where they could hear the rest of the carpenter's tale.

Tibbits drew a deep, shuddering breath and continued. "The bastards opened fire, but it must take forever for those big guns to reload. We was stunned, but we had all the red-side guns manned, and we fired right back. Ol' Guns, Mr. Barlet, he let 'er rip, right through our hatch covers, with four above, and seven below. Thirteen 12-pounders, all loaded with double shot at point-blank range can do the Elder King's own damage sir! As we was pullin' off, we hit them again, and then again, all on what we'd call their green-side. We musta hurt the bastards, but all the shots was into their hull, none of their masts or riggin' was damaged much, so it didn't seem to slow them down any."

"Chips, this may be very important," Melville said, gripping the old sailor's shoulder. "As you remember it, do we have an advantage of height in the waist?"

"Aye sir, over a yard's height advantage, all the way across, except where there was a funny little half a quarterdeck. It's really more like a connin' tower on the corner, astern. Above, their quarter-deck is on the red-side, while below it's on the green-side. They have a little jollyboat on davits hangin' off the quarterdeck on each side, so it'd be tricky to board from their rear quarter. That boat'll keep you from gettin' close.

"Their guns are rigged all weird, too. On the green-side they have the guns all for'ard above the plain of Flatland, and all astern below. On the red-side, all the guns below are for'ard, while the ones above are squished back astern."

"Good. As I understand it, the jollyboat would hamper boarding astern, on either side. But on the red-side, above, they don't have a gun for'ard. And we could board her from there, from the for'ard upper red quarter, without worrying about those guns?"

"Aye . . . aye, I guess so, sir. Unless they swing that gun up for'ard, as a bow chaser. But so far they haven't done that above, just the one gun below. It must be damnable hard to swing the gun up front, and they probably want a full broadside on at least one side. I know I would, if I only had four guns to a broadside.

"But, Lootenant," Tibbits continued, "the ones below will rake us like hell's own furies."

"Aye Chips, but we won't *be* below. *They don't know that our Ship is dying.* We'll smash our bows together, red-side to red-side. Everyone, including the cook and her cat, will be hidden away, ready to board from that one quarter. Even if we begin to sink from the impact, it won't matter, because *we'll all be on their Ship.* Meanwhile, down below, they can board our Ship, and *they'll die with the Ship!* Can you think of a more fitting end for the bastards?"

"Aye, sir," said the old carpenter, looking up through his tears with a faint glint of hope in his eye.

"Now, you say we had double shot in the first volley. Did that volley penetrate their hull?"

"Aye, sir. Punched clean through the hull on this side. I don't know where they went after that."

"And the other volleys? Did they penetrate?"

"Aye, sir. Best I can tell they did."

"Good," said Melville. "And did they have a lot of their Goblan 'allies' up in the rigging?"

"No, sir. No, they made it look all peaceful like. Almost no one was in the riggin'. That was most of why we managed to get away. Everyone, curs and ticks both, musta been packed in below decks. You think we mighta chopped them worse than we can know?"

"Oh, aye, Chips. Aye." Melville knew that he was also speaking to nearly a hundred listening ears as he said,

"Read here the moral roundly writ
For him who into battle goes —
Each soul that hitting hard or hit,
Endureth gross or ghostly foes.
. . . blown by many overthrows,
Half blind with shame, half choked with dirt,
Man cannot tell, but Allah knows
How much the other side was hurt!"

"Dear Lady Elbereth," said Tibbits, "I *hope* we made the bastards pay for what they did to poor old Rick Crosby and the others."

Melville knew that, in the words of Lord Wavell, "When things are going badly in battle the best tonic is to take one's mind off one's own troubles by considering what a rotten time one's opponent must be having."

"You tell me Chips. Fifty-two 12-pound balls bouncing around inside that Ship. Each one must have created hundreds, thousands of splinters as it busted its way in. You can *bet* the doggies and their Goblan 'ticks' were sucking shot and splinters that day. Aye, we made the bastards pay, and we'll make them pay *even more*! Now, wrap up quickly and tell what happened after that."

"Well, then came the weird part, sir. We ran straight east, 'cause that's how we lay when we was snookered by that bastard. We spotted a line of Guldur Ships, stretched out to the north and south, all headed west, toward Stolsh. It was an invasion fleet! The biggest damn fleet you ever saw. Mostly transports, runnin' real slow, but there was a sizable batch of frigates with them, too.

"We figured they must be plannin' to take out the whole Stolsh Empire in one punch. The one we ran into musta been part o' their scout screen. Their job bein' to get rid of anyone who could warn the Stolsh. That's got to be why they did for us like that, the bastards.

"We veered off from them pretty easy 'cause they was goin' so slow. We slipped around that vacuum scummer what sucker-punched us, 'cause you know those Guldur can't sail worth a damn. But with the damage we took we couldn't put stress on the mainmast or the Keel, and so we couldn't pull far ahead of the bastard. We seen him signal to his fleet, so he must've told them not to worry about us, 'cause we was hurt bad. The bastard probably didn't want to share any of the loot and glory.

"Lootenant Fielder said we could escape to this world here. That it was our only chance. So here we are, and that bastard of a Guldur vacuum sucker is right behind us, sir."

"Can *Kestrel* fight, Chips? Can she handle a boarding action?"

"Aye, maybe she can hold out for a little while. She could take a solid smack in the bows and it might just compress the Keel, but anythin' from the side is apt to crack that Keel the rest of the way. But how can we fight that bastard's guns? They swung one of those monsters up front, for a bow chaser, on the lower side, and what we saw would curl your hair. They was shootin' at us at ranges *two times* what our 12-pounders can do. How can you fight guns like that?"

"Chips, did they ever hit us?"

"Well, no sir. Except for a few that passed through our sails and our riggin'. One of those took out the sailin' master."

"I'm sorry to hear that. He was a good man. Our captain, first mate, marine lieutenant, sailing master *and* our bosun. The enemy has *much* to answer for. But do you see? Those guns are inaccurate as hell at long range, and slow as hell to load at close range." The old carpenter looked at him with hope smoldering in his eyes.

"Chips, an ancestor of mine, Herman Melville, wrote that, 'Mishaps are like knives that either serve us or cut us, as we grasp them by the handle or the blade.' By the Lady, we can do it. We can close with those bastards and board them! We shall grasp this dark deed by the handle and plunge it into the enemy's breast! *We have no choice.* To fight is our duty. Do *you* want to kill your Ship and rot below? Or do you want to avenge her?" A ragged cheer broke out among the surrounding sailors.

Melville didn't wait for an answer as the carpenter looked at him openmouthed, bewildered, amazed, and . . . hopeful. "Mr. Aquinar!" he shouted.

"Sir!"

"Get me the gunner, asap!"

"Aye, sir!"

The *Kestrel* had four warrant officer positions, each responsible for the operation, repair and maintenance of their portion of the Ship. The carpenter, Mr. Tibbits, was responsible for all the wooden parts of the Ship. The sailing master was responsible for all sails and rigging, but he was dead, and so was his senior NCO, the bosun. The gunnery warrant, Mr. Barlet, was responsible for her forty 12-pounders. The purser, Brother Petreckski, was responsible for the cargo and the holds. In order to get the *Kestrel* ready for combat Melville needed to get these section leaders and their personnel into action.

Melville's next priority was to get a quick exterior look at the damage to the lower half of the Ship. *Wise-nose* was specifically designed for maintenance tasks such as this. At the bow, stern and flanks of the cutter there were steps that permitted access directly to Flatland. Melville moved carefully as he lowered himself down to this level, since gravity and warmth increased as you got closer to Flatland.

At the upper levels of the rigging, gravity was around a quarter gee and it was uncomfortably chilly. At the crow's nest it went up to a half gee and cool. The constant cold at that height was why they used enclosed crow's nests instead of open fighting tops.

On the maindeck of the Ship it was about one gee, with warm and balmy temperatures. Right at the plain of Flatland, where Melville was, the Ship was hot, with around 1.5 gees, and you had to move with some caution.

Melville knelt on the platform, and dipped his head through the opaque blue plane of Flatland. From this position he could see the half of the *Kestrel* that was "below." Basically, the Ships of two-space were like two old-time sailing ships with everything below the waterline cut off, and then joined together at the "waterline" formed by Flatland. The end result was that you had two ships arranged so that one of them was "upside-down" to the other.

When he turned his head briefly, he could see that the cutter beside him was exactly the same on a smaller scale. Two equal sides, balanced above and below Flatland, except the cutter only had one small mast to a side.

Masts and sails had to be equally placed, above and below the vast plain of two-space. If the "balance" between the upper and lower part of a Ship got out of adjustment, the Ship could tip over. If an old-time sailing ship tipped over it sank into the deep blue sea. When a Ship in Flatland tipped too far it would also "sink," popping *out* of two-space and *into* the cold, hard vacuum of interstellar space.

As soon as Melville's head popped through, "down" became "up" for the portion of his body that was on the other side. All forces pushed him "down" from both sides into Flatland, that impossibly thin layer that represented the thickness of the entire galaxy.

From here it was as though his head was sticking out of water. He could see the two gaping holes where the enemy's cannonballs had punched through the gundeck, and down into the Keel. Hanging immediately above him were the constellations of the "lower" sky. Dominating all was the great pinwheel that sailors called the Andromeda Galaxy. Which Earth astronomers swore had nothing to do with the "real" Andromeda Galaxy.

After taking a quick look, Melville pulled himself back up to the deck of the cutter. There was one other entity that Melville needed to consult before he committed them to combat. *Kestrel* herself.

Hans and Broadax helped Melville pull himself up to the maindeck. He strode to the hatch, just for'ard of the mainmast, down the ladder (a land lubber would have called it a set of stairs, but aboard a ship, stairs are always called ladders), and through the upper gundeck. The warm yellow light given off by the Elbereth Moss guided him through the wrack and ruin of the shattered decks. He went down a second ladder to the upper hold.

Beside him, running fore and aft down the floor of this deck was the Keel, a round beam covered with pure white Elbereth Moss. Lovingly placed around the Keel were the crew's most delicate instruments. These were mostly the locks and barrels from many muskets and pistols. The cannon, muskets, and rifles that fired in two-space were somewhat protected by their "Keel charges," the small, modified version of the Ship's Keel, that provided the projectile force for the gun. But the gunpowder weapons used in three-space needed the protection provided by close proximity to the Ship's Keel whenever they were transported in two-space.

Beside the Keel they also stored some of the carpenter's equipment (much of which was now in use), some navigational equipment, a few carefully tended block-and-tackle, and some of the surgeon's instruments. Here, closest to the Keel, the corrosive effect of Flatland on technology was at its least. With daily maintenance these few pieces of crude three-space technology could continue to exist.

In slots in the deck, further out from the keel, the swords were stored. They were kept parallel to two-space, their blades essentially "floating" in that impossibly thin plane. The influence of Flatland worked to pull the blades "flat," atom by atom. The effect was that the edges of the blades were "drawn" into supernatural, almost monomolecular sharpness.

Melville could see where the Keel was mortally damaged by the impact of two great cannonballs fired at point-blank range. All around him men were working to shore up this vital area of the Ship.

At the foot of the ladder lay an open hatch surrounded on three sides by a ladder-like railing. This was the opening to the "lower" half of the Ship. Flatland couldn't be seen here, in the same way that the waterline is invisible from inside a ship. But the gravitational effect could be felt. If you eased feet-first through this hatch you'd sink halfway down. Half of your body would be pulled "down," while the other half, the half below Flatland, would be pushed "up." Like floating in water, with gravity pulling you down and buoyancy pulling you up. Except in this case it was gravity pushing from both directions.

Instead of easing in, Melville dove through the hatch, headfirst, like diving into water. His momentum carried him most of the way through, and he pulled himself out using the railing on that side. From here he could see the damage to the keel from the other side. It didn't look any better.

He knelt carefully in the 1.5 gees and grasped the shattered Keel shards in his hands. <<Kestrel?>>

<<C A P T A I N ?>> She replied with deep, slow, strong, ponderous thoughts.

<<Yes, I'm the captain now. Can you hold on long enough for us to fight them?>>

She was in pain, preoccupied and distracted. But she was the product of over a century of fellowship with human beings. Her sentience was her own. Her heritage was human. Communicating with her was sometimes ponderous, but she knew how to transfer complex concepts in a concise manner.

<<. . . F L A N D E R S . . . F I E L D S . . . >>

Melville understood immediately, and was rocked to his core by what she was saying. Aloud to the men around him, and to his Ship (*his* Ship, by God, for a little while it was *his* Ship), he replied:

"<<We are the Dead. Short days ago
We lived, felt dawn, saw sunset glow . . .
Take up our quarrel with the foe!
To you from failing hands we throw!
    The torch; be yours to hold it high!
    If ye break faith with us who die!
We SHALL NOT SLEEP!>>"

Kestrel replied with a pulse of energy so powerful that it was felt by every crewman who was in contact with the Elbereth Moss that coated much of the Ship.

In that moment the young lieutenant became the avatar of his Ship. *Kestrel*'s ancient voice tore his throat raw as the Ship replied. "<<Y E S ! !>>"

<<B U S Y N O W,>> the Ship concluded, and cut the connection. Melville slumped to the deck.

What had just occurred was remarkably rare. A Ship had cried out to her whole crew, sending a message of despair and anger, a request, an order, a *demand* for vengeance. No captain of a Ship ever had a greater mandate thrust upon him. The men around him looked stunned. The crew of the *Kestrel* might not *want* to seek what they thought was certain death, but trapped between the steely will of their Ship and the orders of their captain, they had no choice. They would obey.

With the help of Broadax and Hans, Melville staggered to his feet. He looked down at his hands, which were torn and bleeding from clutching the ragged shards of his Ship's soul. In a daze he began moving toward the ladder.

The gunner and his gunnery sergeant stood beside little Aquinar. "Mister Aquinar, find out where the captain's remains have been placed. Bring them, his hat and his jacket to the upper quarterdeck, immediately. Gentlemen, the rest of you come with me." Sergeant Broadax and Chief Petty Officer Hans were no gentlemen. *They* were NCOs. They grinned at each other with the superiority and confidence of career NCOs and began to saunter off in another direction. Melville stopped and turned to them. "That means you two as well. Broadax, you are promoted to lieutenant of marines. Hans, you are now the sailing master. You *are* now gentlemen . . . er . . . gentlefolk."

The two ex-NCOs were dumbstruck. Their confidence, poise, and security in life revolved around being noncommissioned officers. Under ordinary circumstances they would have rejected a commission. In fact, they'd both done so repeatedly, scorning officers, their manners and their airs. Because, as one old ex-sergeant once put it, "When it's all said and done in this old world, after everyone panics, there's got to be an NCO there to pour the piss out of the boot." But now, with their Ship's current plight, they couldn't say no, and the joke was on them.

Damn, Melville thought, *it felt* good *to do that to them!* There were times when it was *good* to be captain. He turned and dove back through the hatch and through the plain of Flatland, to the upper portion of the Ship. He strode up the steps of the ladder, two at a time, past the gundeck and onto the maindeck, followed by the others. They turned astern, through the waist, and up the short flight of stairs to the quarterdeck.

The helmsman was standing by the wheel with the old quartermaster keeping careful watch over him. Lady Elphinstone, Mr. Tibbits, and Midshipmen Crater and Archer joined them on the upper quarterdeck. Crater reported. “Sir, all the wounded have been evacuated onto Broadax’s World.”

“Very good, thank you, Mr. Crater.” Melville now stood on the quarterdeck as captain of his Ship. Lieutenant Fielder, the two rangers, and Brother Petreckski came to join them. Fielder looked angry, but given the Ship’s mandate, it was clear that he wouldn’t confront Melville’s authority at this time.

Aquinar stood at the foot of the ladder with their captain’s remains. A bloody bundle wrapped in sailcloth. So little of the body remained that a boy could hold it in his arms. Atop the bundle rested the captain’s second best blue jacket and gold braided hat. He’d been wearing his best uniform when he was blown to smithereens. Every eye was on the boy and the bundle.

As Melville looked on his murdered captain’s remains, words came to mind.

> I’ve lived a life of sturt and strife;
>   I die by treachery;
> It burns my heart that I must depart
>   And not avenged be . . .
> May coward shame disdain his name,
>   The wretch that dares not die.

He didn’t speak these words to the crew; they applied only to him. It was *he* who must “dare to die.” For them all. It was *he* who would have “coward shame disdain his name,” if he did not.

These words rang in his mind as he stood at the rail of the quarterdeck. His officers behind him, much of his crew before him. They looked at him with a frightening mixture of fear, dread, reproach, and hope. Melville understood that most of them believed he was taking them to their death.

It would be so very easy to bow to the desires of these men. It would be an enormous relief to escape to the world below with these shipmates whom he’d come to know and love. Even if his plan succeeded, many of them would die. If it didn’t succeed, then probably all of them would die.

It was hard. So very hard. Truly he was, “One nameless, tattered, broken man.” Who was *he* to send these men to their deaths? Who was *he* to lead this mighty Ship into battle? To be a good leader you must love your men. To do your duty meant you might have to kill that which you loved. In the end, duty was a harsh mistress.

His men stood waiting for him to say something. He didn't disappoint them. "Mr. Aquinar, place the captain's remains atop the ladder." Every eye moved to the bloody bundle.

Melville looked over his shoulder at Petreckski questioningly. The purser had served nobly once before. Did he have Words for the crew in this dark hour? His look asked the purser, but it was the purser's alter ego, Brother Theo the monk, who nodded calmly back. Being assured of the answer ahead of time, Melville formally asked. "Brother Theo, would you say Words for us, our murdered captain, and our fallen comrades?"

Petreckski nodded and stepped forward to the railing. Then he spoke to the crew, once again leading them in Words. In an ancient hymn that tapped deep into the roots, the common heritage of these men. A hymn that reminded them of dark days in eons past, and the Judeo-Christian ethos and the spiritual collective consciousness that had overcome and transcended such sad, dark times.

Once again Brother Theo began, in his clear, pure tenor, and the men joined in.

"Soft as the voice of an angel,
Breathing a lesson unheard,
Hope with a gentle persuasion
Whispers her comforting word:
'Wait till the darkness is over,
Wait till the tempest is done,
Hope for the sunshine tomorrow,
After the shower is gone.'

"Whispering hope, oh how welcome thy voice,
Making my heart in its sorrow rejoice.

"If, in the dusk of the twilight,
Dim be the region afar,
Will not the deepening darkness
Brighten the glimmering star?
Then when the night is upon us,
Why should the heart sink away?

When the dark midnight is over,
Watch for the breaking of day.

"Whispering hope, oh how welcome thy voice,
Making my heart in its sorrow rejoice."

That was it. The funeral service for their fallen, the prayer for their success. Now it was Melville's turn to speak. To speak for their murdered captain, for their Ship, and for himself. He looked his men in the eye and paced the rail as he said,

"Oh yesterday our little troop was ridden through and
through,
Our swaying, tattered pennons fled,
a broken, beaten few,
And all a summer afternoon they hunted us and slew;
But to-morrow,
By the living God, we'll try the game again!"

Then the young captain gave his orders, and hundreds of men swung into action. *Kestrel* was going forth to die.

CHAPTER THE 5TH
Approach: The Joy of Courage

Alone amid the battle-din untouched
    Stands out one figure beautiful, serene;
No grime of smoke nor reeking blood hath
    smutched
    The virgin brow of this unconquered queen.
She is the Joy of Courage vanquishing
    The unstilled tremors of the fearful heart;
And it is she that bids the poet sing,
    And gives to each the strength to bear his part.

"Courage"
Dyneley Hussey

Melville stood beside the quartermaster on the upper quarterdeck. A strange calmness was upon him as he maneuvered the *Kestrel* toward their foe. His eight-legged spider monkey clung to his back, peering cautiously over his shoulder. He stroked the monkey's little neck, and found himself completely resigned to the fact that today was a good day to die.

He wasn't going to die easy. He had no death wish. *The Mirror for Princes*, written in Persia on Old Earth in the eleventh century, commanded warriors, "reconcile yourself with death . . . be bold; for a short blade grows longer in the hands of the brave." Melville was reconciled to death.

Dag Hammerskjöld, a famous twentieth-century statesman, put it like this, "Do not seek death. Death will find you. But seek the road which makes death a fulfillment." All his life Melville had sought that road. Now he'd found it. He was *on* that road, and he was at peace with himself and the universe.

Melville had read about military leaders who entered into this state. They weren't suicidal, indeed, just the opposite. But once the plan was made, once all possible preparations were taken, and you're about to see how the dice settle, there can be an enormous peace.

"We are going to attack and board the doggies," he'd told his officers. "Only they aren't 'doggies' any more. That's what we called them when they weren't our foe. I *like* dogs. The Guldur like to think of themselves as wolves, but they're nothing but curs. From now on that's what we will call them, and by the living God we'll neuter these curs!"

Indeed, that was what the Guldur looked like. Huge dogs, giant mutts, standing on their hind legs. They had opposable thumbs on their paws, and were as varied in color and coat as the dogs of Mother Earth. It was strange, the power that existed in words. Calling them "curs" would make it easier to kill them, and some serious killing was now required.

"In spite of what everyone seems to think, we *will* win. We are going to meet the enemy bow to bow on the red-side. The curs *like* boarding actions. Their honor and their doctrine won't let them deny us a boarding if we come at them with an equal force. They will also think this approach is advantageous to them. Boarding from this direction will bring their lower red-side guns dead against us. What they don't know is that they have already killed our Ship, so their guns can't do us much further harm, and we *want* them to board the lower side. Meanwhile, we'll all be in the upper bows, where their guns can't reach us. Then they will reap what they sow, as we leave them to die on the Ship that they killed."

The midshipmen lay under a tarp in the upper bow of the *Kestrel*, nibbling on bits of ships biscuit. Beside Crater, Archer and Aquinar were the three other midshipmen who had remained on the *Kestrel*. The three who'd been part of the away party to

Broadax's World all had their spider monkeys with them. The little creatures still refused to leave their newfound friends and there was no sense in leaving them behind on a dying Ship. Everyone who was adopted by a monkey worried that the creatures might get in the way in battle, but they didn't see any real choice. And there was something about the little monkeys and their past actions that led the crew members to trust them.

Waiting with the six middies were Josiah Westminster, with the rangers' remaining dog; Brother Petreckski; and the vast majority of the crew. Melville offered Josiah and Petreckski an opportunity to remain on Broadax's world, since their duty as purser and ranger could be interpreted to give them an excuse for missing the battle.

Melville smiled at Josiah and put it this way, "How about it, John Carter, you want to play with your Tarka friends some more?"

Josiah grinned his mischievous grin and replied, "Throughout mah life I've never turned from the glory road. You sir, are on the glory road, and ah shall follow."

Melville laughed aloud. He'd opened with Burroughs, and Josiah trumped him with Heinlein.

When he put the matter to Petreckski, the purser simply replied: "'Here I stand. I can do no otherwise.'" Melville grinned to hear the words of Martin Luther come out of the monk at this time.

All the cutters were away under Lieutenant Fielder's command. In place of the cutter that usually filled the *Kestrel*'s bow, a phony cutter of canvas and wood scraps had been constructed. Busted spars and tangles of rope and sail were artfully placed to make the area a confusing mess. Under this camouflage the crew waited patiently.

Two 12-pounder cannon were also hidden here under a heap of dirty sailcloth, with a double load of grapeshot, poised to fire down into the enemy's deck. Gunnery Sergeant Don Von Rito lay between the guns with a few hand-picked gunners. Gunny Von Rito was a marine who was the gunnery warrant's senior NCO. These two 12-pounders would only get one shot before they recoiled back across the deck. Von Rito was determined to insure that this one blast of grape would get maximum "payback" for the cowardly, treacherous attack that had murdered their captain and first officer.

The majority of their marines were under the command of Corporal Kobbsven. They were the only ones in view on the upper deck, crouching along the railing, looking like a "normal" boarding party.

Their new captain had put it clearly. "Unless I specifically say otherwise, every swinging, living creature on this Ship, including the cook and her cat, will go across the upper red-side bow in the boarding party." Indeed, somewhere in the party was the one-eyed old cook, Roxy, her cat, all the other cats, *and* all the ship's dogs. Many of the crew lay on the maindeck, under artfully draped tarps or inside the phony cutter. Those who couldn't find room on the maindeck waited below, on the upper gundeck, ready to swarm out the for'ard hatch and join the boarding party.

What was about to happen wasn't a boarding, but a mass exodus from a dying Ship. For all they knew, the ship's rats also sat poised to join them.

Lady Elphinstone was one of those who waited below on the upper gundeck. Lieutenant Melville had offered her an opportunity to remain below, with the wounded, on Broadax's world. Her response was simply to say, "My duty is to tend our wounded. Where thou art going, there *shall* be wounded, and so I must go."

She and her "lob-lolly girl," Mrs. Vodi, held their medicine bags. Their two medical assistants, or "corpsmen," Pete Etzen and Thadeaus Brun, stood by with even more medical equipment packed on their backs. Under ordinary circumstances Elphinstone and Vodi would never be in the boarding party. That was Doc Etzen and Doc Brun's job. But anyone who stayed behind on this Ship could expect nothing but certain death. The only hope of survival was in rapidly boarding the enemy's Ship. Something the curs were apt to violently resent and resist.

A cloud of distraught, distressed cats milled around Elphinstone and Vodi. For many hundreds of years a systematic effort had been dedicated to breeding dogs and cats for intelligence. The cats and dogs assigned to the Westerness Navy were the cream of the crop of a centuries-long breeding program. The result was that the cats had some idea what was going on, and they didn't like it. Not one bit. The whole thing seemed completely beneath their dignity.

The dogs also had a good sense of what was going on and, as usual, thought it was all a great, glorious game. "Fetch boy! Go get the ship!"

Darren Barlet, the gunnery warrant, strode the lower gundeck. Black as a gun barrel, whipcord lean, with a ramrod posture and a shaven head, Barlet was a wizard at long-range gunnery. His men joked admiringly that if all else failed they could lay him on a gun carriage and use him as a cannon. All he had to do was put a cannonball in his mouth and *command* it to seek the enemy. His men were certain that the ball wouldn't dare disobey.

"Switch guns to get as much firepower as you can up for'ard on the red-side, above and below," Lieutenant Melville had ordered. "Run painted logs out as Quaker guns to fill any gaps, so that the enemy won't know what we're doing. Load nothing but grape or canister in every gun."

"Aye, sir," the master gunner replied quietly.

"Your job is to suppress the enemy's guns. Every hit they get on us is another chance they might knock the Keel loose. Keep the pressure on them. Fire canister and grape into those big gun ports as long, as hard, and as *fast* as you can."

"Aye, sir," again, quietly with a nod.

"Guns, at first the danger will be from the bow chaser on the lower green-side. Focus our two lower bow chasers there. Then, as we close up, bow-to-bow on our red-sides, I want you to suppress those two guns on the lower red-side. On the upper side, have the bow chasers try to clear the ticks out of the rigging. No ball shot, you understand? You'll just damage our Ship, for *that* is what the enemy's Ship is. *Our* Ship by God. Aye, and the curs owe us one! As soon as we come alongside, give one or two last shots of grape into those lower gun ports, then all the gun crews race up and join the boarding party."

"Aye. Oh, aye, indeed, sir." There was nothing but steely determination in those brown eyes. If anyone could pull this off, it would be his master gunner.

Now Mr. Barlet and a few hand-picked crews stood ready to fire the guns that would come to bear in the coming battle. The rest of his gunners stood by with pistol, boarding ax, and the straight swords of two-space sailors, waiting beside the medics below the for'ard hatch on the upper side, or concealed on the upper maindeck with the boarding party.

Mr. Hans (no longer "Chief" Hans, much to his dismay), hung in the upper rigging beside Valandil, the Sylvan ranger. Each of them had a rifle cradled in one arm. When Melville gave Valandil the opportunity to remain below on Broadax's world, the ranger's answer was yet another literary quote, said with the barest twitch of a smile, "'Faithless is he that says farewell when the road darkens.'"

Hans' monkey scampered and frolicked next to him, apparently untroubled by the chill, and completely delighted by the quarter gravity of the upper rigging. Like the monkey, Valandil exulted in the dizzying heights and low gravity of this realm. The Sylvan race lived high in the huge trees of low-gee worlds. The ranger's skill in battle was superb in any terrain, but here he was a supernatural fighter, and the sailors were heartened by his presence.

"I need a crack crew in the rigging, and your best quartermaster teams on duty at the wheel, above and below," Lieutenant Melville had told Hans. "They need to respond quickly, and bring us to a gentle stop right at the enemy's bow. The crew in the upper rigging has a special job. I want all of them to stay up high where the gravity is light. Swarm into the enemy's rigging as fast as you can, stay high, head to the enemy's stern, and drop down on their quarterdeck. Have sailors hidden in the crow's nests to reinforce this action. Cut through or bypass any pockets of Goblan resistance in the rigging. Meanwhile, all the crew in the lower rigging will come up as fast as they can and reinforce the boarding party."

Newly commissioned "Lootenant" Broadax stood with a quarter of her marines in the bow of the lower maindeck, smiling, caressing her ax, and humming to herself. She wasn't sure about this "ossifer" business. Ossifers had to do a lot of talking and directing of folks, and she'd never been good with words. She always found it easier to hit people with something. But this battle now. *This* was something she could handle. Her monkey clung tightly to her back, making little squeaks of concern and protest.

"You will be in charge of the defense of our lower decks," their new captain had told her. "Except I don't want the lower decks defended. I want you to lure them in. Take the bare minimum force you need for the job. We will be in contact with the enemy only at the bow, so the space they can come across is fairly small. Detach the rest of your marines to support the boarding party on the upper deck." Broadax nodded placidly and sucked in on her cigar as he continued.

"Hold at the bow just long enough for the crew in the rigging to escape through the hatches. Stand for a minute at the for'ard hatch, then give them the gundeck, taking all the gunners down with you. Drop down into the hold and dog the hatch. I want to give them full run of the lower-side maindeck and gundeck, but *not* the hold. Then immediately evacuate Mr. Tibbits and your whole crew to the upper maindeck and reinforce our boarding party." Again she nodded, exhaling a cloud of noxious smoke that formed a small, low-lying fog bank.

"Do *not* let them into the hold. If you run the curs *will* chase. Their instinct, their 'honor,' and their doctrine demand it. But if they get into the hold and see the condition the Keel is in, they'll run back to their Ship like their tails were on fire." Still Broadax said nothing, only pulling in a drag from her cigar and rolling it to a corner in reply.

"Lieutenant Broadax," Melville continued, looking down into her beady, bloodshot eyes, "I want you to try very hard to avoid getting yourself killed. That's an order. I need you and your marines to reinforce the main boarding effort. Is that all understood?"

"Yes, sir!" the Dwarrowdelf replied, fondling her ax and exhaling deeply, adding fresh reinforcements to the toxic fog bank at her feet. "Minimum force below ta draw the curs in. The rest'll be under Corporal Kobbsven up here. Down below we'll let the blueboys in the rigging git out, then give the curs the maindeck. Then we git the gunners out, an' give 'em the gundeck. Dog the hatches shut, an' don' let 'em in the hold. Git back ta the upper deck an' come join the party." She added with a saucy wink and a gap-toothed grin, "An' don' git me ossifer ass bit by no mutt."

Old Hans shot a stream of tobacco overboard and laughed admiringly at this little joke at their new captain's expense. Broadax seemed truly delighted with her role in this caper. You'd never know that she'd just been given the most dangerous mission in what was already a forlorn hope. Kind of a suicide mission within a suicide mission. And she loved it.

Tibbits sat in the hold with a hand on the Keel of the Ship. The old carpenter was sobbing unashamedly.

"Mr. Tibbits," the captain had told him gently, "you stay in the hold and keep the Ship company. Once Lieutenant Broadax has cleared out, ask the Ship to hold for just another few seconds. Then immediately join the boarding party. Chips?" Melville continued, looking the old carpenter in the eye. "Resist the temptation to go down with the Ship. That's an order. Your skills may be vital to convincing this new Ship to accept us. The survival of everyone on this Ship may depend on your being with us."

Melville lowered his voice to a rasping whisper, husky with unshed tears, "Just tell her good-bye for us. Let her know we love her, and we will avenge her if she can hold on for a little while longer. If we do this right, old *Kestrel* herself will personally kill half of the enemy for us. Okay?"

The old man raised a tear-streaked face to his new captain. Not caring what the young lieutenant saw. He replied softly, almost inaudibly. "Aye, sir. Aye."

Lieutenant Fielder was in a black funk as he stood in the upper stern of *Fatty Lumpkin*, which usually served as the captain's barge. The other three cutters, *Sharp-ears*, *Wise-nose* and *White-socks* were sailing slowly along beside him, making an intentionally poor job of getting away from the coming battle.

"Put a skeleton crew in each cutter," Melville had said. "Move away as though you were trying to escape, but make a poor job of it and stay reasonably close. Come around to the far side of our boarding, and take the curs in the rear, on the green-side of their upper maindeck. You'll kick them in the tail, while we hold their noses!"

" 'Kick them in the tail,' " Fielder muttered to himself. He was too depressed to respond with anything more than a scowl. Their little handful of crewmen couldn't conceivably have any impact on the battle. To add injury to insult, Melville had loaded each cutter down so that they couldn't possibly make any speed. "We should be able to put three 12-pounders in each cutter, if we lift the cannons from their carriages and store them separately. The curs may have killed our Ship, so we'll take theirs, but we'll save the cutters and as many of our cannon as we can."

Like the rest of the Ship's crew, they'd scrambled madly to prepare for Melville's insane scheme. That was the problem with the navy. Put an idiot in charge, and you had a Ship full of idiots. Following a deranged dreamer's daft scheme to the letter.

There was a very good chance that the *Kestrel* would die long before they boarded, in which case everyone on board would die. Or she might die during the boarding, in which case most of the crew would die with the Ship, and the rest would be butchered by the Guldur. The only ones with a chance of surviving were those in the cutters. Maybe, if they split up, some of them could escape the Guldur Ship. But loaded down like this, even that was a remote possibility. They were gonna die. . . .

Theoretically, you should be able to see forever across the vast, flat plain of Flatland. However, it seemed that the gravitational pull of the entire galaxy was so great that it actually pulled the light waves "down" toward the plain of Flatland within a fairly short distance. Or at least that was the dominant theory. Whatever the reason, the enemy Ship had been out of sight for several hours. Now its topsails were in sight, and it bore down on them relentlessly. The crew of the *Kestrel* could have used a little more time camouflaging their positions in the upper bow, but when the enemy drew into sight they were about as ready as they were ever going to be.

The Guldur grapeshot had chewed most of the way through their mainmast on the *Kestrel*'s upper side. Melville had the carpenter's mates pull away the spars and tightly wound rope that had been put in place to reinforce the mast around this damage. Then they chopped at the damaged section until their mainmast was completely severed. Now the severed butt-end of the mast was resting on the deck. The mast and topmast were still united at the cap and the trestle-trees, suspended by the shrouds. When the enemy saw this they assumed that the mainmast had finally broken and their elusive foe had turned to fight a weak, desperate delaying action. While her cutters, filled with much of the crew, tried to escape.

Both Ships slowed down for a boarding action, coming at each other head on.

The bow chaser in the Guldur's lower section fired one shot, which went high and cut through the rigging.

Down in the lower gundeck, Mr. Barlet looked at the Guldur marksmanship with disgust. The curs loved to board and didn't pay much attention to long-range gunnery. He yearned to get his hands on one of those huge guns. *He* would show them how to use it to its *full* potential.

The forwardmost 12-pounders, on the red- and green-sides, above and below, could be swung around as a bow chaser. Thus a total of four guns could be brought to bear toward the front. Now it was time for these guns to start paying the bastards back.

The bow chasers were all loaded with canister, which was like grapeshot but held together so that it didn't spread as fast. The Guldur liked their gunnery close. "Go for the throat" was the curs' motto. Their usual, preferred method of combat was one quick blast and then board the enemy, continuing to bang away with the guns while the boarding action was in progress. None of this dancing around and playing with long-range gunnery for them. It was just "wham-bam, thankee ma'am" for the curs.

It was a little surprising that they even took the one long shot. But the range of the Guldur guns, combined with the slow speed as the two Ships approached each other, would give the curs ample time to reload. Under ordinary circumstances.

The curs clearly planned to get one more shot with the bow chaser on their green-side below, at close range. Once they met bow-to-bow on the red-side, they'd have a point-blank shot with the two guns on the red-side below.

Usually the goal in a Ship-to-Ship battle like this was to damage the other guy, with minimal regard for the damage he does to you. In this case Melville had to do everything humanly possible to reduce the chance of taking a hit that might cut the circuit on *Kestrel*'s Keel. This meant that below the plain of Flatland, where the enemy had a bow chaser in position, they would use their guns to fire at the enemy's guns.

Mr. Barlet hunched over the lower green-side bow chaser. The two lower bow chasers should each be able to fire three times before the huge Guldur gun was reloaded. He wanted to use every shot to put canister balls through the huge gun hatch before the Guldur could fire again.

Barlet was hunched over in the odd, contorted position of a "sniper." The gun would recoil violently upon firing, so he had to stand to the side of the carriage. But he needed to look down the barrel to aim. That meant he must face the gun from the side, bend over, turn his head to the left, and rest his cheek on the gun barrel as he sighted down it. His left hand was above him, grasping a handhold in a support beam, while he shouted commands to the crew and used his right hand to signal fine adjustments.

Gunpowder didn't work in two-space. Flatland operated by its own laws, its own logic. If you wanted to propel something from a pistol, rifle, or a cannon in two-space, it had to be from a muzzle-loader with a Keel charge set in its base.

When the gun was ready to fire Barlet lifted his cheek up off the gun barrel and touched the Keel charge which stuck out from the cannon's end, like a nipple protruding from the end of a baby bottle. It always grew a layer of Lady Elbereth Moss, and it was somewhat sentient. When his hand touched the Keel charge it initiated the force, the *energy* that sent the cannonball flying. Touching the keel charge was almost like patting a dog. He "felt" the gun speak to him and he tried to "talk" back, telling it exactly where to fire.

<<Yes!>> the gun responded, like the yelp of joy from a dog that was released to chase a rabbit. "CHOOM!" <<Takethat!>> He barely had time to snatch his hand back as the gun recoiled against its restraining ropes, and the load of canister splattered against the green-side of the Guldur Ship. Like some huge shotgun blast, it slammed twelve pounds of half-inch balls into the enemy's hull. But the range was long for canister, and by the time it reached the target the pattern had spread so widely that it would have taken some significant luck for one to go in the hatch.

With the gun recoiled all the way back, all Barlet had to do was to stride forward, stepping over the taut restraining ropes, to the red-side where the other bow chaser waited. He leaned forward again and put his cheek against this gun, repeating the aiming and firing process. <<Yes!>> "CHOOM!" <<Takethat!>> Again the canister shot splattered against the green-side. Hopefully a ball or two went into the gun port and slowed down the enemy's loading process.

The green chaser's crew of four gunners had their 12-pounder loaded and run back up to the gun port. Barlet ran around the back of it to assume his original position. The Ships were approaching each other rapidly, and now the range was better. Again he fired the green chaser. <<Yes!>> "CHOOM!" <<Gotcha!>> This time the cluster of shot was much tighter as it impacted around the enemy's open hatch. There could be little doubt that it was making life miserable for whoever was trying to load that gun. Again, with the red chaser. <<Yes!>> "CHOOM!" <<Yippee!>> Then the green. <<Yes!>> "CHOOM!" <<Gotcha!>>

The enemy gun port was chewed into an irregular opening, and there was no movement to get their huge bow chaser back into position. *This* gun was silenced. The enemy bow chaser on the lower green-side had done no harm. Now, as they approached the Guldur Ship, the goal was to put the same kind of pressure on the guns on the enemy's lower red-side. Those guns couldn't bear on them yet, but as they approached bow-to-bow for boarding, they might be able to get off a shot.

Guns couldn't fire through the plane of Flatland. What Mr. Barlet was doing on the lower gundeck had limited impact on the upper half of the Guldur Ship.

On the upper side they were moving into the enemy's dead space. No enemy guns could hit them here, so the goal of the upper bow chasers was to kill as many of the enemy as possible, in support of the boarding operation. Like the guns below, these bow chasers had time to get off three shots each before the two ships met. They each fired one canister followed by two of grape. Each shot sent another twelve pounds of half-inch balls sweeping through the enemy rigging.

A veritable sleet of shot swept the enemy's masts and rigging, killing swarms of the Goblan "ticks." These "allies" were actually more like vassals or slaves. They lived and worked high up in the Guldur Ships where the "curs" didn't like to go. Clearing the Goblan out of the enemy's upper rigging helped clear the way for Hans, Valandil, and the sailors who would "take the high ground" and sweep down on the enemy's upper quarterdeck.

A hail of shot rattled the enemy rigging, and a rain of black Goblan came down. Like decayed fruit falling from a dying tree, they landed with a wet, crunching "thud!" on the deck, or they fell into the sea. Into Flatland. Those who hit Flatland bounced through once, bobbed partially back out again, and then disappeared into the vacuum of interstellar space.

The battle wasn't all one-sided. The Guldur in the bow of the upper and lower sides fired volley after volley of muskets at the approaching Westerness Ship. The Goblan in the rigging were savaged by the *Kestrel*'s cannon fire, but they too sent down a hail of musket balls directed at the marines who were visible and exposed as they crouched in the upper and lower bows.

The marines' job was to draw the enemy's attention away from the hidden boarding party waiting behind them . . . and to stay alive. So most of them weren't invested in exposing themselves to return fire. They simply crouched behind the railing, praying or swearing, as was their individual inclination.

Private Jarvis had been mauled by an ape in the last battle. He'd recovered enough to be released for duty. Now here he was again, with musket balls bouncing around him and wood splinters flying into his exposed flesh. Sergeant (oops, Lieutenant) Broadax might enjoy this stuff, but he'd never been so miserable in his life. At least the apes didn't shoot at you. Once again his bladder control was failing and "leg sweat" was darkening his trousers. He felt his bowels loosen and it was all he could do to maintain control of his sphincter.

In training they'd been told about a survey of combat veterans in World War II, back on Old Earth in the twentieth century. About half the veterans who saw intense frontline action admitted to wetting themselves in combat. In the same survey almost a quarter of these combat veterans admitted to messing themselves. Jarvis was one of many combatants since then whose cynical response to that data was, "Hell, all that proves is that the rest were liars."

Up in the rigging, it was important not to look too strong. To accomplish this, many of the Westerness sailors were hiding, packed in the crow's nests. The rest were firing rifles. In two-space, loading and firing was much easier. No need for powder here. A little Keel charge plugged the breech of each barrel. Insert two minié balls into the double-barreled muzzle, drive them home with the double ramrod, re-set the ramrod beneath the barrel, touch the Keel charge at the base of the barrels with your thumb, and "Crack!" the minié ball slammed forward.

The white, Elbereth Moss–coated Keel charges of the muskets and pistols were much smaller than those of the cannon. When you touched them off there was a small sense of sentience, like a purring cat.

On the upper quarterdeck Melville's job was made much easier by the effect of *Kestrel*'s grapeshot on the Goblan in the upper rigging. The enemy was having trouble fine-tuning their sails, so they simply dropped all sails and let the Westerness Ship board, just as she pleased. Just where he wanted. If the *Kestrel* wasn't so obviously crippled, with her mainmast shattered, the Guldur might have feared that she would try to trick them with some maneuver. But under the present circumstances it was obvious that they could only be coming to board. And that was just fine with the curs.

As they drew near, it became obvious that the boarding would come off as planned. Melville called a final command, "Let fly the sheets!" Once upon a time, in the old, wet navy, that meant to release the bottom half of the sails. Then the sails could "fly" in the wind, without providing any more forward momentum. While sailing the endless seas of Flatland this command still meant to release the bottom half of the sails, but now the result was that the constant downward "wind" of two-space made the sails hang loose, straight down, so that forward momentum ceased.

The quartermaster's mate echoed the command through the voice tube to the lower quarterdeck so that the sails would be equally trimmed on both sides. This prevented any chance of "tipping" which could lead to "sinking." In the rigging, above and below, the sailors released the sails that were giving forward thrust. Their headway quickly dropped off, and the quartermaster used the rudder to fine tune the final approach.

Melville left control to the quartermaster, grabbed a double-barreled pistol in each hand and ran to the bow to lead the boarding party. Both his monkey and the eery calm still clung to him. Sweet as kiss-my-hand, the two Ships moved toward a gentle meeting, right where Melville wanted.

Lieutenant Fielder sat out in *Fatty Lumpkin*, watching the Ships pull together. "The bastard," he muttered to himself. "The goofy, gonzo, poetry-prating, prat bastard. He might actually pull this off. He might just do it. Come on, you bastard."

Fielder moved down to where the deck was close to the plain of Flatland. He lay on his side and stuck his head in, like you might dip your head into a pool of water. He held one eye above and one below Flatland, which permitted him to see both the upper and lower portions of each Ship. Anyone other than a sailor would be driven to distraction, if not insanity, by the operation. But for someone who had spent his childhood and teen years as a midshipman it was a normal procedure.

From this position Fielder could see the comparative lack of sailors and marines on the lower side. And that mad, demented, berserker Broadax stood in the lower bows waving her silly hatchet, glaring out from beneath the obligatory iron Dwarrowdelf helmet. On the upper side the crow's nests were crowded and the bow was packed with marines.

Melville, the damned fool, had left the quarterdeck and was moving to the front of the marines on the upper deck. A single blue jacket in a sea of red, showboating as he waved two big, double-barreled pistols in the air. All sails hung free on both Ships, and they coasted gently together. *Kestrel*'s upper guns were blazing away at the Guldur's upper rigging. Her lower guns were hammering the enemy's lower guns. If only they could prevent a blast from those big guns that would shake the *Kestrel*'s Keel loose.

"Come on, you bastard. Come on." For the first time in many days, hope began to kindle in Fielder's heart. "You know," said Fielder to no one in particular, "when trouble arises and things look bad, there's always one individual who perceives a solution and is willing to take command. Very often, that individual is quite mad."

Down in the lower gundeck, as they approached the Guldur, red bow to red bow, Mr. Barlet got one last shot off with the red bow chaser. <<Yes!>> "CHOOM!" <<Takethat!>> He put a load of grape into the enemy's red-side gun ports. Then he moved back astern, firing the first four red-side 12-pounders as they came to bear on the same gun ports. <<Yes!>> "CHOOM!" <<Gotcha!>> <<Yes!>> "CHOOM!" <<Haha!>> <<Yes!>> "CHOOM!" <<Ohboy!>> <<Yes!>> "CHOOM!" <<Gotcha!>>

He put hundreds of canister balls into the enemy in a desperate attempt to stop them from firing into the crippled *Kestrel.*

Stopping a gun from loading is really not too difficult. Stopping a loaded gun from firing is far more difficult. Good as he was, Barlet and his gunners weren't able to stop one of the enemy's guns from firing. Just as they drew together with the enemy, the huge cannon fired.

"CH-DOO-OOM!!!" The *Kestrel* shuddered from stem to stern. Her severed mainmast shuddered and swayed as it hung in the rigging. The butt end of the shattered mast ground into the decking. Those with their feet or hands in contact with the Elbereth Moss felt their Ship groan in agony and effort.

Down in the hold Mr. Tibbits moaned in pain as he held onto the shards of the Keel, lending his spirit and soul to that of his Ship. He was using his body as a living conductor to link the sundered pieces of the Keel. The soul of his dying Ship ran through him.

The blast tore through the hull in the lower red bow and came out the lower green bow. The shot was devastating, but it didn't touch the Keel. *Kestrel*, the faithful Ship that had served the men of Westerness for over a century, was able to hold on for a few minutes more.

Melville raced across the fo'c'sle to join the marines waiting patiently in the upper bow. All around him men lay still in hiding, beneath heaps of sails and ropes, and inside the phony cutter. Most of them clutched double-barreled muskets with fixed bayonets. Random musket balls from the enemy's rigging punched through their cover and hit some of the sailors lying beneath, wounding many of them, killing some. But there was never a sound or a twitch that would give them away as they lay in hiding, bleeding and dying.

Melville leapt over and around many of them, stepping on a few. Again there was no sound from them. A strange, awesome and powerful joy was building in him. He'd abandoned all options but one. His plan was working, and now it was time to kill.

His monkey slipped down the back of his jacket, down his pant legs and onto the deck as Melville moved to the forefront of the boarding party. He was relieved to see the little creature get out of harm's way, but now he was worried that it might be left on board the *Kestrel* when she sank. This worry was relieved and the original concern returned when the monkey scampered up his back with a wooden belaying pin clutched in its upper two paws. The marines around Melville grinned and cheered at the little monkey's mock ferocity as it waved the belaying pin in the air above the young captain's head.

Melville looked at the marines crouched at the railing and he looked at the sailors hiding around him as he thought,

> Biding God's pleasure and their chief's command.
> Calm was the sea, but not less calm was that band
> Close ranged upon the poop, with bated breath,
> But flinching not though eye to eye with death.

The enemy was massed at the railing, a demonic, canine mass of Guldur. A wall of fur the color and hue of every dog on earth, and some never seen on earth. Most of them were crisscrossed with white bandoleers. Furred claws clutched muskets, pistols and swords. Atop it was a sea of slavering snouts, yellow fangs, howling red mouths, and glaring eyes. Above that were the gray furred Goblan ticks, perched on the curs' backs. Their smaller fists clutched smaller swords, pistols and rifles, with their big-eyed, big-eared heads glaring out from on high.

As this howling mass drew near, a little piece of Kipling occurred, unbidden, to Melville:

> But now ye wait at Hell-Mouth Gate
> and not in Berkeley Square.

The Ships came within arm's reach. Grappling hooks flew over from both sides to hold the vessels together in a death grip. But *whose* death?

Chapter the 6th

Boarding Action: I Shall Not Die Alone, Alone

High in the wreck I held the cup,
I clutched my rusty sword,
I cocked my tattered feather
To the glory of the Lord.
Not undone were the heaven and earth,
This hollow world thrown up,
Before one man had stood up straight,
And drained it like a cup.

"The Deluge"
G.K. Chesterton

Gunny Von Rito was lying inside the canvas "cutter," peering through holes in the sailcloth. Just as the enemy was ready to leap at them he touched off the two 12-pounders hidden under the canvas. A bullet-headed, barrel chested, broad shouldered man with a criss-cross pattern of scars on his face and bald head, he looked as though his past assignments included serving as the regimental battering ram. His arms reached out far enough for him to simultaneously touch the Keel charges of both the cannons that flanked him. <<Yes!Yes!>> "CHO-OOM!" <<Gotcha!Takethat!>>

The two guns held a double load of grape. The enemy was at point-blank range, with no cover at all. Each cannon belched out twenty-four pounds of half-inch balls, blasting through the sailcloth camouflage and exploding into the approaching mass of Guldur. The big guns recoiled back across the fo'c'sle with stunning force. The sailors had avoided hiding in this area, lest they be smashed by their own guns. The for'ard gun recoiled so hard that it punched through the green-side railing and fell into the sea, where it bobbed once and sank, disappearing into interstellar space.

Melville stood between the cannons, with enemy musket balls whizzing past him. For him the cannon blast was as though he'd blinked his eyes and suddenly the enemy was no longer there. Only a red mist hung in the air where they once stood. An instant before there'd been a barking, slavering mass of enemy troops. Now there was a yelping, whining, groaning, mass of twitching bodies and slick red fur.

Before the stunned enemy could fill the gap, Melville and the men of Westerness began the process of violently abandoning Ship.

Lieutenant Broadax stood in the lower bow, clenching her cigar in her teeth and roaring her defiance at the furry mass confronting her. The curs and their ticks up in the rigging were terrible shots, but the sheer volume of enemy fire had already dropped several of her marines as they crouched behind the railing. Some died where they lay. Some of the wounded crawled back to the for'ard hatch and dropped down. Other wounded marines lay moaning and helpless, sick with fear that they might be left behind on a dying Ship when it was time to retreat.

Broadax hadn't been able to remove the little spider monkey from her back. Now it clung to her, gibbering with apparent terror, "Eekeekeekeek-ah! eekeekeek-ah! eek-ah! eekeek-ah!" as it waved some silly chunk of a broken spar around with its two upper hands.

The curs were holding their fire for one last point-blank volley. Broadax heard the bark of their commander, which was the signal for them to hit the deck.

Hitting the deck like this was a "dishonorable" act that distressed the curs greatly. But, as Broadax had put it to her marines, "Always remember, boys, incomin' fire has the right of way!" Most of the Guldur volley whizzed over their heads. Then the men of Westerness leapt up and each marine emptied both barrels into the wall of fur in front of them.

Already the Westerness sailors in *Kestrel*'s lower-side rigging were down on the deck and scurrying through the hatches. A wave of ticks came across from the enemy rigging, close on their heels. The sailors quickly closed and secured all the hatches except for the one immediately behind the marines in the lower-side bow.

Broadax swung her ax in a glittering, lethal figure-eight, and all the marines put in one solid bayonet thrust. Then they fell back around the hatch that led down into the gundeck below, crouching to pull their wounded and dead with them as they went. They didn't always succeed. In trying to rescue their wounded, several others were killed or injured, lying in bleeding, red-jacketed heaps.

The ladder to the gundeck below had been removed and the marines simply fell down through the hatchway, one-by-one, trusting the sailors below to catch them. The sailors held a piece of stout sailcloth stretched taut between eight of them. When healthy marines hit the cloth they were unceremoniously flipped off. When wounded marines hit they were rolled gently off where they were immediately carried down to the lower hold, through the plain of Flatland, and into the rear of the main boarding party. There the ship's boys and the lightly wounded would help them in evacuating to the enemy vessel.

Broadax went last, backing into the hatchway. With her left hand she reached out and tossed two marines back through the open hatch behind her, while cutting the knees out from under a row of Guldur with one powerful sweep of the ax in her right hand. "To the axeman, all supplicants are the same height."

A wave of fur, fangs and steel came at her and she simply fell back through the hatch, covered with a mountain of snarling, clawing, slashing Guldur. Her ax flashed in an intricate, deadly pattern as she fell. Her spider monkey clung tight with six legs. The club in its two uppermost legs delivered a flurry of blows all around Broadax's head as they fell backwards, the monkey gibbering all the while. A despairing "Eeeeeek!" trailed behind them along with a wisp of cigar smoke and spray of blood.

Broadax's body, covered with a mass of curs and ticks, hit the outstretched canvas held taut by the sailors.

"Thump! Eeekeekeek!"

The weight was far too great and the impact snatched the canvas from the sailors' hands. The whole mess hit the deck with a sickening thump. "Whumph! Urr . . . urrk . . . urkk?" A flurry of bayonets skewered the mass of Guldur and Goblan, flicking them off of the pile like pitchforks might toss hay bales.

The Guldur above hesitated for one split second as they looked down into the open hatch. The pile of bodies shuddered and shifted as Broadax struggled to her feet and staggered out from under the hatchway with a small mountain on her back. Her marines continued to flick curs and ticks off of her. Her monkey broke free of the clinging attackers and renewed its flurry of blows with its chunk of wood, slapping away anything that approached Broadax's head, while its sharp teeth snapped at anything in reach.

"Ye damned blueboys!" Broadax bellowed.

She pitched one hapless Goblan against the bulkhead with her left hand ("Thump! Urk!"), thrust the haft of her ax back and down into the gut of a Guldur ("Thud! Huuuu!"), then thrust the blade up into the conjunction of several others ("Yelp! Ark!") as she smashed her face into a hairy dog face, extinguishing her cigar in an enemy's eye ("Aaaargh!").

"Ye only had one job," she howled, continuing to harangue the unfortunate sailors. "Just one thing. Hold the damn tarp. Was that too damned hard fer ye?"

"Mumph? Mumph!" her monkey added. Its comment muffled by the Goblan neck in its mouth.

The wounded and most of the sailors had already retreated down through the next hatch, into the hold. After one brief hesitation the Guldur continued to hurl themselves through the maindeck hatch, and the marines continued to stab and slash into the mass of Guldur and Goblan bodies as they fell and slid down. Again the marines backed into the next hatchway, falling through one-by-one, dragging their dead and wounded with them into the lower hold.

Once again Broadax was the last one through. This time there were fewer Guldur besieging her, since the first hatchway formed a bottleneck that limited the number who could come through.

She actually had the situation reasonably under control as she chucked a wounded marine back into the hatch behind her and fell back into the hold with only a handful of enemy clinging to her.

"Eeeeeek!"

The hatch was propped open above her, and as soon as she fell through onto the canvas ("Thump! Eeekeekeek!") the prop was pulled out and the hatch slammed down into place. Or almost into place, since there were various bits and pieces of screaming, yelping Guldur and Goblan protruding from the seam, where they'd been trapped as the hatch slammed shut. Bayonets flashed and they quickly became, in a very real sense, dead weight.

Here in the hold the Keel generated around 1.25 gees, and again the weight of Broadax and her entourage of curs and ticks was too much for the sailors holding the tarp. They hit the deck with a thump, "Whumph! Urk . . . urk . . . urkk?"

Broadax bellowed, red faced as she swept the luckless sailors with blazing eyes and a mangled stogie. "Oh ye bastards. Ye damned bluebelly bastards," she howled, rolling the smashed remains of her cigar in her teeth. "I'll get ye for this. I swear I will."

"Eek. Ge-eek-eek-ook!" Her monkey added threateningly.

Together she and her marines quickly dispatched the Guldur that had entered with her. Broadax stood in resplendent, gory red glory. Her red marine jacket and sailcloth trousers had been slashed to a few tattered ribbons. Only her round iron helmet and her coat of fine Dwarrowdelf chain mail remained, but they were again covered with a red jacket. As were her hair, face, head, arms, and legs. A solid layer of red blood coated her from head to toe. Her monkey, too, was like a sticky red wraith, barely discernible from the rest of her body as it moved about. Indeed, the monkey blended in with the rest of her like some bizarre, macabre extension of an alien being. Together they formed a symbiotic fellowship that was a living incarnation of death.

Above them the Guldur were pulling up on the hatch. Several ropes suspended from the hatch. Numerous sailors and marines hung from these ropes, using their weight to keep the hatch down as the ropes were secured to tie-off points on the deck.

Meanwhile a mass of marines flicked their bayonets up at the protruding bits of Guldur. They expertly removed the fragments of organic debris that blocked the hatch from seating firmly, like a surgeon would use a scalpel to remove the debris and decay that stopped a tattered wound from sealing tight.

The hatch finally fell fully into place and was dogged down firmly. They made one last check of all the hatches and flipped a piece of canvas so that it concealed the exposed, shattered Keel. Above them the enemy was already hacking at the hatch covers, but it would take time to cut their way through. They dove through the hatch to the upper hold where they would pick up Mr. Tibbits and make their final departure, posthaste.

Melville leaped joyfully onto the railing and hurled himself into the gap created by the cannon blast, grasping a double-barreled pistol in each hand. His bare feet slipped and skidded on the writhing, moaning, yelping mass of bloody fur as he landed. His monkey clung to his back with six legs and swung its belaying pin around with its top two legs.

To his left were Corporal Kobbsven and Gunny Von Rito. The massive Kobbsven bore a mighty, two-handed claymore, and Von Rito had only an ancient K-bar fighting knife in his hand.

To Melville's right was the ranger, Josiah, with Valandil's dog at his side. As soon as he stood up, Josiah threw his rifle to his shoulder and fired two shots. <<prrrrrr-rrrr>> "Crack-Ack!" He moved as quick as thought, the two shots coming so close together that it was almost impossible to tell them apart. Two officers on the enemy's distant quarterdeck each took a rifle bullet to the head. The .50 caliber minié balls exploded out the backs of their heads and launched the ticks from their shoulders. The ranger's dog barked with joy as Josiah moved forward smoothly, dropping his rifle and drawing two pistols from his sash.

Petreckski followed immediately behind Melville, already firing the pistol in his right hand, with more ready in his belt. <<prrrr>> "Crack!" The shot was fired over Melville's shoulder, instantly dropping the first cur who stood in their way. The midshipmen came along behind and beside the monk, each of them with pistols in their hands and more tucked into their sashes.

The majority of the *Kestrel*'s marines were fanning out to their left and right, followed by wave after wave of her sailors, ship's boys and ship's dogs. These were followed by the cook, the medicos, the wounded, and a furry mass of very irate cats.

The goal was to gain and maintain momentum. They couldn't permit themselves to be trapped in the bow of the enemy's Ship. They needed to spread out so that their superior numbers could be brought to bear. It was vital that they make a space for the entire crew to escape. Each crewman aboard the enemy Ship was another life saved and another warrior who could hurt the enemy.

Melville ran forward across the dying, writhing, yelping mass and pointed his pistol at the first Guldur to raise up in front of him. The curs stood on their hind legs, and their clawed paws gripped swords and pistols every bit as well as a human could. But their heads were purely canine . . . or lupine. The men of Westerness preferred to think of them as canine. Curs and mutts, not wolves. However, the distinction was moot when one came at you with its fangs bared, a sword in its paw, and a Goblan tick on its back.

The curs' size varied greatly. Most were slightly smaller than a human. Some were quite a bit smaller. With a gray tick on their shoulders, even the small ones formed a fearsome fusion of species that was taller than a human. The ticks hung on with their legs, while their arms usually held a long knife in each hand.

A few curs were considerably larger than humans and they tended to carry an extra large tick. These were usually Guldur officers and it was just such a creature that rose up in front of Melville as he raced forward.

Melville didn't hesitate. Muttering "Front sight, front sight!" to himself, he thrust his right pistol forward. The Guldur were still disoriented by the sudden blast of the cannon. The ones who had survived needed just a split second to adjust themselves to what happened. Melville was determined not to give them that split second. Tempo, tempo, tempo. The momentum of the attack was everything.

He superimposed the pistol sight over the enemy's throat, brought the front sight briefly into focus and thumbed the Keel charge. <<prrrrr>> "Crack!" Since it was propelled by a small Keel charge instead of gunpowder, the sound of a rifle or pistol in two-space was much smaller. Melville noted that the effect of auditory exclusion, the tendency to shut out noises, was also greatly reduced. He distinctly heard this smaller sound, whereas in his last battle he'd tuned out the larger sound.

Regardless of how it sounded, it placed a high-velocity .50 caliber ball precisely up through the top of the cur's throat, shattering the base of its skull, traveling on through and slamming into the chest of the tick on its back. Guldur were notoriously hard to kill, but no creature survives a bullet to the base of the brain. The cur crumpled back like a toppled statue. Its tick went down with it, a miniature parody of its Guldur mount, arms spread wide and face turned upward as it fell.

The ease with which he dispatched this huge enemy officer was reassuring to Melville. He continued to take each of his three remaining pistol shots with calm precision as he moved swiftly forward. <<mmmmm>> "Crack!" <<prrrrrr>> "Crack!" <<mmmmm>> "Crack!"

He had a vague impression of Corporal Kobbsven's great sword slashing red havoc among the enemy ranks to his left, and Josiah and the dog weaving an intricate network of red death to his right. *What* was *the dog's name?* Melville thought. *How odd to think of that question now!*

All around him the sailors and marines of the *Kestrel* fought in swirls of blue and red jackets. Most of them had fired both barrels of their muskets early on in the battle. They were now little more than pikemen, fighting with their bayonets.

Around their feet the ship's dogs snapped and bit, confronting the ticks that tried to attack and infiltrate the battle line down low to the deck. Beside them were the ship's boys, also joyfully gutting ticks, and hamstringing and "neutering" the curs with their razor-sharp knives.

There were even a few ship's cats mixed into the melee. Greatly distressed, irked, outraged cats. The ship's cats *never* participated in boarding parties, and seldom participated in combat at all. Their job was to control the rats, mice, cockroaches, and the other, alien, critters that tried to hitch a ride on the Ship. Now they found themselves mixed into a boarding party and they didn't like it. Not one bit. The ship's dogs and boys responded to the battle with their customary boisterous, gleeful spirits.

Immediately behind Melville, Petreckski was performing his usual, splendid dance, emptying his pistols and then turning to precision sword work. Many times throughout the battle Melville saw a sword blade dart under his arm or beside his head to strike home into the enemy. Once it even darted out from between his legs and into the groin of the enemy in front of him. A macabre phallus of death. It never occurred to Melville to worry that the blade might harm him. He knew that *this* blade was guided with superb skill and speed, and it was dedicated to keeping the path in front of him clear.

Also behind him were the midshipmen, each with a double-barreled pistol in each fist. One of them was wounded even before crossing to the Guldur ship, and another fell with a musket ball in the head as soon as he crossed. But the remaining four were still behind him, including all three of those who had landed on Broadax's world. Periodically they took shots with their pistols. Shots carefully chosen to aid and protect him. Having the young middies shoot from behind him *was* something that concerned Melville and he reminded himself to have Petreckski take charge of their pistol marksmanship training in the future. Assuming there *was* a future.

As Melville and Petreckski fought with their swords, their left hands were usually back behind them in a fencer's stance. As the middies' pistols ran dry their job was to reload, and then place the loaded, cocked pistols into Petreckski and Melville's outstretched left hands. Periodically during the battle, Melville and Petreckski gained added momentum when a double-barreled pistol was suddenly slapped into their hand.

> Quoth he, "The she-wolf's litter
>   Stand savagely at bay:
> But will ye dare to follow,
>   If Astur clears the way?"

Well, he was no "Astur," or any other hero of ancient legend, but Melville's sense of duty did put him at the forefront of the battle, in the most dangerous position, so that he could "clear the way." That didn't mean that he had to do it stupidly. His best fighters, Gunny Von Rito, Corporal Kobbsven, and Josiah, were to his left and right. Petreckski was immediately behind him, and the middies were also lending their assistance. The net effect was like the vanguard of a military attack, supported by artillery and the covering fire of all the units behind him. Even his monkey seemed to be adding its two bits, as it gibbered madly and flailed its belaying pin around with amazing speed and agility.

Archer and Crater had a special task in this attack. These two senior midshipmen had each been issued a powerful flashbang concussion grenade, to be used if the attack stalled. These terribly expensive devices were one of the Kingdom of Westerness' most closely guarded secrets. They were powered by a little piece of Keel contained in a special lining. The concussion and flash contributed by these devices wasn't much of a "secret weapon" but it was the best that Westerness could do, and it could make a critical difference if used correctly.

The momentum of the attack bogged down as the enemy forces mustered and met the warriors of Westerness in a solid line to the left and right of the mainmast. These curs and ticks were fresh, and organized two deep. The Westerness boarders were beginning to tire, and they weren't able to get their superior numbers into play along this straight line.

Melville was hard pressed. He was dodging blows from his enemy's sword and from the short sword of the tick on the cur's shoulders, although his monkey seemed to be helping a lot with this latter threat. Immediately behind this foe was another cur with a long boarding pike, thrusting and stabbing at Melville in a very proficient manner.

He considered calling for a flashbang . . . if he could just get a free second! Then one sailed over his head. Behind him the four middies began to chant, "ONE-thousand!, TWO-thousand!, THREE-thousand!, FOUR-THOUSAND!" On the last count there was a sudden flash and a loud "BLAAMM!" behind the enemy's line. There was a heartening chorus of yelps, and for one split second the enemy was surprised, stunned, and distracted. Even after that effect passed, the enemy remained slightly cowed and dismayed.

In the early twenty-first century, some obscure pioneer in the field of warrior science introduced the concept of the Bigger Bang Theory. "In combat, all other things being equal, whoever makes the bigger bang will win."

Napoleon said that, in war, "The moral is to the physical as three is to one." That is, the psychological factors are three times more important than the physical factors. One of the most important of these "moral" or psychological factors is noise.

In nature, whoever makes the biggest bark or the biggest roar is most likely to win the battle. Bagpipes, bugles, and rebel yells have been used throughout history to daunt an enemy with noise.

Gunpowder was the ultimate "roar." It had both a "bark" *and* a "bite." First used as fireworks by the ancient Chinese, later in cannon and muskets, gunpowder was a noisemaker that provided sound *and* concussion. Concussion is felt *and* heard, and gunpowder also provides the visual effects of flash and smoke. Often a gunpowder explosion, or its drifting smoke, can be tasted and smelled. Thus gunpowder provides a powerful sensory stimulus that can potentially assault all five senses.

This is one of the primary reasons why the early, clumsy, smoothbore, muzzle-loading muskets replaced the longbow and the crossbow. The longbow and the crossbow had many times the rate of fire, much more accuracy, and far greater accurate range when compared to the early smoothbore muskets. Yet these superior military weapons were replaced, almost overnight (historically speaking) by vastly inferior muskets. Inferior at killing, that is, *not* inferior at psychologically stunning and daunting an opponent.

Back on Old Earth, in the incredibly violent world of the early twenty-first century, the police forces often encountered criminals who would surround their houses with dozens of vicious dogs. The police tactical teams found that the best way to counter this problem was with a flashbang concussion grenade. One of these, tossed into the yard, seemed to "take the fight right out of them." It was like the dogs were saying, "Whoa! That's *some* bark you got there, fellow. I give up." The men of Westerness had hoped that, if they ever went to battle against the Guldur, the effect of a concussion grenade might be the same.

In two-space it was very difficult to get a true concussive explosion. The Keel charge of a 12-pounder did make a significant noise, especially when the cannonball slammed into your Ship's hull. But it was nothing like the concussion, flash, and smoke that a gunpowder weapon of similar size can create. Rifles and pistols in two-space provided significantly less noise than an equivalent gunpowder weapon. So the wise men of Westerness, steeped in the lore of warrior science, were determined to find something that would provide a true concussion effect in two-space. The result was the flashbang.

On the deck of the Guldur Ship the curs were surprised by the flashbang, but every Westerness warrior was cocked and primed to strike on the middies' count of "FOUR THOUSAND!" Every warrior within reach of the enemy thrust home a blow at the instant immediately after the explosion. Melville cut down and left to deflect the pike, using the recoil from that blow to deliver a powerful backhand slash that decapitated the cur in front of him.

And out the red blood spouted,
In a wide arch and tall,
As spouts a fountain in the court
Of some rich Capuan's hall.

As the cur's blood fountained upward into the face of its tick, Melville continued the sweep of his sword, bringing it around and to the right. He stepped in and to the right of his headless foe, before the body could even fall. The Guldur with the boarding pike still held his weapon on the other side of the corpse, which was now crumpling to its knees. Melville was completely free to thrust his sword up and to the left, into the torso of the cur with the pike.

Melville was vaguely aware of the fact that Kobbsven and Von Rito, to his left, and Josiah, to his right, were having similar success. Kobbsven's mighty sword was threshing Guldur like wheat. His huge size, his terrifying strength, the awful pallor of his face, and his way of foaming at the mouth, all made him a dreadful incarnation of berserker rage.

Von Rito still fought with only his ancient fighting knife. Gunny Von Rito had been the Westerness Marines' primary trainer in hand-to-hand combat, and he had demonstrated that, one-on-one, a man with a knife would defeat a man with a bayonet more than nine-out-of-ten times. The gunny practiced what he preached, and his fighting knife combined with Kobbsven's huge claymore to form a long-range, close-range team that was a joy to behold. All along the battle line the curs' defense was giving way and the boarding party again began to move forward.

At that instant, Melville also became aware of Fielder and the men from the cutters hitting the enemy in the flank. Initially they took them silently from the rear. Fielder demonstrated extraordinary ability at lopping off heads from behind, slaying many of them before the enemy even knew he was there. When the enemy finally began to turn to face this new threat, he combined excellent sword work with supernatural pistol skill. *He's a consummate bastard* thought Melville briefly, *but he's also one hellacious pistol shot.*

Fielder seemed to be truly peeved. No, he was flat pissed off, and was now screaming incoherently at the top of his lungs. He'd always been a bully, a cad and a bounder. At heart he knew he was a coward. Now, against his nature he'd been drawn into suicidal battle. His latent rage and fighting instincts took over his usual cynical self-serving nature. He was seriously irked and feeling abused about it all. He was a bellowing, flailing, flashing paragon of berserker death and destruction, urging his men into desperate battle, and his impact turned the tide completely. *He might be a "wicked contumelious discontented forward mutinous dog,"* Melville thought with an appreciative grin, *but lord that man could fight like a trapped ferret when caught in "death ground."*

Hans, Valandil, and a party of elite topmen fought their way through flocks of Goblan in the upper rigging. Hans' monkey clung to his back, chittering and screaming exultantly.

Never in his long life had Hans seen anything remotely like what Valandil was doing in the upper rigging of this Ship. First the ranger stood on the end of the yardarm and fired both barrels of his rifle with deadly accuracy, picking off what appeared to be the Goblan captains of the foretop and maintop. Then he ran forward, leapt onto the enemy yardarm and fired all four barrels of his two pistols, picking off the four nearest Goblan, all before the rifle he dropped had time to fall halfway to the deck below. Then he dropped his pistols and drew his sword in a blur of motion. Then the real show began.

It defied description. The Sylvan flew, spun, sailed, and flipped in an astounding display of low-gee acrobatics. All the while his sword was a flickering, flashing red scythe that left Goblan falling from the rigging like overripe fruit shaken from a tree.

The Goblan in the enemy's upper rigging fled Valandil like cockroaches caught in the sudden light of a torch. Those who were too slow, or too brave, died like moths caught in a torch's flame. But he was just one warrior and the others were less successful at fighting the Goblan.

The battle in the upper rigging was slow and painful. If not for Valandil it would have been a failure. Even after being savaged by the *Kestrel*'s grapeshot, there were so many, many ticks. Some sailors were shot by Goblan. Others were overwhelmed by a swarming mass of the nimble ticks. Dead, wounded, or simply tipped off balance, the fate of combatants on both sides was usually the same as they fell, spinning, cursing and fighting, to their deaths on the deck below.

Hans' monkey was like a gibbering guardian angle, flying along beside and above him. All eight arms expertly fended off Goblan attacks and constantly assisted Hans in maintaining his balance and his grip. On several occasions Hans found himself stabilized by his hair, as his monkey held onto his thin, wispy gray locks with two hands, while clinging to a line with four others, and fending off the enemy with its remaining two hands and its flashing white teeth.

Hans had one additional weapon in his arsenal, a stream of tobacco juice. Spat out in this light gravity, it had excellent range and effectiveness as it splashed with superb accuracy into hapless Goblan faces.

Finally, after much heart-wrenching battle up in the dizzying heights where a slip meant certain death, they reached the enemy's mizzenmast. Then the remaining sailors of Westerness, led by Valandil and Hans, spun, slithered, slid, and spat down the rigging, to land with a "thump!" en masse, to visit sudden death and destruction on the small fortress of the enemy's upper quarterdeck.

Lieutenant Broadax flipped through the hatch and led her marines into the upper hold. Mr. Tibbits, the old carpenter, still knelt, weeping, holding the shards of the Keel.

"Chips," said Broadax, as gently as her harsh, rumbling voice was capable of speaking, "we must go."

"Aye," said Tibbits, looking up at the short, red, viscera-coated apparition that stood before him. He sent one last message of love and gratitude to a faithful servant of his race, asking her to hold on for just a few more minutes. Then he picked up a small shard of the shattered Keel, reverently laid a piece of canvas over the Ship's gaping wound and left. As they were leaving, through their bare feet, through the Elbereth Moss on the deck, they felt the reply to Tibbits' message of love.

In the upper fo'c'sle of the *Kestrel* Lady Elphinstone knelt to help evacuate a wounded marine. As she touched the deck, she too felt the Ship's response to Chips' final message. The ancient Sylvan healer paused in wonder, that this young race should be worthy of such a message from the spawn of the Elder King. And she kept this thing, and pondered it in her heart.

As the bows of those two great Ships rubbed together, the white Elbereth moss of those two sentient vessels was in contact, and the Guldur Ship also felt *Kestrel*'s final message. A fierce, slow, strong pulse of deep affection and loyalty surged across. The Guldur Ship was a young Ship, a new Ship, freshly and roughly constructed. Her spirit and soul was still unformed, and what she felt coming across from the *Kestrel* rocked her to the depths of her being.

Broadax raced up the ladder from *Kestrel*'s upper gundeck, leaping onto the maindeck with a wounded marine draped over each broad shoulder. The marines moaned, groaned and grunted with every step. "Be quiet, ye wimps!" said Broadax, ever the soul of sympathy and compassion, mourning her eradicated, disintegrated cigar. "Would ye rather I left ye?"

She and the few remaining marines, most dragging an injured comrade, moved quickly onto the upper fo'c'sle just in time to join Lady Elphinstone and evacuate the last wounded warriors.

On Kestrel*'s lower gundeck the Guldur finally break through the hatch to the hold. A mass of them leap down through the hatch to the lower hold. They and their Goblan riders are wide-eyed with terror at the prospect of meeting the ghastly Dwarrowdelf that has been defending every hatchway with such ferocity. Instead, there is nothing. No one. They look around in wonder, expecting an ambush.*

More and more curs and ticks leap down to join their comrades. The Guldur first mate drops down to join them, barking orders. The curs dive through the hatch, through the plain of Flatland, to the upper hold, still expecting resistance. One pops back through and tells the first mate that the enemy have disappeared. Out of curiosity the Guldur officer reaches down and removes the piece of tarp that covers the Keel. He yelps in fear when he sees what is under the tarp.

Kestrel *sends one last message, up through the Guldur's paws where they touch the deck:* <<G O T C H A, S U C K E R*!!*>>

Broadax is the last to leave the Kestrel. *As she leaps across to join the boarding party, the noble old Ship begins to sink. From above and below the plain of Flatland, the view is exactly the same as the Ship seemingly melts into the sea, leaving two-space and entering interstellar space.*

The two Ships are tied together at the railing, above and below. The Kestrel *sinks and the Guldur Ship stands fast. The railing is torn and shattered, with splinters flying. Soon only the* Kestrel's *masts can be seen. Finally they too disappear, somewhere into the hard vacuum of deep space.*

On the enemy's upper deck the boarders maintained the momentum of their attack. After the one volley of the precious flashbang grenades and Lieutenant Fielder's unexpected flank attack, the enemy was falling back on all fronts. As Melville approached the ladder to the enemy's upper quarterdeck a huge, brown cur, with large black spots, reared up in front of him. It was the biggest Guldur he'd ever seen and on its back was the biggest tick he'd ever seen.

The huge creature in front of him had to be the enemy's captain. It looked at Melville's monkey and said, with a bizarre, lap-tongued doggie grin, "I sree rrou have a tick! Hrrold strrill, rrI'll get it!"

Melville responded in surprise, "Tick?!"

The monkey echoed, with outrage, "Kick!!?"

Von Rito, Kobbsven and Josiah were all occupied. For once, Petreckski was busy elsewhere. No loaded pistol was available. The middies were madly reloading.

Melville had just dispatched a loose Goblan with a downward slash, and it took him a split second to dislodge his sword from the body. The oversized cur in front of him swung a ferocious, overhand sword stroke at his head, and he was out of position to block it.

At times like this the senses can become acutely, intensely clear, seeking to find any escape or alternative. Besides the obvious one. In this case the information provided by that vivid clarity served only to confirm the fact that Melville was doomed.

I shall not die alone, alone,
    but kin to all the powers,

As merry as the ancient sun and
fighting like the flowers.

So, *thinks Melville,* This is how it will come. This is how I will die. This is the being who will kill me. *He is astounded to find that there is no anger in him, not even resignation, just wonder and . . . a fierce joy!*

One sound shall sunder all the spears and
break the trumpet's breath:
You never laughed in all your life as I shall
laugh in death.

His sword comes up in slow motion. He can tell that it will be too late. The rest of the battle doesn't exist. All sound is gone, only eery silence remains. His tunnel vision permits him to see only his opponent's head, torso and upper arms. He doesn't see the sword tip crashing down. Sword tips move too fast to follow, best always to watch the enemy's arms and project the position of the sword.

His sword is still moving up. Too slow, too slow! He is looking upward. At the edge of his vision he sees his monkey's belaying pin, a tattered, splintered, torn, beautiful belaying pin, meet and slightly deflect the huge Guldur sword. The long, straight, sword is deflected to his left! He jerks his head and body to the right. So little time. Time to move just slightly right. The enemy sword clips his hair, clips off the top of his left ear and slices deep into his left shoulder. He is alive!

Funny, he feels no pain as the sword slices through his flesh. Only the pressure of the blade cutting through the muscles of his shoulder. He also feels the pressure of his sword in his hand, coming up, thrusting forward. His left leg thrusts his body forward. His right knee bends. His sword point, a gory, dripping, hungry red sword point, lunges home:

Through teeth, and skull, and helmet
So fierce a thrust he sped,
The good sword stood a hand-breadth out
Behind the Tuscan's head.

The enemy drops, with Melville's sword through its brain, protruding out the back. Its tick leaps down to the deck where it dies, almost casually, anticlimactically, sliced in half as the tip of Corporal Kobbsven two-handed claymore begins an upward sweep.

Melville watches his enemy, his noble, noble enemy, fall.

How white their steel, how bright their eyes!
I love each laughing knave,
Cry high and bid him welcome to the banquet
of the brave.

Melville asks himself, "Why are there tears in my eyes?" Water for the dead. Water for the brave. He has killed the enemy captain. Brave, brave captain.

Yea, I will bless them as they bend and
love them where they lie,
When on their skulls the sword I swing
falls shattering from the sky.

Hans and Valandil are coming toward him from the enemy's quarterdeck. Only a handful of Guldur and Goblan are still on their feet. It's only a matter of time now and this mighty Ship will be his. The rightful fruit of honorable combat. Melville drops to his knees and looks down at his fallen foe.

The hour when death is like a light and
blood is like a rose,—
You have never loved your friends,
my friends, as I shall love my foes.

Somewhere in the darkness of interstellar space, a wooden ship drifts. Perhaps, in the unthinkably long lifetime of the universe, some alien race will find that ship. Inside this bizarre wooden vessel they will find the corpses of many doglike creatures, and gray, goblinlike beasts, all dehydrated and mummified by the vacuum of space. As they examine these corpses, if they look closely at their faces, and if they understand such things, perhaps they will be struck by the fact that all of them appear to be very, very surprised.

Chapter the 7th

Recovering from Battle: Lief Should I Rouse at Morning

> Could man be drunk forever
> With liquor, love or fights,
> Lief should I rouse at morning
> And lief lie down at nights.
>
> "Could Man be Drunk Forever"
> A.E. Housman

Melville was hung over. Seriously, seriously hung over. He hadn't touched a drop of liquor, but he felt like a sailor the morning after he got knee-walking, commode-hugging drunk, got beat up in a bar fight, and *then* got falling-down, belly-crawling drunk.

He'd been going on a physical and emotional high from the minute the apes attacked him on Broadax's World, up until the capture of this Ship. Man could *not* be "drunk forever, with liquor, love or fights." Now, finally, things were slowing down, and he must pay the price.

During combat an effect called vasoconstriction makes the veins constrict. The arteries are wide open, but just before the capillaries the return flow is cut off and the veins collapse. This is why a person's face will go white under intense stress. The blood pools in the body core and in the large muscle masses. Blood pressure skyrockets and, unless an artery is hit, bleeding from wounds can be very limited. In effect, the whole outer layer of the body becomes a layer of armor. Immediately afterward a powerful backlash can occur. Vasodilation sets in, the veins are wide open, and the face turns red and flushed.

For Melville that meant the blood loss from his shoulder wound was limited, initially. Shortly after combat was over and he relaxed, the blood began to gush from his wound and he christened the deck of his new Ship with a fair amount of his blood. The last thing he remembered, before he slept and woke up with this incredible "hangover," was Lady Elphinstone applying a little psychological first aid as she staunched the bleeding and plied her Sylvan skills to stitch up his wound.

He was lying on the deck where he had collapsed after slaying the enemy captain. His shoulder was a blaze of pain. Anesthetics and pain relievers *did* work in Flatland, but any complex chemical compound that wasn't part of a living creature tended to slowly break down. Thus, over time, the effectiveness of pain numbing medication grew weaker and weaker as it sat in storage. The *Kestrel* had been at sea for a long time and the stuff he'd been given was very weak.

He'd once read an early twenty-first century book entitled *Ether Day*, about the invention of anesthesia. The book fortunately survived the Crash since it was deemed fit to include in military archives, which the paranoid military types kept religiously separate from the vast interlocking Info-Net. A certain line from that book stuck in Melville's mind. "When one speaks of 'pain' during an operation without anesthetics, it is a word with ragged tails of meaning and imagery that permanently dye the mind: the peculiar red of one's own blood, the echoing blue of a limb dropping to the floor." Yep, that was about right. There was a lot of that going around today. Pain is relative. It doesn't get any more intense than when it's related to you.

The warriors of Westerness had found mind control tools, based in warrior science, to help them handle their pain. In the early twenty-first century, elite military units learned to apply the precepts of "Lamaze" to combat. Lamaze was initially a tool that was used to permit women to go through the *very* painful process of childbirth without pain medication. Soon the basic process of breathing, relaxation, visual concentration, and listening to a coach were applied to a wide variety of situations where individuals were in pain and medication wasn't immediately available or effective.

Melville was applying his Lamaze skills diligently. He was doing his breathing. He was working consciously on relaxation, avoiding the tension/pain/more-tension/more-pain cycle. He was listening very intently to Lady Elphinstone. And he was concentrating his vision intensely on a focal point, a knot in a rope far above him as he lay flat on the deck of his new Ship. Lovely, fascinating, remarkable knot. The combined effect was such that so many senses were being used, and so much thought processing was going on, that there was little mental capacity left over for feeling pain.

It really did work. One author called this the "ceremony of diminution," quite rightly stating that, "this stoical appearance of indifference in fact diminishes the pain."

It really did work. Melville kept telling himself that. Trying hard to believe it.

Next to him Lieutenant Broadax, coated in drying blood, was looking up into the stars with a blissful smile and a fresh cigar. She gave new meaning to the term "crusty old Marine" as she said to no one in particular, "Aye, this is wot I joined the Marines fer. Travel the galaxy, meet exotic creatures . . . *and kill 'em!*"

"Captain," said Lady Elphinstone as she worked on him, "lives have been lost, and thou must take care, lest thou shouldst feel some guilt in the aftermath of this combat. Dost thou hear me?"

"Yess . . . my lady," he gasped in reply. The wound in his shoulder was deep enough that she had to apply her stitches in two layers, a few stitches in deep to hold it together, and then a layer on the surface to close the wound.

"Thou hast no cause to feel guilt. Thou hast done well. Most importantly, thou hast done thy *duty*, and there is great healing in that. Hast thou read the Bhagavad Gita? 'Twas written on thy world in, I believe, the fourth century B.C."

"No," replied Melville, breathing hard, concentrating hard, relaxing hard, and trying to ignore the pinwheels of pain coming from his shoulder as she worked on him. "I . . . haven't read it. Tell me, how doesss-sss-sss it apply . . . to the current haah-aah! sssituation?"

"It says that, 'Valor, glory, firmness, skill, generosity, steadiness in battle and ability to rule—these constitute the *duty* of a soldier. They flow from his own nature . . . If you perform the sacrifice of doing your own *duty*, you do not have to do anything else. Devoted to *duty*, man attains perfection.' Dost thou hear me?"

"Yesss."

"Captain, thou hast done thy *duty*. For a little while, today, thou didst attain perfection. Go now and rest, for thou art weary with sorrow and much toil."

"Th-thank you, Doctor," said Melville, gasping with relief now that she was finished. "Any additional medical advice?"

"Yes. Thou must never, under any circumstances, take a sleeping pill and a laxative on the same night. Now sleep. Sleep." There must have been a dose of hypnosis in the healing skills of that good Sylvan surgeon. When she said "sleep," even as Melville was grunting in disgust at the very idea, he found himself drifting off. . . .

He awoke to the great-grandmother of all hangovers. His body shook like a sick dog. His stomach, no, his entire digestive tract, was a gurgling churning mess. His very *soul* ached. Every muscle was wrenched and every movement was pain incarnate. Every *breath* was pain. If only he could stop breathing. Yes, that might help. . . .

Melville was flat on his back. His left arm was strapped to his side. His left shoulder ached. His left ear ached. He reached up with his right hand to push the sleep mask up on his forehead, wincing as it caught on his wounded ear. The Elbereth Moss provided a constant soft yellow light anywhere inside a mature, healthy Ship of two-space. To really sleep well you needed to be in the dark, so those who slept below decks usually wore a sleep mask. Someone had kindly put one on him.

With the mask removed, Melville could see that he was in a cabin in his new Ship. His spider monkey slept, curled up beside him. He knew they were somewhere in the stern cabin of the Ship, directly below the quarterdeck. He could see the eternal constellations of Flatland, through what were obviously stern windows. Under his pillow he felt the butt of his pistol: a short, squat, black, double-barreled, over-and-under, .45 caliber "security blanket." In two-space he was never without this old family heirloom that seemed to grow better and better across the centuries as its Keel charges adapted to Flatland. He hadn't used it in his last battle, but it had been tucked into his belly sash like a lucky rabbit's foot. A rabbit's foot with *teeth*.

A portly sailor looked kindly down at him. "Captain," he asked, "how are you feeling?"

Duty. Duty was still ringing in his mind. Elphinstone said he was doing his duty. That made it okay. All he had to do was keep doing his duty. That would make everything okay.

He pulled at his blanket and looked down at himself. He was naked. Can't do your duty naked. At least not his duty to Westerness. He might *just* be able to do his duty to his nation *if* he could find some clothes. But the kind of duty he might perform while naked was definitely outside his ability at the moment. Fortunately *that* was not his pressing need.

"Dresh me." His mouth was dry. His voice was slurring. He worked some saliva into his mouth. His monkey looked up with sleepy curiosity.

"Sir, you can't get up!"

"I'm . . . captain. Dress me. Dammit. Or you're fired." Portly One's eyes got big and he began to scramble about obediently while Melville stifled a moan.

It hurt. It hurt bad. Melville made a visit to the head in the little quarter-gallery hanging out over the blue plane of Flatland, voiding his bladder and bowels out into interstellar space as he rested on the seat of ease with his head swimming. He looked in a mirror mounted to a bulkhead. The fellow looking back at him didn't look like the winner in a battle. (Yeah, yeah, "You shoulda seen the other guy." Sure, sure.) The top half of his left ear was missing. His face was white and pasty from loss of blood. His monkey sat on his right shoulder, like a huge, fawn-colored tarantula, with its legs splayed out in all directions.

Finally he was dressed in white trousers, shirt, black belly sash, and blue jacket. Tucked in the sash was his ugly little pistol. He would have felt naked without it. He was weak, depending heavily on Portly to accomplish even the simplest tasks. His steward had somehow manifested a steaming cup of tea that Melville eagerly sipped down. What was his name? He'd seen him before. Used to be Captain Crosby's steward. Should remember his name. Brain not working right . . . "What's your name, sailor?"

"McAndrews, sir."

"Aye. Thank you, McAndrews."

And so he went out on the deck of his Ship. *His* Ship.

As soon as he poked his head out he could tell that his cabin was under the upper side quarterdeck, which is where the captain's quarters should be. A marine stood on guard at his door. All sails were furled and the Ship appeared to be docked.

"Are we at Broadax's World?"

"Aye, sir," McAndrews replied. "We've moved all the dead below. They've been buried and Words said. Lieutenant Fielder said we needed to move fast, to avoid the main Guldur fleet and warn the Stolsh."

"Good. That's right." Fielder. He felt a knot of fear and dread in his stomach. Would Fielder try to rob him of his Ship? *So far* everything Fielder had done was appropriate. Best to confront the issue immediately. Mostly Melville wanted to crawl back into his bunk and keep sleeping, but *duty* called him. "Where is Lieutenant Fielder?"

"Here, sir. I'm right here."

Melville turned around and there was Fielder, standing above him at the railing on the upper quarterdeck, where the officer in command should be. He'd called him "sir." That was a good start.

He looked carefully at his first mate. Lord he looked bad. He didn't look defiant, or angry. Just tired. His dark hair hung limp and loose. His usually florid face was pale. He probably hadn't slept for a very long time. "Mr. Fielder, how long until we will be ready to set sail?"

"I think it will be about another hour, sir."

"Very good." Now for a situation report. "Give me a sitrep."

"Chips has established commo with our new Ship. She appears to be willing to tolerate us for now. The carpenter's mates have no significant problems in preparing the Ship to sail, since we only fired grape and canister at her."

Good. At least that part of his plan worked. He nodded for Fielder to continue.

"Guns has most of our 12-pounders on board. They're lashed down but we haven't begun to cut gun ports yet. I wanted to check with you first."

"Good. No immediate rush on that. We'll give it careful consideration. Tell Guns to prepare a recommendation."

"Yes, sir. Mr. Hans has the rigging and sails in order. He says he's ready to go. He still has to finish loading the last two cutters onto the deck. There should just be enough room for them."

"Good."

"*Lieutenant Broadax* has the enemy prisoners in the lower hold, well away from the Keel." Fielder's face was a steely, emotionless mask, but you could see his mask slip and a sneer slithered out when he mentioned the Dwarrowdelf's name. Well, that problem could wait. Odds were that Broadax could take care of herself. They *were* technically the same rank now. Melville nodded for him to continue.

"Mr. Petreckski says that there is adequate supply of water and food, even if some of the curs' chow might not be to our liking."

"Good." One less problem to worry about. They'd brought the cutters over with full water barrels and lots of food, but it wouldn't have been sufficient if there wasn't an adequate supply already on the enemy Ship.

"And the surgeon has the wounded in the lower quarterdeck cabin. All wounded from ashore have been brought aboard and our dead have been buried. Lady Elphinstone insisted that we not wake you up, so I proceeded with the burial." No apology there. Just a statement of fact. Overall, Fielder's actions and his demeanor were about as good as Melville could have asked for. Indeed, a compliment was in order.

"Well done, Daniel. Well done. Now I'm going to go ashore. I'll be right back." Fielder nodded and Melville left.

He was lowered onto Broadax's World in a bosun's chair; then he walked down to the graves. It was a blur of pain, both physical and emotional. McAndrews stood beside him. Melville dropped to his knees before the graves of his shipmates. So many, many graves. God, if he could only stay drunk with combat. *Duty*. He'd done his duty. A dirty, four-lettered word. Like kill. Like hell. Like damn.

It was raining. The new graves were slick mounds of wet earth. The graves of those killed by the apes already had grass sprouting from them. Young boys and old salts rested here. Some he knew well, many he didn't.

Melville generally disliked poetry that didn't rhyme. Somehow it struck him as cheating. But if that was so, then Walt Whitman cheated and got away with it. Privately, with only McAndrews and a small guard of marines there, Melville said Whitman's benediction upon his friends.

"A child said *What is the grass?* fetching it to me
with full hands . . .
I guess it is the handkerchief of the Lord . . .
And now it seems to me the beautiful uncut
hair of graves.

"Tenderly will I use you curling grass,
It may be you transpire from the breasts
of young men,
It may be if I had known them I would have
loved them . . .
It may be you are from old people, or
offspring taken soon out of their mothers' laps,
And here you are the mother's laps.

"What do you think has become of the young
and old men?
And what do you think has become of the women
and children?

"They are alive and well somewhere,
The smallest sprout shows there is really no death . . .
All goes onward and outward, nothing collapses,
And to die is different from what any one supposed,
and luckier."

Melville stood on the upper quarterdeck. They were moving out toward Stolsh space to warn them of the vast, slow moving Guldur fleet that was approaching. He'd sent Fielder and the middies to bed for four hours. Each of the sections also bedded down everyone they could, keeping only a skeleton crew on duty. For four hours Melville stood on the quarterdeck of his Ship (*his* Ship!) and rejoiced. He forced himself to eat and drink. His body ached. His soul ached, but the naval officer that was his core, *his* Keel, was rejoicing.

Above him the off-white sails were like clouds blocking the view of the starry heavens. The mizzenmast, mainmast and foremast all had three sails spread. Beneath the sails he could see the bowsprit pointing the way toward their navigation mark. Beneath the bowsprit another sail was spread.

There was little for him to do as he watched the sand trickle out for four turns of the hourglass. Every hour the glass was turned and they calculated their speed by the age-old process of casting the log. He wanted to test the new guns, but not now. He wanted to play with the sails and rigging, but not now, not with this skeleton crew. It seemed that every living creature who wasn't on duty was sleeping. Mostly he listened to the beautiful distant music, the song of Flatland, and just . . . was.

In four hours Fielder relieved him, the skeleton crew was rotated, and the men continued to sleep. Melville made a short visit to the hospital, where Elphinstone and Vodi escorted him as he visited the wounded.

Heavy gravity could be deadly to injured men, so it was vital to get them as far up above the plain of Flatland as reasonably possible. So they'd put the hospital in the cabin below the lower quarterdeck. The great windows in the stern looked out on the beautiful constellations of two-space, which was a balm to the soul of every sailor. They lay stacked up on pallets, wrapped in blankets.

They were hurt so very badly, these warriors of his. Many had lost limbs and were now destined to live a maimed and crippled life. Some might not last through the day. In the corner, slightly out of the way, removed from the others, one sailor was gasping out his last few breaths. They were brave, but in the end they were so frail, so very fragile.

> Too delicate is flesh to be
> The shield that nations interpose
> 'Twixt red ambition and his foes —
> The bastion of liberty.

Their efforts had saved all their lives, had given them victory in battle against a base, cowardly foe. But somehow, at moments like this it all seemed so hollow. Melville found himself overwhelmed with affection for these men, these *brave* men, these *noble* warriors, this "delicate flesh" that had followed him into battle and made their victory possible.

> Was there love once? I have forgotten her.
> Was there grief once? Grief yet is mine.
> Other loves I have, men rough, but men who stir
> More grief, more joy, than love of thee and thine.

The men were in remarkably good spirits. They seemed to take particular joy from his monkey. Cats and dogs were there to keep them constant company, but they considered the monkeys to be a particular talisman of luck and success. Wild tales of the monkeys' contribution to their battles were already circulating. Melville's monkey seemed to take the cautious stroking and petting as its rightful due.

> Faces cheerful, full of whimsical mirth,
> Lined by the wind, burned by the sun;
> Bodies enraptured by the abounding earth,
> As whose children we are brethren: one.

The hardest part was knowing that they would probably have to do it again. These men, of whom so much had already been asked, would have more to do. They would mend and heal their bodies, only to do it all again. Worse yet, their enemy could attack them at any moment, before they were healed, and these brave men would have to huddle helplessly in the hospital, where death could still find them.

His job was to protect them. How could he take them into harm's way again?

> And any moment may descend hot death
> To shatter limbs! Pulp, tear, blast
> Beloved soldiers who love rough life and breath
> Not less for dying faithful to the last.

Melville moved to the corner, where he knelt and held the hand of the dying sailor. It seemed like a very long time as the sailor shuddered out his last few minutes of life.

O the fading eyes, the grimed face turned bony,
Opened mouth gushing, fallen head,
Lessening pressure of a hand, shrunk, clammed
  and stony!
O sudden spasm, release of the dead!

He held the cold, dead hand for another moment, then let go, as Lady Elphinstone moved to cover the sailor's face. The room was silent, dead silent, as her assistants removed the body.

Was there love once? I have forgotten her.
Was there grief once? Grief yet is mine.
O loved, living, dying, heroic soldier,
All, all my joy, my grief, my love, are thine.

The warriors of Westerness dreaded burial in the cold vacuum of space. This body would be lovingly sewn into a sailcloth bag, and then lowered on a line into the "sea," into interstellar space. Sometimes there was a whole "stringer" of these strange, sad, frozen fish, to be hauled up and buried upon landfall.

The sailors gave a few last loving strokes to his little monkey. Others held their dogs and cats, pups and kittens, nurturing and treasuring the lives in their hands, as death went past. There were a few last words. Inconsequential words, comforting, supporting words. Then he left. He went to his cabin and wept . . . and slept.

It was eight hours later when he awoke. Most people go through a kind of panicky, preconsciousness checklist upon awakening. "Who am I?" "Where am I?" (And, upon occasion, "Good god, who is she?") Perhaps this is because they exist in a miasma of constant doubt and dread. Doubt and fear were what propelled them through life.

Melville had developed an ability common in most successful sailors and soldiers. With the exception of last time, when he'd been put to bed while unconscious, he woke up every morning knowing exactly who he was, where he was, and what he had to do that day.

He lived completely in the present. He knew where he was yesterday, he damn sure knew where he was today, and he had a pretty good idea where he'd be tomorrow. If you wanted anything more than that he'd have to check his log books or calendar.

He never had to "find himself" when he woke up in the mornings because he knew exactly who he was. He was, by God, the man in charge.

Again he made a trip to the head in the quarter-gallery, and again McAndrews had a cup of tea ready for him. Lots of sugar and lemon, just as he liked it. He still ached, but when he saw McAndrews there and smelled the tea, he was willing to suffer the portly, unctuous steward to live another day. Periodically his monkey stretched its neck out and took a drink of the tea. It closed its eyes and shuddered comically with the first sip, then it came back for more.

The cutters had been loaded with everything from the old *Kestrel* that they thought might be needed. Melville had tossed in a small bag of his own personal gear. Some books, tea bags, and a bottle of lemon juice. Somehow his steward had found the bag and put the contents to good use. Yes, Melville thought, I might just permit him to live a while longer. With McAndrews' help he managed to get dressed and went out on the deck, just in time to join the day watch for breakfast.

Over the centuries a rhythm had developed in the Ships of the Westerness Navy. The sailors on the "day" watch slept on the deck while the "night" watch was up and about for twelve hours. The night watch did most of the daily maintenance in the hold, worked silently, and respected their shipmates' sleep.

Then the "day" watch went on duty, and the sailors on the "night" watch slept in the hold or gundeck for twelve hours. Their new Ship had no separate gundeck, so the night watch all slept in the upper hold, while the marines and the Guldur prisoners were berthed in the lower hold. The day watch was boisterous and loud as they worked in the rigging. They did all the maintenance on the deck, and tried to limit how much they disturbed their shipmates in the hold.

Twelve hours could be a long shift, but a sailor's life was usually an easy, paced life, with plenty of time for breaks, and all three meals taken on duty. Out on the maindeck, in preparation for breakfast and dinner meals, their old cook, Roxy, would have her mates set up their "burners." These were yet another special adaptation of a Keel, which were designed, in this case, to release their energy as heat.

One day Cookie would set up on the upper maindeck, and the

next day she'd set up on the lower maindeck. This made the upper and lower crews socialize during meals, which contributed to the cohesion of the whole Ship. The only meal that wasn't served on the maindeck was the night watch's lunch, when the cooks set the kitchen up in the hold, so as to avoid bothering the day watch as they slept on the deck.

The watches "blended" into their duties at shift change. First the day watch formed up for duty and were inspected by their section chiefs. Then half of them had breakfast on deck, while half the night watch ate dinner at the same time. Finally the other half of the watches had their meals. At the end of the watch the process was reversed. This permitted the day and night watches to constantly intermingle and cross-level information.

Even with all these shared meals, if the captain wasn't careful, the "upper" and "lower" crews could become almost two separate ships. In order to prevent this, a constant rotation was in place. Periodically the lower night watch would become the upper night watch. In a few days the upper day watch would trade off with the lower day watch.

Westerness officers sometimes ate, or "messed," with their sailors out on the deck, but in the normal process of duty they preferred to eat in the wardroom. The petty officers and marine NCOs also ate together in a separate mess. The captain often ate alone in his cabin, in splendid solitude. Soon they'd set up an area in the hold to use as a wardroom. For now Melville stood on the upper quarterdeck, eating some kind of scrambled breakfast concoction with Lieutenant Fielder, Lieutenant Broadax, his surgeon, his midshipmen, his two rangers (who were accounted by the captain as officers on *this* Ship), and his four warrant officers.

The crew was lounging around on the unfamiliar maindeck. Messmates gathered in groups around the guns, clusters tucked into corners, and clumps sprawled out on the deck, as they began the process of making themselves at home. They were enjoying a leisurely meal, and during the meal they went about the age-old process of "debriefing" after combat. With each telling of the events of the battle they "multiplied their joy," emphasizing the valor, the courage, the sacrifice, the professionalism of their mates, living and dead. And they "divided their pain," working through the memories and "delinking" them from the physiological arousal.

Some would imagine that these sessions would be a kind of "koom-by-yah sob-fest," but nothing could be further from the truth. Across the centuries, warriors learned that the men who grew weepy and could not control their emotions were the ones who would not be there the next year. It was okay to weep, to mourn briefly and intensely at the funeral of a friend, but it was not acceptable for a warrior to weep at the memory of combat. Perhaps you would weep the first time, but you were ashamed of your weeping, and the next time (and the next, and the next) it was expected that you would talk about your combat experiences and remain calm. You *must* talk, and you must remain calm, in order to "make friends" with the memory.

Across the countless centuries warriors have taken their cues from the "Old Sarge." There was *always* an Old Sarge. He was the veteran of twenty battles, and he was *calm*. Weeping and becoming emotional at the memory of combat was not acceptable because, across the countless centuries, warriors found that the way to continue performing the desperate, wretched, debasing, dirty job of combat was by controlling your emotions, dividing your pain, and making friends with the memories. Every night, around the campfire, or over hot food with their messmates, this age-old process continued.

In these sessions the men also sorted out what had actually happened. In Alexis Artwohl's twenty-first-century law enforcement research, almost a quarter of the combat veterans she interviewed had memory distortions. They actually "remembered," sometimes with vivid intensity, something that did *not* happen. And half of these veterans had experienced memory loss, with significant gaps in the memory of what happened. Left to their own devices, there was a tendency to "fill in the gaps" with guilt-laden acceptance of responsibility, sometimes even a greatly exaggerated sense of guilt. "Its all my fault." "I let my buddies down." "I was a failure." These were the kinds of responses felt by many men after combat. Only their mates, the ones who shared the event with them, could help them fill in the holes accurately. And only their friends, their comrades who had shared the searing experience of combat, only they could give understanding, acceptance, and forgiveness of the events that had occurred.

Every day, day after day, this is what occurred. *This* is what warriors did.

~ ~ ~

Melville's left arm was slung securely to his side, but his left hand was free. He held the plate in his left hand, propped on a railing as he spooned the mystery glop into his mouth with his good right arm. Periodically, as a spoonful was on its way to his mouth, his monkey would reach out a three-fingered paw with amazing speed and dexterity to snag a handful. Sometimes Melville would lift up a spoonful and be momentarily disoriented when it arrived empty at his mouth. The other crew members with monkeys were experiencing the same thing. No one seemed to begrudge the little creatures their small tariff on the goods that went from plate to mouth.

"Shipmates," Melville began. "We have a course and a mission, so now I think the first order of duty is to establish the name for our new Ship. Mr. Petreckski, I understand you have been interviewing the Guldur prisoners. What did they call this Ship?"

"Well, sir," replied the purser, leaning against the railing in his brown robes, "I think I can show you better than I can tell you. Valandil, if I may use your dog as a demonstrator?"

"Certainly," replied the ranger, looking down at his dog with mild bemusement.

Petreckski dropped down on one knee and patted the dog on the side. "Cinder, I need to show the captain your teeth, please."

Cinder, thought Melville to himself, *her name is Cinder. Why didn't I know that?*

The Sylvan dog looked up at Petreckski in amiable compliance, as the purser peeled back her lips and showed the captain her teeth. "Do you see this lower right canine tooth?"

"They named the Ship after a fang?"

"No sir, not a fang, although they have a specific word for each of the four fangs, two upper and two lower. Actually, the Guldur have a very specific word for every single tooth in their head. Their teeth are very important to them. Do you see the little gripper teeth in between the two lower canines?"

"Yesss . . ."

"Well, sir, the second one from the left is what this Ship is named after. Apparently this whole class of Ships has each been named after one of these little gripper teeth."

"Hmm, I don't think that we can name our Ship 'Her Majesty, the Queen of Westerness' Ship, the Second Little Gripper

Tooth in from the Canine.' Since we only have one of these Ships, instead of a whole class of them, I propose that we shall name her *Fang*. Does anyone see a reason why this would be a problem?"

"No sir," responded Mr. Barlet, the gunnery warrant, "but that still leaves open the class of Ship she represents. I think that the cannonball these big guns fires is close to a 24-pounder, so may I suggest that we call her 'Her Majesty, the Queen of Westerness' 24-Pounder Frigate, *Fang*."

"Very good," responded the young captain with a smile, "and so it shall be!"

Of course, he didn't have the authority to take this action. It would have to be approved by the Admiralty. When the time came his actions would be judged, and his only real defense would sound something like, "Hey, it followed me home. Can't I please keep it?" But right now, what other option did they have?

"Chips," Melville went on, looking at his carpenter, "at the end of the day watch I intend to go down and talk to the Ship. Would you be so kind as to come with me then?"

"Aye, sir," Mr. Tibbits replied. He appeared benumbed, still in deep shock and mourning from the loss of *Kestrel*. It reminded Melville of an Edgar Allen Poe poem,

> For, alas, alas, with me
>   The light of life is o'er!
> "No more—no more—no more—"
>   (Such language holds the solemn sea
> To the sands upon the shore)
>   Shall bloom the thunder blasted tree,
> Or the stricken eagle soar!

Truly something ancient and magnificent had been lost. The stricken falcon would soar no more, no more. She was lost to mankind, and lost to the *Kestrel*'s old crew. But Tibbits had been in close daily telepathic contact with the Ship for many long years. For him it was like losing a spouse, a soul mate. Only the duty of coordinating with this new Ship seemed to be keeping him afloat.

"Now, gentlemen, there is one more task I want to take care of before we begin our first full day watch aboard our new Ship.

A happy task. I'm going to give Midshipman Archer and Midshipman Crater field commissions to acting lieutenant. Lieutenant Fielder will have the night watch and I will take the day watch. Each of us will now have a lieutenant to command the lower quarterdeck, while we command the upper deck."

Melville looked at the two young men. Jarad Crater was a tall broad-shouldered lad with an open grin and a scraggly wisp of beard on his chin. He'd seen Crater in action and the boy was very good, but he still managed to communicate an image of gangly awkwardness. Buckley Archer was a slender lad of average size, with brown hair, and elegant red sideburns and goatee. He carried himself with an air of self-confidence and poise, but there was always an underlying note of wary concern. They were both academy graduates and extraordinary young men. They were fully proven. Given their skills and the current circumstances, Melville felt completely justified in giving them field commissions.

"Lieutenant Archer. Lieutenant Crater," he said, looking them each in the eye and shaking their hands as he said their names. "My congratulations to both of you. You understand that this commission may not be approved upon our return to Admiralty authority, but regardless, it will look good on your records." They both nodded their stunned reply.

"My friends," he continued, looking at his officers, "now we must replenish the ranks of our midshipmen. Look for ship's boys that you can nominate to be midshipmen. Give me your suggestions at the end of the watch. We'll put them right to work and begin training them immediately. When we get the chance, we'll nominate them for the academy."

Melville looked around at his officers and could see that they were thinking about the young men under their command. "We should also draw from our seamen and perhaps even our petty officers for midshipmen. Most of you know that I began my career as a seaman and a young petty officer, before being selected for the academy. Mr. Fielder also spent some years as a seaman before being selected as a midshipman and then receiving a field promotion to lieutenant. I think," Melville continued with a grin and a glance at Fielder, "that we can agree that some quality officers can come from the ranks."

Melville looked at young Midshipman Aquinar. He could guess the boy's thoughts. Archer and Crater were promoted to lieutenant.

Midshipman Faisal was in the hospital and Midshipman Chang was dead. Aquinar was now the senior midshipman.

The monkeys had developed a habit of stretching out their accordion necks and placing the top of their heads on their master's shoulder so that their upside-down face was now right-side-up. Perhaps this was an attempt to look more like their friends, or simply their impish sense of humor. The result was that it appeared as though a small, second head was growing from your shoulder. Now Aquinar's monkey was doing that, and it was mildly disconcerting as both heads looked at their captain with wide eyes.

"Mr. Aquinar, you are now the senior midshipman. The midshipman berth will be empty except for you, but it will fill up soon. Some of them will be quite a bit older than you, but I expect you to remain in charge. If you need any assistance, don't hesitate to ask any of the officers." Both heads looked at him and *both* nodded in solemn, silent understanding.

Melville looked over at his own monkey's face. It was resting on his shoulder just like Aquinar's, and he could swear that its right-side-up face winked at him as it also nodded.

" . . ." Blink. " . . . Yes, well, then let us get to work. This is the beginning of day watch. Mr. Crater, you take command of the lower quarterdeck. Mr. Aquinar, you'll be assigned to assist the carpenter in his duties; tomorrow you'll have a new crew of midshipmen to break in. Mr. Fielder, Mr. Archer, you have the night watch, we'll see you in twelve hours. Sleep well."

Melville stood and rejoiced in his first full watch as captain. He stood beside a young helmsman, who stood at the Ship's wheel. Under the watchful eye of the quartermaster, the boy was looking carefully across the maindeck, keeping the Ship on course by keeping the bowsprit pointed at a specific star. Melville still ached, but his body was young, as was his soul. Body and spirit seemed to be working together, in spite of his wounds, to find some enthusiasm for his duties.

At the beginning of the watch they'd measured the Ship's speed by heaving the log. Melville, as the officer on duty, stood holding a timer. He said "Go," and turned over the small half-minute glass. The "log" consisted of a small piece of Keel attached to a line, since anything other than a Keel wouldn't remain in two-space but would sink into interstellar space. On his command the quartermaster threw the log off the back of the quarterdeck. The log hit the sea, bobbed once and began to recede into the distance as the Ship sailed away. A young quartermaster's mate stood holding the reel as the line raced off, marked periodically by knots in the cord. When the last grain of sand ran out of the tiny glass, Melville said, "Stop," and the young sailor stopped the cord.

"Just a tad under ten knots, sir," said the quartermaster, looking down at the reel. The quartermaster's mate began to reel the log back in as the quartermaster looked up at his captain. "Not near as fast as old *Kestrel*, sir, but not too bad. As we tweak the rigging, hopefully we can do a bit better than that."

Hans, in his role as sailing master, was working hard to get every bit of speed out of their new Ship. "Aye, sir," he told his young captain as he handed up a chunk of chewing tobacco for his monkey to bite a chaw off of, "the ticks is piss-poor sailors. Damned fine topmen, mind ya, but their idee of arrangin' sails 'as got no finesse, no art to it, if ya take my meanin'."

A two-space Ship typically had ten sails. A mainsail, topsail, and topgallant sail on each mast, and a spritsail on the bowsprit. They all ran perpendicular to the length of the Ship. The strange "wind" or gravity effect of two-space was caught by the sails. Since it always came from directly above there was never any need to shift the angle of the sails, which made their rigging quite a bit simpler than it was in the old sailing vessels. Which was good, because any kind of pulley, as would be found in a block and tackle, was quickly made useless by the technology-eroding effects of Flatland.

Spankers and jibs, sails that ran more parallel to the length of the ship, contributed little to the forward movement of a Ship. So they were used only rarely, to facilitate sudden direction changes.

"The curs made a damned fine Ship, sir," added Hans during one of his periodic consultations with Melville. These conferences were really more diplomatically conducted education sessions than consultation, as the master sailor explained what he was doing to his young captain. He *and* his monkey spit streams of tobacco juice over the side of the railing as he continued. "She has some o' the strongest masts I've ever seen on a Ship. By God, I think 'er sticks are stout enough 'at she might be able ta stand some royals *and* a spritsail-topsail, if we do it real careful like. We might work on those later, but fer now we have at least a week's worth o' work in front of us, sorting out this rats' nest of a riggin' the ticks 'ave been usin'."

Every turn of the Ship's glass marked an hour, and each hour the bell was rung, up to twelve bells. Then the night watch would begin the cycle again. At one bell they heaved the log again. "Just a hair *over* ten knots this time," the quartermaster said with a satisfied grin.

Shortly thereafter a nervous young ship's boy approached the quarterdeck. "Beg pardon sir," the young man said. "But Mr. Petreckski and Lady Elphinstone say there's som't'n int'restin happenin' in the surg'ry, if the Cap'in has time to come look."

"Thank you. Tell them I need to speak with Mr. Barlet first and then I will be there directly."

"Aye, sir! You'll be with Mr. Barlet and then to the surg'ry direc'ly." The boy saluted and scurried off as Melville turned to the quartermaster on duty. "Do you feel that all is well here?"

"Aye, sir," he replied with a confident grin. "All is well." Above them Mr. Hans' sailors were working like a great, chattering flock of dirty white birds, adjusting the sails and coordinating well with the quartermaster throughout the process. Hans respectfully coordinated with his captain, but it was immediately obvious to Melville that the new sailing master (and ex-chief) had a mastery of sails and rigging that he would probably never equal. Melville resigned himself to the fact that he'd never be a Jack Aubrey, tweaking the sails of a Ship to get the greatest possible speed. He counted himself lucky to have Hans as a sailing master and was content to leave such things to the real expert.

"She's a sweet Ship," the quartermaster continued, "if a little slow and sluggish compared to *Kestrel.* Some of the changes Chief, er, Mr. Hans is making will make her even sweeter."

The quartermasters were all experienced and trusted petty officers, assisted by two mates, one of whom served as the helmsman. As a former petty officer himself, Melville remembered how much he enjoyed it when the officers left him in charge. It was rare that there wasn't at least a midshipman in nominal "command" and the quartermasters were enjoying their moment in the sun. Melville hoped to find a few good midshipmen from among the ranks. Although technically a promotion, it was often hard to convince a good career NCO to take the step from godlike NCO powers to lowly midshipman. It was sometimes easier to move them to a warrant position, as he had done with Chief Hans, but even then it was hard to get a good NCO to step "down" from being the big frog in his comfortable little pond, to being a middle-sized frog in a bigger pond.

Melville returned the young petty officer's grin. "Very good. I'm going to coordinate briefly with Mr. Barlet, then I'll be down in the surgery."

It wasn't hard to find the gunnery officer. He, Gunny Von Rito, and their mates were on the lower gundeck, crawling all over the big guns that Barlet had designated as 24-pounders. "Guns," said Melville as he walked up, "what do you think of these cannon?"

"Sir, they're simply magnificent," replied the gunnery officer, with joy shining from his dark face. "Did you know that they were actually *brass* under this black coating the curs put on their guns? *Brass* cannons, by the Lady!"

He scowled and continued, "But the sighting system stinks! It's like building the biggest, finest ship ever imagined, out of the finest possible material, and then not putting a rudder on her. It's just like the curs, but I can't really blame it all on their stupid, slam-bam-thankee-ma'am tactics. The problem is that this gun is too big to lean over and sight down when you fire it, and anyone who stands behind it when you touch her off will be crushed. So you have to sight her from behind the barrel, step back, tap the Keel charge, then jump back fast. Bottom line is that whenever you shoot, you're always firing from old data."

Then he grinned with the joy of a true craftsman, the feral grin of a master gunner facing a problem that he was born to solve. "I think I have a solution. It'll be tricky but I think we'll be able to use these guns in a way the Guldur never dreamed possible."

"Good!" Melville responded. "That's our top priority. Let me know what you need to get the mission accomplished. I'm also eager to do some test firing, so let me know when you're ready. Our second priority is to get the 12-pounders we brought from *Kestrel* into position. Do you have a suggestion as to their placement?"

"Yes sir, I do. I think we can put a pair of 12-pounders forward of each pair of 24-pounders, two above, two below, on both the green and red sides. If we do it right, then on the upper green-side and the lower red-side we can swing the for'ard-most gun around and use her for a bow chaser at need."

"That will account for eight of them, what of the remaining four?"

"Well, sir, I'd like to put two each in the cabin right below the quarterdeck, above and below, as stern chasers." His brows furrowed and he looked askance at his captain, warily, judgingly. "The only problem is that you'd have to give up a lot of space in your cabin."

Melville laughed out loud. It was plain to see that in Barlet's eyes this was a test of the new captain's character, but for Melville it was no test at all. "Aye, Guns, great minds do think alike. That's exactly the solution I came up with. I don't give a hoot in hell about space in my cabin! But what I do want is to give a load of grief to anyone who chases us. I figure with a Ship this slow we're more apt to be the chasee than the chaser. So having some firepower back there may be useful. Tell Chips where you want the gun ports put, and make it happen! We have the wounded in the lower quarterdeck cabin, so do that last, and give the surgeon plenty of warning before you do it."

"Aye, sir!" Barlet nodded happily as Melville turned and strode toward the surgery. If only all of his tests were that simple. If only all of his men were that easy to please. His good mood evaporated instantly and anxiety gripped his stomach as he thought about the fact that there would be times when he'd have to make hard decisions, decisions that they wouldn't like. All their support and amiable nods might dry up in an instant in the face of their young, inexperienced captain.

The glow of the Elbereth Moss provided steady light. Within the Ship, if nothing was placed in the way, the combined light from the ceiling, bulkheads and floor could be almost as bright as daylight. But it was rare to have a room with nothing in the way of the Moss. Usually there was furniture, great quantities of equipment hanging on the bulkheads, and hatches in various bulkheads and decks.

The surgery was a walk-in closet, just off the lower quarterdeck cabin, where the glow of Lady Elbereth's Gift flowed freely. Nothing was hung on the bulkheads. There was no furniture except a table and no hatches except for one small door. Outside this small door was the hospital, where many of the wounded were stacked up in stretchers.

Many of them were sitting up in their pallets to peer into the surgery. A large bloody bundle sat outside the door and Doc Etzen, the day watch corpsman, stood outside the door. A strong stench of decaying flesh was in the air.

The captain ducked into the surgery. As he bent over to go in it became clear that the putrid smell was from the bundle sitting outside the door, and from inside as well. The strange, constant, downward "wind" of two-space drove their sails. It also pulled a draft down through vents in every room, then exited the Ship from vents just above the sea. Even with this constant flow of air, the smell was almost overwhelming. Gagging slightly at the stench, he found Petreckski, Lady Elphinstone, and her assistant, Mrs. Vodi, gathered around the operating table, the latter two with their usual small cloud of cats at their feet.

The Sylvan was wearing her traditional buttercup yellow dress with grass green sash. Her long blond hair was braided behind her. Her hands were covered with blood and ichor, but her garments were spotless.

Vodi was in a dowdy black shift, her gray hair up in a bun. She was gummy as a baby, with a face like a large, self-satisfied, golden raisin. She kept a large chaw of tobacco in her cheek and a spit cup in her bloody hand. As he watched, she spat a stream of juice into the cup. "Psssuttt."

"Sir!" said Petreckski. His pale blue eyes were shining with excitement in his heavyset face. His thin, straw colored hair was in disarray, and he had a smear of blood on his cheek. Smears of blood and ichor could be detected on his brown robe. "Look at this."

On the table before them, spread out on a piece of sailcloth, was the dissected body of one of the little spider monkeys, spread-eagled on the table. If eight legs, a tail and a head splayed out and sliced open in every direction could qualify for that term. On Petreckski's shoulder sat his monkey, alive and well, peering down at the body without any apparent distress or concern over the process. Indeed, the little monkey seemed as intent and interested as its master. Melville looked over at his monkey, which was craning its neck to look at the operating table, apparently sharing the interest, as Petreckski continued. "I saved the corpse of an ape and several spider monkeys from Broadax's World, and we just finished dissecting them."

It occurred to Melville to be concerned that precious space on their cutters must have been tied up with such items during the boarding process. But collecting cargo and knowledge was the purser's job. That was *his* contribution to Westerness and Melville trusted him to know what constituted valuable cargo. In the old days of sailing ships the purser wasn't often a popular officer, since he was notorious for stealing from the ship. In those days "purser's tricks" was a term for any kind of swindle with food or supplies. But today, in the Westerness Navy, the purser was a highly respected professional who helped make sure that the Ships turned a profit as they traveled. A profit that was shared by all the warrior-traders onboard the Ship.

"This little fellow is one of the ones that fell from the trees while they were fighting the apes," Petreckski went on, pointing to the bloody remains. "He really didn't have too much damage, just some internal trauma and broken bones. Of course, he and his bigger playmate out there *have* gotten a little ripe."

Melville found himself fighting a wave of nausea at the sight and smell in the confined area. The purser went on, oblivious to his captain's discomfort. "We could have put them on a line and hung them down into space. But the freezing and vacuum would have done even more damage, and then we'd be working with a frozen body, so this is really best."

"I assume," Melville asked, "that the reeking bundle outside the door is this little fellow's larger cousin?"

"Well, yes and no," Petreckski replied. "That *is* the bundle containing the ape, but he isn't even remotely a relative of this little monkey," gesturing at the bloody mass on the table. "Perhaps Lady Elphinstone can explain it best, since this is really her area of expertise."

Nodding at the purser, the Sylvan healer took up the account. Beside her, her lob-lolly girl, Mrs. Vodi, spat some tobacco juice into her spit cup, "psssuttt," causing Melville's stomach to heave again.

Elphinstone was "still waters" that ran *very* deep, but even she was reflecting a little of Petreckski's excitement. "Captain, I need to begin by telling thee that the large apes are very crude, simple creatures. To put it plainly, they are very unevolved. The one we dissected was clearly male, but cursory inspections of their bodies after the battle also identified many females."

She went on, her fingers flashing a probe and a scalpel to demonstrate her points. "The spider monkeys, inside, are as different as night is from day. They have the same three-fingered paws as the apes, but one of *their* fingers is capable of wrapping around and acting as an opposable thumb. Thou canst also see that these little ones have a *very* highly refined neural system. And look, thou canst tell that their brain is quite well developed." Melville could tell no such thing, but was content to take her word on it. "Everything about them is evolved, or developed to the very highest degree. But here is the most remarkable thing. They have absolutely no sexual or reproductive capability."

"So," said Melville, since something seemed to be expected of him at this point, "the spider monkeys are the dominant species of the world, while the apes are some distant, unevolved branch."

"Captain," Petreckski interjected, shaking his head thoughtfully, "these two creatures are as different from each other as a squid is from you and me. Different number of limbs, different reproductive process, different nervous system, and totally different levels of development. They *look* similar, but they couldn't possibly be any more different. That's why it's so *very* strange that they look so much alike!"

Melville looked at him blankly. Elphinstone went on, trying to make it clear. "Think of it as though two civilizations set out to build an automobile. One is crude, industrial age technology, making a Model-T Ford. The other is the highest technology thou canst think of, making a state-of-the-art land vehicle. Inside, *nothing* is the same, so why bother to make it *look* like a Model-T?"

The excitement and enthusiasm in these two was mildly infectious. Melville found himself beginning to share their interest. Then they gave him the one bit of information that was truly electrifying. "But," Elphinstone continued, her blue eyes sparkling with relish, "if they have no reproductive capability, and they *don't*, then how dost thou explain the two baby monkeys that arrived last night?"

"Babies?" Melville asked.

"Two that we know of," said Petreckski. "Both are with the wounded. Hakeem and Ivanov both report waking up with a little bundle of fur nestled beside them. They say they thought it was a puppy, or kitten at first, but when they found out it was a monkey, just like yours, they were delighted."

"Well, let us take a look at these 'babies,'" said Melville, delighted to have an excuse to leave the malodorous surgery. He didn't think he could last another few minutes without embarrassing himself. To add to his discomfort, Mrs. Vodi spat a squirt of tobacco juice into her cup again. "Psssuttt."

The young captain looked at her and must have appeared particularly green.

"Yes, Captain," said the ancient lob-lolly girl. "I know it's a nasty habit. I tried to kick it. 'Get Thee behind me, Satan!' I said, and a scant minute later I heard a deep voice say, 'Nice Ass.' Oh, well, Take 'em where you can get 'em. That's my motto."

"..." Blink. Gulp. Blink. Melville looked at her ample bottom and gulped again. Mrs. Vodi didn't just derail his train of thought. She ripped up the rails and tied them in knots over roaring fires made of the railroad ties, burning the station and the bridge for good measure on the way out. "... Um. Yes. Well, let us see these 'babies,' shall we?"

"Wait, Captain," said Petreckski his voice growing low and conspiratorial. "Before you go, I have one last thing to show you." He reached behind him and pulled up a cloth sack. Inside the bag was an assortment of shattered belaying pins and chunks of wood. "These are the pieces of wood that our little friends were waving around in battle. Please look carefully at them and see what you notice."

Melville looked, picking each one up and examining it in the bright light of the surgery. The hair began to stand up on the back of his neck. "Yes... Each of them does seem to have an inordinate number of musket balls in it." That was an understatement. Several of them were riddled with imbedded musket balls, and deep grooves indicated where many more bullets had been deflected.

Petreckski continued as Melville stood transfixed by what he was holding in his hand. "Captain, you and Lieutenant Broadax, in particular, were real bullet magnets. Right out in front. Every enemy musket was firing at you. The Guldur are rather bad shots, and the Goblan are even worse, but not *that* bad." He pointed to two particularly tattered chunks of wood. "This is the one your monkey carried, and this belonged to Broadax's monkey. Truth is, you should both be dead, several times over. But somehow, it would appear, our monkeys may have been . . . blocking bullets. I don't know any other way to put it. Perhaps it's just a coincidence, or perhaps our little friends have a lot to answer for."

Now his whole skin was a mass of goose bumps. The stench of the surgery was forgotten. Melville stared at his monkey, and he could swear that the little creature looked him in the eyes and shrugged. "Perhaps," replied Melville, still looking at his monkey. "For now, let us keep this quiet." He reached up and scratched behind his monkey's soft, furry ears in a way that the little creature seemed to enjoy. It arched its back, closed its eyes and pushed gently against his ministering hand.

Melville continued, "Broadax and Fielder need to know about the results of your . . . research." He gestured at the bullet encrusted belaying pin in the purser's hand, "And about the . . . bullet stopping. Otherwise, this stays within this room. Understood?"

Elphinstone, Vodi, and Petreckski all nodded solemnly. So did Petreckski's monkey.

" . . ." Blink. "Right, then," he continued as he ducked out the door, "let's see these 'babies.'"

Standing out in the main hospital area, Melville took deep breaths as the others came out to join him. He wanted to say something about getting rid of these stinking corpses, but then realized that a few ship's boys were already taking charge of that task, dragging the bundles away in a manner that was oddly furtive.

The two tiny monkeys did look like little dappled kittens or puppies, all curled up, but with way too many legs stirred into the equation. Their "masters" were inordinately proud of them. Melville shuddered to think how possessive they might be if they suspected the monkeys' bullet-stopping skill.

No one had a clue where they came from. "Why, from momma monkeys, of course!" said one sailor and they all laughed. Melville and Petreckski looked at each other knowingly.

Melville knew he was running out of gas. He was already "smoked," as they would say of an exhausted warrior. By the end of his twelve-hour shift he was going to be useless, or "smoked like a cheap cigar," as the saying goes. There was something he needed to do first. Something he'd been putting off.

A young ship's boy, third class, was assigned to the quarterdeck, and when Melville returned to his duty station he called him over.

"Sir!" said the boy, wide eyed and tugging his forelock in salute.

"Find the carpenter and ask him to come meet me here, when he has a chance."

"Aye, sir! When the carpenter gets a chance, 'e's to come meet you here."

Tibbits arrived shortly. "Aye, sir?"

"Mr. Tibbits, I've been putting off talking to our Ship. Do you think that now is a good time?"

"Aye, sir. She'll talk with her carpenter, but in the end everythin' depends on her relationship with the Cap'n. Now is as good a time as ever. If you wait too long she may feel insulted, or it may look weak."

"Aye, Chips. My thoughts exactly."

"Aye, and there's one other thing," said the old carpenter, pulling a white Moss-coated piece of wood from his pocket. "I saved a shard of *Kestrel*'s Keel. A bit of her's still alive here," he said. "I reckon you can decide what to do with it, but maybe it'd be a good idea to put it next to the new Ship's Keel. Maybe they can . . . talk . . ."

"Aye," said Melville, taking the sliver of wood and immediately feeling the comforting, distant sense of an old friend. "Between this and *Kestrel*'s cutters sitting on her decks, *Fang* will have something to think about. Let's go."

Down in the hold Melville and Tibbits stood over the Keel of Her Majesty, the Queen of Westerness' 24-Pounder Frigate, *Fang*. This was a vital moment. If the Ship didn't accept them, they might well be dead. There were several ways that *Fang* could kill her occupants, and none of them were pleasant ways to die. The captain's relationship with his Ship was the key. "Chips," Melville asked, "do you have any advice before I speak with her for the first time?"

"Well, Cap'n, I'd be real gentle. She's a young Ship, and she seems kind of stunned by the whole business. She swapped Moss with old *Kestrel* during the boarding, and our four cutters is in direct contact with her. That seems to be havin' an effect. The curs don't treat their Ships real nice. Seems like there's not much love there. Our relationship with dear old *Kestrel* seems to be something new to young *Fang* here, and she's tryin' to adjust. Just be gentle, Cap'n and in the back of my mind I'd be thinkin' a little about old *Kestrel*, as background noise, so ta speak."

"Thanks, Chips." Melville sat down carefully in the 1.25 gees of the hold. He took several deep belly breaths. Now wasn't a time to show fear. Then he placed a hand on the Keel.

Speaking aloud *and* through his telepathic link to his Ship, Melville introduced himself. <<"Fang. I'm your captain. On behalf of our old Ship, the *Kestrel*, and our entire crew, I thank you for your hospitality.">>

<<C A P T A I N? F A N G?>>

<<Yes, we have translated your old name as *Fang*.>>

Melville had a sudden vision of a wolf lunging. In his vision there was particular emphasis on the wolf's canine tooth, its fang. Bright fang. Strong fang. Ripping fang. Good fang. <<F A N G G O O D.>>

Melville heaved a sigh of relief. She *liked* the name.

<<C A P T A I N G O O D F I G H T E R. K I L L C A P T A I N.>>

<<Yes, I killed the old captain.>> It suddenly occurred to Melville that, in *Fang*'s mind, that might be key to his mastery of this Ship. Especially by Guldur tradition, that made him the rightful master. He suddenly felt a shudder of fear when he thought about the quirk of fate that permitted him to meet and defeat the captain of this Ship in honorable combat.

With almost puppylike excitement *Fang* went on. <<G O O D F I G H T. G O O D B L O O D!>>

Yes. His blood had flowed freely on the deck, where the Elbereth Moss soaked it up. As it did most blood, but not any other fluid. What did that do? What did it *mean* to the weird amalgam of Moss and Guldur-based memories that formed *Fang*'s sentience? Whatever it meant, it seemed to be good.

And then, with a strange sadness and yearning, something was added . . .

<<G O O D S H I P.>>

Melville felt a thrill as he understood that his Ship was talking about *Kestrel*. Their old Ship had left them with one last gift. The respect and awe of this young Ship. Keeping his hand on the Keel, Melville reached into his pocket and pulled out the Keel shard from *Kestrel*. He placed it lovingly next to *Fang*'s Keel charge, wedging it in a little. One hand on the shard and one hand on the Keel, he felt a surge of interest and empathy. Something deep and profound was happening, something he could barely understand.

Fang repeated herself, saying again, with new depth of feeling, <<G O O D S H I P. S A F E N O W.>>

<<Aye, *all* of us are safe now, thanks to you.>>

<<G O O D P U P S! P U P S S A F E T O O.>>

Again, Melville understood through their telepathic bond that *Fang* was speaking of the cutters, *and* the real dogs treading the decks of this Ship. *And*, strangely enough, the young midshipmen and ship's boys whose bare feet trod the decks. Yes, thought Melville, with his eyes misting up just a little. They were *good* pups.

Then he realized with a shock that *Fang* included him as a "pup." *Great*, he thought with a smile, *it's the classic tale of a ship and her boy!*

Then *Fang* got down to coordinating daily business with her captain.

<<W H E R E G O?>>

The young captain smiled and looked up at Tibbits. "We're home, Chips. We're home." Brave *Kestrel*, their brave dogs, and the courage of their brave lads had bought them a home.

Chapter the 8th

Establishing Routine: To Guard from Hurt

. . . then dreams o'ertake
His tired-out brain, and lofty fancies blend
To one grand theme, and through all barriers break
To guard from hurt his faithful sleeping friend.
"The Battlefield"
Sydney Oswald

Melville completed his discussion with *Fang*, telling her where they were headed and why. She didn't seem in the least concerned that they would be informing the Stolsh about the approaching Guldur fleet. It was obvious that his Ship could be counted upon to be loyal and steadfast to him. And to her "pups."

Melville flipped down through the hatch, and checked on Mr. Crater as he conned the lower quarterdeck. To go through the area where gravity "flips" wasn't particularly arduous or difficult. Easier even than slipping into water, especially for someone who'd done it from his youngest days. But still he did it cautiously, protecting his injured shoulder.

Young Crater was doing fine. He'd been the 2IC, or second in command, of the quarterdeck on many a watch. He had often been left to con the deck while the duty officer went about his many responsibilities in other parts of the Ship. An experienced quartermaster with over a decade of sea duty under his belt was there to assist. Above them an experienced petty officer directed the seamen in the rigging. They seemed to take delight in breaking in their new "lootenant."

Then Melville flipped back through to the upper quarterdeck, kneeling to say a passing hello to *Fang* as he passed the Keel.

The rest of the shift went by in a dull blur for Melville. He had barely begun to recover from his wounds and was quickly exhausted. Hans insisted on rigging a deck chair for him to sit on, something that was unheard of in ordinary circumstances.

At six bells he went below, where McAndrews had fixed him a hot lunch. The portly steward appeared to be an unimaginative cook, but Melville wasn't a picky eater.

Hans, in his duties as sailing master, was reworking the rigging and sails to conform to Westerness standards. He bounced back and forth between the upper and lower decks, keeping a good eye out for young Lieutenant Crater on the lower quarterdeck. Hans' monkey perched on the sailing master's shoulder and seemed to delight in everything they did. The little tobacco-chewing creature was now the darling of the topmen.

Finally, his long watch was over and Melville went into his cabin. Again McAndrews prepared a meal, which he shoveled down. It was hot and it felt good, whatever it was.

They had an adequate supply of water, with resupply expected fairly soon, so he was able to grab a quick sponge bath. He stood in a wide, shallow basin designed to catch the precious water, sponging himself off while McAndrews held a pan of hot water for him. The steward had heated the water, and it felt good. The unctuous sailor was definitely beginning to grow on him. Ordinarily he didn't get hot water to bathe in, another advantage to being the captain. There *was* an up side to the responsibility. There wasn't enough water to wash his entire body, but he could soap and rinse his "pits." The arm pits and the whole region between the thighs and buttocks that academy cadets jokingly referred to as the "leg pit."

His monkey hopped off during this process, and watched from McAndrews' shoulder. The steward delighted in this honor, and

Melville found himself feeling slightly jealous. Then he felt foolish about feeling jealous of a monkey.

Lady Elphinstone tapped at his door and stepped in at that moment, seeming to have sensed that she could find her patient naked.

How does she do that? thought Melville. *Sylvan magic? Doctor's instinct?*

He was slightly embarrassed to be standing naked in front of a beautiful lady, but she was also ancient, and wise, and Sylvan, *and* she was a doctor. Somehow this all combined to make it perfectly all right, even to a sailor who had been sailing the seas of two-space for entirely too long.

She unwound the dressing and proceeded to prod and cleanse his wound, "tutting" like some omnipresent, universal healer archetype. "Thou art healing well, Captain, but thou may not go into the rigging, and thou must continue to pace yourself. I saw thee resting on the quarterdeck. That is good."

She stood back and looked at his naked body with a clinical eye. He tried not to suck his gut in. He found himself settling on a half relaxed, half poised position, shoulders back, hands at his side, as she examined him. It wasn't much but it was all his dignity could muster, as she went on. "Healing is strange in two-space. Some fester and die who should not, and others live when they probably should not. I would guess thee to be the healing type. I'll keep an eye on thee. In a few weeks thou shouldst have thy old strength back. In a month or so thou shouldst have the full use of that arm again. *If* thou dost pay attention to what I say. Dost thou understand, Captain?" she asked, no, demanded, as she replaced the dressing.

"Yes, indeed I do, my lady. I'll do my best to follow your guidance." There, that was a good way to put it. Because they both knew that he would damned well do what the situation called for, even if it killed him.

"Indeed thou *shalt*, thou *silly* man," she said, not unkindly and with a slight smile. "Unless thee *wants* to die?"

"I *do* happen to be the captain, you know," said Melville, with as much dignity as a naked man could muster.

With a slight, mocking nod she corrected herself, "Thou silly *captain*, sir."

"Thank you."

"Very good, now go to sleep, Captain. All is well here. All is well."

All is well. Those words rang in his ears as McAndrews helped him slide into a long sleep shirt. He pulled a sleep mask over his head and stretched out on his bunk. He felt his monkey hop in next to him, and as it snuggled warmly in beside his head he drifted off to sleep.

The next morning, after sleeping for over ten hours, he found life felt almost worth living. He leaned back while McAndrews shaved his sparse beard. Two-space would keep a straight-razor supernaturally sharp, but proper handling of such a razor was an entirely different matter. That's why many sailors chose to wear beards. McAndrews was doing an excellent job, but it occurred to Melville to ask the steward to let the blade grow just a *little* bit dull.

The steward helped him dress and did his magic with tea, sugar, and lemon. His supply of tea and lemon juice was limited, but it was *good* while it lasted.

Then he went out on the deck of his Ship (*his Ship!*) with a steaming mug in his right hand. His monkey leaned out, stretching out its long, accordion neck to get sips of the tea.

It was just after eleven bells in the night watch when he walked out onto the deck. All was still and quiet. This was the most serene, peaceful time of the day on board Ship. It was almost as though the men of Westerness had recreated the sleepy hour just before dawn, here in the timeless depths of Flatland. Even the illumination from the Moss seemed subdued during this period, as though the Ship itself took on that rhythm. The day watch slept on the deck, wrapped in blankets on thin pads. A few members of the night watch worked quietly in the rigging; some were working below with the carpenter's mates.

Fielder stood on the quarterdeck. Melville nodded to him, finishing his tea in peaceful solitude, and went below to check on Lieutenant Archer.

Around the lower quarterdeck a few of the cook's mates quietly set up their burners and pots, preparing breakfast. Meals had been served on the upper side yesterday, so today the Ship's crew would gather on the lower side. Even with the activity of the cooks, things were quiet, still, and sleepy. The lower day watch were sleeping on the deck. Part way up the ladder, from the shadow of the hatch, Melville stopped and watched Archer standing beside the helmsman on the quarterdeck.

Around no fire the soldiers sleep to-night,
But lie a-wearied on the ice-bound field,
With cloaks wrapt round their sleeping forms,
to shield
Them from the northern winds. Ere comes the light
Of morn brave men must arm, stern foes to fight.
The sentry stands, his limbs with cold congealed;
His head a-nod with sleep; he cannot yield,
Though sleep and snow in deadly force unite.

The young lieutenant's face shone by the glow of the deck. His eyes were heavy and his head was nodding. Like everyone else he was exhausted, and it was always hard getting your body adjusted to night shift. There were no winds here, and there was no ice-bound field, but as he looked at the boy standing watch over his mates, those ancient lines about the young sentry came to life.

Amongst the sleepers stands that Boy awake,
And wide-eyed plans brave glories that transcend
The deeds of heroes dead; then dreams o'ertake
His tired-out brain, and lofty fancies blend
To one grand theme, and through all barriers break
To guard from hurt his faithful sleeping friend.

Or perhaps those words applied to Melville himself. Guarding not just his "faithful sleeping friend," but his *friends*. To guard *all* his beloved crew. *That* was his "one grand theme."

But to truly guard them, he must form them into a fighting ship and then take them in harm's way. It was a truism of war that no one was ever really safe on the defensive. Against an aggressive, hostile enemy, if you sat and huddled on the defensive, or if you ran and hid, in the end you'd die. Only in attack, only by defeating the enemy, could you ultimately be safe.

If they'd run with their crippled Ship they would have been hunted down and killed. If they'd scuttled their Ship and tried hiding on Broadax's World, they would have been as good as dead. Several hundred men and a handful of females, marooned forever on an uncharted planet. Only by attacking their enemy were they able to survive.

In the wars of Old Earth, most of the time, it was only by attacking that the free nations could be triumphant and secure. Whether it was the twentieth-century wars against Nazi Germany and Imperial Japan, or the twenty-first-century wars against terrorism, if they'd sat and done nothing, they would have died in the end. Even in the Cold War against Soviet Russia in the late twentieth century, it could be argued that the democracies of Old Earth won by waging an economic war, and a war of ideas, while constantly preparing for real war.

You were never truly safe on the defensive. To be a great military leader you must sincerely love your men. But to keep your men safe, all too often you had to give them orders that would result in their deaths. That was the great paradox of military leadership. A paradox that destroyed many good men, and now it hung heavy upon Melville's heart.

He stood on the ladder and watched Archer for a few more minutes, then he returned to the upper quarterdeck. Fielder still stood there, looking better than he had in a very long time.

"Good morning, Daniel."

"Good morning, sir." Good. That "sir" appeared to come out completely without irony or resentment.

Melville was amazed to see the head of a tiny spider monkey peering out of the first mate's jacket. "Where did *that* come from," he said pointing at the little head peering at him owlishly.

Fielder seemed disconcerted, even a little embarrassed as he looked down at the little creature. "Sir, I don't have a clue. It just appeared. I took off my jacket for lunch in the area we've designated as the wardroom. When I went to put the jacket on, there it was. It must have crawled in during my meal, but no one saw it."

Melville walked back to the relative privacy at the rear of the quarterdeck, motioning Fielder to follow him. Lowering his voice he continued, "Did someone fill you in on what the surgeon and purser learned?"

"Aye, sir," Fielder answered, looking a little apprehensive. "Lady Elphinstone told me while I was down there visiting the wounded. Several more monkeys have shown up down there, and in other places. It's all very strange. But I must say, knowing about that, I'm pleased to have one. I think." Looking down with a strange mix of wonder, suspicion, and admiration in his voice, the cynical, embittered lieutenant added, "Cute little bastard, ain't he?" The monkey looked up at him and flicked its tongue out momentarily.

"Yes. Truly cute as a button. Congratulations, I give you joy of your monkey." Melville reached down and scratched behind the creature's ears. "So, can you give me a sitrep?"

"Aye, sir. We seem to be settling into a good, healthy routine." Fielder appeared to actually have some satisfaction, perhaps even pleasure, in his voice as he outlined the ongoing activities.

"The surgeon reports no deaths. They thought they might lose a few more of the severely wounded, but everything has been going very well on that front."

Melville nodded. "Excellent. We've had enough funerals for a lifetime."

"Aye. Meanwhile, the carpenter is ready to go ahead with the gun ports for the 12-pounders. I didn't want to do it during the night watch, the day watch needs their sleep too badly, but by the end of the day watch he thinks they can have it all done. I directed the marines to give all their assistance to the carpenter, all possible prep work has been done, and the project should go quickly. All but the stern guns are already in position."

The marines were the jacks-of-all-trades in the Westerness Navy. They needed time for training in their own skills, but they were also a reserve of able bodies available to assist wherever they were most needed. Over the years they'd developed many skills. They could be of assistance to the purser as stevedores and assistant cooks. They were also litter bearers and orderlies for the surgeon, and ammo bearers and gun handlers for the gunner. Even for the sailing master they could be of use in simple tasks demanding muscle power.

Now their marines' abilities were focused on helping the carpenter and his mates with their many tasks. The first priority was getting the new guns into position, then rearranging the compartments in the hold. Finally, after everything else was finished, they would set up partitions in the quarterdeck cabins, creating a decent wardroom and a suite of cabins for the officers. All sailing ships traditionally carried a good supply of spare spars, raw lumber and partitions. Since this ship was setting out on the first stage of a long war, it was particularly well equipped. Indeed, most of the partitions they needed were already there, but they'd been struck down into the hold when the Guldur cleared her for action.

"Good," Melville responded, "as soon as we get the guns in position I want the gunner to get his crews working on firing drills for the 24-pounders. We don't have much ammo for the 12-pounders, and that's okay because we know how to use them. But it's vital that we get good with those 24-pounders, asap. Anything else?"

"No, sir. That about covers our primary area of progress during the watch. I think the staff can fill you in on their areas during breakfast."

"Very well. And how has Lieutenant Archer been performing?"

Fielder's face took on his usual hard, cynical smile, but there might have been just a hint of fondness there. "He's doing well. He worked a lot during the day watch, helping to get things settled in, and by now I suspect he's ready for a good sleep. After that he should be pretty much on his way to having his body clock set for night watch. The men seem to respect him, and I've no immediate complaints."

"Good. Anything else of interest?"

"Most of the ship's boys seem to be sick. The proverbial dog's breakfast heaved over the side, most of 'em. Must be something they ate disagreeing with them. Elphinstone says they'll live and probably be the wiser for it. The damned fools."

As they were talking, the glass was trickling out the last sands of the twelfth hour of the night watch, and the Ship was coming alive. Most of the day watch was awake. They were rolling up their sleeping pads and stowing them in the netting along the Ship's sides, where they could stop a musket ball and slow a cannonball. In a green or ill-disciplined Ship the bosun's mates would have to waken them, but in this Ship they tended to get up on their own, or with a few nudges from their friends.

It was traditional to pass the con to a midshipman while the officers went to meals. Now, since there was no midshipman, the quartermaster filled in as they went below to breakfast.

Once again, Melville and his officers stood by the quarterdeck rail, eating breakfast and discussing the day's activity. This morning, though, it was the lower quarterdeck. The crew of each deck worked hard to get their area in good shape for "company" on the morning when it was their turn to host meals. With a newly captured Ship and so much to be done, getting truly shipshape wasn't possible, but the lower crew had done their best.

Everything was routine, or as routine as possible on a newly captured Ship in time of war. The mark of a professional was the ability to quickly establish routines.

Lady Elphinstone reported that she'd released a few of the injured to serve as outpatients, and could make room for two 12-pounders. Brother Petreckski had little news to report, and was ready to begin schooling the new midshipmen. The carpenter was set to cut the gun ports and put the new guns in place. Lieutenant Broadax's men were ready to help the carpenter and the gunner with their task. The two rangers, as usual, said very little. They could be counted upon to be where they could help the most.

The sailing master reported that he was about finished with his rerigging of the Ship, and was ready to tinker with putting "royals" in place. These sails, high up on the masts, above the topgallant sails, would be small but they would have tremendous leverage, and could contribute significantly to her speed. "Aye," said Hans, "we logged nigh onta eleven knots last time we 'eaved the log, an' I think 'at's about as good as we're gonna do, as she stands now. But I tell ya, sir, I ain't never seen such stout sticks on a Ship. If we can put royals on 'er, an' maybe even a sprits'l-tops'l, we might squeeze twelve knots out of 'er!"

Twelve knots was a respectable speed; the old *Kestrel* could maintain fifteen knots when her sails, rigging and masts were in good shape. The Guldur probably never imagined that their Ship could attain anywhere near their current eleven knots. That was what *real* sailors could do.

"Aye," said Hans as he and his monkey gave a synchronized spit overboard. "Ya know, the story 'as it, that royals was first proposed by King 'enry the Eighth, of old England, in the 1500s. The captains back in those days thought addin' a fourth sail high up on each mast was a silly idear, so they only put the sails up when they thought the king might be watchin'. So the sailors took to callin' 'em 'royal' sails! In the followin' years they became pop'lar. We know Captain Aubrey used 'em a lot, but ye seldom see 'em in two-space. The point bein', they ain't nothin' new. No innervation, jist reintroducin' a fine old concept, seein' as how this ship'l bear it."

This was important, since new inventions went deeply against the fundamental philosophy and the ingrained technophobia of their culture and civilization. "Good," said Melville. "Then we're not really committing an innovation. If they were good enough for Captain Aubrey, they're good enough for me."

"Aye, Cap'n. Ya know I'm dead set agin progress. Progress jist means bad things happen faster."

"And," added Melville, "I think the Ship will like it."

"Aye," said Tibbits, with a gleam in the old carpenter's eye. "She *feels* the speed, and she *likes* it. You can feel it in her bones. She's a young Ship, a wolflin' Ship, and she does like to go fast. If she wasn't happy with her lot before, she is now. I suspect those royals will tickle her pink."

Everyone grinned with pleasure at hearing this report from the carpenter. If the Ship was happy, then everyone on her was happy. "A happy Ship is a happy ship," as the saying went, "and a happy Ship is your only right hard-fighting ship." It also cheered them up to see the old carpenter taking joy in life.

"Very good, my friends. Everything is progressing well, and I thank you for all your hard work. Now, have each of you thought about nominations to fill our empty midshipman slots? I'd like to have at least four more middies, and we'll begin a selection board this morning."

Each of his officers made a few suggestions from their sections, and they were directed to have the candidates stand by to report to the upper quarterdeck at one bell into the day watch.

"Mr. Fielder, I'd like to ask you to assist me with the board."

"Aye, sir," nodded the first mate. With twelve hours in his off watch he could perform this duty and still have plenty of sleep time. It was important to have the first mate agree on the middies.

"Brother Theo," Melville continued, "I'd like for you to serve on the board as well."

"Yes, sir." As the purser, he was one officer who wasn't too deeply involved in the ongoing work on their ship, so he could be pulled off other duties without too much difficulty. He was also the primary school teacher for the middies, and a very learned and respected officer.

"One last thing," Melville added as they began to break up. "I want to invite all the officers for dinner tomorrow evening in my cabin. I fear that McAndrews, my steward, has demonstrated himself to be an uninspired cook. Does anyone have someone they'd recommend as a chef? Whoever it is will have to try to find a way to prepare our Guldur provisions into a pleasant meal. A significant challenge for any cook, I dare say."

"Yes, Captain," answered Lady Elphinstone immediately. "My loblolly girl, Mrs. Vodi, is an excellent chef. She seems to excel at making exotic meals. The men in our hospital have certainly been enjoying what she has prepared."

"Excellent!" replied Melville. "Do you feel like you could release her from her duties for this task?"

Elphinstone nodded agreeably. "Yes Captain, I can."

"Good, please be so kind as to ask her to report to me at her earliest convenience."

The morning flew by as the midshipman's board selected four individuals to serve in the wardroom. Melville was pleased that he, Fielder, and Petreckski seemed to work well together, making their decisions with relative harmony. Between these three, no one could question the judgment of his promotions. A captain could make such selections by himself, but his decisions would ultimately have to be approved by the Admiralty. It was always best to follow proper procedures whenever there was time.

During the proceedings Melville also came to know his clerk, Archibald Hargis. He was a large, introverted man of great intellect. Hargis was a veteran of many such boards, and his assistance was of significant value. Throughout the process he seemed to be distant, dreamy, and not completely present. But the report that he produced was deemed first rate by all three board members.

In the end, they selected two ship's boys and two young crewmen to be promoted. The board was looking mostly for demonstrated bravery and brains. Not only did they interview the candidates, but they interviewed the petty officers who supervised the candidates, to see how each individual fought in the recent battle and how they performed their duties during the long months on the *Kestrel.* Given the raw ingredients of native courage and intelligence, plus a record that was clean of lying and theft, the navy could give a young midshipman everything he needed to be a suitable officer. Many such young men existed on every ship, but promotion opportunities such as this, "opportunities" created by the deaths of so many superior officers, were rare in peacetime.

One of the ship's boys and both of the crewmen came from the sailing master's crew. This wasn't unusual, since the brightest and most ambitious crewmen were usually drawn to prove themselves high up in the rigging. If a man didn't work out there he was quickly moved to another section.

One of the two crewmen they selected was Hezikiah Jubal, an able seaman and topman who served with distinction in Hans' party in the upper rigging during the boarding action. The other was Lao Tung, an ordinary seaman who had proven himself to be a ferocious fighter in the battle line. He was also remarkably well read.

The two ship's boys were Kande Ngobe and Ellis Palmer. Ngobe was a boy, second class, and Palmer was a boy, first class. Both of them had proven themselves to be quick-witted, with above average intelligence, and they endeared themselves to the hearts of the crew by scampering among their legs during the boarding action. Working down beside the dogs, they'd killed ticks, while hamstringing and "neutering" the curs with their razor-sharp knives. Palmer had been working for the sailing master. Ngobe had been assigned to the ship's carpenter, where he showed great promise in his understanding of the Ship and her inner workings.

Westerness was colonized by the men of Old Earth over four hundred years prior, in the Earth year 2210, almost a century after Mankind's first, disastrous entry into Flatland in 2119. The computers on board that first foray into two-space brought back the Elder King's Gift, a devastating, two-dimensional virus that caused a complete and irrecoverable collapse of the world-wide Info-Net. Within two hundred years of its colonization, Westerness grew to become the dominant force in Mankind's activities in Flatland. By 2420, Westerness assumed control over the worlds of Man. For the last two centuries the Kingdom of Westerness ruled peacefully over the far-flung realm of Man.

The original colonizers of Westerness came from all corners of the Earth, but the majority of them hailed from Britain and North America. Over the centuries it became increasingly rare for anyone to carry distinctive racial characteristics. Thus Mr. Barlet's gunmetal black skin was fairly unusual, as was Lieutenant Archer's red beard. If Midshipman Ngobe was coffee colored, it was coffee with lots of cream, while Midshipman Tung had only faint traces of his oriental ancestry. What was important to the navy was *not* their appearance, or their ethnic background, but that they were brave and smart. With luck, brains, and lots of hard work these four young men might become commissioned officers in the Westerness Navy.

After the proceedings were closed, the board congratulated the new middies, and put them immediately to work. All of them would have four hours of schooling from Petreckski each morning, starting tomorrow. As the first mate, Fielder would also assign them on a rotating basis to the day and night shifts, with one midshipman assigned to each quarterdeck at all times except for school. Formal recognition among the officers would occur tomorrow evening, at the captain's dinner. At Sunday afternoon formation they would be formally presented to the whole crew. For now there was little more than a handshake and a pat on the back, as they moved to assume their new duties.

After they completed the board proceedings Melville, Fielder and Petreckski stepped out onto the deck. Melville noticed Lady Elphinstone's lob-lolly girl waiting patiently. "Mrs. Vodi! Thank you for coming. I've been informed that you're a prime chef. The men of the sick bay all speak very highly of your efforts. They say you've done wonders with the stock of Guldur and Goblan food here on the ship. So I wonder if you'd do us the honor of preparing a meal for my officers and myself tomorrow evening."

Mrs. Vodi had left her spit cup behind to come speak with the captain, but she still kept a chaw in her cheek. "Yes, Captain. I'd be glad to."

"Good! I do sincerely thank you. My steward, and any other resources you may need, are at your disposal. Is there any other way that I can assist you?"

"Yes, Captain, there is. I need a Guldur to assist me. Right now I don't have a clue what I'm working with. I test all the food items on myself first, but some of it might actually be poisonous. A native guide would be very useful. I understand several of them can speak English, and I'd like your permission to release one to be my assistant."

"Of course. I'm on my way to our little brig to check up on the prisoners. Would you like to come with me?"

"Certainly, Captain."

"Good. Brother Theo, would you come with us? I understand that you speak their language?"

"Yes, sir," responded his purser. "But it really wasn't necessary for me to tap into my limited Guldish. I found a translator early on, and used my limited skills to be sure that he was translating faithfully. Their officers all died in battle and they've been very cooperative."

Down in the lower hold they found the Guldur, sitting disconsolately, truly hangdog in their appearance, guarded by two marines. Melville moved among them. At first he found his heart pounding as he remembered the battle and their despicable ambush of the *Kestrel*.

> When first I saw you in the curious street
> Like some platoon of soldier ghosts in gray,
> My mad impulse was all to smite and slay,
> To spit upon you—tread you 'neath my feet.

Then he looked again, and the mental process he went through was one that might have been as old as warfare itself. It made him think of Lee's "German Prisoners."

> But when I saw how each sad soul did greet
> My gaze with no sign of defiant frown,
> How from tired eyes looked spirits broken down,
> How each face showed the pale flag of defeat,
> And doubt, despair, and disillusionment,
> And how were grievous wounds on many a head,
> And on your garb red-faced was other red:
> And how you stooped as men whose strength
>   was spent,
> I knew that we had suffered each other,
> And could have grasped your hand and cried,
>   "My brother!"

Very quickly Vodi, with Petreckski's assistance, picked her assistant. He was a buff-colored Guldur who had been a purser's mate. He claimed to be familiar with the ship's comestibles, where they were stored, and how they should be prepared.

It was sad to see how eager they were to be selected for any duty that would take them away from their current, depressing conditions. All of them were willing to give their parole and serve as trustees among the ship's crew, apparently undisturbed by any sense of loyalty to their old masters. Their lives had been harsh, and they seemed truly doglike in their willingness to give their loyalty to anyone who would offer kindness, structure, and meaning to their lives.

Mrs. Vodi went to work exploring the foodstuffs that were stored all over the ship. She, the captain's steward, and their Guldur guide poked into every corner of the ship. Her usual entourage of cats kept their distance, looking with dismay and distrust at the Guldur. She was particularly intrigued by barrels of brains that were stored in a brine solution. "Well, Fido, what do we have here?"

"Rit's prig brains! Grrood struff!"

"Pig brains. Well, well, well, Rex. Combined with those nuts and that bottled green stuff we found, I do believe we'll treat the captain and his guests to thrice cooked javelina brain with crunchy pecan coating and sweet leek sauce. Or a reasonable facsimile thereof." She was happy to find such an excellent food source, but McAndrews didn't see it that way.

"You call that food? I wouldn't feed that to a hole in the ground!"

Vodi spat in her cup ("spputt") and eyed him at a cross angle: "Aye, that's food and some of the best at that."

"Rats right! Grroood strufff!"

McAndrews took a cautious step back. He was half convinced that the old woman must have been hit on the head in their recent battle, and was inclined to poison them all.

Vodi sneered, "You tell 'im, Spot." Stepping forward and leaning into McAndrews' face she continued with bravado. "When I set it on the board for you to feed to that noisy hole in your face, boy, I expect you to take the first bite because I said so, but the second, oh, I think the second bite you'll take on your own and with many a thought towards how much you can get before it disappears into the other holes seated around the table."

Their meal the next evening was a roaring success, a vital step in the process of bonding them all together as a team and establishing a new routine in their new ship. The thrice cooked javelina brains were a resounding hit, and outside the dining room

McAndrews did indeed vie with Vodi's Guldur assistant to sneak in bites whenever he could. Cats also kept slipping in, mewling for tidbits of whatever it was that smelled so good. They all competed with the ever-greedy ship's boys coming in and out on errands, grabbing bites at every opportunity and constantly being whacked by Vodi's wooden spoon. "This shur beets that dam' munky meet," muttered one as he snagged a morsel while ducking a swipe from Vodi.

At the head of the table Melville sat with his monkey on his shoulder. He was dressed, like all the sailors, in his blue jacket over a white cravat and white trousers. To his right, in the place of honor, was Lady Elphinstone, in her normal yellow gown with emeralds in her hair. By tradition that seat should have gone to the first mate, but a beautiful lady of noble lineage was gladly given precedence. Her grace and charm added much to the evening as their dinner wound its pleasant course. Across from her sat Fielder and his monkey. To her right was Archer, and across from him was Crater, both with monkeys perched on their shoulders. Their two brand-new lieutenants were uneasy with their new positions, but the natural goodwill and the freely flowing Guldur beer combined with their youthful cheer to make them good guests.

To Archer's right, and considerably lower even though she sat on a thick book, was Broadax. The last of their commissioned officers, she was a splash of bright marine scarlet that balanced out Elphinstone's yellow amidst the sea of navy blue. For once Broadax left behind the obligatory helmet and omnipresent cigar. Her monkey seemed slightly bewildered as it peered out from amidst the stiff locks that splayed out in disarray from her scalp. Across from her was Hans and his monkey, both with discreet chaws of tobacco in their cheeks. Although he had the least seniority among the warrant officers, his position as sailing master gave him traditional precedence among them.

Broadax and Hans were both uncomfortable at the beginning of their first formal dinner as commissioned officers. They were more accustomed to quaffing their drinks, which they firmly held to be a lot like drinking, except that you were allowed to spill more. But, like Archer and Crater, they too quickly adjusted and, much to their surprise, were able to enjoy themselves.

To Broadax's right was Petreckski in a clean brown robe, then the gunner, followed by the carpenter. The two rangers in soft, beaded buckskins completed the party. These were all old hands at such dinners and they kept the conversation, the alcohol, and the food flowing freely.

Each of them had a servant standing behind them. The table was set with a gleaming sea of Guldur silver service that they'd found on board, all polished to a brilliant luster by Melville's steward, McAndrews, who now stood contentedly behind his captain. The service was only silver plate, of very little real value, but it added significantly to the pleasure of the evening.

It was a large party for so small a cabin, but with the table set athwartships and the two 12-pounders trundled into the captain's office and sleeping cabin, it could be done. To Melville's left were the windows looking out on the vast blue expanse of Flatland with the shimmering galaxies hanging above. On the other three sides were white, Moss-coated bulkheads. Immediately behind Melville the bulkhead was adorned with a star-shaped array of quite utilitarian pistols and swords. At the opposite end was a bookshelf. To his right was the doorway, flanked by a coat rack and a chart locker.

The meal was that odd mixture so common in military life. Elegance mixed with mundane necessity. In this case it was Vodi's gourmet thrice cooked javelina brains, "or-a-reasonable-facsimile-thereof," combined with ancient ship's provisions. The whole affair was enlivened by Vodi's amiable commentary as she brought each dish to table.

"Now, gentlefolk," she said as she brought the soup in, for once without her chaw of tobacco, "I'm not all that much of a reader, but I do read everything I can about food and cooking. Captain Aubrey's biographer once referred to a similar meal. 'This liquid is technically known as soup,' as he put it. May I ladle you out one full medical dose? 'It is pleasant enough to see the remnants of peas so aged and worn that even the weevils scorned them and died at their side, so that now we have both predator and prey to nourish us.' " This was especially humorous since it was a fairly accurate description of the daily fare provided for them by the ship's cook. However, in this case the weevils did appear to have been assiduously separated out and replaced with a most pleasant mélange of spices. "What is pleasanter still, is to see the infamous brew spooned from this gleaming great silver tureen, the gift of the previous residents of our humble abode.

We are informed that 'however poor you are—and nobody could be much poorer in reality than sailors in a ship without any stores—what crusts you may scrape together eat with more relish in handsome silver.' " And indeed it was true.

"Next, gentlefolk, we have a truly villainous piece of mystery meat, that has traveled the galaxy in its time, growing steadily more horny and wooden as the years went by. But we shall eat it without concern, for we have all grown and thrived on worse."

Finally came the *piéce de résistance*, accompanied by Vodi's own family history. "An ancient family recipe tells us the background of this dish. Family tradition has it that one of my ancestors actually included this in a book called *The Contented Poacher's Epicurean Odyssey*. Great-great, many-times-great-gramma Vodi, mayshe-restinpeace, tells the true tale about the hunting of one particular wild pig. A very large and dangerous creature indeed, nicknamed 'Major' who was in the habit of ordering people the hell out of his domain. Apparently, the sacred honor of the Great Apes was in eternal jeopardy if they could be bested by a pig. One fine hot and misty morning five guys and seven dogs set out to bring Major down. But there's many a slip twixt dress and drawers, as Gramma used to say. Some time after the fight started in earnest, the survivors straggled out to tell their story. One man lost his leg, another his life!" Here you could see her mouth twitch as she yearned for a chaw of tobacco to spit for emphasis at this point.

"They had shot him once for each of the dogs he gutted and flung into the bushes and once again for the fella whose leg he ripped to the bone. The guy with the ripped leg and the three other survivors waited in the trees until Major bled to death on the ground. The moral of the story seems to be something along the lines of 'I am not now, nor was I ever that hungry, and if chicken's for dinner I'll take chicken and be glad of it!' Me, I'm glad to have so many excellent javelina brains provided at someone else's expense."

At the end of an excellent meal combined with quality commentary and conversation, the cloth was drawn and the wine bottle made its rounds, along with a plate of ship's biscuits. Melville automatically tapped the biscuit on the table causing a few weevils to race out and hide, peering out from under his plate. For centuries sailors have stoically put up with creatures in their biscuits, and the Ships of Flatland were no different.

Usually the weevils elicited no comment, they were just a part of shipboard life. But in this case Melville brought it to the attention of his purser and surgeon, both of whom were fairly new to navy life. "Doctor, Brother Theo," he began, catching their attention, "have either of you ever been instructed in the naval protocol for the selection of weevils?"

Both of his guests looked somewhat confused, and the other sailors sat back with anticipation and pleased smiles on their faces. "No, Captain," said the monk. "There are so many nautical concepts and rules that I have yet to learn, and I fear that this one hasn't been brought to my attention. Doctor, do you know of which our good Captain speaks?"

"Nay, sir," replied Elphinstone with an enchanting smile. "Pray, tell us."

"Well," said Melville, "of these two here, trying to hide under my plate, which would you be inclined to choose?"

"I would guess the larger," replied Brother Theo, "or perhaps the faster, or perhaps the only good one is a dead one?"

"All excellent guesses, but the truth is my friends, that in the navy you must always select the lesser of two weevils."

The guests laughed appreciatively, but the sailors laughed with even more delight. It was an old, old joke, come alive and afresh each time it was inflicted on the uninitiated, establishing the kind of heritage and tradition that they deeply valued.

Eventually their talk turned to one of the oldest of all subjects in the navy: the mystery and wonder of Flatland. Several discussions were flowing freely back and forth when a conversation between Petreckski and Valandil caught the attention of the group. Petreckski was speaking of the nature of the Keel. "A mechanism that provides entry into two-space, with a side effect of heat, that would almost be what you expect."

"Yes, and what of the gravity?" asked the Sylvan ranger as he leaned back in his chair.

"That probably comes from Flatland, representing the gravitational pull of the galaxy. Which is also what you might expect. All of this is acceptable to the rational mind. But a life-form that just happens to provide light and air? Light and air tailored precisely to our needs? It defies imagination, sir. It is just too much. So bizarre that we had to 'invent,' or anthropomorphize some godlike creature to create it. They say that Lady Elbereth gave it to us as a 'gift,' just as the ignorant Greek peasants could only understand the sun as a chariot in the sky brought to us every day by a god. No, the Elbereth Moss is too much to ask a reasonable person to accept."

"And so?" asked Elphinstone with keen interest.

"So, my lady, we've proven that it doesn't and cannot exist."

This was greeted with wry grins, groans and expressions of polite disgust.

"Or!" continued the monk with a grin on his cherubic face, "it is intentional. A symbiotic life-form. It's alive, and intentionally adapting to us, just as we adapt to it. The reason why it's exactly what we need is *because* that is what we need. A sentient life-form is *trying* to provide, to the best of its ability, just what we could have wished for."

"Now that really does defy imagination!" interjected Mr. Barlet with a raised eyebrow and a friendly grin on his ebon face.

"Does it, my worthy Master Gunner?" replied the monk, returning the smile. "Does it indeed? We live, we've found it. It lives, and it has found us. That's what life does. It finds what it requires for existence. Furthermore this theory explains one other mystery. Why is the Ship sentient? Perhaps it's a colony, a vast colony of life- forms, working together to give us what we need. When the captain or the carpenter 'talks' to the Ship, he isn't talking to a creature, he's talking to a whole vast nation. Or, perhaps, to the elected representatives of that vast nation."

"Aye," said their carpenter. This was his area of expertise, and he warmed to it. "It has been proposed before. That would explain why the larger the amount of moss the more intelligent it is . . . and the slower it is. The little bit on a rifle or pistol's Keel barely musters a purr, like a tribble. While the cannon is like a dog. The cutters are like children and the Ship, why the Ship is every bit as intelligent as us, yet slow and ponderous in her thinking."

"Could that 'life-form' be what caused the Crash?" asked Crater.

"That's the dominant theory," the monk replied. "The reason why the Elder King's Gift was able to destroy Earth's Info-Net was because the 'virus' was two dimensional. Inside the computer world it could exist, even thrive, in three-space—as a living body makes it possible for a virus to survive and thrive. It got into the computer brought into two-space by the first explorers. They brought it home and it reproduced exponentially, destroying everything in its reach. Brought into three-space, this two-space life-form became a parasite or a virus when it found a suitable environment. Like any deadly virus, as it destroyed its host, it also destroyed its habitat. In the end, both the virus and the host no longer exist."

"But," said Melville, intrigued by the direction the conversation was taking, "in nature a virus continues to exist because it can move on to other hosts. It's communicable."

"Yes, sir, but who says this virus isn't communicable? Most other civilizations that have entered two-space report having similar experiences. 'Spores' of the virus appear to be out in two-space. If you're foolish enough to bring a computer into two-space, and then bring it back home and connect it to a network, it will do what any virus does. Reproduce, live, thrive in one great blaze of glory, and then die, pulling its host down with it."

"Okay," said Melville, "back to the Elbereth Moss. What could be the purpose of the 'symbiosis' with us? What do *we* give to *it*?"

"Perhaps travel?" interjected Elphinstone. "As a cocklebur would attach itself to a dog, to be transported and planted miles away?"

With a grin Melville added, "Or a flea, or . . . maybe a bedbug. An anonymous ditty comes to mind:

"The June bug hath a gaudy wing,
The lightning bug a flame,
The bed bug hath no wings at all
But he gets there just the same."

There were appreciative grins and chuckles all around, then Elphinstone continued. "So, it could get transportation. Or, like a flea, or bedbug, it might get sustenance from us. Perhaps it gets companionship, as thou wouldst get from a dog or a cat. Maybe it gets shared information and knowledge, like a fellow sentient species might give to us. There are four viable options. Mindless transport, sustenance, friendly companionship, and equal partnership. Or possibly some combination thereof. *Or* something completely different."

"Indeed," said Petreckski. "On Old Earth there is something called a slime mold. It exists as individual cells when it's in a favorable environment. Yet when things start to go bad, some of them put out a chemical signal, which is picked up by the others.

They group together and form a multicellular animal, a worm of sorts, which crawls out of the drying slime, up to the highest point around. It grows a stalk on top, which forms a bulb of spores that launch themselves into the wind, in search of a better home. Our 'moss' might have a similar lifestyle, traveling from planet to planet in two-space. Given enough time, it seems to have developed into an intelligent creature."

"Aye," said Melville as he handed a tidbit up to his monkey. "An intelligent creature that has become our friend and companion. If some superior alien species should ever judge us, perhaps we have this to our credit, that we could become friends with something so very strange. The bottle stands by you, Mr. Crater."

As the wine bottle came round to Melville, he made a formal cough and said, "Mr. Fielder, the Queen."

"Ladies and Gentlemen," said Fielder, "the Queen of Westerness," and they all drank deeply.

Valandil added, "Sisters, brothers, the King of Osgil," and they drank again.

"Aye," added Melville, "God bless them both. And may I propose a toast to our fallen comrades, and to the good Ship *Kestrel*, which although gone, still lives on.

"Bind her, grind her, burn her with fire,
Cast her ashes into the sea, —
She shall escape, she shall aspire,
She shall arise to make men free;
She shall arise in a sacred scorn,
Lighting lives that are yet unborn."

"Well said, sir," replied Lady Elphinstone, turning to Melville when she'd done her loyal duty to both rulers and *Kestrel*. "That was a delightful dinner, but before we go, wouldst thou permit me to give a toast? To the dear *Fang*, and may she long continue to *bite* the queen's enemies."

"Hear her, hear her," said one and all, as they drank. Then, led by Melville's spontaneous act, they all splashed a dollop of wine onto the deck of their ship. To their amazement it quickly disappeared, like blood soaked up by the Elbereth Moss.

CHAPTER THE 9TH

Forging a Weapon: Beat Out the Iron, Edge It Keen

O dreadful Forge! if torn and bruised
The heart, more urgent comes our cry
Not to be spared but to be used,
Brain, sinew, and spirit, before we die,
Beat out the iron, edge it keen,
And shape us to the end we mean!

"The Anvil"
Laurence Binyon

Her Majesty, the Queen of Westerness' 24-Pounder Frigate, *Fang*, sailed westward into a "pleasant illusion of eternity." The days flowed by with quiet sailing under a perfect, unchanging sky. They sailed constantly toward a golden horizon that blended into a band of purple twilight. A horizon that remained perpetually ahead, never nearer. Above them the starry galaxies hung.

Below them the plane of Flatland flowed past. Flatland was a deep, dark blue, except when they passed a star or planet. Then, beside them or beneath them would flow the vast brilliant yellow, white, red or blue glow of a star, the huge expanse of an orange gas giant, or the reds, browns, whites, blues and blacks of uninhabited planets. Rarest of all was the swirling blue, green and white that indicated a world which might support human life. In this region of the galaxy there were many stars and many planets, but none of them were known to be inhabited. The first inhabited planet would be Pearl, a Stolsh colony that was their destination.

The great twenty-volume biography of Captain Jack Aubrey, one of the most famous mariners of Old Earth, was preserved on one of the military data nets that survived the Crash. Like the volumes of the magnificent Hornblower biography, only the raw text was loaded in, and even the names of those great writers were lost. They were lost to the ages even more surely than Homer or Shakespeare, ever to be a source of controversy and academic discussion. But that great, nameless writer of the Aubrey biography had gained immortality like few men among the sailors of Westerness, and he wrote well and true when he spoke of this illusion of eternity.

"The immemorial sequence of cleaning the upper decks in earliest morning . . . piping up hammocks, piping hands to breakfast, cleaning the maindeck, piping to various morning exercises, the solemn observation at noon, hands piped to dinner, grog piped up [or, in this case, Guldur beer], the officers drummed to the gunroom dinner, the afternoon occupations, hands piped to supper, more grog [or beer!], then quarters, with the thunderous roar of the great guns flashing and roaring in the twilight." This timeless ritual, "punctuated by bells," was indeed "so quickly and firmly restored that it might never have been broken."

The passing of the weeks was marked by religious services on Sunday mornings for those so inclined, led by Brother Theo and consisting mostly of a few favorite hymns. On Sunday afternoon the crew would assemble for the captain's inspection formation, followed by his formal inspection of the ship. These endless days could almost have been an idyllic time if not for the fact that they'd recently lost so many comrades. And every one of the ship's company knew that the hosts of hell were following at their heels.

Their Guldur prisoners were being used as parolees, or trustees, for various duties throughout the ship. A careful eye was kept on them, but it soon became clear that there was no evil in them. As a final assurance of their trustworthiness, the Ship herself vouched for their good intentions. Their bare paws padding about on her decks couldn't lie to her, and the warriors of Westerness trusted their Ship's judgment. At first the crew held some resentment toward their former enemy, but the Guldur's willing spirits and eagerness to please soon won over their shipmates.

The Guldur were of no use in the rigging, but elsewhere they were dispersed among the crew. Melville would have liked even more hands to bring them up to strength, but with the Guldur fully integrated into their crew he felt like they had a fighting chance if they met another enemy scout ship of this class.

The baby monkeys continued to appear mysteriously, turning up on the shoulders of more and more crewmen, and they were warmly welcomed. Many of the sailors' tasks were solitary. On lookout high up in the rigging or on watch in the wee hours, it could get lonely, and the monkeys were welcome companions. The senior officers viewed the situation with concern but no real alarm since they were accustomed to dealing with alien pets and bizarre life-forms as passengers and cargo. Just as their earlier, earthly counterparts had dealt with parrots, apes in the rigging, and a host of other pets. Both *Swish-tail* and *Fang* had vouched for the little creatures' goodwill, but Melville was certain that there must be more to the monkeys than met the eye. His primary concern was to rope them in and bring them under navy discipline as soon as possible. Everyone enjoyed the monkeys' antics, but on one occasion they stepped across the line. Melville took the opportunity to assert his authority and make them full, trustworthy, obedient members of the crew.

The monkeys loved to ride on the dogs' backs, and after some initial adjustment to the idea the dogs seemed to enjoy the experience. The dogs chased each other around the decks, their monkey jockeys screeching with joy and egging them on as canine ears flapped and tongues lolled out in joyful doggy grins.

The cats, on the other hand, had absolutely no patience for the monkeys. And the little eight-legged creatures seemed to delight in tormenting their feline fellow travelers. On several occasions the monkeys dropped from above onto an unsuspecting cat's back, where they'd ride the tormented creature like a bucking bull. The cats were having a hard enough time without this abuse, since the Guldur Ship was infested with a wide variety of exotic vermin that made the usual cockroaches, mice and rats seem mundane. It was the cats' job to hunt down all vermin. They'd been bred and selected across the centuries for this ability, and they took their job, and themselves, quite seriously.

No skylarking was ever permitted on the holy quarterdeck. The ship's cats, dogs, and boys all learned this lesson at an early age. The monkeys seemed to immediately understand the limits of what they could get away with. But off the quarterdeck their antics could be a source of pleasant entertainment for all.

So it was that Melville was standing his watch on the upper quarterdeck. A big tomcat was taking a well deserved nap on the green-side railing down by the waist. Hans' topmen were crawling about the rigging like huge spiders, most of them with a smaller spider upon them. Melville's twisted sense of humor brought to mind an old ditty that he shared with Hans:

> "Big bugs have little bugs
> On their backs to bite 'em,
> And these bugs have smaller bugs,
> And so on, ad infinitum."

Hans grinned, "Aye, sir. If you think of *Fang* as bein' alive, which she is, then that 'as par-tic-u-lar appleecation."

Hans and his lads were putting the finishing touches on a set of studding sails, small sails that extended out on booms from the sides of their regular sails. Hans' royals were answering well. And the spritsail-topsail, which was another, smaller, square sail further out the bowsprit, was adding its extra thrust. Now with these studding sails aloft and alow, they were moving at almost thirteen knots. All of these were quite rare in the ships of two-space, and their combination together on one ship was unheard of. As the speed of the ship increased, the tones of the rigging (the stays, shrouds, backstays and cordage) rose and rose to a triumphant pitch that seemed to harmonize joyfully with the strange, constant background music of two-space.

The crew was universally pleased and excited about these additions and Hans was talking to Melville about how "those massy yards and damn'd stout sticks'l bear it, by the Lady," when suddenly a monkey dropped from above onto the back of the sleeping cat. The sailors had a rough sense of humor, and everyone grinned as the startled cat howled and leaped up.

But the situation stopped being funny when the tormented cat launched itself off the end of the rail and into the blue plane of Flatland. The monkey on its back ejected up into the rigging, but the poor cat sank and then bobbed up once, its head popping out with a desperate "Wrrarr?!" Then it disappeared into the depths of interstellar space. From the bottom side of the ship a few startled observers watched an upside-down cat pop feet-first out of Flatland, and disappear.

"Bugrit!" swore Hans.

On the top side the crew all watched in silent dismay and Melville knew that he needed to take immediate action. He pointed up at the monkey and called out, "Whose monkey is that?" The monkey fled up into the rigging to crouch on the back of a topman. "Izra Smith! Is that your monkey?"

"Aye, Cap'n," the sailor called back timidly.

"You, your monkey, and your division officer report to my cabin immediately." Melville moved down the quarterdeck steps and turned into his cabin. Various options flashed through his mind as he waited. This was an accident. It was horseplay gone awry, with no evil intent. Indeed, he felt that it was partly his fault since he hadn't taken action earlier when the monkeys first began to tease the cats. He was sitting at his writing table when Smith, accompanied by Midshipman Aquinar, was shown in by the marine guard at his door. Smith stood wringing his hands while his monkey peered cautiously over his shoulder. Aquinar stood beside him with a worried look on his face as *his* monkey peered over his shoulder.

"Smith," began Melville, looking at the unfortunate owner of the miscreant monkey, "what do you think this ship would be like if all the monkeys got out of control and drove their fellow crew members over the edge?"

"Aye, Cap'n, it'd be bad. Parful bad," said Smith, looking at the floor.

"Aye, indeed. So you agree that we must ensure that our new crew members exhibit proper navy discipline?"

"Aye, Cap'n."

"Good. Well the best way I can see to administer discipline is to stop the creature's food and grog. Your monkey is on bread and water for a week, starting today. You will not permit him to partake of any beer, or anything except bread and water, during that period.

If he so much as snags a handful of your food, or anyone else's, it will be *you* on bread and water. Do I make myself clear?"

"Aye, Cap'n."

"Good, now, put your monkey on the table in front of me. Mr. Aquinar, you do the same." Then he reached up and grabbed his own monkey.

"Huurkk? Heek?" said the surprised monkey as Melville set it down in front of him. The other two monkeys were placed beside it, and Melville stood up and looked down at them sternly, leaning forward with his hands on the table. All three of the monkeys crouched on the table with their eight legs pulled in close and their heads drawn up in their thorax. Only a trace of their eyeballs could be seen peeking out at him, and above the eyeballs their mouths were chittering silently.

"Now you lot listen up," Melville began. Smith and Aquinar looked at him incredulously. *What the hell am I doing,* thought Melville. *I'm lecturing a bunch of damned monkeys! I swear it's See-no-evil, Hear-no-evil and Speak-no-evil.* "Those cats are members of our crew, just like you. They serve a function here, and I will not tolerate any further harassment of the cats. Do I make myself clear?"

"Krw?" said his monkey.

" . . . Aye," replied Melville. Now," he continued, pointing his finger at his monkey as it crouched back away from his remonstrating digit. "From this point on you, sir, will be in charge of discipline among the monkeys. You are the captain's monkey, and you'll be in charge of monkey discipline. When I want something done among the monkeys, I will tell you, and you will by God ensure that it is done. Is that understood?"

"Aiee kptnn," responded his monkey faintly, its head nodding inside its thorax. The other two could be seen nodding their heads as well. A strange effect since it caused their eyes to blink in and out of sight.

Damn, thought Melville, *I knew it! They really do understand.*

"Good. If there are any other occurrences like this, you and all the other monkeys will be put on bread and water. If you cannot submit to authority you will be put off at the next port. Do you understand?"

"Aiee, kptnn." Now their heads crept back out of the thorax and this statement by Melville's monkey was accompanied by a chorus of nods from the three monkeys.

"Good. Very good. Now, what the cats do for us is to hunt down vermin. From this point on I want all of you to start earning your keep on this ship by helping to hunt down vermin. Not only do we have some rats, mice, cockroaches, and weevils, but we have all kinds of weird Guldur infestations. The cats are driven to distraction by having to take care of these critters, and you'll help them. Can you do that?"

Now their heads were extended well out on their accordion necks. There was an eager nodding and a chorus from all three that a good imagination might take as "Aye Captain."

"Good. Now move out!"

Smith and Aquinar saluted while the monkeys spun their necks 360 degrees to watch them. The monkeys mimicked the salutes almost perfectly and scampered to the appropriate shoulders. On their way out the monkeys looked at each other and exchanged relieved glances and a brief chittering. Melville could have sworn that they thought things could have gone much worse and perhaps they had gotten off lightly.

"Damn," said Melville quietly as they left, reaching up to scratch his monkey behind the ears. "I wonder if I should feel sorry for the vermin?"

There were two additional groups that still needed to be integrated into their crew. One was the huge, semi-sentient 24-pounder cannons. The other was Cinder's litter of puppies.

Sired by Josiah's dog, born of Valandil's Cinder, this litter of pups represented some of the finest canine bloodlines known to Sylvan or human kind. For centuries mankind had bred their dogs for intelligence and physical ability, as had the Sylvans. To the best of anyone's knowledge this litter was the first cross between these two mighty breeds. At some time in the primordial past, many of the worlds in the galaxy appeared to have been seeded, perhaps repeatedly, by some elder race, or races. Indeed a strong case could be made for a continuous exchange of genetic material between many planets, so that life coevolved at the same time on all of them. It was generally believed that Sylvan and humans could interbreed. Here was further proof that interbreeding was possible between similar species from far distant worlds.

Melville looked with wonder at the little furry blobs mewling at the proud mother's flank as they nursed with dogged perseverance.

Above him the monkeys in the rigging were batting around some poor crayfishlike vermin they'd caught, until finally one of them batted it off into the blue plane of Flatland with a belaying pin and a cheer. Melville picked up a pup, with an audible pop as he pulled it from its mother's teat, and stroked its little blind head. Here was another new thing. An ancient Spanish blessing went, "May no new thing arise," but for him many new things had arisen. The monkeys, the Ship, the pups. And he found them all to be a source of great joy in his life.

Melville probably should have realized that Cinder was gravid when they came off of Broadax's World. In retrospect it was pretty obvious, but somehow there were always other things to worry about. He was sincerely surprised when the pups were born, and deeply moved when the rangers presented one to him. He immediately began to bond with the puppy, but the rangers, and Cinder, took responsibility for training the pups. Having seen how splendidly the rangers' dogs performed in combat, Melville asked them if they would assist in training all the ship's dogs. They readily agreed.

The puppies were easily incorporated into the crew. Mankind had vast centuries of experience to draw upon when it came to dogs. It was in the genes of both species to adapt to each other, and this process even seemed to apply to the Guldur. But when it came to integrating the huge cannon, the task wasn't nearly so simple and straightforward.

When you put your hand on the 24-pounder's Keel charge you felt a feral yearning to lash out and destroy. This was true to a lesser extent of their 12-pounders, but in this case there was an intensity and a viciousness that was mildly disturbing. Like the difference between a hunting dog and a feral wolf. All the gun crews for the 24-pounders fired a round early on. When they touched off the cannon the response was something like <<killhurt!>> or <<smashdie!>>, as the carriage screeched back on its greased ramp and the breaching ropes twanged deeply. It was hard to tell if what they yearned to destroy was some target in front of the gun, or the human behind it as they recoiled with stunning violence against the restraining ropes.

Accurate firing of a Keel-charged cannon in Flatland was accomplished through a bonding with the cannon. The gunner *willed* the cannonball to hit what he was sighting on, and the Keel charge was capable of adjusting itself to hit the target. The cannons were capable of astounding accuracy *if* the gunner was experienced, and *if* the cannon was trained, and *if* they had practiced together as a team.

The problem with these cannons was that they were so large that the gunner couldn't sight down the barrel and concentrate on his target as he touched off the Keel. Thus the gunner had no choice but to stand to the side as he touched off the cannon, or he'd be crushed by the recoil. But their master gunner, Mister Barlet, had a solution to that problem. His plan was to build a platform over one side of the gun, and the gunner would lie on that, looking down the barrel, making hand motions to the assistant gunners on each side of the carriage. They would pry the gun to left and right according to these signals. Once they got this all in place the result was amazing.

Since nothing but a Keel would "float" in two-space, and Keels were precious and expensive, the process of setting up a target for gunnery practice required significant ingenuity. Their standard procedure was to send out one of the cutters with a target suspended from a boom held out astern. The boom was long, as long as they could manage to lash together, with support lines up to the cutter's masthead, but still there was danger of a missent cannonball hitting the cutter. At first the cutter was kept in close as they learned the guns' ability, range and accuracy. The results astounded them. With a few weeks of daily gunnery practice they were able to run the cutter out farther than one of their 12-pound balls could even reach at maximum elevation. Their 24-pounders were still hitting the targets, usually a few suspended barrels, with deadly accuracy.

There was a full stock of round shot, canister and grape for exercising the 24-pounders, but there was only a limited amount for the 12-pounders. All of the ammunition for the 12-pounders had come across from *Kestrel* in the cutters, so the supply was necessarily limited. This was acceptable, since the 12-pounders' crews were well trained and competent.

Within a few weeks Cinder's pups were small balls of pure energy, gamboling merrily about with out-of-control limbs and a sheer love of life that was simple, pure and complete. They had thick, fluffy, tan and black fur, huge feet, floppy ears, and long, thick tails that wagged their whole bodies. They had the sailors in stitches as they romped back and forth across the decks in a great, hairy horde. The crew dearly loved and appreciated the pups for making them laugh. After the horror of their recent battles the puppies' zest for life and boundless affection was healing, renewing and reenergizing, and most of all contagious.

Burned from the ore's rejected dross,
The iron whitens in the heat.
With plangent strokes of pain and loss
The hammers on the iron beat.
Searched by the fire, through death and dole
We feel the iron in our soul.

They'd been forged in fire and death, but now the fire was quenched in laughter, just as the white-hot sword is quenched in water. They were stronger for the quenching and there was, indeed, iron in their souls.

Soon the puppies each carried a baby monkey, a true kindred spirit riding gleefully upon their backs. The inspired naughtiness and boundless energy of the puppies seemed to be reflected perfectly in the monkeys. Together they persistently went about the serious business of play, attacking the toes of the barefooted sailors, chewing at the railing, and mounting combined-arms offensives on the mops that flogged the decks each morning. Like the cats, the puppies needed to be taught to use the heads, dropping their urine and feces into interstellar space. This batch of puppies seemed to be learning particularly quickly, apparently helped along by their monkeys.

Every day the great guns fired and, like the monkeys and puppies, they too were learning how to integrate themselves as full-fledged members of the team. And each day the crew members were drilled extensively in combat craft. For the sailors, that meant rifle practice and bayonet drill. For the midshipmen, it meant extensive pistol training.

Petreckski was in charge of most aspects of the midshipmen's training. He was their schoolmaster, teaching them in the classics and many other areas, but he took particular delight at training them in pistolcraft. With a battle pending he saw this as a priority task.

"Gentlemen," said the monk to his students as they began pistol practice on targets hanging from the yardarms, "I cannot emphasize enough how important it is to focus your eyes on the front sight of your pistol. You *want* to look at the target, but even though you look with all your might, it will accomplish nothing. You cannot influence the target one little bit by looking at *it,* but you *can* influence your pistol by focusing on the front sight." He looked at Hezikiah Jubal and shook his head sadly. Jubal was an excellent sailor but he was adjusting poorly to using a pistol.

The middies stood facing the targets suspended over the dark blue plain of Flatland. The targets were chunks of wood and canvas carefully shaped and painted to look like human beings. In front of them was a rack of pistols. Petreckski stood to the left of the line, facing them. "Each of you pick up a pistol from the rack and face the target in the low ready position. The pistols have been loaded.

"Now, think of yourselves as artists. Your pistol is your brush. The artist uses the brush to paint with. He moves the *brush,* not the painting. He focuses on the tip of the brush to get the stroke right. What you are painting, my friends, is literally a masterpiece of life and death. Life for you and your friends, death for the enemy who is trying to kill you. All painted on a canvas of flesh with your little front sight. Do you understand?"

"Aye, sir," they answered in chorus. The new middies had all acquired monkeys. Now each middy had a monkey on his back, nodding in unison with its master. Petreckski also had a new monkey. It had quickly acquired a comical air of dignity and grave wisdom. It looked like a little Buddha sitting on his shoulder, folding its hands on its thorax, and comically mimicking the monk's gravity.

"Gentlemen, today I have a special drill to be sure you focus on your front sight. A number has been painted on each of your front sights. No, don't look! It's very small, and the only way you can read it is to focus very carefully on the front sight. So now, one by one, you will raise your pistols and place the front sight on the target. Then focus on the number, calling it off as you fire. Do you understand?"

"Aye, sir . . ." they said, with some uncertainly.

"Starting from the right. Mr. Jubal, ready, fire."

Jubal raised the weapon up to point at the chunk of scrap wood that was his target. Beneath them were the floorboards, before them the railing, behind them stood the mainmast, above them hung the mainyard. *All* were coated with Moss and glowing like vast florescent bulbs. By this ample light he brought his pistol up onto the target and read the number painted on the sight as he slipped his thumb over the Keel charge. "Three." <<purr>> "Crack!" It was a dead hit that flipped the target back on its ropes.

"Good! Did you see how that worked?"

"Yes sir! That was amazing! *Now* I understand what you meant about focusing on the front sight."

"Good," replied the monk with a pleased smile, folding his hands on his ample belly. "We will all do that, reload, switch pistols, and do it again and again."

Later, as the excited and pleased middies took a break after their drill, Tung asked, "Sir, why do we fire at targets shaped like people? Why not Guldur, since that's what we are likely to face?"

"Ah, grasshopper," replied the monk with a smile. "That's because anyone can kill a member of another species. That's easy. But inside the midbrain of most healthy members of most species is a hardwired resistance to killing your own kind. Animals with horns fight each other head-to-head in their territorial and mating battles, while they try to gut and gore any other species. Piranha, a breed of fish that is essentially teeth with fins attached, fight each other with flicks of the tail, but they will devour anything else that hits the water. Rattlesnakes will sink their fangs into anything and everything, except each other . . . and lawyers," he added with a blissful smile. "Any species that didn't have this resistance would soon be driven extinct by their own territorial and mating battles."

The midshipmen sat on the deck, leaning back against the railing and listening intently as the monk continued. They were sore from days of pistol practice. Their arm and shoulder muscles ached. Their hands were rubbed raw from the recoil of thousands of rounds of ammunition, and they were happy to take a break and exercise their ears and their minds for a change as their teacher leaned against the mainmast and continued. "In the twentieth century, mankind became aware of this resistance when research showed that the vast majority of soldiers in combat wouldn't fire their weapons at an exposed enemy, even to save their own lives.

"Now, my friends, the question you should ask yourself at this point is . . . what?" Then he waited, and the tension built as the midshipmen looked at each other.

"Well, sir," said Tung, frowning with concentration, "If it's so hard for humans to kill each other, how did we fill so many military cemeteries over the centuries?"

"Excellent, Mr. Tung! You win the big 'no prize' for today. Consider, gentlemen, that we weren't born with the ability to fly, yet we have this brain that permits us to overcome that limitation. And although we may have some innate difficulty in bringing ourselves to kill members of our own species, the entire evolution of military history has been a process of ever better mechanisms to enable us to kill. Groups, leaders, distance, all these things are effective and useful at enabling killing, but nothing beats training.

"Remember, you might have to shoot in an ambush, gunning down your enemy in cold blood before they even know you're there. Anyone can understand shooting to protect themselves. You give me five minutes and I'll make any sentient being in the galaxy mad enough to shoot me. The real question is, will they have that much time in a fight? The time to decide whether or not you can calmly gun down an enemy soldier, *before* they have a chance to kill you, is *now*, before the battle. Your life, and the lives of your comrades depend on it.

"Thus you must always practice on the most realistic simulator possible. A simulator of the thing that is hardest to kill. Perhaps we will face human pirates, or some species so similar to ourselves that our brain is tricked. We must prepare for these eventualities, but mostly it's the principle of the matter. Anyone can kill a member of another species, but only a well trained warrior can kill members of his own species in cold blood."

"But, sir, isn't that dangerous?" asked Aquinar. His monkey, sitting wide-eyed on his shoulder seemed to nod in agreement.

"Yes, it can be dangerous, but failing to prepare your warriors to kill in combat is far, far more dangerous. Ultimately the safeguard is discipline. Every warrior has two values pounded into his skull from the very earliest days. Violence, and discipline." The midshipmen nodded and many of the sailors were finding nearby tasks to complete so they could listen. The whole ship felt honored to have such a "learned cove" as their purser, and *this* was a subject that interested them greatly.

But not everyone *could* stop what they were doing and listen to the lecture. "Johanson, ya witless booby!" shouted the bosun to one distracted sailor. "I swear you shall never shite a true seaman's turd! If ya leave that stirrup like that the next person on it might fall through to their death. Now get back up there and finish the job. Then go up to the masthead and stay there and consider the magnitude of yer sin until I tell ya to come down!"

Not in the least distracted, the monk continued his class. "Violence and discipline. First is violence. Violence is your *duty*. If you're not capable of violence at the moment of truth, then you are a failure and all the effort and energy expended to equip, train, and transport you was wasted. And you'll die like a dog. Worse than that, you will have failed those who are depending on you for their lives. But if you are capable of violence and you have no discipline, then we've created a monster, a danger, a threat to our civilization. Discipline is your *honor.*

"Violence and discipline. *Duty* and *honor,* in service to your *country*. *Duty, honor, country*. *That* is what makes a warrior, and discipline is the safeguard. We don't require the uniforms and the haircuts for fun. We do it because if you cannot submit your will to authority about little things like how you wear your hair, at *least* for a short period of time, like in basic training, then you can never truly be trusted to submit your will to authority in big things, like attacking the enemy and not committing atrocities. Most great warrior cultures used some kind of distinctive haircut as a symbol of separation and submission to authority." The warriors gathered around him, along with the monkeys on their shoulders, all nodded. *This* was good stuff. This was what warriors wanted to know about.

"Think about it. In the twentieth century, probably the single most violent century in human history, democracies like the United States sent millions of men to war. (I use the word democracy in its broad sense here, since the U.S. was actually a republic or a representative democracy.) In World War I, World War II, Korea, Vietnam, the Gulf War, throughout the century, they sent millions of men to distant lands. They gave those men weeks, months, *years* of practice at killing people. They were *very* good at killing. But when they came home those men were *less* likely to use that skill inappropriately, less likely to murder, than nonveterans of the same age and sex. Those who were taught leadership, logistics and maintenance came home and used those skills to build a nation. But those who were taught killing didn't use that skill. Why?"

He paused and scanned his audience, then nodded as he answered his own question, his voice echoing with authority. "Discipline. Discipline. Discipline. Discipline, grasshoppers, is the safeguard. In this realm the captain has the power of life and death in the application of his discipline, and that keeps us alive. It also keeps our society safe from trained killers released into their midst.

"As I said, the other half of the equation is violence. Basic training is essentially a form of brainwashing. You participate willingly. You want and need the skills they are teaching, but it's still essentially brainwashing. They own you day and night for months on end. The Stockholm Syndrome sets in, and you identify with your captors." Here the monk grinned slyly and wiggled his eyebrows with a clever point that seemed to go completely over his students' heads. He sighed, made a mental note to teach them later about the Stockholm Syndrome, and continued.

"You accept the discipline, and you also accept the violence. You *know* that there are people in this world who will hurt you, and your drill sergeant is at the top of the list." Another pause and some appreciative chuckles, this was a bit of humor that struck home. Every one of these warriors was a product of some form of basic training and *this* was a concept they could understand. "And you become convinced that violence is an acceptable response to those who will hurt you."

"That's one of the things that went wrong in the late twentieth and early twenty-first centuries. Children were exposed to violent visual imagery. A constant barrage of it in the form of movies, television, and worst of all, the violent video games. I think that most of you have been exposed to these on mid- or high-tech worlds. If not, then you may get a chance later.

"For the little ones this violence was *real,* and like soldiers in basic training it convinced them, beyond a shadow of a doubt, that there were people in this world who would hurt them. Most of them just became fearful, but some of them also became convinced that violence was an acceptable response to a violent world. Most of those became bullies, but a few became murderers. This was done not to military personnel, with discipline, but to *children.*"

Petreckski's monkey, which had been sitting benevolently on the monk's shoulder, now began to look at his master with what seemed to be attentive horror.

"Many children were also bereft of discipline, just at the same time that combat simulators were developed; ever more *realistic* combat simulators in the form of 'games' became the primary pastime for many of them. You've all participated in training on high-tech worlds, using combat simulators, and you know what they do for us. This was military-killing enabling, without the discipline, and given to children. The result was horror. All-time record juvenile mass murders. Events unprecedented in human history. Body counts each year eclipsing previous years. The amazing thing was that it took them so long to figure out what their toxic culture was doing to their children."

"Sir," said Ngobe, with wide eyes, "they didn't really provide combat simulators to kids, without any structure or adult discipline, did they? Why? Why would they do that?"

"Money, grasshopper. Money. The same reason men once enslaved their fellow men and fought wars to keep doing it. The same reason men once fought to keep selling alcohol and tobacco to children. 'The love of money is the root of all evil,'" concluded the monk, suddenly looking old and tired.

"We know that real change began to happen in the early twenty-first century, when they began to release the brain scans showing the destructive, deadening effects of violent television and video games on the human brain. Once upon a time the doctors showed an X-ray of a smoker's lung next to a nonsmoker's lung, and from that point on the tobacco industry, with all their lies and lobbyists, started to be reined in. Next they showed the brain scans of a healthy brain, compared to that of a person exposed to high levels of TV and video games, and the effect was stunning. In the following decade the television and video game industry, and all *their* lies and lobbyists, were slowly but surely reined in. And our civilization took a step back from the brink of disaster.

"Technology provides a constant font of new innovations, each a potential blessing and a possible curse. Somehow the same basic lesson of caution and restraint has to be learned over and over again. Every time, those who would gain money at any cost lead the charge. Only afterwards do other, wiser heads clean up the shattered lives, families, and nations."

The monk reached up and gently rubbed his monkey behind the ears as he continued. "There is another path though. A path that our civilization has been blessed with for centuries, and that path is retroculture. *That* is why we study the classics. Dickens, Dumas, and so very many others show us how to *live* in a retroculture. The secret is to draw from the past, the *best* of the past, accepting anything 'new' with great caution and suspicion. You don't *have* to accept the latest fashion, the latest gadget. The fool is the one who flocks to the latest fad, while the wise man taps into the roots of his history.

> "All that is gold does not glitter,
> Not all those who wander are lost.
> The old that is strong does not wither,
> Deep roots are not reached by the frost."

"We 'wander' the galaxy gentlemen, but we are *not* lost. Warriors like Broadax, Westminster, Valandil and our good captain are solid 'gold,' but they hardly glitter. We tap into the '*deep* roots' of our civilization, and they *are* strong: the '*old* that is strong,' strong enough to form the greatest civilization ever known to man, perhaps the greatest in the galaxy.

"But we know that we need two things to prosper: *roots,* and *wings.* And so we also study the great works of the twentieth and early twenty-first centuries, the truly magnificent genre known popularly as 'science fiction' and 'fantasy' and they give us *wings.* Thucydides tells us that 'The state which separates its scholars from its warriors will have its thinking done by cowards, and its fighting by fools.' So, my friends, you must be warriors *and* scholars. You must exercise your minds *and* your bodies. And science fiction teaches us how to *think.* Not *what* to think, but *how* to think in the face of the unknown and unexpected. Most of those writers were only writing to make a living. They probably had no idea that they were writing timeless classics that would be venerated in the centuries to come, not just by their own civilization, but by others as well.

"As one great man put it, 'Science fiction lets us play out our nightmares and dreams in the theater of the future before turning them into reality. . . . It inspires us and warns us: The future can be better, but be careful what you create.' And I might add that the readers of science fiction are best prepared to handle the future. Indeed, the influence of Earth's science fiction and fantasy has been so great that many cultures have learned English in order to read these works in their original format. Over the period of the last four centuries our language has become the *lingua franca* of trade and culture. Much as Greek culture conquered the Romans, so has our culture, and the 'all conquering English language,' as Churchill called it, conquered much of the galaxy.

"Murder mysteries, romances, westerns, contemporary novels . . . bah. Bah to them all. They were wood, hay and stubble, to be washed away by the tides of time and left far, far behind. But those who turned their minds to what might be, and how to deal with it, *they* were opening the door to the future. Taking the next major developmental step in our civilization, our species.

"When the Crash came, all books and essentially *all* writing was on the net. There was no such thing as printed books any more. We lost virtually all the literature of the late twenty-first and twenty-second centuries. The works of the twentieth century and early twenty-first century were printed on such poor paper that *most* of them decayed within a century or so. During the chaos of the Crash most of the few remaining collections were lost. The nineteenth-century works were published on better quality paper, so we have most of them, but we might have lost almost all of the twentieth century's works, with all that incredible classic science fiction and fantasy, if not for the Cockett stash. It was carefully and very luckily preserved in the mountains of Wyoming, a land so deserted and desolate that even insects shun it." The monk smiled, thinking on the happy coincidence that preserved the books that meant so much to their civilization.

"Aye, sir," said Tung thoughtfully, "I wouldn't want to live in a world without Heinlein, or all the other great masters."

"Well said, Mister Tung, well said," replied the monk with a nod. "But we almost did lose it all. There were odds and ends of all genres preserved, but really only the Cockett stash remains as any major body. All we know is the name, 'Charles Cockett' written in each book. The funny thing is, we know less about Mr. Cockett than we do about Shakespeare or maybe even Homer. One scrap of information says that Cockett had one child who went on to do great things, but another reputable source says he had thirteen 'half-witted' children. As usual, the truth probably lies somewhere in between these two extremes."

The two rangers, Josiah Westminster and Aubrey Valandil, were leaning against the railing listening to the monk, with a pack of dogs and puppies around them, taking a break from their dog training. Looking up at them Petreckski asked, "Josiah, do you have anything to add before we get these young gentlemen back to their training?"

"Well," drawled the ranger with a grin, "the whole situation can be summed up in a parable about a young marine." The extended audience now sat back with great pleasure. The usually laconic ranger was also a shameless storyteller. Everyone loved a good marine joke, and they all looked appreciatively at the few red jackets among them.

"O Lor'," said one old marine, "'Ere we go again."

"There was this ranger on a vacation at the beach," Josiah began, scratching a worshipful dog behind the ears. "He was running a little low on cash when he saw a note on the bulletin board that said, 'Ocean Cruise: Five Dollars.'

"'Ocean cruise, five dollars,' says the ranger, 'that's just mah speed.' The note said to go to room 222 in the hotel so he went up, walked in and said, 'Hey! Ah'm here for mah ocean cruise!'

"'Bam!' someone smacked him on the head and took his wallet, and he woke up strapped to a log floating out in the ocean.

"'This is so embarrassing,' thought the ranger. 'All ah had to do was check at the front desk, conduct a proper recon and see what ah was getting mahself into.' Then he noticed that, strapped to a log right next to him, bobbing on the wave next to him, was a young marine! 'Waal,' he says to himself, 'Ah can't let this marine know this has got me down.' So he looks over at the marine and says, 'Hey buddy!'

"The marine says 'Wot?'

"'Do you suppose they're gonna serve us any food on this here five-dollar ocean cruise we signed up for?'

"The marine looked up and said 'Well, they didn't last year.'"

The whole group laughed appreciatively, poking their marine friends in the ribs.

"The moral of the story," continued the ranger, "is simply this. Always conduct a proper recon, and if you had a hard time last year, dear Lord, let's not do it again! Mah friends, ah reckon we've conducted a recon of the route the high-tech worlds are headed down. We've seen their sick cultures, and we'll be damned if we ever take *that* ocean cruise again!"

"Sir," asked Midshipman Faisal, sensing that the break was ending and wanting to extend it, "one last question. Why do you call us 'grasshopper.'"

For the first time the monk looked perplexed. "Because it has ever been so," he said with a frown, "now enough dawdling! Back to work." They groaned but Petreckski made the situation clear to them. "No sniveling, gentlemen. If we survive these next few weeks we will have years to educate you fully, but right now all that matters is preparing you for the battles that await us. And I will be damned if any of you die because I didn't take every available opportunity to prepare you, in sinew, smarts, and spirit."

The next day, the monkeys started showing up with bizarre, military haircuts, and across the endless seas they trained. Lieutenant Fielder trained the midshipmen on grenades. "Gentlemen, once his pin is pulled, Mister Grenade is *not* our friend." The captain trained the middies in navigation, and the lieutenants trained in sword *and* pistol. While the crew trained endlessly with rigging, sails, emergency drills, and fighting with cannons, bayonets, and rifles.

Broadax particularly delighted in torturing the crew during rifle and bayonet drill as she walked around in a short cloud of toxic cigar smoke: "When I tell ye to open fire, I expect ye ta shoot what's available, as long as it's available, until something else becomes available. An' if yer *not* shootin', ye should be loadin'. If yer not loadin', ye should be movin'. If yer not movin', someone's gonna *cut yer stinkin' head off and put it on a stick!*"

In many ways the ship was coming together quite nicely as they approached their destination, but Melville was aware of a certain tension among his officers. He didn't know its exact cause, but everyone else on the ship knew that it was set off by an incautious remark made by Lieutenant Fielder in the wardroom.

"She thinks she's a Weber!" Fielder had said as he slouched over his wine. "A mighty, beautiful, indestructible female warrior from a high-gee world who can lick any man through her superior strength and exotic martial arts training! Complete with the critter around her neck! Well, gentlemen, now you see that in the real world, a Weber is ugly, fat, bearded, and would be clobbered by any equally trained man from her home world."

A more indiscreet remark had seldom been uttered, since Broadax happened to have stepped back in and was standing behind him. For such a heavy person, she moved very lightly. Fielder had a brief intuition that something was very, very wrong, probably communicated by the wide-eyed looks of horror on his messmates' faces, just as Broadax cuffed him alongside the head, stunning him. Fielder's monkey flipped up to cling to a ceiling rafter as he fell. Broadax's monkey clung to her, its head deep in its thorax, making faint, confused moaning sounds. Broadax grabbed Fielder by the collar and flipped him around to face her. She drew herself up to her full height, which was hardly worth the effort, and shook him like a rat. Since she was so much shorter than her victim this lost some of its effect as his numbed feet and knees rattled on the deck.

"Aye," she replied, her cigar stub clenched tightly in her teeth, "ye look at me an' ye see no Weber. A *real* heavy worlder female is short and ugly by yer standards. An' aye a warrior from me own world would like as not defeat me every time in fair combat. But the warriors of the Dwarrowdelf seem t' like us well enough to 'get their brats on us. An' I don' see any of 'em around to defeat me at the moment. So jus' who's gonna prevent me from twisting ye into a ball and bouncing yer ugly body against the bulkheads!"

"Urk, urrk, urk," Fielder replied with all the dignity he could muster as Broadax dropped him and stormed out in a cloud of smoke. "Did . . . anyone," he gasped, "get the license number of that truck?"

In a small community such as a ship there are very few secrets. Only the captain remained unaware, for he didn't cultivate tale-tellers or snitches, and he had no interest in nurturing such creatures. As their captain sat in a solitary splendor and blissful ignorance, the rest of the ship waited with bated breath for the next act in this drama.

But nothing happened. In essence, Fielder was a rotter, an old fashioned unvarnished cad, and he was now well and truly afraid of Broadax. He had absolutely no intention of challenging her to a duel. Like all the Dwarrowdelf she was a terrible shot, so Fielder would happily gun her down with impunity if *she* challenged *him* and he got to choose weapons. But the old NCO was too much of a pragmatist to do that. If *he* challenged *her*, then she got to choose the weapons, and Fielder shuddered to think how *that* would turn out.

So a duel wasn't an option for either of them no matter how much they tormented each other. Fielder knew he was in the wrong and couldn't press charges, so he chose to act as though the event never happened. In the wardroom the two of them simply ignored each other. Fielder *always* sat with his back to a bulkhead, and everyone walked a'tiptoe 'round them. The tension was broken when they finally arrived at the Stolsh frontier world that was their destination.

They approached Pearl, gradually passing through the deep blue of interstellar space into the sunrise blue region where the system's star illuminated the immediate area. This was a water world, manifesting itself in Flatland as a large, aqua tinted mass with indistinct streaks of green land and white clouds.

Pearl's Pier protruded from the horizon as they sailed into this aqua-colored realm. As they approached it, the Pier grew into a white mass that was bigger than a ship, with cannon barrels protruding out in all directions. Pearl was a frontier world and their Pier was the equivalent of a frontier fort, suspended from the world below on multiple, Moss covered pilings.

A sailboat came in to circle their ship. The Stolsh crew consisted of handsome, tall, brown males and females, calling out to them happily, apparently amazed by their royals, studding sails and spritsail-topsail. The Stolsh sailed their slender, elaborately carved white craft, with its single yellowed sail, around the *Fang*. They were all naked except for short kilts, their females freely exposing an extra set of sharp, pointed breasts, placed down the ribcage like a dog's teats. All of them had webbed feet and hands, as well as faint blue gills under their chins.

The Ur-civilization that seeded so much of the galaxy made only minor modification to a basic stock. Human, Sylvan and Dwarrowdelf were minor variations for gravity differences. The Stolsh were a slightly greater variation, with the addition of gills and webbed hands and feet.

"Mr. Archer!"

"Sir!"

"You may commence the salute."

"Aye, sir!"

The forward cannon on the upper green side roared out the first of Fang's compliment, and the fort began its reply. They were close enough that the Pier's cloud of atmosphere had merged with Fang's, and the sound of their salutes rolled back and forth between them, nation extending its respect to nation in all courtesy.

In very short order *Fang* was tied up amidst a small orchard of masts. There was no Westerness or Sylvan consulate on this frontier world, so Melville immediately reported to the port admiral and passed on his message: The Guldur were coming, like the host of Mordor on his tail.

The tall Stolsh admiral nodded sadly, breathing in deeply through his thin, aquiline nose. He looked like some tall, dignified, deeply tanned human except for the blue gills in his throat that pulsed faintly. "Welll," he began in his deep, resonant voice. "We haave expected this, loong and loong."

The typical, slow Stolsh accent always sounded to Melville like the woebegone complaints of some deeply depressed old man, but he knew that they were a fierce, proud race. "This muust be their western force," the admiral continued. "If the projections are riight, thaat means thaat Ambergris is proobably aalready besieged by the force cuutting northwest. Thaat would explain why the mail paacket waas late. We will mobilize, aand we caannoot thaank yoou enough for warning us. Loong will your claan be hoonoored heere. Where do yoou go noow?"

"We carry Sylvan crew members with us," replied Melville. "Ours is the first joint Westerness and Sylvan expedition. Our orders are to report to the nearest senior officer on Ambergris upon accomplishing our mission or upon encountering serious trouble."

The Stolsh port admiral nodded gloomily, politely not asking what that mission was. "The neearest seenior Sylvan authoority is in chaarge of their expeditionary foorce at Aambergris, aand the nearest Westerness embassy is aalso there. The commander there is proobaably desperaate to waarn us. Yoou woould doo us a greaat boon to let them know thaat we aare waarned. I need every ship I haave right here."

"Aye, sir, I can do that. I guess I'm actually following my orders by moving in that direction. Technically the Guldur should respect the neutrality of our flag."

"Hooo, hooo, hooo!" laughed the old Stolsh admiral, leaning his head back and pulsing his gills. "Even if yoou weren't in one of their ships, I doon't think they would let yoou go. If yoou go yoou might haave to break thruu their blockade."

"Aye, sir. My orders didn't anticipate this kind of situation. I really don't have much option but to go to Ambergris, and frankly I'm honored to be of further assistance in your hour of need. But I'll need a massive resupply, and fast."

"Aaye, yoou'll haave it. Aaye."

Fang was a busy, busy ship. Melville had been given *carte blanche,* and he worked constantly, using every ounce of authority and prestige granted to him by the port admiral to pry resources and maintenance crews from the dockyard facilities. The sailing master, carpenter and gunner worked closely with their captain in this endeavor, rummaging through the vast resources of the dockyard for anything that would or could be of value to their ship and its mission. Then they supervised their divisions and the Stolsh dockyard maties who would stow these supplies. Meanwhile Lady Elphinstone and her mates were given free run of the hospital to replenish their greatly depleted medical supplies.

Lieutenant Fielder, as first officer, stayed with the ship, working with great competence and zeal to supervise the loading and stowing of the vast quantity of supplies. Melville watched Fielder, and he saw an enigma, a paradox. His first officer was heavy, dark-faced, rude, and domineering, but never, ever inefficient or incompetent. Coming steadily on board were 12-pound shot, canister and grape; biscuit, beer, rum, salt beef, and salt pork; linear miles of various ropes and cordage; square miles of sailcloth; bosun's stores, carpenter's stores, and medical stores to include several casks of common rhubarb purgative.

Their water casks were currently coming aboard, rising up from the Pier and swayed into the hold with many a cry, as ancient as the sea, "All together now, handsomely there, damn your eyes! Half an inch, half an inch, mate," and then vanishing into the hatchway to be stowed below with muffled but equally passionate cries. Meanwhile, Gunny Von Rito was carefully stowing deadly little copper-ringed, wooden barrels of gunpowder and percussion caps, inert in two-space but vital to survival on land.

Broadax was worn to a frazzle as she and her marines protected the crew and the ship from the ravaging hordes of Stolsh dockside idlers who would steal incoming supplies. Given half a chance, the Stolsh would also sneak on board. Sometimes these boarders would be Stolsh prostitutes who would happily couple with anything faintly humanoid, and whose presence was constantly aided and abetted by sailors. Sometimes they were simple and blatant thieves who would sneak back off the ship with anything that wasn't nailed down. Often they were both. As old Hans put it, "They'll git ya comin' and goin'."

Their purser's first task was to clear customs.

"Doo yoou haave any boooks of licentioous oor lewd naature, any haallucinoogenic substaances, oor any laarge quaantities of aalcoohoolic beveraages intended foor resaale?" asked the customs inspector.

"No," replied Petreckski.

"Aare yoou suure?"

"Yes."

"Woold yoou like soome?"

Sigh.

The customs formalities satisfied, the purser's detail then gathered all available "trade goods." This consisted mostly of bizarre items they'd scrounged from the hold of the Guldur ship. These were taken to the ubiquitous bazaar that always waited just outside the Pier. Like every Westerness ship, the crew made a side income from trading. The Queen, the Admiralty, and the crew shared from whatever they earned from the goods transported in their hold. They'd lost their cargo with *Kestrel* and were starting over from scratch, trying to establish the bones of a grubstake with miscellaneous Guldur weapons and equipment.

Their sad assortment of trade goods barely rated them a spot in a side alley that was, as Broadax put it, "If'n not a dead end, it's at least mortally wounded." Their primary trade goods were kept in barrels, with sailors and marines sitting on them, guarding them from the teeming Stolshanity that swept around them. The bartering was carried out first by Petreckski, who set the initial rate for each item. (Guldur muskets seemed to bring a particularly good price.) Then that price was used as a basis for trade by the more experienced crew members.

Although he wasn't entrusted to barter, Corporal Kobbsven *was* assigned by Lieutenant Broadax to be in charge of security. A duty which he accomplished primarily by looking huge and intimidating in his red jacket with a pistol tucked into his belt and the hilt of his huge two-handed sword sticking out over his shoulder.

A light, warm rain was coming down, and off in the distance between the low mud buildings they could catch a glimpse of the sea, for the amphibious Stolsh were never far from water. In the opposite direction, the Moss-coated pilings of the Pier could be seen. From here on the ground the bulk of the Pier was invisible, but its pilings looked like an orchard of white telegraph poles, each with attendant ladders and stairways, all ending abruptly like Aladdin's magic rope as they entered two-space. Periodically people and cargo appeared and disappeared, as they came in and out of two-space.

A motley crowd of Stolsh moved around them, leavened by Guldur, Goblan, and other creatures from throughout the frontier region. One cute Stolsh girl squatted in the muddy street directly in front of them, wearing only a short kilt. She was giggling and jiggling, making a great show of prodding at a small frog as her four breasts did interesting things and other intriguing things winked from beneath her single garment. All the guards were intently watching her.

Kobbsven was far, far from the sharpest knife in the drawer. (Indeed, by that classification standard he was more in the fork or even the spoon family.) But he had the virtue of single-minded dedication to an assigned task, combined with a deep veneration and even deeper fear of Lieutenant Broadax. It slowly dawned on him that his men were neglecting their duties, and suspicious hooded characters seemed to be sidling in from several directions. Furrowing his brows in the painful process that passed for deep thought (making his one eyebrow beetle up like a cockroach conference), he snatched up a jug of the cheap local wine that they'd been drinking. Then he strode over, scooped up the frog, and swallowed it in one gulp with a swig from the bottle.

The Stolsh girl's eyes went wide and she began to jabber to all who would listen, while Kobbsven ignored her. A few of the cloaked figures who were shuffling in toward them began to advance on him. He drew his two-handed sword from over his shoulder in one smooth motion, looked nonchalantly at them, and they thought better of it. He went back to scowling at all passersby. His sword was still out, but he wasn't "flourishing" it. Men who truly know what to do with weapons never bother with flourishing them. In the end it was more intimidating that way.

"Corporal," said Petreckski, distracted from his bartering, "this girl says you ate her frog. Did you swallow her frog?"

"Aye, sir. Her and that damn'd frog was distractin' da troops. One uf them had to go." Furrowing his brow in concentration he looked down at the monk, "Ya reckon I made a bad call, sir? Ya suppose I shoulda et her instead?"

The purser blinked distractedly. " . . . No, Corporal. No, she seems to have lost interest, and all's well that ends well." Then he left them to begin purchasing food.

They had brought their strongbox across from *Kestrel,* and there was a small supply of gold from the captured Guldur strongbox as well, so some funds were available. The grateful Stolsh admiral had already freely contributed water, ships provisions and miscellaneous cordage, spars and lumber. Their purser's primary goal was to purchase greenstuffs for the ship, as well as livestock for the wardroom and for their captain. With him were "Ducks" and "Butcher." These were individuals who, like "Chips" and "Guns," took their names from their position. Ducks was responsible for their poultry, and Butcher had authority over the four-legged food stock, which consisted mostly of pigs and a few goats kept for milk.

After a short and intense period of bartering, a menagerie of huge white geese on leashes; coops full of gray pigeons and small brown hens; low, hairy brown swine; and tall, slender black nanny goats were all herded to the Pier alongside carts full of greenstuffs. The pigs and goats were hooded and swayed up into Flatland one by one, where they loudly communicated their distress at the process and their strange new surroundings. The livestock was penned up in the lower forecastle until quarters below could be prepared for them.

Once the food was purchased, the harried purser set out to find a cargo that would be of value in Ambergris, which was their next stop. Ambergris would probably be under siege. (As would this world, but the general population didn't know that yet.) And Ambergris was a world low in phosphates. Thus a load of saltpeter was the purser's goal, and he was pleased with the deal he cut. He used the last of their gold to lock in the deal, quickly moved to the alley where the last of their trade goods were being sold, took that money and the security detail to get the saltpeter, and completed one of the most exhausting and satisfying trading days in his life. There was something special about starting from the ground up, and having inside knowledge about the pending invasion gave him an advantage that he savored.

"Well, Captain," he asked as they were pulling away from the Pier, "are you satisfied with our stop?"

"Aye," said Melville. The two of them were standing with their hands on the quarterdeck railing, looking at the far horizon. "We even picked up a few stray hands to fill in some of the holes in our crew. How did it go on your end?"

"Well enough, sir, well enough," his purser replied. "It's a miserable backwater port. No one will ever make their fortune here. Even their plagues are half-hearted. The best they could muster was a Plague of Frog, but the redoubtable Corporal Kobbsven was able to dispatch it for us. All things considered, I am satisfied."

And so they left Pearl, the sails sheeted home one by one, placing the strain slowly upon the masts and rigging, until *Fang* again gained her splendid speed of almost thirteen knots. Properly supplied and equipped, they sailed toward Ambergris and the likelihood of combat against the forces that were probably besieging or invading that world.

Melville had done as much as he could to prepare his ship. His men had faith in him, based on his victory on Broadax's World and his cunning scheme that gained them their current ship. In their eyes he was responsible for not just snatching victory from the jaws of defeat, but actually yanking a *Fang* from the slavering jaws of defeat. He knew that his men expected more miracles from him, and he felt unworthy of their trust. He tried to explain his philosophy one day while most of his officers were his guests at dinner.

"It's called maneuver warfare. It was first developed by the Germans in the early and mid-twentieth centuries, then picked up by the United States military late in that century. There were many pioneers in the field, but one of the greatest was Robert Leonhard. In his book, *The Art of Maneuver*, he put it this way, 'Maneuver warfare is, to put it simply, a kick in the groin, a poke in the eye, a stab in the back . . . Maneuver warfare puts a premium on being sneaky rather than courageous, and it is not at all glorious, because it typically flees from an enemy's strength. It takes its name from its most common practical application: outmaneuvering the enemy.'"

"Aye, Captain," said Hans, admiringly, "'Ats wot ye did ta the curs all right! Poke 'em in the eye an' kick 'em in the balls! Is 'at wot ya plan ta do at Ambergris, too?"

"I'm not sure, Hans," Melville replied scowling thoughtfully. "I hope to use surprise and our superior accuracy. We'll take down all the new sails and cruise in looking like one of their ships. We bluff our way through if we can. Westerness policy is to remain absolutely neutral. We can only attack them if we are attacked, so we will have to wait for them to fire first. When they do, we'll run up the Westerness colors, set all sail, and let them know that Westerness is here. And a world of hurt is coming with us."

With the exception of Fielder, who was his usual cynical self, most of the officers at the table nodded, looking at him with cautious admiration. "Aye, sir," said Mr. Barlet. The gunner was thinking happily about what his guns would do to the enemy. "*If* they try to mess with us we'll show them what those 24-pounders can *really* do!"

Melville looked with pleasure upon his officers. He possessed something that few other officers in the Westerness Navy could claim. Military victory. In their heart of hearts the navy sometimes feared that they might just *be* Hokas, playing games with their traditions drawn from the old British Royal Navy. The long centuries of Westerness history included many ground actions on frontier worlds, and a few brushes with pirates, but no real frigate actions like the one they'd just survived.

Now, after centuries of preparation, their first true naval engagement had ended in victory against overwhelming odds, and Melville had won the loyalty of these veterans by demonstrating his competence in combat. They were willing to spend their lives for a cause, but they *desperately* did not want their lives to be wasted. A leader who had proven his worth in battle was the most precious of all assets. A man to be truly cherished by his men. Melville had accomplished that now, but it was far harder than anyone who hadn't been there could ever understand. First, the opportunities to gain such credibility were so very rare. Second, once it was gained, it was a fragile substance, since one "dammit" could delete a lifetime of "attaboys" in the bank balance of battle.

Starting in the late twentieth century, combat simulators began to make it possible to develop "pre-battle veterans" *and* leaders who could demonstrate their ability to their men, at least in the simulators. When the military used these they were combat simulators, which honed battle skills. When that same technology was put in the hands of children, the games they played became "mass murder simulators," and like Ender in Orson Scott Card's *Ender's Game*, the games the kids played became horrifyingly real, resulting in unprecedented mass murders as the children turned their sad games and conditioned reflexes into dark tragic reality. Melville and most of his crew had trained long and hard on such simulators on Old Earth.

Still, combat simulators were never the same as real combat, and every leader yearned for the battle experience that would give them the only true credibility in their profession, while simultaneously dreading that combat would prove to the world that they were a fraud. When a warrior leader *was* successful in combat, there was a new fear. Now they feared that *next time* they *would* fail. For every military leader knew that, no matter *how* good he was, in the end so very much depended on luck. And *next* time, luck might not be there. Melville felt that fear, and now the danger was that he wouldn't want to risk his fragile reputation, but instead would avoid battle and rest on his laurels.

Thus military leaders *could*, in the end, be the most insecure of all human beings. In truth, every leader knows in his heart that he's no better than his men. Melville knew that somewhere out among his crew there was someone smarter, faster, stronger than him. So by what right was *he* in charge? Who was *he* to send these men to their death? There were ways to handle this. Like Alexander or Gustavus Adolphus you could put yourself in danger and perform acts of great valor to prove yourself "worthy." In peacetime that opportunity to prove yourself isn't really there, and there is a need to convince the leader that he *is* something special. Thus the salutes, parades, fancy uniforms, inspections, and elaborate displays of respect.

The strange thing is that in some ways this was a two-way street. All that pomp and circumstance could convince the leader *and* his men that he was special. The captain on a ship is an extreme example, dining and living in splendid isolation. Very little exists across the centuries of "the ultimate social Darwinism" of the battlefield without good reason, and the "need" for this kind of ceremony and ritual is a two-way street. Egalitarian democratic armies limit this a little, and veteran units in combat can relax it a little, but it was still there and probably always would be.

Military leaders in wartime, successful military leaders in the true test of combat, could transcend this need for phony reassurance and replace it with the greatest balm of all to the soul of the military leader. Victory, honor, and glory. Melville had a little of that now and, God help him, he wanted more. This was another risk for combat leaders. He had tasted *honor* and *glory* and it was *good.*

> The fewer men, the greater share of honour . . .
> By Jove, I am not covetous for gold,
> Nor Care I who doth feed upon my cost;
> It yearns me not if men my garments wear;
> Such outward things dwell not in my desires;
> But if it is a sin to covet honour,
> I am the most offending soul alive.

Honor, and glory. The next battle would decide, and the next battle was soon. To the best of his ability he'd forged his ship and crew into a fearsome weapon. He could run, yet the enemy was closing in from almost every direction and his duty was in Ambergris. Once again the odds might be overwhelming, but what the hell . . .

> A thousand shapes of death surround us,
> and no man can escape them, or be safe.
> Let us attack—
> whether to give some fellow glory
> or to win it from him.

Chapter the 10th
Sea Battle: Lords of Helm and Sail

On our high poop-deck he stood,
And round him ranged the men
Who have made their birthright good
Of manhood once and again—
Lords of helm and sail,
Tried in tempest and gale,
Bronzed in battle and wreck.
Together they fought the deck.

"The River Fight"
Henry Howard Brownell

They were sailing into Ambergris. The two-dimensional sea they sailed upon shifted from the midnight blue of interstellar space, passing through imperceptible gradations to a pure royal blue and then a light cerulean as they entered the solar system. A swirl of aqua, white, and green marked the plane of the planet itself. In the distance the off-white topsails of many ships could be seen.

Although it was still a comparatively young colony, Ambergris was already a major world with two large Piers, one above the plain of Flatland and one below. As the world spun, these Piers slowly shifted in relationship to each other in Flatland. On the world itself the Piers were hundreds of miles apart on opposite ends of a vast mountain range. But in the condensed, compressed environment of two-space you could sometimes see them both from the same ship, the Upper Pier from the upper deck and the Lower Pier from the lower deck. Most of the rest of the world was dominated by oceans, archipelagos, and swamps, the kind of world that the Stolsh loved. Given a few more centuries they would build it into a rich, heavily populated planet.

Melville cut a course for a point between the two Piers, trying to discern the status of the Guldur invasion. As he drew closer he could see only Guldur ships clustered around the Lower Pier. Around the Upper Pier the scene was a shifting, swirling mass of sails, some Guldur, and others clearly Stolsh and Sylvan. Faintly, over the endless, distant music of two-space, they could hear cannon fire coming from that location. They changed course and moved toward the sound of the guns.

On board *Fang* the scene was the same on both the upper and lower decks. First the crew was well fed. Then they beat to quarters, a daily ritual that the crew had performed countless times in the past, but this time it was for real. The men of the gun crews, supplemented by a sprinkling of Guldur, crouched motionless. Each gun captain lay over his gun on a platform, glaring down the barrel. At each gun the muzzle-lashing was coiled exactly and made fast to the eye-bolt above the gun port lid. The mid-breeching was seized with precision to the pommelion of the cannon. Handspike, crow, ram, bed, quoin, train tackle, round shot, canister and grape were all neatly arranged. "Slush," the fat carefully collected from the cook pot, was applied to grease the path that the gun recoiled back onto. A small bucket of slush was held in reserve beside each gun. Swords and pistols were in racks close to hand. The guns were organized into four batteries, consisting of the two 24-pounders and two 12-pounders on each side. Each battery had an officer or midshipman as battery commander. The gunner, Mr. Barlet, stalked the gun line on the upper deck, checking his guns and their crews. Gunny Von Rito did the same on the lower deck.

Behind the gun crews, the officers and midshipmen acting as battery commanders were exactly spaced. The decks were cleared for action. Everything that could be disassembled was struck down into the hold. Scuttlebutts full of fresh drinking water were centrally located with dippers hanging from them. Roxy, the one-eyed old cook stood by with her mates, ready to refresh the scuttlebutts and to act as litter bearers. The upper and lower cabins were stripped of internal partitions and furniture so that the two 12-pounders in each cabin could be manned without obstruction.

High up in the rigging, the topmen stood with pistol and sword at their hips, ready to adjust sails, repel boarders, or attack the enemy rigging. On the upper side old Hans stood with the topmen. On the lower side the bosun did the same. Marine sharpshooters manned the crow's nests. Gathered aft and beside the upper quarterdeck, Lieutenant Broadax and the remainder of her marines served as a ready reserve. In the same location on the lower side, Petreckski and a handful of purser's mates stood with the two rangers, forming an additional reserve.

Their surgeon was moved down into the hold. The operating table, consisting of sea chests lashed together and covered with tightly drawn sailcloth, was centrally located beneath an expanse of radiant white ceiling. Dressings and coil after coil of bandages sat beside the leather-bound chains sometimes required to lash down patients. An array of grim saws, retractors, scalpels, forceps, trephines, catlings and other mysterious torture instruments were arranged with loving care by Mrs. Vodi. Elphinstone and Vodi both wore starched aprons, bib and sleeves, and white caps over their startlingly different dresses. one buttercup yellow and one drab black. Buckets and swabs waited in the corner. Buckets full of water to swab the decks when they became bloody, buckets full of sand to spread on the slick wet decks, and, most ominous of all, empty buckets to hold amputated limbs and body parts. Etzen and Brun, their two corpsmen, stood at the upper and lower hatches with their heavy aid bags, ready to provide immediate, lifesaving medical attention, and to direct the evacuation of the wounded.

Deep in the hold the carpenter and his mates formed a damage control party, standing by to provide repairs to the precious Keel, brace up structural damage, or to sally up and assist Hans or the bosun with repairs to masts, yards and spars.

By now almost every crew member, and most of the dogs, had a monkey. And most of the monkeys held a belaying pin. Even some of the Guldur crew members had been adopted by a monkey and they delighted in the little creatures, finding them to be in every way the opposite of the hateful little Goblan they'd been forced to carry into combat. The process of monkey procreation and reproduction was still a mystery, but everyone was happy to have them on board. The little spider monkeys all chittered apprehensively to themselves as combat approached, with heads pulled in and eyes peering out anxiously. Except for Broadax's monkey, which chittered and screeched excitedly in a cloud of cigar smoke atop her helmet, flailing its belaying pin in intricate figure-eight and cloverleaf patterns with such speed and power that it hummed and whistled as it sliced through the air.

The dogs were excited and happy, pacing the decks like an eager bird dog that sees its master pull the shotgun from the rack on a crisp fall morning. The puppies were all gathered into the surgery, out of the way, but they looked for any opportunity to escape and join the fun. The cats also lingered in the hospital, curled up in corners or peering out from beneath bunks. They had absolutely no intention of joining in the dogs' fun. An old, one-eyed, three-legged cat, down to his last life and his last ear, sat at Vodi's feet and loudly, plaintively made the position clear. *If* the enemy boarded, and *if* they brought vermin with them, and *if* said vermin made it to the surgery, *then* and *only then* would the cats deem it their responsibility. They'd already participated in one boarding action, thank you very much, and that was enough for all nine of *their* lives.

During combat Melville's place was on the quarterdeck with his coxswain, a quartermaster and two mates. Hargis, Melville's clerk, was also there to time and record the battle, and little midshipman Ngobe served as a runner. On the lower quarterdeck Fielder commanded with his own quartermaster team, a clerk's mate, and a midshipman. If anything happened to Melville, Fielder would take over. If both quarterdecks were wiped clean, Hans would drop down and take command until one of the lieutenants in command of a gun section could join him.

Prior to combat, as he was trying to assess the situation, Melville went up in the foremast crosstrees with Hans, where they engaged in quiet discussion and contemplation. It was bitter cold up at this height, and they were refreshed periodically by the devoted McAndrews, who came aloft carrying a stained tin pot of coffee slung from his teeth by a loop of cord. McAndrews' monkey gripped his shoulder with six hands and carried the cream and sugar in the other two. "'Offee shir," said McAndrews through the cord as his head came up level with the crosstrees. Both he and his monkey were rolling their eyes in mute terror at the fall beneath them, and at the glare from Melville's coxswain.

Melville's new coxswain stood beside him in the crosstrees, balanced like a cat on the slim yard with one hand up in the rigging. Assigned to Melville by Hans, up until now the captain and his coxswain hadn't worked together. The coxswain was a petty officer with other duties, who was pulled out to command the captain's boat crew as needed, to serve as the captain's personal bodyguard during combat, and to accept other duties as the captain saw fit. An ill-tempered, ill-faced, shrewish man named Ulrich, he was quick as a grasshopper and mean as a mantis. A perpetual suspicious expression was as much a part of his equipment as the pistols, knives, and a wicked little short sword that hung from his belt.

In private Hans confessed to one of his old petty officer cronies that, "I've never known a real rat-pizzened, murderous little killer of a hater who would talk like 'at man, think like 'at man, move like 'at man, even shoot like 'at man. 'E's tailor made ta save our innercent young captin's life, dam me if 'e ain't."

Melville was convinced that Hans had inflicted Ulrich on him as punishment for promoting the old CPO to "ossifer" rank. There were many angry men in the world. Fielder was angry when the world didn't go his way, which was most of the time. Broadax was angry at the enemy, and let them know it. But Ulrich was just flat pissed at everybody and everything, and was itching for the opportunity to let the world know it. Fielder would run from a fight if he could. Broadax would run toward a fight whenever she could. Ulrich *was* the fight, and now he belonged to Melville, like a pet pit bull who couldn't be trusted around the children.

Like the rest of the crew, Ulrich carried a monkey, but it seemed to be a mangy, discreditable, sullen example of the species, always looking suspiciously over its shoulder. His monkey carried a wooden belaying pin, which was now standard-issue. But this was the only monkey to also wield a small dagger, carried in one paw with an air of casual insolence that seemed to reflect its master's attitude perfectly.

As they approached, they could see a widely spaced ring of Guldur 24-pounder frigates, *Fang*'s sister ships, firing into the melee from a distance. On the Guldur side the main battle was being conducted by a fleet of the curs' 12-pounder frigates, which were poorly constructed versions of their old *Kestrel.* They were mixing it up with a combined Sylvan and Stolsh fleet defending the Pier. Once the defending fleet was finished, the 24-pounder frigates could move in and eliminate the 12-pound guns on the enemy Pier with impunity.

"Aye, Hans," said Melville, handing his coffee cup down to be refreshed by McAndrews and sweetened by the steward's monkey, "there is one serious battle brewing out there. We'll cut through the gap between those two 24-pounder ships. I'll delay raising our flag as long as I can. Once they fire at us we'll hoist the Westerness flag and we'll play long bowls with them. When we cut into the main battle I don't think we can avoid a close-in exchange with those 24-pounder frigates that are engaging the Sylvans and Stolsh." He flashed a feral grin as he continued, "We'll see how *they* like those 24-pounders at close range. So, as soon as they open fire we hoist the colors and put up all sail."

"Aye, sir," said Hans, mirroring his captain's grin. "As soon as they fire, we hoist the flag and hang out all the laundry. Win I do that, y'll see my 'piss da resistance' y'will, sir. I been savin' it, I 'ave."

"Good." The cold caused steam to waft up from the fresh hot coffee in his mug. He breathed the warm steam in deeply as he lifted it up for a sip and then continued, "I'll go down and have one last talk with *Fang,* and then we're as ready as we can be." As the young captain headed down, Hans began to relay the orders through the foremast speaking tube that ran from the upper crosstrees to where the bosun waited at the lower crosstrees.

So it was that the entire ship stood ready. Even the few remaining much-persecuted and oppressed mice, rats, roaches and other, more exotic, vermin knew that something was afoot. Through the white Moss that coated most of the Ship's wood, every creature could *feel* the eagerness of their ship to be at battle.

They approached the battle around Ambergris' Upper Pier, pulling between the two distant 24-pounder Guldur frigates. Melville had all the gun crews run their pieces in and out a few times to loosen their muscles, and then they waited to see what the Guldur would do. They didn't have to wait long. The flanking ships both ran up a recognition signal consisting of two red flags, combined with firing a single gun. The response was probably some combination of flags and guns, so Melville had their signal yeoman act as though the lines were fouled, a stratagem to buy them a few more minutes.

When no responding flag came up, both enemy ships fired another gun for emphasis, but still no response came from the stranger in their midst, except for more fussing with the lines. The tension built as they passed the nearest point between the two ships, hoping they wouldn't fire on a ship that was so clearly one of their own, even if it didn't know the recognition signals. But the Guldur were slaves to a harsh master, and they would gun down a fellow ship if that was what their orders said to do. Suddenly the ship to their right fired in earnest, and two 24-pound balls came at them, one above and one below the plane of Flatland, which was now a swirl of green, blue and white from the world beneath them. Then the enemy ship on their left did the same.

The enemy had run two guns to the forward ports, and two guns to the rear, covering all bases, as it were. In this way they could bring two of the big 24-pounders to bear, one above and one below, in every direction. The enemy's forward guns had been taking longshots at the melee in front of them.

Everyone aboard *Fang* watched the two enemy ships fire at them with a careful eye, especially Mr. Barlet, their gunner. He looked with scorn and disgust as the two upper-side balls went wide. Word came through from the speaking tube that on the lower side one round had torn through some lower-side rigging, doing minimal damage, and the other had been a clean miss. As soon as the enemy fired, the flag of Westerness, a brilliant pinwheel galaxy on deep blue, was run up the main.

McAndrews, his steward, had found some tea *and* some lemon on Pearl, bless him. So Melville was now standing on his quarterdeck with a steaming mug of hot tea in his hand. "Fire as they bear, Mr. Barlet!" called the captain. They were out of range of the 12-pounders, but a deliberate broadside from their 24-pounders erupted from each side. If four guns per side, two above and two below, qualified as a broadside. <<Yes!>> "Cha-DOO-OOM-OOM-OOM!!" <<Kill-ill-ill-ill!>> and a flashing stab came from each gun combined with the concussion, the shriek of the deadly recoil, and a smell like ozone in the air as though they were discharging lightning bolts, accompanied by a copper taste in the mouth. The crews, most of them stripped to the waist, many with kerchiefs around their heads, remained intent on the loading, not watching the fall of the shot. It was deadly serious business. Checking the recoil, ramming home the new ball and running the ton of wood and metal back up against its port with a "blam!" while the gun's captain followed the strike of the ball and aimed the gun for the new strike. Throughout it all, the shrouds vibrated and the decks trembled with fierce joy.

Everyone who wasn't intent on loading guns or rigging sail cheered as they watched their balls hit home. At this range the gun captains weren't able to direct exactly *where* in the enemy ship the round would strike, but hanging over the gun on their platforms they were able to aim with deadly accuracy, and they were well enough bonded with their guns to mentally assist in directing the strike of the shot. Every 24-pound ball hit the enemy. Most punched through the enemy's sails and rigging. A few hit their hulls, causing the ships to shudder and sending a cloud of debris into the air.

At the same time, Hans and his topmen hung out all the "laundry." Fresh unbleached white studdingsails, royals, and spritsail-topsail bloomed into position beside the other, yellowed, older sails. His "piss da resistance" was a set of royal studdingsails, and then a handkerchief-sized moonsail above the royals. Which may have been a bit "over the top," as Melville observed, but surely stirred the heart of any creature that ever sailed the endless seas of Flatland. The ship surged forward with the kind of speed the curs never imagined it could achieve, just as *Fang*'s second broadside cut loose from each side.

<<Yes-s-s!>> "Cha-DOOM-OOM-OOM-OOM!" <<Die-ie-ie-ie!!>> Again the 24-pound balls sunk home, only one from the red-side missing, as rigging and masts began to tumble and collapse on the enemy ships. Melville called over the speaking tube to Fielder on the lower quarterdeck, "Mr. Fielder! How do they fall?" and then put his ear to the tube.

Faintly he heard Fielder in a tone he'd never heard from the sour first officer. "Ha! Take *that* you sons-o-bitches! Play long bowls with us, will you! Ambush *our* ship will you!"

Melville grinned grimly and repeated into the tube, "Mr.

Fielder! How do they fall?" and again put his ear to the mouthpiece.

"One miss from the red-side on the first broadside, looks like one miss from the green-side on the second. The curs have masts and rigging falling like rain around their ears!"

"Good!" They were pulling quickly away from the two enemy ships as Melville ordered, "Give them one more, then rest the crews and direct your attention to the front."

"Aye, sir!"

One last volley, again mostly striking home, with no response from the enemy. They were moving far enough ahead that the guns could not swing back to bear on the enemy, so Melville called out, "Avast firing," as the last gun fired. "Load and run them up. Now take a breather. Well done, shipmates!" The quartermaster immediately relayed each command through the speaking tube to the lower side quarterdeck.

Men and Guldur all straightened, grinning at each other. The humans glistened with sweat, the Guldur's tongues hung out as they panted. Most went to the scuttlebutts for a long, gasping drink.

They watched as the enemy ships desperately slacked sail to balance the thrust from above and below. Both ships were dead in the water as their crews scrambled to make repairs.

Melville continued, in a voice suited for the battle deafness of the hands, "Now shipmates, here is the real test. We are going to cut through that mass of ships before us, cutting straight for the Pier and firing at every Guldur ship that comes in range."

"Dear God, there's a lot of Guldur ships out there," muttered Melville's clerk beside him.

"Aye," replied Melville, then, to himself, and to the quarterdeck in general. . . .

> "Shall I retreat from him, from clash of combat?
> No, I will not. Here I'll stand,
> though he should win; I might just win, myself;
> the battle god's impartial,
> dealing death to the death-dealing man."

That drew grim smiles from his men, and they sailed on, into the mass of Guldur 12-pounder frigates that were battling the defenders on the Pier and the small Sylvan and Stolsh fleet that was assisting in the defense. These few defenders were all that protected the citizens of Ambergris from the brutal tyranny of the Guldur.

On high-tech or mid-tech worlds an invading force, with its technology limited by the strange dynamics of Flatland, could seldom do more than occupy or destroy the Pier. But Ambergris was a thriving low-tech world, with two major cities centered around the two Piers. The invading force already controlled one Pier. If they conquered the second Pier, the people stood little chance against the Guldur's mighty armada and its countless troopships. The enemy would also have secured an important base of operations close to the major Sylvan world of Osgil.

The 24-pounder Guldur ships they'd engaged were already within range of the battle, and now so was *Fang*. But at this distance Melville couldn't discern friend from foe in the swirling mass of ships in front of him, and he wanted to give his men a breather. Best to use this time for planning and coordination, rather than fire blindly into that mess.

He called out from the quarterdeck rail, "Gun captains, battery commanders, and sailing master rally on me! Lieutenant Broadax, you too," he said, looking down to his left where the marines waited in reserve. "Quartermaster, relay the command to the lower side, and ask the bosun and the first officer to come as well." As an afterthought, remembering that Petreckski was in charge of the lower reserve he added, "And the purser also."

"Aye, sir, gun captains, battery commanders, bosun, purser and first officer to the upper quarterdeck."

"Good. Mr. Ngobe," he continued, turning to the midshipman by his side, "Go quickly to the carpenter and ask him to come to the upper quarterdeck."

"Aye, sir," replied the boy with puppylike eagerness. His excitement and pleasure at their success was infectious, and brought a smile to Melville's lips.

Within minutes, his key leaders were present with him on the quarterdeck. "Just at the outer limit of 12-pounder range is when we will open fire." He was speaking to the leaders, but he knew that many others were listening. "From that range every 24-pounder should be able to get solid hits on their hulls, and even have a fair chance of hitting their Keel and sinking them, like they almost did to our *Kestrel.*"

He continued with a feral grin, "My friends, we are entering into a 'target-rich' environment." That brought a lot of smiles. "In the absence of any other instructions, you're free to fire at the closest enemy in your sights, and keep on firing. Be *sure* they're enemy, and then hammer them mercilessly."

He continued, looking at Hans and his bosun, "I intend to yaw to bring the red-side to bear first, then the green-side. I want a spanker and a jib ready to aid in rapid movement." That brought a grin from old Hans; he loved nothing better than fancy sailing. Melville smiled back. "We'll use them to bring our broadsides to bear as needed. With our superior guns and superior aiming, we should be able to sink several of the enemy ships. We *will* repay them, manyfold, for our *Kestrel*!" That got a cheer, then he concluded, "Quickly now, back to your stations, and when we open fire the bastards won't know what hit them!"

Minutes later everyone was at their stations. The swirling confusion of battle began to sort itself out into individual ships as they drew nearer. Melville could see two Guldur ships directly in front of him, their flanks exposed, sending thunderous broadsides into a Sylvan ship. Hans gave him a thumbs-up to indicate that the topmen were ready, and Melville gave the command to yaw to the green-side, his left, in order to bring the red-side batteries to bear on the enemy.

Suddenly, above and below, a jib and a spanker appeared. These were sails that ran roughly parallel to the main axis of the ship, directing their thrust to the side. The spanker extended out from their rear and was oriented to catch the downward "wind" of two-space to pull the stern to the red-side, Melville's right. The jib extending out to their front was oriented to pull the bow to the green-side, or Melville's left. The result was a rapid "left turn," combined with considerable slowing of forward motion.

"Fire as they bear!" called Melville. The quartermaster echoed his command into the speaking tube, and the 12-pounders came on target first as the ship spun. His command was answered by a steady, <<Yes!>> "CHOOM!" <<Gotcha!>> and <<Yes!>> "CHOOM!" <<Yippee!>>, from the smaller cannons, and then <<Yes!>> "Cha-DOOM!!" <<Kill!>> and <<Yes!>> "Cha-DOOM!!" <<Die!>> from the great guns.

She reached our range. Our broadside rang,
Our heavy pivots roared;
And shot and shell, a fire of hell,
Against her sides we poured.

The men cheered as two 24-pound balls punched holes in the enemy's hull, sending a cloud of debris into the air. One of the two 12-pounders, firing at the extreme end of their range, also made a hit on the enemy's hull. Through the speaking tube the lower side reported similar damage to the enemy.

"Bring the green-side to bear!" shouted Melville to Hans. Then, to the gundeck, "Green-side batteries serve the same ship again, I want to sink the bastard!"

Again the quartermaster echoed his command into the speaking tube, the ship spun, and once again the guns rang out with joy and malice, above and below. Somewhere within the enemy ship the bracing for the mainmast gave way, and it began to fall, slewing the enemy ship around and bringing her dead in the water. She wasn't sunk yet, but it was time to deal with the other.

This time they were slightly closer, as they took a series of slow "S" curves toward the enemy. Their cannonballs wrought even more damage on the enemy, sending two of their cannon flying like matchsticks and dropping masts and rigging around their heads. But now the Guldur were returning fire, and a few of the enemy's 12-pound balls were punching through *Fang*'s sails and rigging. One punched a hole in the green-side upper bow.

The red-side came to bear again, making a shambles of the same enemy, but still the Guldur fired back. The Sylvan ship the enemy had been attacking was now relatively free from fire and they rapidly moved out of harm's way, traveling in a wide arc and scrambling to make repairs as they went.

Now the green-side hammered the enemy at close range, close enough that the enemy was able to get a volley of canister into them at the same time, dropping several of *Fang*'s crew members from their guns and bringing several sailors plummeting down from the rigging. But this was the volley Melville had been waiting and hoping for. Through some combination of luck and skill *Fang* sent a ball straight through the enemy's Keel. Almost instantly the ship began to "sink" into Flatland, entering inexorably, silently into the cold hard vacuum of space. The only sound was the bloodcurdling, horrifying screams of the doomed crew.

Now the enemy ship that they'd wounded first was regaining headway and sending fire into their red-side as they progressed toward the Pier. The red-side batteries gave this ship their undivided attention. The enemy ship spun around, out of control and unable to bring any guns to bear.

Now, for the first time, Melville's four 12-pounders in the stern, two above and two below, could come to bear. They began to hammer the enemy as *Fang* drew away. The Sylvan ship they'd rescued came around in a long arc, firing at the enemy ship as they went, and then joined in behind *Fang*, forming a two-ship line of battle.

"Mr. Ngobe!"

"Aye, sir," answered the eager midshipman.

"Run down to the carpenter, and ask him for a report on the condition of our Keel, and the bracings for our masts." These were the foundations of the ship, hidden below decks. Their condition was an important factor in his coming decisions.

"Aye, sir!" said the boy over his shoulder as he scampered down the quarterdeck ladder.

Now there were two clusters of ships slugging it out in front of them, one to the left and one a little farther to the right. Melville charted a course between them and began to fire on the enemy as they came to bear. In a few minutes they'd sunk another enemy ship and crippled two more. They had also picked up another allied ship in their ad hoc line of battle. But the enemy was pounding them hard, and the Guldur ships kept trying to come around to engage in boarding actions.

Finally, one enemy ship bore down upon them with relentless fury. The red-side gun crews had taken a disproportionate number of casualties, so Melville swung *Fang*'s green-side to fire at the approaching ship, whose prow was filled with eager boarders. The green-side gave a volley, but the enemy came on undaunted.

On, on, with fast increasing speed,
    The silent monster came;
Though all our starboard battery
    Was one long line of flame.

"Yes, Mr. Ngobe?"

"If you please, sir, Chips says . . ."

"What was that, Midshipman?"

"Beg pardon, sir." He responded, smiling, buoyant and eager-eyed, completely undaunted by his captain's best reproof. "Mr. Tibbits says that ever'thin's sound as a pound!"

"Good," said Melville quietly, "because we may be in trouble here."

The red-side was reloaded now, so they spun to bring its guns to bear. The aftmost 24-pounder, right in front of Melville, was almost completely depleted of crew. Their captain was being evacuated down to the hospital.

The dead and dying round us lay,
    But our foemen lay abeam;
Her open portholes maddened us;
    We fired with shout and scream.

Melville dropped his empty mug, stripped off his jacket, and called out to Broadax and her marines for assistance as he leapt down to captain the gun. Ulrich, his coxswain, worked beside him with diligence and professionalism.

And when a gun's crew lost a hand,
    Some bold marine stepped out,
And jerked his braided jacket off,
    And hauled the gun about.

As he climbed up on the platform to aim down the barrel of the gun, Melville thought about Mister Barlet and felt a renewed appreciation for the sighting system his master gunner had devised.

Now was the moment of truth. His reserves had been deployed. On the lower side, Petreckski and the two rangers were also manning a gun beside a bunch of cooks and purser's mates. He was the final reserve, and now he was committed, up on the platform, leaning over the 24-pounder in an exposed position as Ulrich and the marines shifted it in response to his hand signals.

From captain down to powder-boy,
    No hand was idle then;

Two soldiers, but by chance aboard,
Fought on like sailor-men.

When Melville judged the gun to be on target, he reached out to touch the Keel charge that would set it off. Suddenly, something remarkable happened. His left hand reached back and down, making contact with the Ship's Moss that had recently grown on the platform. His right hand was in touch with the Keel charge of the 24-pounder. He "felt" *Fang* to his left, like a deep, powerful entity; like being in the mind of some vast, intelligent, feral warrior. He also "felt" the Keel charge to his right, like being inside the mind of some savage, vicious, slavering beast, straining at the leash in its lust for blood and death. He was in touch with them both, and through him they were in touch with each other.

The cannon delayed firing for an instant that seemed like an eternity to Melville. He could feel *Fang* rejoice as it was able to directly take part in the killing, but this was a calculated, deliberate malice. For an instant the three of them became one. One being, with one intent, to throw a 24-pound cannonball through the enemy's hull and directly into their Keel. To *sink* the enemy and send them into oblivion, into *hell* where the murderous bastards belonged!

<<YES!>> shout three minds in unison, "Cha-DOOM!!" they scream to the world as death incarnate belches from their maw, and <<DIE YOU BASTARDS!!>> they chorus in triumph. For a brief instant they are *the cannonball. They punch through and true. Straight as an arrow. Straight as a thought. The enemy Keel is crushed, instantly snuffed out of existence. Just as the enemy's prow, its bowsprit loaded with eager, bloodthirsty boarders, is approaching* Fang's *railing, they sink, sink . . . sink into oblivion. The enemy faces are masks of horror and despair as they sink, sink . . . sink into the hard, cold, pitiless depths of space.*

Remember, *said a little voice,* remember *that they would have killed us, and all that we love, without remorse. . . .*

Melville came up in shock, as from a plunge under cold water, as from a deep sleep, as from death. Death of being. Death of individuality. The pure, feral joy of battle and killing was still singing through his veins, and he looked for another enemy to kill . . .

Over and over again they screamed together as one, <<die! Die! DIE!>>

Melville captained the 24-pounders throughout the rest of that famous run to the Upper Pier of Ambergris. A run that will be recorded in the annals of warfare, to be remembered for as long as there are minds to recall and hearts to inspire. He found that the 12-pounders wouldn't perform in the same way. They were perfectly willing to hit the enemy, to harm the enemy, but they didn't have the same feral, malignant urge to kill as the 24-pounders. Nor did they have the ability to punch straight through to the Keel for the killing blow.

Melville realized that here was a unique combination. Westerness ships were products of civilized minds. No other ship of their navy could desire, could *yearn* to kill like his feral, vicious *Fang*. *Fang*, combined with *these* cannons, under *his* control, formed a team unlike anything ever seen. Somewhere in him there was a kindred spirit, a killing spirit, guided and shaped by a steely resolve to do his duty.

So he sought a gun, any 24-pounder, whichever one was loaded and ready. Acting as a human conduit between the awesome computing power of his ship, and the feral killing power of his cannons, Melville became an avatar of death. He *willed* the gun to strike the enemy Keel, and it *did*, each time taking hundreds of lives with it. He sailed into a vast forest of Guldur masts, followed by an ever-growing tail of allied ships who picked off the few enemy ships he only maimed. If it had been a fleet of enemy 24-pounder frigates he might not have survived, but against their 12-pounders he was like a lion among wolves. Everywhere he went he killed and he killed. His cannonballs ran true and straight. His gun captains willingly ceded their guns to him, watching in awe.

And always at his side there was Ulrich, his killer cox'in. If Melville was a counterpart to his ship, Ulrich was a living analog to his feral, malignant cannons. As his 24-pounders fell completely under his dominion in their lust to kill, like dogs obeying a master who will take them to the hunt, so too did Ulrich fall completely under his captain's sway upon that day.

Also making a special contribution were Melville's two rangers,

Josiah and Valandil. They operated on the lower deck, while Melville fought mostly from the upper deck. Although they had to man a cannon upon occasion, they were always quickly relieved and sent back to what they did best. Many an enemy officer, or quartermaster standing at the wheel, or topman adjusting sails, became painfully aware, at a critical moment, that they were facing two of the finest rifle marksmen in the known galaxy. A brief, fleeting, final awareness in many cases.

Cinder sat beside them, barking with feral joy every time their musket balls struck home. A group of ship's boys clustered round them, loading double-barreled muskets for them and echoing Cinder's savage pleasure every time an enemy topman fell, spinning down with balletic grace. The two rangers shared calmly in the pleasure, with the deep satisfaction of a true professional, quietly calling out targets, and congratulating each other's better shots.

Together Melville, his crew, his Ship, and his guns formed a team so superior to his foes that the enemy fell everywhere they turned. Some snipers or tank crews in World War II on Old Earth accomplished such a state of superiority, reportedly racking up hundreds of kills. More famous than that were the fighter aces of World War I and World War II, some of them killing over a hundred, two hundred, three hundred and, in one case, as many as 353 enemy aircraft.

The vast majority of the fighter pilots never shot anyone down. Many never got the opportunity, and those who did often found out, too late, that they didn't have the killer spirit. One of the greatest fighter aces of all said that most of the time he killed men who never knew he was in the sky with them. This is what it must have felt like. The finest pilot in the finest machine with the finest crew, all utterly devoted to death. Completely committed to killing. Death incarnate, sweeping down. Melville laughed aloud. Laughed with joy. Joy of victory, joy of life. They were truly "Lords of helm and sail, tried in tempest and gale."

But each time, the enemy got in a few hits before they died. They always went down fighting, doing as much damage as they could.

His gun crews took tragic casualties. There wasn't a gun that didn't have at least one marine or a purser's mate filling in for dead and wounded comrades. When the captain wasn't there to fire the gun, and the majority of the time he couldn't be, then the crewmen fired them, and fired them well. But they could never match the preternatural, lethal accuracy of their captain, his Ship, and his guns working together as one.

His topmen also suffered dearly, yet their ever-thinning ranks performed feats to rival Melville and the gun crews on the deck. When the upper mizzen topmast was shot away, they made heroic efforts to rapidly clear the debris, while calling down through the voice tubes. These were hollow tubes running beside the masts, from upper to lower decks, and down these tubes came the orders for the lower mizzen topsails to hang free, so that the sails' thrust was equal. When the lower maintop was shot off, the lower mizzen topsails were pulled taut again so they would pull again and balance the thrust. Again and again they performed such balancing acts, all while hacking away the hanging, dangling debris, and taking incoming fire.

Finally there were no more enemy to kill. The foe were fleeing, fleeing. Even as they fled Melville turned *Fang* to sink one last ship, to mercilessly, ruthlessly send a few hundred more sentient beings into the frigid embrace of outer space. And then, when there was nothing left to kill, he stopped, reeling and staggering like a drunk man. On his back, his monkey gave a feeble, "eek." Bits of flesh and blood splattered them. Some of it was his blood. He tested his body. Everything seemed to be working. Just minor wounds from flying wood splinters and falling debris, things his monkey couldn't block. They began to ache. *Have to see the doc soon*, he thought. *She'll help.*

He stood on the gundeck and looked around at the tattered remnants of his beautiful ship and his proud crew in stunned, amazed horror. . . .

> Then the dead men fouled the scuppers and the
> wounded filled the chains,
> And the paint-work all was spatter-dashed with other
> people's brains . . .

His shell-shocked crew stood around him, looking at him in silence, with stunned, thousand-yard stares. Duty, he told himself. There was solace in doing his duty. He was obeying orders, protecting his nation's allies from a foul invader, preventing tyranny and oppression. It was his duty.

No heed he gave to the flying ball,
No heed to the bursting shell;
His duty was something more than life,
And he strove to do it well.

He staggered up the steps to the quarterdeck. *Damn. Damn, damn, damn,* thought Melville, looking down at the crumpled, still form of Midshipman Ngobe at his feet. Ngobe's monkey was a smear of blood and fur mixed in with the midshipman's body. The little creature had died trying to deflect the cannonball that had killed his master.

Melville's monkey crooned softly, mournfully. Melville sunk to his knees with tears welling up in his eyes. *Duty. Here is the price of duty. Here is the price of victory. . . .*

Victory! Victory! . . .
And there at the captain's feet, among the dead and dying,
The shot-marred form of a beautiful boy is lying.
There in his uniform!

Once he stood, buoyant and eager-eyed,
By the brave captain's side . . .
Into the battle storm!
There in his country's uniform.

Laurels and tears for thee, boy,
Laurels and tears for thee!
Laurels of light, moist with the precious dew . . .
And blest by the balmy breath of the beautiful and the true;

And laurels of light, and tears of truth,
And the mantle of immortality;
And the flowers of love and immortal youth,
And the tender heart-tokens of all true ruth—
And the everlasting victory . . .
Dear warrior-boy for thee.

CHAPTER THE 11TH

Siege: Hark to the Call of War!

Far and near, high and clear,
    Hark to the call of War!
Over the gorse and the golden dells,
Ringing and swinging of clamorous bells,
Praying and saying of wild farewells:
    War! War! War!

"The Call"
Robert Service

Melville and Fielder stopped as they came down from their ship and looked out from the bluffs where the Pier was located. As always the transition from star-swept Flatland skies to a sunlit world was sudden and dramatic. In this case it was a sweltering tropical world, under a clear, brass colored sky. The visual impact of the light and the physical blow of the heat were joined by the additional sensory impact of a veritable nasal explosion of smells.

Before them, across the River Grottem, was the vast, low, teeming city of Ee. On their side of the river, high on the bluffs, encompassed by gray city walls and fortifications, was Ai, nicknamed

"Bluff City," with its vast Pier, lofty villas, and proud municipal buildings. Both cities were swollen with refugees from Scrotche, the city surrounding Ambergris' Lower Pier, several hundred miles away and now conquered by the Stolsh invaders. All around them the twin cities swarmed and bustled with mobilization and preparation for war.

"There it is," said Melville with a sardonic smile. "Proud Ai and pestilent Ee. AiEe, *pearl* of cities!"

"Oh, aye, sir," replied Fielder. "*This* is indeed an annoying impurity, covered with the slimy secretions of an irritated, mindless sea creature. If I ever saw one, this is it."

Melville grinned. "Our lovely refuge in a storm doesn't appeal to you, Daniel?"

"I'll say this for it, sir. I've traveled the galaxy, man and boy, and I've seen prettier cities, and I've seen bigger cities, but no city can rival fair AiEe for its smell. Ancient Katmandu and far Qualth were ripe indeed, but even these classic samples of olfactory poetry were mere doggerel when set against the full gagging glory of AiEe." Looking down at a region of fetid sludge at the bottom of the bluff he continued. "And behold the River Grottem, which oozes between the proud twin cities. Reservoir, sewer and morgue, it serves each citizen from womb to tomb. Hastening the journey considerably in many cases."

"Aye, Daniel, and if the Westerness consul tells us to, we will fight for it unto the death."

"Damn," said Fielder, with a scowl, "I hate it when you talk like that. We've been shot to hell, sir. Twice. No, dammit, three times! Four if we count your battle on Broadax's World! Now we've accomplished a feat unprecedented in the annals of modern warfare. You yourself received a dozen minor wounds, and there are few men on board ship who aren't at least lightly wounded. We've done enough, sir. It's time for us to go home."

Then, for just an instant, Fielder looked into the eyes of a man who wasn't quite human, and he suppressed a shudder. Melville had grown. Leadership responsibilities and combat experience had forged him into a warrior. His deep communion with his Ship and cannons had also left a lasting mark, changing him into a killer. He'd "swapped moss," exchanging neurons with savage, exotic beings, and the thoughts of alien, feral creatures now echoed in Melville's brain. There is a streak of madness in anyone who spends quality time inside an alien mind. Only the demands of duty kept him on the slender rails of sanity, and the call of duty carved into his haunted soul was all that balanced the lust for blood. No living creature would keep him from his duty. If his duty was to kill, then that was good. That was very good.

Melville's coxswain, Ulrich, stood glowering beside him. They'd become virtually inseparable in the short period since the battle. Ulrich always made Fielder's blood run cold. The "murderous little killer of a hater" was as efficient and eager a killer as a sociopathic mongoose, and now he'd found his master. Fielder realized with a chill that the man who mastered such a killer was the one who truly deserved to be feared.

The butcher's bill wasn't as bad this time. Less than when they'd been ambushed by the Guldur. Far less than resulted from their boarding action. Most of their casualties were wounded, with only a handful of dead. It would have been much worse if AiEe's superb medical facilities had not been immediately available. Although Ambergris was a low-tech world, AiEe's upper city did have some superb mid-tech medical facilities, facilities which Lady Elphinstone was already putting to full use. Also, high up on the Pier, where the gravity was light, a hospital had been established where the wounded could recover in a low-gravity environment. Combining mid-tech medical treatment with low-gravity recovery facilities created a powerful, lifesaving synergy.

"Start getting the ship in order, and find us some replacements, Daniel," said Melville quietly. "There are humans here, many of them sailors who may be willing to sign on with us. Perhaps some Sylvans could be convinced to join. We know that they make great topmen. Meanwhile, I will talk with the port admiral. I'll pass on the message from Pearl, and try to get support for our repairs." He added with a sardonic smile, "They will hopefully feel grateful to us."

"Aye, sir. Aye they should," his first officer replied with a fierce scowl.

"After that I'll go to the consul. If he tells us to fight, then we will fight, and that's all there is to it."

High and low, all must go:
    Hark to the shout of War!

Leave to the women the harvest yield;
Gird ye, men, for the sinister field;
A sabre instead of a scythe to wield:
War! Red War!

Corporal Kobbsven was the commander of Melville's small escort as he went to make his visits. In this case that meant that Kobbsven was the battering ram, flanked by two large marines, punching a path through the fear-maddened, refugee-clogged streets of a city preparing for war. Women wept, children cheered, men marched or cheered or wept, and insanity reigned. In the background a cacophony of bells, bugles and horns proclaimed, "War! War! War!"

Melville stayed right behind Kobbsven and his two flankers, while Westminster and Valandil, his two rangers, stayed behind their captain in a kind of wishbone formation, with Cinder trotting between them. They were ready to serve as countersnipers, or as a reserve force if need be. Immediately behind them were Gunny Von Rito and Ulrich protecting their rear. Von Rito was here in his capacity as the ship's armorer. If all went well, there would be a need for him.

It was a rather large entourage, but Melville wasn't in the mood to take any chances. He was developing what some would call paranoid tendencies, but in the mind of a warrior this was the kind of SOP, or standard operating procedures, that would keep you, *and* the people around you, alive.

They had just returned from the funeral for young Midshipman Ngobe and the others who had died in their approach to Ambergris. They'd also buried the handful of shipmates who had died in sickbay since their last planetfall. Those corpses had been kept in cold storage, towed along behind their ship in interstellar space. Now they had been pulled up and lovingly planted in the living earth of Ambergris. Melville and the crew had grieved intensely but briefly for these shipmates, and now they were ready to get on with business. The first order of business was a visit to the port admiral.

They pushed through the crowds to the port office, and Melville was shown directly in to the admiral. His entourage waited outside, Ulrich and his monkey making a fine game of staring down and intimidating everyone in the outer office, while Melville was escorted in to the admiral. He found himself in a spacious, sunny, corner office high upon a prominence. In one direction it looked out upon the immense expanse of the port, a seemingly endless orchard of Pier pilings, ropes, stairways and ladders, all disappearing up into nothing. In the other direction a wide window looked down upon the vast, teeming, lower city of Ee across the river.

The Sylvan fleet admiral was already there, slender and elegant, his long blond hair streaked with gray, standing in fine green silks with intricate yellow and red piping. His Stolsh counterpart sat behind an ornate desk, a tall, dark, dour individual swathed in complex layers of blue, green, white and brown, the colors of a world as seen from space. His look of calm and dignified control was belied by the steady pulsing of his gills. Both officers carried swords at their hips. Swords with well-worn, sweat-stained hilts.

A servant brought in a tray of refreshments, with two huge chairdogs trotting obediently behind him. The dogs curled up and Melville and the Sylvan admiral each took a seat. Melville was grateful for the opportunity to relax his battered body into the perfectly adjusting contours of the big, plush, warm, contented beast. His monkey delighted in the new experience of the chairdog, and the little creature was even further distracted by the fine Stolsh cheeses and Sylvan wines that were served. Then Melville made his requests.

It was as though some demigod had descended from above. There was nothing he could ask for that they weren't willing to give. The gratitude of these two battle-hardened old sailors was sincere and gratifying.

"No one can be completely sure," said the Sylvan admiral, "but we believe that thou hast personally destroyed over a dozen enemy frigates, and damaged at least as many more. The ships that followed thee in thy line of battle destroyed several more. There can be no doubt that the enemy abandoned the attack because of thy actions."

The Sylvans had the bulk of the naval forces around Ambergris, and the Sylvan seemed to accept it as his responsibility to personally acknowledge and thank Melville. "We were cut off by their 24-pounder frigates, as thou hast termed them, and probably could not have escaped. The Osgil fleet, *and* our Stolsh allies here in Ambergris, were all facing certain doom. We had reconciled ourselves to our deaths when thee didst descend upon them like a hawk among crows, turning our greatest defeat into our mightiest victory. Truly, we owe thee a debt of gratitude that can never be repaid."

Melville and his monkey both nodded somberly in response. Then Melville replied simply, "I am honored to have been of service in your hour of need." He was just too weary to think of anything else to say.

The two admirals didn't know what to make of this heavily bandaged young barbarian who had come to succor them, literally out of the blue, in their darkest hour. He was an enigma sitting before them in his faded, tattered uniform, with his strange pet beast sniffing and peering into the patient chairdog's eyes, ears, nose and mouth while periodically stealing tidbits and sips of wine. But they were warriors, veterans of many battles and skirmishes in distant corners of the galaxy. They understood that *here* was something beyond the ken of past experience. Something to be appreciated, supported, and perhaps even placated. Every resource of the vast dockyard was extended to him, and they also agreed to help find human sailors to fill out his crew. The Sylvan admiral even promised a draft of crack Sylvan topmen.

> Prince and page, sot and sage,
>   Hark to the roar of War!
> Poet, professor and circus clown,
> Chimney-sweeper and fop o' the town,
> Into the pot and be melted down:
>   Into the pot of War!

His ship and men cared for, Melville and his entourage then fought their way through the weeping, cheering, cursing masses to the Westerness Consulate. Again Ulrich and his monkey very successfully performed their intimidation act in the outer lobby while Melville was shown directly to the consul. A bald, potbellied, bespectacled little man in a drab black, pinstripe suit sat behind his desk in a wide, expansive office. No seat was offered, no refreshments provided. It was like a house in mourning. The drapes were drawn on all the windows, as though that would protect them from the hostile world outside.

The Honorable Milton Carpetwright sat looking at Melville with eyes full of dread. He was as small in spirit as he was in stature. Here was a man in a quiet job, at the pinnacle of a quiet career, who suddenly found himself deep in affairs far beyond his ability. "No risks, no gambles, no chances," was his petty little life's motto. When a violent, harsh, unpredictable world intruded, as it inevitably does, he was completely bewildered and unprepared.

Now he was confronted with a wild-eyed, bandaged, tattered young captain with an exotic beast upon his shoulder. Both of them looked at him with a casual ferocity that made his bladder loosen. He was cut off from his immediate superior, who was the ambassador in the Sylvan capital world of Osgil. In the absence of other guidance his top priority became his personal survival. In his high-pitched voice he told Melville that he wanted to use *Fang* to immediately evacuate the consulate to Osgil.

"Yes sir, I can try to do that," answered Melville slowly. "But we've been shot up badly and will need a lot of repairs first. And we'd be on our own against the entire enemy fleet. I think we've proven that we are good, sir, very good, but chances are that we would all die if we tried to break out without the entire Sylvan and Stolsh fleets supporting us."

Carpetwright's eyes grew wide and his jaw quivered as Melville continued. "I think our chances are far better if we wait to see if the enemy ground forces are defeated. If we beat them on the ground here, then we are safe, and sooner or later they will have to pull off most of the forces besieging us. If we lose the ground battle then we will have to evacuate, but we will have the entire fleet here to support us. Probably some relieving forces from Osgil will also be available to link up with us by then."

The consul nodded. This did make sense. Here was wise advice.

"Basically, sir," Melville continued, "I'm under your orders. If you accept my advice to stay here, then the only question is, should my men support the ground defense of the city? They *have* attacked our Westerness flagged ships repeatedly, in a totally unprovoked manner. Essentially, they have declared war upon us, whether we want it or not. In a legal, diplomatic sense, would that make us justified in defending ourselves here?"

"Oh yes, yes indeed. Defending ourselves. Very important. 'The right of self defense is never denied.' "

"Then sir, again, the question is, *do* we participate in the defense of the city? I think we could contribute a lot, could significantly increase the chances of victory. The question is do we do it, and if so how thoroughly should we commit ourselves?"

Sweat beaded up on the little man's forehead as *he* committed himself. "If it will help us stay alive, then I want you to participate in the defense."

The diplomat is able to pull his head out of his . . . shell, thought Melville as he nodded to the consul, *and make a decision.*

"But under no circumstance should your forces become decisively engaged. Your priority is to prepare your ship for evacuation," he concluded, with a note that almost sounded like decisiveness.

Ah, but he is, in the end, still a diplomat. If the pig flies, don't blame him if it's only a little ways, and if the landing is rough.

"Aye, sir. Will do," said Melville standing up. "Now, sir, if you'll permit me, I must attend to your orders."

"Indeed, Captain, indeed."

"Oh, sir," said Melville, as though it were a minor afterthought, "I recommend that your Marine guard should stay here to secure our noncombat personnel." *As though this sad little man would have it any other way. His handful of marines wouldn't make that much difference anyway.* "But I wonder if we could tap into the consulate's emergency supplies. It will greatly increase our chance of success."

"Oh, yes, indeed, Captain." Carpetwright was obviously relieved that this wild-eyed, young man didn't try to take his personal marine guard. *Great military minds must think alike,* he thought, preening and rebuilding his wounded ego slightly. *Here is a man who thinks like me, someone I might be able to trust.* "You have my permission to make any military decisions in that area. Just, again, my marines stay with me, and do not become decisively engaged."

"Yes sir, I agree completely." And in truth, he did. He had no intention of fighting to the death here, on land. But he *did* intend to hurt the enemy as much as he could, and the consulate's "emergency supplies" might make all the difference.

Women all, hear the call,
    The pitiless call of War!
Look your last on your dearest ones,
Brothers and husbands, fathers, sons:
Swift they go to the ravenous guns,
    The gluttonous guns of War.

~ ~ ~

"Aye, sir. Here they is," said the consulate's little marine armorer, Corporal Petrico. "Each one made by hand from raw steel, with tendur luvin' care, acrost several decades, an' then carefully tested an' retested. M-1911A1, .45 caliber, semi-ottermactic, recoil-okerpated, magalzine-fed, gummernt modul pistuls. The finest pockin' low-ta-mid tech hand weapon efer inventud."

"Aye. Ahhh, aye, indeed," said Gunny Von Rito, holding one reverently in his hand. "Essentially using nineteenth century, Victorian era metallurgy and technology, it was developed in the early, early days of the twentieth century and first used in combat in 1916 against Pancho Villa. And yet *over a century later* it was still the dominant handgun of its time. Hell, until them la-tee-da blasters and phasers were developed, centuries later on high-tech worlds, there really was no better weapon for one man to hold in his hand. You'll seldom see any weapon with that kind of staying power, throughout the annals of history."

The bullet-headed, scarred old NCO was in a state of near religious veneration as he continued. "Can you imagine what kind of technology base it would take to develop blasters or phasers! And when you're done, you still will never have the psychological impact, the noise, concussion, flash, and smell of a .45. With just a minimal tech base this baby gives you maximum lethality. And, most importantly, when properly built, *this* is one of the most reliable, dependable guns ever built. In the mud and the blood and the beer, this baby will never let you down. All skill is in vain if the angels piss in the flintlock of your musket."

"Aye, Gunny," said Petrico, as they both paid homage at the altar of the .45 auto. "'At's God's Gun."

"Aye, that's God's own gun," the Gunny replied. "The perfect gun. There's some that'd disagree, but I'm not one."

"Now," said Petrico, with reverence as he held the gun in his hand, "six hundert years later, it's da standart three-space weapin fer da hole pockin' Westerness forces any time they gets a chance ta develerp a perduction base. When wurd come out fer da marines ta develop small arms at each embassy an' consulate, waddaya suppose we turns ta? Saint Browning's pockin' masterpiece, thas wat. This baby wouldn' last fife minutes in two-space, but da plans, printed on paper, dey travels jis fine. Firs' we made da tools ta make 'em, an' then we begun ta work, buildin' 'em, one-by-one.

Lots o' spare time the Marines have on consulate an' embassy duty. Wot better way ta spend it. I'm not even shur them pockin', mawdikker diplermats knows or cares about 'em. But we knows, we pockin' knows, ay gunny?"

The ceremonial guards of Westerness' embassies and consulates didn't waste a lot of time on spit and polish. Some fancy ceremonial guards spent all their time polishing their fancy ornamental armor. The marines did look good on duty, and everything that could be polished was *well* polished, but they hated being thought of as the kind of people who wore stupid ceremonial armor. They saw it as a kind of "gilt" by association. Thus they had a fair amount of spare time, but they believed in investing it. Physical fitness and combat training was important, and whatever time was left over, across the years, was spent handcrafting firearms. Mostly they built .45 autos, but they also built a few of Saint Browning's other masterpiece, the M-1918 Browning Automatic Rifle, or BAR, invented in the same general time frame. The technophobia of the Westerness Empire was able to stretch just enough to embrace these two, magnificent, *almost* Victorian era weapons, both of which were used in World War I.

"You know, Gunny, Corporal," said Melville, nodding to each of the old warriors respectfully as he held his own .45 up beside his ear and heard the satisfying "thok" of the reset as he put it through a function check, "The idea isn't new. Even in the twenty-first century, on Old Earth, there were craftsmen in Pakistan and other parts of Asia who could handmake a replica of almost any gun you brought to them. Give them a working model, and in weeks they could have an exact copy, made entirely by hand. The only thing that would stop them is if you needed something with fancy metallurgy, or with tight tolerances."

"Aye," replied Von Rito. "No fancy metals or tight tolerances here. Just a fistful of death and destruction. With the twenty-two .45s and the two BARs the boys can release to us, plus all the ammo they've ginned up, we'll make the Guldur mighty sorry they ever landed on *this* world."

"Aye, indeed, Gunny," said Melville grimly. "They *might* conquer this world, but if they do I intend for it to be a *hollow* victory. If I have my way, this arm of the invading force will have nothing left to attack any other worlds. And they'll think long and hard before they ever attack the Westerness Navy again."

~ ~ ~

Training their troops with the .45 wasn't something to be taken lightly. All of them had familiarized with the weapon in basic training, but this was the first Westerness force to use them in true combat, and the first force to tap into a consulate's "emergency stores." There was a responsibility to make sure the troops did a good job, and that meant *intense* training.

The BARs weren't a problem. Gunny Von Rito and Corporal Kobbsven were both instructor qualified with that weapon. Some might think that their two best marksmen, Westminster and Valandil, would be the best men to assign to the BAR. But proper use of a heavy automatic rifle is as different from a normal rifle as a submachine gun is from a pistol. The BAR required specific training and skills, which these two NCOs possessed in spades. The effective use of the massive BAR in crowd-clearing, close-range operations also required a big man, a *strong* man, and Von Rito and Kobbsven both met the standard there.

The real problem was making sure the .45s would be used to the maximum possible effect. They had several thousand rounds of ammunition for each weapon. For the BARs that meant the .30-06 ammo had to be held back, used conservatively. Firing at a cyclic rate of around 550 rounds per minute, the automatic rifles would burn a few thousand rounds, or fifty twenty-round box magazines, in a matter of minutes. There was no need to waste the BAR ammo for anything other than a quick test-fire, since they had experienced, highly trained gunners. But it took a *long* time to burn a thousand rounds of .45 ammo from a pistol. They could afford to fire a thousand rounds per man in training and *still* have a thousand rounds for combat. And so they did.

To Melville's surprise it turned out that Lieutenant Fielder was the best qualified individual to train their troops on the .45. He was instructor qualified and, according to his records, had even survived a gunfight with a .45. The specifics were vague. When asked about the incident Fielder's answer was, "The people you kill aren't important. What matters is the ones who *fail* to kill *you*." He'd even trained at Gunsite, the famous desert world where the monks at the Gunsite monastery followed the teachings of Saint Cooper. Thus he was called upon to be the lead instructor for the .45 training. And he did so, in his own, inimitable style.

He taught misfeed drills, tactical reloads, speed reloads, and one-handed reloads. Marksmanship wasn't as critical since most of his students were already extensively trained with two-space pistols, and with three-space, muzzle-loading, double-barreled pistols. But they still fired many, many rounds of ammunition to fine-tune their shooting skills with these weapons. What *was* important was the new philosophy and science of combat with a semi-automatic pistol. *That* was Fielder's specialty.

"Gentlemen," he began, "you are holding in your hands the universal translator. As the ancient wise man, Saint Clint the Thunderer, once said, 'You can say "stop" or "alto" or use any other word you think will work, but a large bore muzzle pointed at someone's head is pretty much the universal language.' I will teach you how to use your universal translator, and I will teach you much of the wisdom of Saint Clint and the other ancient wise men from the time of the great warrior Renaissance in the late twentieth and early twenty-first centuries."

They were standing in the sweltering heat of a Stolsh firing range as Fielder paced the firing line, looking at his twenty students. They each had a .45 holstered at their side. "The first thing we want to do is to *avoid* a fight! The First Rule of a Gunfight is *don't*! As a last resort, you *use* your weapon, your 'universal translator,' to *communicate* to your opponent that this is all a misunderstanding, and they *really* don't want to mess with you. The Second Rule of a Gunfight is, if you can't avoid it, bring enough gun. An armored vehicle with automatic weapons can be considered barely enough gun. But the enemy has forced this fight upon us, and you hold in your hand the biggest, best gun we can provide. So let us use it to communicate the *most effective* message possible!"

Melville and Petreckski stood to the side of the firing line with the remaining two .45s holstered comfortingly at their hips, listening, assessing, observing, and learning. Broadax stood beside them, scowling. Like most of her race she was essentially useless with a firearm, so she'd be conducting this battle with her trusty, faithful ax. Melville was beginning to wonder if it had been a good idea to pull his first officer away from the Ship's repair and refurbishing for this training. But, in truth, what Fielder was saying *did* make sense.

"If you can choose what to bring to a gun fight, the most important thing to bring is a friend. Bring lots of friends. Bring a whole damned platoon! And be damned sure *they're* well armed and well trained!"

Fielder gestured to the left and right. "Look around you. Look carefully." Lieutenants Archer and Crater, their four surviving midshipmen (the unfortunate Faisal was wounded again, and poor Ngobe was dead), twelve marines, and two corpsmen obeyed, looking quizzically at each other. "These are your *friends.* Do *not* shoot them! They *are* well armed, and we will make *damned* sure that they're well trained. It doesn't do any good to have a well-armed, well-trained partner and then shoot 'em! Although," he added, quietly and introspectively, "I've had some partners I'd *like* to shoot . . ."

Breaking out of his reverie, he continued. "Teamwork is essential. For one thing, it gives the enemy someone else to shoot at. As a team player, shooting at your friends should be considered a major *faux pas*! Guaranteed to get you taken off their Christmas card lists. The only thing more accurate than incoming enemy fire is incoming friendly fire, and it's guaranteed to make you *very* unpopular!"

Taking a weapon from young Midshipman Aquinar, Fielder held it before them as he continued. "The primary thing that makes this weapon different from the weapons you're used to is the fact that it has *lots* of bullets! One in the chamber, and seven in the magazine. *And* we have *lots* of extra magazines. When I get done with you, you'll be able to change magazines in a fraction of a second, without conscious thought. So you have, essentially, an endless supply of ammo. Endless, that is, until you run out of magazines. But it's your commander's job to make sure that we break off before we get to that point. Since Captain Melville will be commanding you, I think we can all agree that you are in good hands when it comes to such matters."

Melville was mildly surprised by this vote of confidence from his first officer, and warmed by the chorus of agreement from the class.

"So, you have lots of bullets. That means you can afford to be generous! The First Rule of Target Engagement is this. Anybody worth shooting is worth shooting twice! *But* don't be wasteful! In a 'target-rich environment' such as this one, where a whole army will probably be charging at us, double-tapping each target is probably about right. *Unless* someone has singled you out for personal attention, at close range. *Then* the rule is, 'when in doubt, empty the magazine!'

"The bottom line is this: you're going to make your attacker advance through a wall of bullets. You may get killed with your own gun some day, but by God he's gonna have to beat you to death with it, *because it's going to be empty!* You must understand that, in the end, *anything* you do can get you shot, including doing nothing! So you might as well be putting lead downrange."

Then he got deadly serious. Even *more* deadly serious than before, and it became obvious that he was speaking from personal experience. "My friends, you've done a lot of shooting at targets, and you have all been in combat, but I can tell you that a gun-fight with one of these babies in your hand is *real* different when the bad guy shoots back. It doesn't mean you're going to lose, it just makes the story more interesting afterward. To make sure that you do the right thing at the moment of truth, we must drill it into you. Drill it, and drill it, and *drill* it until your fingers bleed and it's burned into your midbrain as muscle memory. You'll hate me before we are done, but that's okay, I can live with that, as long as you're alive to keep *me* alive."

This is a far different Fielder than the panicky popinjay who met me down on Broadax's world, thought Melville as he watched his first officer at work. *I'm learning more about him, but mostly he has grown . . . we've all grown.*

The main enemy attack wasn't anticipated for about a week, which would be just enough time to make the men highly proficient with their new weapons. Melville intended to participate in most of the training, and Petreckski would help instruct when Fielder was needed with the ship. But Melville had another task to participate in. The Stolsh defenders had a special scheme to delay the enemy, a plan to buy that week. These tall, gaunt, dour amphibians came from an ancient race of mighty warriors, and they were grimly determined to make their invader pay dearly.

They'd invited Melville to be there at a "roasting" for the Guldur invaders. How could he refuse?

Rich and poor, lord and boor,
    Hark to the blast of War!
Tinker and tailor and millionaire,
Actor in triumph and priest in prayer,
Comrades now in the hell out there,
    Sweep to the fire of War!

~ ~ ~

The Guldur forces rushed the walls of the lower city in a great, vast wave. Limited by what they could transport in two-space, they had only muzzle-loading cannon and rifles. The Stolsh, limited by complacency and the kind of cultural technophobia associated with most low-tech worlds, had little better. There were some breechloading repeaters used by civilians. It wasn't illegal, just frowned upon. But the Stolsh army was pretty much limited to muzzle-loaders. The result was essentially a battle straight out of the Hundred Years War or the Napoleonic Era on Old Earth.

The scattered cannon on the low, thin battlements of Ee hammered the advancing troops, bringing the attacker's rage to a fever pitch, while expert marksmen on the walls killed their leaders. Just as they reached the walls, just as they were ready to close in honorable combat, the cowardly defenders fled.

From atop the walls the Guldur could see Stolsh women and children in the remote distance, far down the avenues, fleeing from their righteous wrath. All that stood in the way was a handful of defenders manning a feeble barricade in the street. Again a volley of snipers on the rooftops dropped their leaders.

Westminster and Valandil kneel on the roof of a carefully selected building. Before the rangers open fire, Westminster looks out at the approaching enemy horde and mutters those fighting words feared and dreaded across the galaxy, "Y'all ain't from around here. Are ya?"

A group of Stolsh volunteers were reloading their weapons, feeding loaded rifles to the two buckskin-clad rangers as fast as they could fire accurately. Which was *very* fast.

The rangers were the last of the crew to acquire monkeys, as though the little creatures were intimidated by them. These monkeys were quiet, taciturn creatures, much like the rangers themselves. They stayed low and hidden most of the time, giving quiet encouragement while keeping an eagle eye out for bullets to block.

Other teams of Stolsh sharpshooters were performing similar tasks, but none was half as effective as the two elite Westerness warriors. The enemy was evil. What they would do to the innocent Stolsh noncombatants was horrible, it was vile. And so the two rangers found nothing but satisfaction and pleasure in killing the enemy. But they knew, from their contact with the Guldur crew members on board the *Fang*, that the real evil was the nasty little Goblan "tick." And, most of all, the odious leaders and the repugnant system that perverted the average "doggies" into these packs of ravenous beasts.

Thus the rangers took particular joy in killing the leaders. All snipers, throughout history, have found it easier to kill leaders. For one thing, killing the leaders had a much greater impact on the enemy's effectiveness. But there was more to this than the physical, tangible, objective aspect of reducing the enemy's fighting power in the most effective way. There was also the fact that, to the degree that they liked to kill anyone, most snipers liked *killing leaders.*

In most cases the average soldiers weren't too different from each other. It was often hard to get excited about killing them. But the leaders. Ah, the leaders who were sending those poor schmucks to kill you. Killing *them* was a different matter entirely. *This* was something a fellow could sink his teeth into. It was almost as good as killing their damned politicians who started this damned war in the first place.

It was this process of seeking out leaders, the idea of "common" soldiers knocking the muckety-muck nabob off of his pedestal. *This* was what, at least in part, appealed to the sniper. And offended *their* leaders. The idea of contributing to a brand of warfare where leaders were intentionally sought out and killed (nay, murdered!), by lowly, vulgar, baseborn soldiers, was offensive to a certain breed of military commander. Common, peon, pawn soldiers could die by the thousands and that was okay. But a kind of war where people systematically tried to kill *them,* the leaders, from a distance, where you couldn't even fight back? Well, that was something that it was best not to get started!

In this case the Stolsh leadership was able to bend far enough to accept the killing of the enemy's mid-level leaders. After all, things *had* deteriorated quite a bit! The Stolsh might have grudgingly tolerated it, but the rangers took great delight in it. An old saying put it like this, "Fighting with a ranger is like wrestling with a pig. Everyone gets dirty, but the pig *likes* it!"

For those who have never participated in long-range marksmanship, it's difficult to communicate the intense satisfaction that can come from that endeavor. Perhaps the golfer, striving for a lifetime to achieve a hole-in-one, can understand what it would be like if he could make *every* shot a hole-in-one. Even on a par five. And the result of the endeavor isn't to put some stupid ball in some silly hole in some sad little game. *This* game is real. In this game, if you're good, at the moment of truth you can slay a wicked foe and save the lives of your friends. And if, at the moment of truth, you fail . . . you might die. Your friends and family might die. And in the end, your nation may fall.

Josiah Westminster spends a half second scanning the battlefield, picking out the most obnoxious, offensive, insistent pack master whipping his beasts into a frenzy. The ranger chuckles to himself. When he was a boy, "He needed killing," was considered to be a valid defense in a murder trial. Well, here was an ol' boy who just needed killing.

He puts the front sight on the target, sighs, and strokes the trigger. "_____!" As always, when hunting men or beasts, he did not hear his shot. Ahh! The power, the godlike power to smite the enemy from afar. The satisfaction, the intense satisfaction as he watches Mr. Bloodlust R. Frenzy lose interest, gurgle blood, and fall. "Hooah!" says the ranger with satisfaction, then in the blink of an eye he picks another target, brings the front sight intensely into focus, sighs, and strokes the trigger for the other barrel. "_____!" and another leader drops his whip, looks confused, and crumples to the ground. He switches rifles and does it again, and again.

Piss on golf, *thinks Josiah.* "_____!" Piss on basketball. Even baseball and football. "_____!" Those are pathetic little games for dismal little men. *Fresh rifle and . . .* "_____!" Sad, pale replacements for the *real* game. "_____!" The game our ancestors played with stones and arrows, with bullets and lives. *Fresh rifle.* Success in *this* game meant your children wouldn't starve and you could put meat on your family's table. "_____!" Success in this game meant no foe would lightly come to claim your land and defile your family. "_____!" Success in this game meant the difference between life and death. *Fresh rifle.* Piss on golf. "_____!" *This* is a man's game. "_____!"

Now comes the tricky part. Deciding when to fall back to the next position. For the rangers the temptation to stay and kill, and kill, and kill . . . is intense. For the Stolsh helpers and loaders with them there is another temptation: the desire to pull back too soon, before all the juice has been squeezed out of this position. The perfect balance is what a true professional seeks.

The tactical situation is just right when Westminster, Valandil and their helpers pull back. The enemy catch only a brief, fleeting glimpse of buckskin as the foe that has been tormenting them pulls back.

Trotting over the rooftops, across narrow bridges (bridges pulled down after they pass), scrambling up ropes hanging from walls (ropes which are then cut), they fall back to the next position. Westminster looks at Valandil and grins. "I love this job," he says and his Sylvan comrade smiles back.

"Too bad the dog can't be here," he says to his companion, "she'd love this." *They both drop to one knee and scan their sectors for the most deserving leader from amongst the abundant, target-rich array set before them.* Ahh, life is good, *he thinks, as he strokes the trigger . . .*

With a roar, the Guldur headed down into the avenues, squeezing into the streets, packing together in a great raging mass of bloodlust and rage. Then the carefully primed explosive charges in the surrounding buildings blasted out from every window and door, just as the cannons on the barricades fired grapeshot at point-blank range. Nails, screws, and old hinges, lined with high explosive, and set carefully where an inside wall reinforced an outside one. They wanted the city? They got it. Metal bits first. At very high velocity.

Horse-drawn limbers stood by behind each cannon. As soon as the ambush with field-expedient claymore mines was detonated, the cannons fired one last volley of grape, hooked to the limbers, and galloped back to the next barricade.

The sappers who blew the charges slipped off through a series of mouse holes cut through the walls, along prepared routes, back to the barricades. For a little while, on that street, all that was left of the enemy's bloodlust was . . . blood. And still the snipers picked off their officers like a cook might flick the weevils from his flour.

Finally the unstoppable, irresistible mass crawled over the bodies of their dead and dying comrades and reached the hated barricades. Only to find them empty.

On every street coming into Ee, the situation was the same. At great cost of blood and lives they reached the barricades, only to find them empty, with yet another barricade waiting for them a few blocks farther down the street. And always there were the hated snipers, picking off the leaders like lint off a sweater.

In one case the Stolsh gunners were a little too good at killing the advancing foe. They fired one volley too many, and when it was time to pull back, they were too slow and were overwhelmed by the enraged Guldur and torn to ribbons. A reserve element was immediately moved up to the next set of barricades, filling the gap left by these losses.

That one success only fed the enemy's bloodlust. The fury, the wrath, the *rage* of the attacking Guldur was a thing to behold. There was no controlling them. Far in the distance they could see the remnants of the fleeing Stolsh civilians, their rightful prey, crossing the bridges into the upper city of Ai. They yearned to gratify their lust upon those bodies, then satisfy their hunger with their flesh, and slake their thirst with their blood. They charged the barricades and death exploded yet again, from every doorway and window, and the buildings collapsed down upon them.

And still, still the snipers, the thrice-damned snipers, picked off their officers like a fussy child might flick the seeds from a bun.

Valandil and Westminster grin. Happy, contented grins. Like wolves, as they lope back to the next position, their monkeys looking back over their shoulders, ready to block any stray bullets. The right side of their faces are blackened with the gunpowder of hundreds of shots. Hundreds of dead enemy leaders. Their business is killing, and business is good.

Finally, after fighting their way over an endless series of barricades on every street that led directly toward the bridges; finally, after fighting through a living hell of death and destruction; finally, the attackers reached the bridges and swarmed onto them in great, living, raging masses.

Then the bridges were blown, and the attacking masses burst into the sky. Hundreds of Guldur and Goblan became spinning pinwheels, artfully pirouetting up into the air with balletic grace.

Those immediately behind the luckless attackers on the bridges were suddenly faced with a huge gap in the bridge. But that wasn't their major problem. Their major problem was the thousands of other attackers behind them, propelling them into the waters of the River Grottem. Untold thousands were pushed into the river by the enraged masses behind them.

The river. Sewer and morgue, serving from womb to tomb,

hastening the journey helpfully whenever possible. The reeking, stinking river opened its loving arms and embraced an army. All without blinking. All in a day's work. Their passing was marked only by an occasional bubble, rumbling to the surface like the echoes of beans in a bathtub.

An army without leaders is a mob. A mob dies easy. Like sheep. Like cattle driven off a cliff. It might not have worked with another species, but the Guldur's mindless bloodlust made them vulnerable to this approach.

There were too few leaders to stop the enraged attackers from pushing thousands of their comrades into the tender mercies of the River Grottem. And when the attacking mob tired of that, there were still too few leaders to stop the mindless rampage. They spread out into every side street. Into every building. Atop every roof. Into every basement. They sought vengeance. Blood. Flesh to slake their lusts.

All they found was fire.

Westminster and Valandil lope across the bridge, two of the last few defenders to cross the bridge before it's blown. They run with the same tireless stride that carried them across the rooftops, on carefully preplanned and prepared routes, stopping constantly to pick off the enemy leaders. Many Stolsh snipers hunted the rooftops of Ee this day, but the survivors all speak in awe of the fearsome toll taken by the two rangers.

When the bridge is blown behind them they don't even look back, they simply continue to trot up the slope, the monkeys on their backs batting aside a few bits of falling debris. Halfway up the steep road that climbs up to the battlements of the upper city, Gunny Von Rito waits with a BAR slung over his shoulder. Beside him is Cinder, with a monkey on her *back. They have been standing by to cover their friends' retreat if need be. Cinder barks and shimmies with doggy joy upon seeing the returning rangers, while her monkey hops joyfully up and down on her back. They both drop to one knee next to her, turning now to look back while their monkeys scamper onto Cinder's back, to greet each other.*

"Everything go okay?" asks Von Rito.

"Hooah!" replies Westminster with a calm, satisfied smile. "It's been a good *day."*

The Westerness consul, the Honorable Milton Carpetwright, dressed in an elegant black suit, is standing by Gunny Von Rito. His squad of consulate marines are with him as bodyguards. A black bug in the midst of a red blossom, he strides forward to shake the rangers' hands.

"A tremendous job!" he gushes. "Our allies are all talking about you. Our contribution may be small, but you have definitely brought credit upon us. Tell me, what's your secret, how did you get to be so good?"

"Do you play golf?" asks Westminster with a lazy smile as he turns to shake the diplomat's extended hand.

"Why yes. Is it like golf you think?"

"Piss on golf," says the big, buckskin-clad ranger, laconically.

"Eh?"

"You asked me mah secret?" drawls the ranger. "The secret is, you just say, 'piss *on golf.'"*

The diplomat turns without a word and trudges up the hill, his grinning bodyguards trailing behind him.

"Diplomats," snorts Von Rito. "A fully loaded BAR is the best diplomat I know."

The three humans, the dog, and their four monkey compatriots look across the river, watching with contented smiles as the fires begin. . . .

It began in the vats and oil stores in the Merchants Sector and all along the Street of Restaurants, progressing in a blazing series of explosions and fountains that cooked the invading Guldur in a great, malefic skillet. The lower city of Ee usually was a teeming anthill of citizens, but it had been turned over to the enemy after only token resistance. Now it was a great, swarming, seething mass of Guldur invaders, and they were burning, burning.

Sweet, enchanting odors mixed briefly with the burned pork and charred fur smell of incinerating humanoids, as the blazing inferno hit the Perfumers' Market. It was sadly anticlimactic when the firestorm hit the whore pits and brothels of the Court of a Thousand Delights and Perversions. This was partly compensated for when the flaming tide hit the storerooms of the Avenue of Pharmacopoeia, Apothecaries and Druggists. The fumes caused the invaders to have conversations with their gods. Necessarily short conversations. And then they went to meet them.

Sparks drifted like fireflies across the river, where the defenders waited to drown each ember. Smoke from the inferno could be seen from hundreds of miles away, a vast, wind-sculpted shroud for the invading army.

Damn. I wonder if their fire insurance covers that? thought Melville with a grim smile.

Standing atop the battlements in the damp, warm air, the allied commanders watched as their artillery fire plunged mercilessly down on the Guldur masses clogging the gates as they struggled to escape the city. Earlier the same guns, hurling red-hot cannonballs, preheated in furnaces and fired with precision into preselected locations, had started the fires.

The commanders' various staff officers were currently dispatched to help put out nearby fires caused by the swarm of glowing embers that came across the river. For Melville, his "staff" today consisted of Broadax and Hans, along with a squad of armed marines as bodyguards. All of whom were off fighting fires.

Melville stood atop the crenelated ramparts beside the Sylvan and Stolsh commanders, holding his puppy in his arms. If given positive exposure at a young age to things like water, gunshots, wire-mesh stairs, *or combat*, then a dog will have no fear of these things. If his dog was going to be a properly trained war dog, he needed to be exposed to guns, blood, death, gore, and killing at the youngest possible age.

Earlier, one of the elegant, foppish Sylvan staff officers had made an effort at polite conversation by asking the dog's name.

"His name is Boye," Melville replied with a polite smile. "As in, 'Here boy!' but with an 'e' on the end."

"I have not previously heard of such a name. Art thou making some clever historical allusion?"

"He's named after one of the most famous dogs in our history. 'Boye' was a trained war dog that belonged to Prince Rupert of the Rhine. This was during the English Civil War, pitting the 'roundheads' against the 'cavaliers.' The roundheads feared and hated the aristocratic cavalier's fierce war dogs, particular Prince Rupert's Boye. They celebrated when the dog was finally killed in battle. There is a famous nursery rhyme that was originally a poem, mocking the motley, ragtag, cavalier army.

"Hark, hark, the dogs do bark,
The beggars are coming to town.
Some in rags and some in riches,
And some in velvet gowns."

The Sylvan smiled in a polite but confused manner. "But is it not dangerous to have the puppy up here?"

Melville smiled sadly and replied simply, "He knew the job was dangerous when he took it." The bewildered Sylvan nodded and backed away. Then all the staff officers went to put out fires in the immediate vicinity.

Melville's dog looked at the death and suffering across the river with the kind of keen, contented pleasure that a hound would have as it watched a deer being gutted and field stripped. Melville and his monkey both echoed this look of remorseless satisfaction. As his fellow commanders gazed out in wonder and horror, Melville began to recite reflectively, quietly but clearly,

"He said: 'Thou petty people, let me pass.
  What canst thou do but bow to me and kneel?'
But sudden a dry land caught fire like grass,
  And answer hurtled but from shell and steel.

"He looked for silence, but a thunder came
  Upon him, from Liège a leaden hail.
All Belgium flew up at his throat in flame
  Till at her gates amazed his legions quail."

The allied leaders standing next to him on the ramparts looked at him with a kind of horrified admiration. Here was a new twist to the strange, savage, barbarian killer who was their new ally.

The crisis immediately around them had passed, the situation was now under control and their staff officers began to return. Broadax and Hans and their squad of marine bodyguards came staggering up after having barely saved one building. Broadax and Hans moved up to stand beside their commander. Both they and their monkeys were singed and smoldering in various locations. Melville felt guilty about not having gone into "harm's way" with them, but he had decided it was important to stay here with his allied commanders.

"Funny thing 'bout eyebrows," muttered Hans, as he and his monkey launched tobacco juice over the edge of the battlements. "Ya never miss 'em 'til they's gone." Looking out at the blazing cauldron of death and horror across the river, Hans chuckled happily. "Urban renewal," he muttered, "prob'ly an improvement." Then he recited an old sailor's ditty, "Red sky at night, sailor's delight."

"Hah!" chuckled Broadax, she and her monkey both smoking from several places besides her cigar, "Red sky at night, the whole damned city's alight! An' a whole *bunch* of them cur bastards with it."

The Sylvan and Stolsh commanders, and their returning staff, looked in consternation at the human warriors' frank pleasure. "Gentlefolk," said one Sylvan staff officer in a braided, forest green uniform, "dost thou feel no remorse, no empathy for the suffering we have inflicted here today?"

Melville looked at him with feral eyes, thinking of the row of graves on Broadax's World. "A great leader of ours, a man named Winston Churchill, in similar circumstances, put it this way. 'If you will not fight when you can easily win, without bloodshed, and if you still will not fight when your victory is sure and not too costly, you may well come to the moment when you will have no choice but to fight with the odds against you, and you have only a small chance of survival. There may even be a worse case: you may have to fight when there is no hope of victory, simply because it is better to perish as warriors than to live as slaves.' "

The staff officer looked at him with a puzzled yet kindly expression. "We know that a captain's communication with his Ship can have a powerful effect, and we know that war can scar a man. Please forgive me, captain, I mean no offense; but surely, sir, war and communion with thy Ship hast seared thy soul? Otherwise how canst thou say that anyone deserves *that*?"

Melville returned a flat stare. "They'd do the same thing to you, your families, and everything that you love, without hesitation. It does you credit that you have remorse, that's what makes you superior to them. But it also does you credit that you are willing to fight them with every means at your disposal. You didn't ask them to come here. *You* didn't invade *them.* People find in war what they seek. They sought death and destruction, and they have found it." Looking out across the river, he mused,

"Efficient, thorough, strong, and brave—
his vision is to kill.
Force is the hearthstone of his might,
the pole-star of his will.
His forges glow malevolent: their minions never tire
To deck the goddess of his lust whose twins are
blood and fire."

There was a long silence, then he whispered, "Reap what thou hast sown, O enemy mine. Thou hast taught me to hate. Thou hast lusted for blood and fire, now *slake thy thirst.*"

Everywhere thrill the air
The maniac bells of War.
There will be little of sleeping to-night;
There will be wailing and weeping to-night;
Death's red sickle is reaping to-night:
War! War! War!

CHAPTER THE 12TH
Siege: Smote, and Smote Again

So strong in faith you dared
Defy the giant, scorn
Ignobly to be spared,
Though trampled, spoiled, and torn,

And in your faith arose
And smote, and smote again,
Till those astonished foes
Reeled from their mounds of slain . . .

Still for your frontier stands
The host that knew no dread,
Your little, stubborn land's
Nameless, immortal dead.

Laurence Binyon
"To the Belgians"

Now the battle was begun in earnest.

Piers, with their access to Flatland and two-space, usually appear on high ground. Ambergris was an aquatic world with the Piers appearing on opposite ends of the world's one, long, low mountain range. Movement from the Lower Pier to the Upper Pier, here at AiEe, was mostly on high ground where the Guldur were at an advantage. Once they moved off this high ground they'd be in swamps, seas, and archipelagos where the aquatic Stolsh had an enormous advantage.

For hundreds of miles up and down stream, AiEe was the only point where the River Grottem was bridged, the only place where the river didn't have vast swamps on both banks. If the Guldur were coming across the river this was the only place it could be done without months of effort and vast amounts of engineering work to build roads and bridges in the swamps, where the Stolsh would be at a great advantage. The Guldur knew this, and they were *not* that stupid. So they selected the lesser of two evils and attacked head-on, struggling across the water and up the bluffs.

The low gray walls around Ai didn't so much loom over the river as lurk, clinging to the bluffs as though they were worried someone might try to steal them. Now their centuries of paranoid, stony diligence was paying off. They'd finally caught a thief, and they would make them pay.

It was like something out of a ancient epic poem. As Melville and his officers watched in amazement, the Guldur hordes attacked, and died. And died. And died.

> A hundred thousand fighting men
> They climbed the frowning ridges,
> With their flaming swords drawn free
> And their pennants at their knee
> They went up to their desire,
> To the City of the Bridges,
> With their naked brands outdrawn
> Like the lances of the dawn!
> In a swelling surf of fire,
> Crawling higher—higher—higher—
> Till they crumpled up and died
> Like a sudden wasted tide,
> And the thunder in their faces beat them down and
> flung them wide!

The batteries of mighty cannons atop the walls roared out defiance and death for days on end. Their stockpile of shot, shell and powder was immense. But so was the enemy army.

Their packmasters moved immediately behind each wave of Guldur. These were huge, brutal curs with long whips, goading their troops into a frenzy of bloodlust. Little was known about the distant Guldur empire. Even the most basic aspects of their culture and leadership were a mystery. The doggies who were now members of *Fang*'s crew could do little but moan and hang their heads when asked about it. Clearly their leadership was brutal, goading the individual curs into acts that, without their leaders and ticks, they would ordinarily never be capable of.

The ticks were an even greater mystery to the alliance. They were foul-smelling little creatures with nasty habits, apparently not of basic humanoid stock. The Guldur leadership used them to control and incite the doggies, but exactly how this happened was an enigma.

Regardless of how they accomplished it, some highly effective combination of factors made it possible for the Guldur to goad their troops into endless, suicidal attacks. The Guldur hordes attacked in a rainbow of uniforms, each regiment dressed differently, with color-coordinated Goblan ticks on their backs. Each attacking figure needed to be killed twice, cur and tick. And they were. For all their pretty uniforms they died in great, horrid, ghastly gray heaps.

> They had paid a thousand men,
> Yet they formed and came again,
> For they heard the silver bugles sounding
>   challenge to their pride,
> And they rode with swords agleam
> For the glory of a dream
> And they stormed up to the cannon's mouth
>   and withered there, and died.

The might of a vast star empire was wasting away before their eyes. The Guldur members of *Fang*'s crew couldn't bear to come to the ramparts and watch, as the others did on their off hours.

As the Stolsh defenders watched in horror, their resolution began to waver. Even the refugees from Scrotche, the Lower Pier city that had been conquered by the Guldur, were losing heart for the slaughter. Melville, Broadax and Hans found that even *their* fierce lust for vengeance was being fulfilled. The young captain was constantly busy in the councils of the allies. Encouraging them to fight and, yes, to *kill* their foes, *now* while they could. Churchill's admonishment was brought up again and again.

Fielder, self-centered as a tornado, as self-absorbed as a cat, was able to find complete comfort in his pragmatic, egocentric philosophy. "Do onto others before they do onto you" and "Better you than me," had served him well for a lifetime, and he saw no need to change now that a whole army was coming to kill him. But even he couldn't find delight in the enemy's slaughter. Only Ulrich, Melville's fierce coxswain, could continue to watch the enemy's death and destruction with undiluted pleasure.

> The daylight lay in ashes
> On the blackened western hill,
> And the dead were calm and still;
> But the Night was torn with gashes—
> Sudden ragged crimson gashes—
> And the siege-guns snarled and roared,
> With their flames thrust like a sword,
> And the tranquil moon came riding on the heaven's
> silver ford.

All too soon, the tide began to turn. Slowly but surely, inexorably, the enemy fought back. At great cost they emplaced siege guns. Vast batteries, battalions and brigades of siege guns, howitzers and mortars began to strike back at the besieged city. And the tide of public opinion began to turn. Each Stolsh soldier who died renewed the defender's determination, each civilian killed rekindled their hatred.

The curs had taught Melville to hate. Now they were teaching the Stolsh to hate. It was a lesson the Guldur taught well.

Each night the enemy attacked. Each night the assaults grew fiercer, ever more terrible and ferocious. The defenders' guns became worn, the crews grew weary, but the seemingly inexhaustible Guldur hordes attacked fresh each night.

> What a fearful world was there,
> Tangled in the cold moon's hair!

Man and beast lay hurt and screaming,
(Men must die when Kings are dreaming)—
While within the harrowed town
Mothers dragged their children down
As the awful rain came screaming,
For the glory of a crown!

The enemy counterfire became increasingly accurate. The defenders' guns were destroyed. Their crewmen died. Raw civilians filled the gaps and helped man the guns. Women bore ammunition up to the guns. Children carried water to their fathers and brothers.

Melville sighed and shook his head as he watched the defenders respond with shock and anger to their losses. It was as if they couldn't comprehend what their enemy would do to them. As though the reality of death and horror couldn't be grasped until it was upon them.

Early in World War II, back on Old Earth, Nazi Germany launched a series of aerial bombing attacks that became known as the Battle of Britain. These attacks on civilian targets accomplished little except to harden the hearts and steel the resolve of an entire nation, and it was this resolute determination which Churchill embodied in his famous speeches.

Islamic extremists made the same mistake early in the twenty-first century, launching attacks on civilian targets in the United States. These attacks unleashed the vast might of that huge, powerful nation in ways that the terrorists never dreamed possible.

Now the Guldur bombardment of the Ai population centers was having the same result. But the most resolute, determined people in the world could still be defeated. They just made the price higher. So they fought, and they died. And died. And died. Each day, as dusk fell, the ragged, exhausted, shell-shocked defenders wondered how they could survive another night.

It was then that the Honorable Milton Carpetwright chose to call Melville to his office. Closed curtains. No coffee. One question.

"Piss on golf?" a bemused Melville repeated.

"Yes. That's what he said. My marine detail seemed to think it was funny. Just what did he think he was doing, talking to me that way?"

Melville's brain spun, grasping for a way to communicate the concept. "Sir," he began, "you're from a mid-tech colony of Old Earth, so you may not understand the history behind the phrase. 'Piss on golf' is a term, a catchphrase, a political slogan. We studied this at the academy. The concept goes back to 1349 when King Edward III of England told the citizens of London that their 'skill of shooting' was being neglected, and he proclaimed that 'every one of the said city, strong in body, at leisure times on holidays, use in their recreation bow and arrows, or pellets or bolts, and learn and exercise the art of shooting . . . that they do not, after any manner apply themselves to the throwing of . . . handball, football, cambuck, or cockfighting, nor suchlike vain plays which have nor profit in them.' You see sir, the playing of such 'vain' pursuits is considered to be a sure sign of decadence in most worlds."

"Well," he blustered, "that's ancient history! None of the great leaders of any developed world would ever think that way!"

"Perhaps, sir. But many would consider Teddy Roosevelt to be one of the greatest leaders of the twentieth century, and he said, while he was President, that: 'We should establish shooting galleries in all the large public and military schools, should maintain national target ranges in different parts of the country, and should in every way encourage the formation of rifle clubs throughout all parts of the land . . . It is unfortunately true that the great body of our citizens shoot less and less as time goes on. To meet this [challenge] we should encourage rifle practice . . . by every means in our power. Thus, and not otherwise, may we be able to assist in preserving the peace of the world. Fit to hold our own against the strong nations of the earth, our voice for peace will carry to the ends of the earth. Unprepared and therefore unfit, we must sit dumb and helpless to defend ourselves, protect others, or preserve peace. The first step—in the direction of preparation to avert war if possible, and to be fit for war if it should come—is to teach our men to shoot.'"

The consul simply sat, with his mouth open, trying to digest this.

"Do you see, sir? In essence, what Teddy Roosevelt and King Edward III are saying is, 'Piss on golf.'" Melville continued, relentlessly, "most scholars believe that when the population starts playing games with no actual application to survival skills, and when they displace swordsmanship and shooting sports, then that's a certain sign that they have become decayed and are deserving of contempt. That's why, when you asked Ranger Westminster what was his 'secret,' he said the secret was to 'piss on golf.' It might overstate the position for rhetorical purposes, but that honestly *is* the standard answer. If you spend most of your time and energy on such pursuits, then in the minds of many people, it is a waste of human talent."

"Well," said the little man with a self-deprecating smile and a wave of his hand, "in my case, I have so little talent when it comes to golf that I'm not really wasting all that much." For just a moment Melville found himself liking the diplomat, as he continued earnestly, "Do people really think that way? Do they think that we are decayed and worthy of contempt if we aren't into shooting or fencing?"

"Well sir, there is nothing wrong with any sport, but if you spend most of your leisure time and take inordinate pride in these trivial sports then, perhaps, yes. And if your culture considers these 'vain sports' to be a higher good, while suppressing or deprecating the skills that contribute to a society's survival, then yes, across the galaxy such a world is subject to a degree of contempt. You think the Stolsh, or Sylvan, or any other major society respect you when you take them out on the golf course? The truth is just the opposite. Anyway, sir, let us hope the Stolsh have been living by that standard, because very soon now, our survival will depend upon the shooting skills of the average Stolsh militia member."

So the morning flung her cloak
Through the hanging pall of smoke—
Trimmed with red, it was, and dripping with
    a deep and angry stain!
And the day came walking then
Through a lane of murdered men,
And the light fell down before her like
    a cross upon the plain!
But the forts still crowned the height
With a bitter iron crown!
They had lived to flame and fight,
They had lived to keep the Town!

And they poured their havoc down
All that day . . . and all that night . . .

Each morning when the dazed defenders looked out at the swarming, teeming enemy they felt despair, yet still they fought. One night the enemy finally succeeded in gaining a major bridgehead across the river, a salient that couldn't be dislodged, and the Guldur began to work their way up the slopes. Now vast numbers of hastily trained riflemen and musketeers manned the ramparts and added their fire to the withering barrages that swept down the bluffs. Yet still the enemy advanced.

So they stormed the iron Hill,
O'er the sleepers lying still,
And their trumpets sang them forward through the
    dull succeeding dawns,
But the thunder flung them wide,
And they crumpled up and died,
They had waged the war of monarchs—and they died
    the death of pawns.

The sailors—Stolsh, Sylvan *and* Westerness—spent most of their time on board their ships waiting for any possible attack upon the Pier. They were under orders to stay out of the ground battle. They wouldn't tip the balance much on the ground. Barely trained militia could man the ramparts almost as well as a sailor.

Only Melville's two rangers were active in the front lines, happily serving as snipers to wipe out enemy gun crews and key leaders. Technically this was disobeying his orders, but the rangers' unique status as elite, attached, ground troops made this acceptable in his mind. Also, although it was dangerous on the battlements, Melville couldn't bring himself to stay away, and the Stolsh and Sylvan admirals were often there beside him.

As the battle unfolded it became increasingly clear that they would be defeated. The defenders' only real option was to hurt the hateful enemy as much as possible and then evacuate, and only well-trained sailors could do that. Militia couldn't fight through the blockading armada. And soldiers couldn't evacuate beloved family members. But first they would make the enemy pay, and pay, and pay.

But the forts still stood . . . Their breath
Swept the foemen like a blade,
Though ten thousand men were paid
To the hungry purse of Death,
Though the field was wet with blood,
Still the bold defences stood,
Stood!

Then one night at moonrise the Guldur king came to look upon that which he had wrought. He was a huge cur upon a white horse, dressed in a red-trimmed gray uniform. Surrounded by an elite cavalry regiment, he came down to the river's edge. All along the line the Stolsh cannons paused as the mortal personification of their foe looked across the river and gazed up at the bluffs. Arrogantly, without a flag of truce, he surveyed the battlefield.

And the King came out with his bodyguard
    at the day's departing gleam—
And the moon rode up behind the smoke
    and showed the King his dream.

For a moment the grim battle ceased, and only the constant, tragic cry of the wounded echoed down the slope. A writhing sea of maimed and wounded, crawling over the dead, envying the dead, cried out to their king.

Three hundred thousand men, but not enough
To break this township on a winding stream;
More yet must fall, and more, ere the red stuff
That built a nation's manhood may redeem
The Master's hopes and realize his dream.

Beside the Guldur king, riding as an equal, was a figure wearing a hooded black robe. Who could have dreamed that such a target would appear? Melville cursed and wished that his rangers were here, but they were contributing to the battle as snipers now; which was a daylight activity, and they were back at the ship getting some well deserved rest. The two BARs with expert gunners would have cut the enemy force to ribbons, but the precious BARs and their few thousand rounds of ammunition weren't here.

They were being held back out of danger, for a key, future battle. Melville cursed himself. Who could have imagined that an opportunity like this would arise!

He yearned to give the order to strike down that distant figure, but only Broadax and Ulrich and his squad of marine bodyguards were with him. He grabbed a rifle from a nearby Stolsh soldier and took aim. Westminster or Valandil might have made it, but it was virtually an impossible shot for him, or for his marines. Nevertheless, he would try. He would do his best.

"On my command, open fire on the enemy leader!" he called out to his marines, and they eagerly leaned or knelt against the walls to take careful aim.

"No! Don't!" shouted the Sylvan admiral beside him. "We do not wage war on leaders."

Ulrich and Broadax gave synchronized snarls and drew their weapons, turning their backs to their captain, facing the surrounding Stolsh and Sylvan leaders and staff officers. The squad of Westerness marines never wavered as they waited patiently for their captain's order to fire.

"Haven't you figured it out yet?" asked Melville. "War as you know it is over. Now you battle evil itself. Before you is an enemy who is no respecter of kings. They murdered our captain under a flag of truce, and they'll do the same to you. Here is an enemy who will intentionally, remorselessly butcher men, women and children, and then make the survivors envy the dead. You can no longer play by the old rules. Strike! Strike with every gun and pray that you slay your foe!"

The Sylvan admiral and the Stolsh commander exchanged glances. "He is riight," said the ancient commander, sadly. "The oold ways aare goone." With a deep, booming voice he continued fiercely, "Ie willl diee with this cityy, and befoore Ie diee Ie willl killl everyy Guulduur Ie caan! Aalll caannoon, aalll rifles, aat myy commaand, yoou willl fire aat the enemyy commaander!"

Many of the cannon had already been shifted to bear on this new target, the rest shifted eagerly, swiftly. The riflemen waited impatiently. The word rippled down the ramparts. Finally, as the moon rose and the enemy force began to pull back, the old general gave his order, in a deep booming voice, "FIIRE!!" Such a command would have echoed like a gunshot across the wide river valley, but in this case his "echo" was a vast array of cannons and muskets roaring out defiance and hate.

Melville and his bodyguards joined in the fusillade firing at the distant target. The Guldur bodyguards around the king staggered and fell. His mysterious, hooded comrade turned his horse and raced away. The king himself had his horse shot out from under him. He scrambled over the mounds of Guldur dead. He was a little gray louse upon a great, vast corpse. Then he disappeared into the darkness as a cloud came across the moon.

> One barrow, borne of women, lifts them high,
> Built up of many a thousand tragic dead.
> Nursed on their mothers' bosoms, now they lie—
> A Golgotha, all shattered, torn and sped,
> A mountain for those royal feet to tread.

[illegible]

[illegible] the darkness [illegible] and I came [illegible]

One burrow, one [illegible]
[illegible]
[illegible] on their [illegible]
[illegible]
[illegible]

Chapter the 13th

Rear Guard: *Not* the Be-medalled Commander

Not of the princes and prelates with
  periwigged charioteers
Riding triumphantly laureled to lap the
  fat of the years,
Rather the scorned—the rejected—the men
  hemmed in with spears;

"A Consecration"
John Masefield

The next morning a cold rain swept down from the north. On that tragic morn the Guldur's Orak allies joined the attack and the walls of Ai finally fell. As the rain and cold swept away the sweltering heat, so did the Orak forces sweep away the brave defenders of the last Stolsh stronghold on Ambergris, and drive them from their world. No one had known that the Guldur were allied with the Orak, but now they understood who it was that rode beside the King of Curs as an equal.

If the Guldur were canine derived, then the Orak were from porcine stock. Pigs, swine, hogs, and porkers, they were called, but in reality they were like huge boars standing upright, with sword, shield and tusks rending all before them.

The same ancient, Ur-civilization that seeded the galaxy with human, Sylvan and Dwarrowdelf to live on worlds with varied gravities, and Stolsh to live on aquatic worlds, had also chosen to wander farther afield in their genetic manipulation of the basic human stock. The Guldur were a strange cross of human and canine, but they were still far more man than dog, just as the Orak were more human than porcine. Most of these races could, reputedly, interbreed. Just as all the diverse breeds of canines or felines could generally mate and reproduce, although some such matches were reported to produce only sterile "mules."

Little was known about the Guldur, and even less about the Orak. They were from a distant part of the galaxy, far to the galactic east of the Guldur's star empire, and this was one of the elite divisions of that vast distant realm. The presence of this new enemy added a frightening new dimension to the war.

They must have been staged and ready to attack long before their leader came out with the Guldur king to survey the battlefield. Their attack was perfectly equipped and prepared, and it broke the back of the Stolsh defenders in less than an hour.

In the streets of Ai, chaos reigned.

There was one narrow street leading up to the Pier, and he stood astride it like a colossus. He was the biggest Stolsh Melville had ever seen, dressed in full armor, like some ancient knight. Every surface was polished to a mirrorlike luster, reflecting the rainy skies in dismal splendor. When he stepped forward and shook hands it sounded like a brass band rolling gently down a steep hill. Shaking his armored hand was like grabbing a sack of large bolts.

He was Marshall DuuYaan, the commander of the Stolsh rear guard. He'd seen combat on many worlds before, and his people called him the "bravest of the brave." Now Melville and his small force of sailors and marines were attached to him for this final defense. Melville had volunteered his men, and he was accepted with the same admonition that the Westerness consul had given him, "Doo noot becoome decisivelyy engaaged. Yoour ship willl be neeeded sooon."

The sudden fall of the city walls caused their carefully conceived, complex plans to collapse. Most of the preselected refugees had struggled through the panic-stricken mobs to the Pier, but they needed time to board and escape from the rapidly advancing enemy forces. The rest of the city's occupants, the vast majority of the remaining Stolsh population on Ambergris, were fleeing into the hinterland. But they, too, needed time to escape.

Time. It was all about time. Napoleon is reputed to have said, when asked by one of his generals for more time, "Ask of me anything but time." In war, time is almost always purchased with lives.

Much of DuuYaan's ad hoc force was already defeated and destroyed in desperate street battles. They'd traded their lives for time. Time for their wives and children to escape. Elite forces had been held in reserve for this mission, but now the rear guard was a tangled remnant of screaming, dying creatures battling in the street as Melville and DuuYaan looked on.

Melville watched in awe, with tears in his eyes as they died. No one ran, no one panicked. Each defender was a hero to the end. No, it was *not* about the "princes and prelates with periwigged charioteer." It was about *these* men . . .

> The men in tattered battalion which fights till it dies,
> Dazed with the dust of the battle, the din
> and the cries,
> The men with the broken heads and
> the blood running into their eyes.

They'd been pushed back to the final wooden bridge leading up to the isolated high ground where the Pier was located. Engineers were arriving to rig the bridge for demolition. Below them a brook, now flooded with rainwater, gushed through a deep ravine. To their rear, on the far side of the bridge, a battery of light howitzers was being positioned to cover the approaches.

Immediately in front of the two leaders was a four-way intersection. Straight ahead was the battle, behind them was the bridge. Refugees flowed into the intersection from the left and right, and fled over the bridge. These were the ones who had been selected for evacuation. The rest of the city's citizens were headed into the swamps, marshes and coastlines of the outback. There were only three choices in the city that day. Escape to the Pier, flee into the wilderness, or die at the hands of the vast numbers of Orak, Guldur, and Goblan who were murdering, looting, tormenting, burning, molesting, torturing, raping, and eating everything in their path.

The rain pelted down and Melville shivered in his tattered blue wool uniform jacket. After the stifling heat, the impact of the cold front felt even more bitter than it actually was. Added to the shock of sudden defeat, the cold rain seemed to reach in and freeze men's hearts.

Melville's men stood behind him on the bridge, pressed to one side as the refugees flowed past. He and Petreckski, his two young lieutenants, four midshipmen, twelve marines, and two corpsmen all carried .45s. Von Rito and Kobbsven each had a BAR and an assistant gunner carrying extra magazines. Broadax and the two rangers brought up the rear with a reserve of ten marines. Each marine carried a bayoneted, double-barreled muzzle-loader, and a bandoleer of grenades. Each warrior also had a monkey, holding a belaying pin in its upper two hands.

The engineers were scrambling to rig the demo charges on the bridge's wooden support structures. This should have been done before, but the sudden collapse of the city's defenses had caught them by surprise.

"Ie knoow thaat yoou haave oorders too noot becoome decisivelyy engaaged," DuuYaan boomed out to Melville.

Yeah, yeah, he thought. *I'm getting tired of hearing those words.* But they *were* his orders, and he intended to follow them.

"Buut," the huge, gleaming Stolsh commander continued, "wee aapreciaate whaatever yoou caan doo foor us."

"We will be here as long as you'll have us, or until someone makes us go away. Either way I promise it'll be exciting," Melville said with a grin.

Even as he spoke, the flood of fleeing refugees dropped to a trickle, and the defending forces fell back from all directions. Left, right, and center, the retreating Stolsh rear guard now was pushed back into the intersection in one great heaving, dying mass of defenders.

An educated eye could tell that the defenders were losing heart. The engineers needed a few precious minutes to prepare the bridge for destruction. After fighting for every inch of city streets, the Stolsh rear guard was starting to crack. *Dear God,* thought Melville, *they have been magnificent.* But now, when they needed just a few more minutes, they were going to lose it all. That's how so many battles have ended up over the centuries. So close, so very close.

All they needed was a few more minutes. Now was the time for the leader to commit his last reserve: himself.

"Thoose aare myy men, aand theyy aare dyying. Ie muust jooin them," said DuuYaan, drawing a long sword and cinching up his shield. A group of Orak broke through the line and he charged straight into them. The armored behemoth hit the enemy line with an impact that sounded like the brass band had rolled to the bottom of the hill and fallen into a deep ravine. In an instant his gleaming armor was coated with black powder, blood, and viscera. The men around him gained strength from his presence, the line stiffened, and they fought on for a few more precious minutes.

Steven Pressfield wrote historical novels about ancient Greece. He wrote with such scope and power that his works became required reading for military men across the generations. He'd written about what happened at moments such as this. . . .

> Someone put the query, "How does one lead free men?"
>
> "By being better than they," Alcibiades responded at once.
>
> The symposiasts laughed at this . . . even our generals.
>
> "By being better," Alcibiades continued, "and thus commanding their emulation. When I was not yet twenty, I served in the infantry. Among my mates was Socrates the son of Sophroniscus. In a fight the enemy had routed us and were swarming upon our position. I was terrified and loading to flee. Yet when I beheld him, my friend with gray in his beard, planted his feet on the earth and set his shoulder within the great bowl of his shield, a species of eros, life-will, arose within me like a tide. I discovered myself compelled, absent all prudence, to stand beside him."

Yes, thought Melville, *that's what is happening here. I'm seeing something ancient and powerful unfold before my eyes.* This is what Pressfield meant when he wrote: "A commander's role is to model *arête*, excellence, before his men. One needs not thrash them to greatness; only hold it out before them. They will be compelled by their own nature to emulate it."

And so they were. And so they were, for a little while.

DuuYaan was like a lighthouse, his men anchoring themselves around him as they were whirled and tossed by the storm. Then they were swept away and he stood alone.

Melville's men were in a battle line with eighteen .45s up front and a BAR on each flank. He had himself, Petreckski, the two corpsmen, and the rangers immediately behind the line. Broadax and her squad of marines stood in reserve behind them. The two rangers were already picking off enemy sharpshooters who were moving onto the roof lines, firing double-barreled rifles as fast as the ten marines could load them. Behind them the engineers still worked desperately with the demolition charges.

"Ready . . . FIRE!" Melville roared, and the battle line cut loose with a withering fusillade. Each of the eighteen .45-armed warriors on the battle line had a round in the chamber and seven rounds in the magazine. In just a few seconds, 144 .45 rounds were expertly fired into the enemy. It took less than a second to slam a fresh seven-round magazine into place and release the slide, then 126 more slugs plowed into the enemy. Then another mag change, and 126 more.

But the real killers that day were the two BARs, sending magazine after magazine of .30-06 rounds scything into the enemy mass on full auto. Each high-powered, copper-jacketed bullet punched through several bodies, greatly multiplying their contribution to the death that day, as Von Rito and Kobbsven plied their twenty-pound weapons with almost supernatural strength and skill.

Bullets are not magic. If you point a gun and pull the trigger, the bullets will not seek out living creatures with some preternatural, malevolent intelligence. Some people seem to believe this, and those people usually die quickly if they're unfortunate enough to get into a gunfight. In reality, just an eighth-of-an-inch elevation of a pistol barrel (the height of a front sight blade) at five yards is the difference between hitting an opponent between the eyes and having the bullet pass harmlessly over an opponent's head. At twenty-five yards, the same eighth-of-an-inch elevation in the front of the barrel would cause a bullet aimed for the heart to fly ineffectually over an enemy's head, and just a quarter-inch depression of the barrel at that range could cause a bullet to plow harmlessly into the ground. It takes a trained, skilled, determined warrior to kill consistently and well with a pistol, and *that* was exactly the kind of individual who stood on the firing line that day.

Each warrior held his pistol out in a firm two-handed stance, and then gently, carefully, lovingly pressed the trigger. "Two things you should never hurry in life," Fielder told them in their training, "A good woman and a trigger. Both will give you the result you want in their own time. Rush either and you'll be very frustrated." And so they silently repeated the mantra of all armed professionals since repeating firearms were invented: "Front sight, press trigger gently. Repeat as necessary."

Added to the physical effect of the thousands of bullets firing rapidly and accurately downrange was the impact of the noise. Again Melville thought of Lord Moran, the great military psychiatrist, veteran of both World Wars on Old Earth and author of the seminal book, *The Anatomy of Courage,* who had called Napoleon "the great psychologist." And Napoleon truly got it right when he said that the psychological, or "moral," factors were three times more important than the physical.

In this case the physical impact of the lead flying into the enemy ranks was tremendous. But the psychological effect of the sudden noise, flash, and concussion was even greater.

The effect of the two BARs was particularly potent. Its muzzle velocity of around 2800 feet per second, triple that of a .45, created intense concussion and noise for anyone downrange as it punched through the atmosphere at supersonic speeds. Its cyclic rate of fire of about 550 rounds per minute meant that the BAR tore through a 20-round detachable box magazine in under three seconds. Each magazine was like a burst of sustained thunder. Like a shattering, prolonged bolt of lightening.

Melville's tactics instructor, Major Johan Farnham, a master of all aspects of weapons, had taught them about the BAR in the academy. His words came flowing back, in one of those distracting thoughts that can come up in combat. "Aside from its weight, the BAR's only major drawback is its lack of a quick-change barrel. In order to sustain a high rate of fire, a machine gun needs to be able to quickly change barrels, or it needs a water-cooled jacket. I doubt you'll get much more than five magazines out of a BAR at its max rate of fire without risking a stoppage due to overheating." In this case, in order to maintain a sustained fire, his two BAR gunners both burned off four magazines and then started firing in short bursts, picking off particularly aggressive or excessively brave enemy attackers. Firing in careful bursts like this reduced the chance of a malfunction due to overheating.

The enemy line faltered and began to stagger back under this sustained psychological and physical onslaught. Out in front of them, only Marshall DuuYaan still stood among the Stolsh. The members of the firing line all worked hard to prevent hitting the Marshall. The good news was that so far no one had shot him in the back. The bad news was that the area immediately around him contained a high density of surviving enemy troops, and finally he was overwhelmed and brought down just thirty feet in front of them.

The enemy masses began to slowly surge forward again, in spite of the withering fire. Melville looked over at the Stolsh engineer commander. "Five minuutes!" called out the harried engineer. "Dear gods, juust five moore minutes is aall we need!"

It has been proven over and over again, that the attack is psychologically more powerful than the defense. And it is a fundamental principle of combat, that the best time to retreat is after a successful attack. Numerous great commanders, when hemmed in from all sides, have been able to gain a needed respite through a vigorous attack. The Guldur and their Orak allies were on the offensive from the beginning, and thus far they had not been the recipient of any deliberate, decisive assault themselves. Now Melville was determined to buy those five minutes, and to give the enemy a taste of their own medicine. Hell, he could even give his men a mission, an objective to focus the attack around.

"On my command!" bellowed Melville, "the line will rapid fire and advance to within point-blank range of the enemy! The reserve will cut through the center and rescue the marshall, then we will pull back to the bridge." He looked at Broadax, who rolled her cigar to one corner of her mouth and gave him a nod of understanding coupled with a grin of absolute bliss. On her helmet her monkey capered gleefully. All along the line the firing eased as the warriors changed magazines so that they could launch the attack with a full weapon.

The enemy began to surge forward with renewed vigor as the fire ebbed. They were about twenty feet away when Melville stepped through the line, manhandling men to the left and right to create a gap for Broadax and her lads to come through. "Charge!" Melville roared, stepping steadily forward and firing his pistol in a two-handed grip as rapidly as he could bring the sights on target. The shots didn't even register, all that existed was: *Front sight, press trigger. Front sight, press. Front sight, press. Front sight, press. Front sight, press. Front sight, press. Front sight, press. Front sight, press. Change magazines!*

As he drew closer, accuracy became easier and his rate of fire increased. *Frontsight,presstrigger. Frontsight,press. Frontsight,press. Frontsight,press. Frontsight,press. Frontsight,press. Frontsight,press. Changemagazines!*

To his left and right every other individual armed with a .45, including the corpsmen, was doing the same, and on the wings Kobbsven and Von Rito burned several magazines of .30-06 ammo at their max rate of fire.

Against an enemy armed with repeating, breech-loading rifles, a pistol-armed force such as Melville's wouldn't have survived. But this enemy was armed with muskets (most of those now empty) and bayonets, with an occasional sword or muzzle-loading pistol. A force equipped with .45 autos, supported by a few BARs, (not to mention the bullet-catching monkey on each back!) had a tremendous, decisive advantage against this enemy.

The men of Westerness advanced to just outside bayonet range, pressing the trigger as rapidly as they could bring accurate fire, and at this range that was *very* fast. Then the enemy was treated to Broadax, two rangers, their dog, and ten marines sallying forth from the battle line like a high-pressure hose plowing through an anthill.

But before Broadax charged, she had her reserve lob their "cheater." Fielder had put it this way in their training, "The Most Important Rule of a Gunfight is, *always cheat*, because there are no second-place winners in a gunfight." *This* was their cheater.

Ten fragmentation grenades, then ten more, and then ten more soared over the firing line as they advanced. While the third volley was still in the air, but before the first volley exploded, Broadax told her marines, "Boys, we're gonna charge through the gap when the second volley explodes! Then we's gonna snag the lizard in the tin can, an' bring 'im back!"

Private Jarvis, standing at the end of the file of ten marines, began to whimper quietly to himself. *Yer jist the one we needs, Sarge sez. Saw action wit da bayonet on Broadax's World she sez. Good, broad-shouldered farm stock she sez. Jist the sort I needs behind me on this one she sez. Oh God, get me out of this alive and I swear I'll go back to the farm and never leave.*

"Sarge, er, sir," squeaked Jarvis, "I don't think this is a good idea!"

Then the first volley of grenades detonated among the enemy horde, "CHOOM-OOM-OOM!!" with massive concussions hurling Guldur, Goblan and Orak into the air with magical ease.

"Don't try ta think, son, ye'll hurt yerself," said Broadax, patting as far up Jarvis' back as she could reach.

With that, the second volley went, "CHOOM-OOM-OOM!!"

"Come, on, ye bastards!" roared Broadax, "ye wanna live forever? Yeeeeee-Haaaaw!" This was accompanied by the screeching howl of her monkey, standing on top of her helmet and beating its chest with four little fists. Her ax hit the enemy like a machete through soft bamboo, just as the third volley of fragmentation grenades exploded, several ranks back in the enemy lines.

"CHOOM-OOM-OOM!!"

The six guns of the Stolsh light howitzer battery on the other side of the bridge opened fire, ripping canister rounds into the wings of the advancing enemy mass in a rolling volley. "CRUM!CRUM! CRUM!CRUM!CRUM!CRUMPP!"

The enemy was now confronted with a variety of new experiences, all of them bad. Thirty grenades were exploding in their midst. A battery of artillery was shredding them. A firing line full of semi-automatic pistoleros, supported by two automatic rifles, was advancing toward them. And now cold steel was penetrating into their ranks. All without warning, after a series of successful attacks. The only thing most of the attackers had to respond with was a muzzle-loader that they'd previously fired and hadn't yet gotten around to reloading . . . what with the mad rush and all.

Intelligent members of most species could adapt to almost anything . . . given enough time. Indeed, that might be considered one of the major definitions of intelligent life. Adapting fast enough though, that's the trick. It's the unexpected, the unanticipated, that usually gets you in life. Or death.

A fountain of red follows Broadax's path into the enemy as her marines struggle to keep up. The marines quickly fire both barrels of their muskets and are now slashing and thrusting with bayonets, their monkeys working madly to block incoming bullets and blades.

An enemy blade is barely deflected up from Broadax's face to her helmet by the sadly overworked monkey on her shoulder ("urkk!") where it's further deflected up with a resounding "Clonggg!" Her small heavy skull might be confused and over-taxed by the complexities of "ossifer" duties, but it was designed by ages of selective breeding to be remarkably resistant to falling rocks and ax blows. She shrugs off the hit with little more than a brief instant of cross-eyed distraction, and then she eviscerates her opponent with a quick, upward, backhand slash of her ax.

The stunned enemy formation is rocked backward by this combination of unexpected blows. The ones in the front are retreating. The ones in the rear will eventually start pushing back. There is always a potential for compression in most substances, and compression is exactly what is happening to the attacking enemy forces. Many of them are packed together too tightly to fight effectively, almost none of them have room to reload. Can't fight, can't reload, can't run. The remaining option is to . . . die.

"Dear God I do love the Marines!" Broadax cries up to the rain-filled skies, or perhaps to her monkey, as her ax continues to cut great swaths through the enemy amidst a shower of blood and viscera. Emphasizing every sentence with a sweep of her ax, punctuated in gore and cigar smoke, her monkey working overtime to protect her from bullets and blows, in her deep, gravelly voice she continues her battle chant (with her monkey adding its terrified soprano counterpoint). "Every day's a holiday! (Eeek!) Every meal's a feast! (Eeek!) Every paycheck's a fortune. (Oook!) Every formation's a parade! (Aaak!) An' every battle's an adventure! (Urk?) IN THE MARINES!!"

Now she is standing over Marshall DuuYaan. She clears a space with a horizontal, knee-high sweep of her ax. Curs and piggies, pruned at the knees, are pushed back to flop on the ground by a hedge of marine bayonets. Amazingly, the huge Stolsh marshall is still alive, amidst a pile of his dead soldiers. Broadax heaves him to his feet. (The lead cymbalist, who had climbed up the ravine, fell back onto the toiling percussion section.) A broken sword is dangling from his hand. Now they begin to pull back, the stunned, dazed "lizard in a tin can" staggering and stumbling back with them. (. . . causing the brass section to lose their grip, just when they'd climbed halfway up.)

Broadax chuckles grimly as she looks at the bedraggled, reeling marshall, "Did anyone git the license number of that truck?"

Not the be-medalled Commander,
beloved of the throne,
Riding cock-horse to parade when
the bugles are blown,
But the lads who carried the battle and
cannot be known.

Melville began the battle with an ammo bag slung hanging on his left side, chock full of loaded .45 magazines, all carefully set in, upside-down, bullets pointed forward, ready for rapid reload. Now the bag was almost empty.

With Broadax and her marines safely behind the firing line, and a few precious minutes having been bought, they began pulling back to the bridge. Broadax had her boys chuck three more volleys of frag grenades into the enemy mass, "CHOOM-OOM-OOM!!, CHOOM-OOM-OOM!!, CHOOM-OOM-OOM!!"

A huge Orak plows through the enemy mass, hurling his own troops left and right to get to the front. His drug-hazed eyes focus on Melville, and he charges.

Oh no, *thinks Melville,* why do the big ones always have to home in on the leaders?

His foe is charging with a big cleaver in one hand, and a shield in the other. Just the enemy's bloodshot eyes and yellow, bristle-covered forehead are visible, peering out over the top of the shield.

The front sight is covering the forehead and . . . _____! A blue hole appears amidst the bristles in the yellow forehead. Again the front sight comes up, this time he covers the hole (aim small miss small!), and . . . _____! A second bluish hole appears right next to the first. Vivid red blood begins to trickle out of the two holes and the huge Orak's eyes cross as though trying to look up at the wound. But he keeps lurching forward, cleaver still raised.

Melville has a moment of panic and despair. If ventilating his skull didn't work, what would? He'd heard rumors about an Orak battle drug that gave their elite fighters great strength and endurance, and the ability to sustain horrific wounds. Now here it was, literally staring him in the face with bloodshot eyes. Indeed, the dribbling wounds in his forehead gave new meaning to the term "bloodshot eyes." Such drugs have often been used in warfare. Fielder had actually addressed this possibility in his class, quoting the semi-mythical Saint Clint the Thunderer, "People ask, What do you do if the bad guy's on drugs? Shoot 'em! But what if it doesn't work? Shoot 'em some more! More lead, more dead!"

Now the enemy was barely six feet away, staggering forward with a host of other foes following him like the tail on a comet. In a split second Melville would be in range of that huge cleaver. The Orak drops his shield just a little and roars in defiance, exposing his two yellow, upward thrusting tusks. Mouth shot. Front sight. Don't jerk the trigger . . . we will fire no projectile before its time . . . prresss trigger and . . . _____!

Brains explode out the back of the foe's head. He has one last, confused, distracted look on his piggish face, then he falls forward. Melville has to skip sideways to avoid having the cleaver chop into his leg.

Melville stops and takes stock for just a split second as he changes magazines. The other members of the firing line are picking off the remaining close-in enemy. Another volley of grenades explodes in the enemy's midst. The BARs roar. The artillery to their rear thunders.

Keith Kreitman, a veteran of Old Earth's World War II, was once asked to describe pitched close combat in words. "Impossible!" he replied. "Because it is all encompassing, six dimensional, from the front, the left, the right, ricochets from the back, exploding shells from above and shaking ground from below. One actually 'feels' the combat in the body.

"It involves blurred vision from sweaty eyes, the acrid choking smell of layers of gunpowder smoke, ear bursting horrific noises, the kinetic nerve vibrations from exploding mortars, hand grenades and shells, the screams of humans, the cries of the wounded, the piercing whine of ricochets of bullets and shrapnel, hiding behind or stepping over bodies of perhaps someone you know. All at one time.

"No media can ever duplicate it.

"No mere words can ever convey it . . .

"But, once exposed to the heat of it, it welds you into a bonding, not only with friend, but foe, that no one else, no matter how close to you, will ever be able to share."

Yeah, thought Melville, *there was a lot of that going around today.*

There was a brief respite as the enemy kept staggering back. Melville turned to Petreckski, who had just spoken to the engineer commander and was now standing beside him. "Any thoughts?" he yelled.

"Yes, sir," he shouted into Melville's ear "The engineers say they're ready, and there is another 'Thou shalt not,' in the Bible besides the Ten Commandments. 'Thou shalt not be afraid for the arrow that flieth by night, nor for the pestilence that walketh at noonday.' So let us fear not, and get the hell out of here!"

"Volley grenades, and fall back!" Melville shouted, looking back at Broadax to be sure she heard. She smiled, nodded, echoed the command, and the reserve all hurled a grenade.

The reserve, positioned back behind the firing line, was better able to hear and respond to this command. Around Melville the command was echoed, but many members of the firing line were concentrating so hard that they didn't hear the order. These individuals were manhandled back by their comrades, or grabbed by the reserve, and in a matter of seconds the entire line was falling back at a dead run. Melville popped a smoke grenade to cover their retreat, as did Petreckski and a few other leaders.

They raced across the bridge, the medics supporting a few wounded, the BARs bringing up the rear. As they left the bridge, the far end exploded, sending a cloud of wooden shards spinning into the sky. For a brief instant the debris seemed to hang in the sky, and then it came sailing back down. Giving substance to the water drops, and a new meaning to the term "a hard rain."

Melville watched with wonder and horrified admiration as some of the engineers were launched into the air with the explosion. Bits and pieces of them came down with the debris. The rain greatly increased the possibility that fuses might not work, so they didn't take the time or the risk to rig the bridge to be blown from afar. Instead the engineers set off the explosion while some of them were still on the bridge. They'd traded certain death for the absolute certainty that the bridge would be destroyed.

Others may sing of the wine and the wealth
    and the mirth,
The portly presence of potentates goodly in girth;—
Mine be the dirt and the dross, the dust
    and scum of the earth!

They ran their weary way up the final slope to the Pier with a steady, shuffling gait, the healthy supporting the wounded. Behind them the artillery battery was punishing the enemy as they tried to make their way down the steep ravine, across the rushing stream and back up again. Eventually they'd make it, but by then the fleet would be gone.

As he trotted up the road Melville began to realize that he was wounded in several spots, spots which began to ache now that the battle was over. On the way Melville conducted a head count and, miraculously, all their troops were with them, although most of them were wounded. A close inspection of the monkeys' belaying pins disclosed the great number of hits that had been deflected by their little friends. The secret of the monkeys' ability was now well and truly out of the bag.

At the top of the hill the Stolsh admiral, the high commander of the forces on Ambergris, met Marshall DuuYaan. With tears streaming down his face the old admiral looked down the road and then faced his marshall. "Where is myy rear guaard?" he asked.

The marshall tore off his mangled, blood streaked helmet and tossed it to the ground with one final, sad "clunk." Drawing himself to his full height in his dented, besmirched armor, he replied, "Sire, *I* aam the rear guaard."

"'Ere now. Wat about us, damit!" muttered Broadax, "I seem ta recall 'at we was there too!"

"Aye," replied Hans, "an' all the other boys 'at died out there; the great, glorious, God damned, magnificent bastards."

And Melville whispered to himself,

> "Theirs be the music, the colour, the glory, the gold;
> Mine be a handful of ashes, a mouthful of mould.
> Of the maimed, of the halt and the blind in
> the rain and the cold—
>
> "Of these shall my songs be fashioned, my tale be told.
> Amen."

Then they boarded their ship. The Stolsh had considered destroying the Pier with demolitions charges after the last refugees boarded. Denying this valuable resource to their enemy would have been tactically and strategically wise. But they couldn't bring themselves to destroy an ancient, living creature that had served them well and faithfully across the years. They were as likely to destroy their world, another living creature that had befriended and aided them across the centuries. They *would* return, and when they did, old friends would be waiting for them.

Fielder had already taken their share of the refugees aboard. Many new hands had flocked to join *Fang*'s crew during their period on Ambergris, and most of them had already been integrated into the crew. Now the first officer took charge of getting the ship under way while Melville saw to their wounded. The captain would be needed to command his ship if the Guldur opposed the evacuation fleet, but for now he must see to his injured shipmates.

Melville insisted that the worst cases be tended to first. Finally it was his turn. Through the dim haze of his pain he saw Lady Elphinstone and smiled. *Ah, now for an encouraging word. One medicinal dose of ancient, soothing Sylvan wisdom, coming up . . .*

"Thee again?" she said, looking at him with a warm, sad smile that belied her words.

"I think it was George Bernard Shaw who said, 'I want to be thoroughly used up when I die.' "

"That may be sooner than ye think. Hast thou not learned that people die here?"

"Thanks," he replied. Responding to her expression and not her words he returned her smile and forgot his pain for a moment. "I needed an encouraging word. You're a good friend."

"One does what one can. So, can I have thy stuff?"

Chapter the 14th
Transition: The Rose is within the Thorn

O wad some Power the giftie gie us,
To see oursels as ithers see us!

Robert Burns

The honorable Milton Carpetwright didn't make it to the Pier for evacuation. Shutting the curtains and cocooning inside his office meant that he and his staff didn't get sufficient warning of the collapse of the defenses. His squad of marine guards did discover the danger, however belatedly, and tried to evacuate him. He dithered, and then he died, taking most of the consulate down with him. Pretending that the outside world doesn't exist proved to be bad policy. Sooner or later the big bad old world will come knocking at your door, or knocking it down, as the case may be.

Only one of his marine guards had managed to fight his way out, and that was the redoubtable Corporal Petrico. Mighty tales were already being told of his blazing pistol craft, with a .45 in each hand, as their dwindling band of marines tried to carry the diplomat to safety. They had fought every step of the way, but the hapless, incompetent consul had been his own undoing in the end.

"Cap'n, we tried ta keep dat pockin' diplermat alife. We did," said the little armorer in tears. He was stretched out in their operating room as Lady Elphinstone tended to his many wounds. "Bud 'e wass usaless. If'n 'e coulda 'elped jist a lidder bit we mida safed 'im. Bud da pocker dinkent no one end off a pistul frum da udder. He wass dedd wate. Dedd wate. It wass like pissin' up a rope efer step a da way. Wit dem mawdikkers cummin' at us conskantly."

"It's not your fault, Corporal," said Melville kindly. "You did all you could."

"Aye," said Fielder bitterly. "Less time on the golf course and more time on the range. *That* is the recipe for survival. Any man who doesn't follow it deserves what he gets, and God *damn* him for every good man he takes down with him."

Melville hated to speak ill of the dead, but in the end that summed it up and all he could do was nod.

Aside from Corporal Petrico, only one other consulate staff member was successfully evacuated from Ambergris. He was that rarest of creatures, a citizen of Old Earth. Cuthbert Asquith XVI had decided to make a foray into two-space, to see "primitive, exotic worlds." Upon being contacted by the government of Earth, the Westerness foreign ministry was happy to oblige by giving Asquith what seemed to be a safe billet in a sleepy little consulate. So it was that Asquith purged his body of all nanotechnology, reversed some minor gene engineering, and arrived on Ambergris just in time for some of the excitement he thought he was seeking.

He happened to be at the Pier, checking the plans for the consulate's accommodations on board *Fang*, when the world came unglued. Needless to say, he was eager to go home. He was *not* enjoying his little adventure, and was attempting to share his unhappiness as he sat at his first dinner in the wardroom.

"I know all about your precious, low-tech worlds! Every citizen of Earth is taught, from the earliest ages, how you people live. Yes, we know all about how you live. You usually get married in June because you take your yearly bath in May and still smell pretty good by June. But your brides still stink, so they carry a bouquet of flowers to hide their body odor."

The members of the wardroom were enjoying his diatribe. It was the best entertainment they'd had since their marine lieutenant bounced the first officer off the bulkhead.

"Your annual bath consists of a big tub filled with hot water.

The man of the house gets to bathe first, in the fresh, clean water, then all the other sons and men, then the women and finally the children."

"'Ere now!" said Hans in mock indignation. "'Ave you been looking through our windows again?"

Undetered, Asquith continued. "Last of all is the babies. By then the water is so dirty you people can actually lose someone in it. That's where the saying, 'Don't throw the baby out with the bath water,' comes from."

The mess members' faces were aching from their efforts to avoid open laughter. This *was* a guest, and it wouldn't be polite to laugh at him, even if he *was* a total prat.

"Aye," said Hans, leaning back in his chair and shaking his head with a look of mock consternation as he sat at dinner. "'Tis true. We lose more babies 'at way."

"Yes!" said Asquith, oblivious to the derision all around him. "And your houses have thatched roofs, nothing but thick straw piled high, with no wood underneath. That's the only place for animals to get warm in the winter, so all the dogs, and the cats and the mice and bugs live in the roof. When it rains, your roofs get slippery and sometimes the animals slip and fall off the roof. Thus the saying, 'It's raining cats and dogs.'"

"Yeah, it's true," drawled Westminster. "Once, back home when ah was a kid, a big old yeller dawg came skittering off the roof in a hard rain and killed mah little brother. So sad."

Their corporate spirits were high. The blockading Guldur fleet hadn't offered battle. Perhaps in part because of the relieving Sylvan fleet that hung just over the horizon, ready to join in. And in part it was probably the sight of *Fang* closing in on them, with all her vast array of "laundry" hanging out, that convinced them to exercise the better part of valor. The enemy now owned Ambergris, why worry over a few refugees?

With the boundless boorishness and bad manners of the truly well bred, Asquith continued. "Since there is nothing but straw to stop things from falling into the house, this means that bugs and other droppings can fall through. This is especially a problem in the bedroom, so you use a big, four-poster bed with a sheet hung over the top to keep the bugs off. That's how canopy beds came about."

Petreckski nodded his head, poured himself some wine, and said,

"Aye, I hate it when all those bugs fall on you while you're sleeping." The purser was in a contented, cheerful mood. He'd sold the cargo of saltpeter from Pearl at a very good price on Ambergris. Then he had bought a huge assortment of trade goods at fire sale prices from fleeing Stolsh merchants before leaving Ambergris. These would be the last trade goods to come from that world, or any Stolsh world, for a very long time, and they should bring good prices on Osgil. Truly, war had been profitable for him.

"Aye," added young Lieutenant Archer, getting into the spirit. "Once a cat came right through the roof, tore plumb through the canopy netting over their bed, and onto my ma and pa. You should'a heard the howling and shouting that night."

Asquith used a pencil to take a note on the pad that he always had with him, and then continued. "And your floors are bare dirt. Only the wealthy have anything besides dirt on the floor, that's where we get the saying, 'dirt poor.'"

"That's where that came from?" said Tibbits, the carpenter, as he finished off his dessert. "I always thought it was because, during real hard times, when we didn't 'ave any food, sometimes momma used to make us eat dirt."

"'Eat dirt,' mumbled Asquith in fascinated horror as he jotted down more notes, then he continued. "The wealthy have slate floors that get slippery when they're wet, especially in the winter, so you scatter leftover stems of grain, called 'thresh,' on the floor to help keep your footing. As the winter goes on, you keep adding more thresh until when you open the door it can all start slipping outside. So a piece of wood is placed in the entranceway, hence, a 'thresh hold.'"

"I wouldn't know about that," said Barlet, their gunnery officer. "We was all too poor to have any of that fancy stuff. How about you, Mr. Fielder, did you have one of them fancy-pants 'thresh-old' jobbies when you was a kid?"

Fielder wasn't participating in their game. Lamenting the loss of his .45 auto and keeping a careful eye on Broadax was preoccupying him at the moment. The .45s and BARs were brought on board (couldn't leave them to the enemy!) where they'd quickly become pieces of junk. He found comfort in the double-barreled two-space pistol tucked into his sash, and never went anywhere without it. In response to the gunner's question Fielder just waved his hand deprecatingly and said, "the bottle stands by you, Mr.

Crater," as Asquith continued in his fatuous deconstruction of Westerness civilization.

"I suppose it's also true, as reported by many observers, that you cook in the kitchen with a big kettle that is always hung over the fire. Every day you light the fire and add things to the pot, mostly vegetables and not much meat. Usually you eat stew for dinner, leaving leftovers in the pot to get cold overnight and then start over the next day. Sometimes the stew had food in it that's been there for quite a while. Hence the rhyme, 'peas porridge hot, peas porridge cold, peas porridge in the pot nine days old.' "

"Aye, you've got us on that one," said Tibbits. "Matter o' fact, we do that on board ship here. No telling how long the chow you just et's been cookin'."

Asquith actually shuddered in horror as he looked at his empty plate and continued. "Sometimes you get pork, which makes you feel special. When visitors come over, you hang up the bacon to show off. It's a sign of wealth that a man can 'bring home the bacon.' You cut off a little to share with guests and all sit around and 'chew the fat.' "

"Yep," said old Hans, "Many's the evening we sat around chewing the fat with friends. 'Course, when ya ain't got no fat, we could always chew bark."

"Those with money have plates made of pewter. Did you know that food with a high acid content can cause some of the lead to leach onto the food, causing lead poisoning and death? This happens most often with tomatoes, so I bet you still consider tomatoes to be poisonous."

They looked at each other in mock wonder and horror, sipping their after-dinner wine as they listened.

"Most people don't have pewter plates, but instead they use trenchers, a piece of wood with the middle scooped out like a bowl. Often trenchers are made from stale bread which is so old and hard that it can be used for quite some time. Trenchers are never washed and a lot of times worms and mold get into the wood and old bread. After eating off wormy, moldy trenchers, one would get 'trench mouth.' "

"Damn," said Tibbits, "*that* explains it. I'm glad we have high-tech friends like you to enlighten us, Mr. Asquith."

He nodded condescendingly and continued. "Your bread is divided according to status. Workers get the burnt bottom of the loaf, the family get the middle, and guests get the top, or 'upper crust.'

"You see," he continued, "we know all about your 'retroculture' and where it leads. Often lead cups are used to drink ale or whiskey. The combination can sometimes knock people unconscious for days. It's common to mistake such an individual for dead and prepare them for burial. They're laid out on the kitchen table for a couple of days and the family gathers around and eats and drinks and waits to see if they'll wake up. Hence the custom of holding a 'wake.'"

"Aye," said Hans. "I remember when my uncle Bob got in such a state. We thought 'e was a gonner 'til he woke up in the middle o' 'is own wake! Gave us all a start, I tell ya. Then he proceeded ta drink all the likker ever'one brought ta the wake. He said if ya needed the hair o' the dog 'at bit ya fir a hangover, then ya needed the whole damn'd *hide* o' the dog 'at kilt ya!"

"Yes," said Asquith after the laughter died down, "it happens more often than you'd think in your low-tech worlds. We have a report from one area where they dug up coffins to move to a new location. When they reopened these coffins, one out of twenty-five coffins was found to have scratch marks on the inside. They realized that they'd been burying people alive! So that's why you tie a string on the wrist of the corpse, lead it through the coffin and up through the ground and tie it to a bell. Someone would have to sit out in the graveyard all night (this was the 'graveyard shift') to listen for the bell; thus, someone could be either 'saved by the bell' or they're considered a 'dead ringer.'"

All the members of the mess smiled genially as they heard this, but their smiles disappeared when the earthworm continued.

"But the saddest thing about your so-called civilization is this fixation with our long-outdated Earth literature. Especially your infatuation with Jay Tolkien. On Earth we know that he was a kook, a religious fanatic with views and values long since discarded by reasonable people."

Suddenly the members of the mess were deathly quiet. They all set down their silverware or wine glasses and leaned forward in their chairs, looking intensely at their guest, and cutting glances to Mr. Fielder, waiting for him to say something.

"Sir," began Fielder. "As the president of our little mess, I must tell you that you have gone astray. I respectfully request that you drop the topic, or we will reach the point where your only options are a duel or an apology."

"Apology? What have I got to apologize for? If you people can't handle the truth, that's your problem. You should be apologizing for your sad civilization."

Petreckski shook his head and tried to reason with the earthworm. "We are amused by your application of a witty piece of fifteenth-century Earth history to us. The truth is that our culture is based on a society that is several hundred years more advanced, and the field of hygiene and medicine is the one area where we draw selectively from more advanced cultures. You, from your one sad little world can say whatever you want about our kingdom, spanning thousands of worlds. But sir, when you speak of our respect, nay veneration, of J.R.R. Tolkien, it is like insulting our religion. Religion and politics are topics which gentlemen can agree to disagree about, and set aside from polite conversation. In your ignorance you have gone across the line, and a simple apology will be accepted with a willing spirit."

"Apology? You pathetic bunch of neanderthals! Let me just ask you one thing. So where are the Hobbits? Eh? Where are the damned Hobbits in your little delusion, your cultish fixation! You found an existing situation, overlaid this sad Tolkien template on reality, and convinced yourselves you are living it. Deluding yourselves that it is prophecy, but it's really a self-fulfilling prophecy!"

"Very good, sir," said Fielder leaning back in his chair with a pleasant smile. "Then honor presents no option but a duel. As Robert Heinlein put it, 'An armed society is a polite society.' We *are* an armed society, and we *are* a polite society. You of course have choice of weapons. The mess will choose its champion to respond upon the field of honor."

"Duel!? Duel?! I have a life expectancy that's several hundred years long. You think I'm going to risk it in some primitive duel? You can all be damned!"

"Very well," Fielder replied, pointedly leaving the "sir" out this time, his lazy smile still in place. "Then you are no longer welcome in this mess. You can take your meals with the men, but I give you fair warning: try any of this insulting foolishness with them and they will simply thrash you. Now leave, or I will ask the mess steward to throw you out. You are no longer a gentleman, and it is beneath the members of the mess to lay hands upon you. But we will happily ask the steward to do so."

Cuthbert Asquith XVI looked up at the two sailors who materialized beside him, grinning eagerly, looking for any excuse to toss the boorish earthworm out on his ear.

"Yes, I'm leaving," he said, "But I'm going straight to the captain." He stormed out, just as Lady Elphinstone was coming in from making her rounds in sickbay.

"My," she said, "he didn't last long."

Melville was quietly content with his lot in the world. The promised draft of Sylvan topmen were aboard and they were performing admirably, along with the other new crew members they had picked up on Ambergris. *Fang* had received top priority for a full-scale refitting in a major dockyard, and she was happy. They'd turned a tidy profit in their trading. And, in spite of his sincere efforts to close with the blockading fleet, the enemy had declined his invitation to come out and play. He'd led the evacuation fleet and chased away the Guldur blockade without scraping the smallest patch of paint, or harming so much as a single hair on a single crewman's head.

Sun Tzu, around 500 B.C., said that the ultimate trick in warfare was to defeat your enemy without having to fight them. One of the commentaries several hundred years later said, 'But if you do, who will declare you valorous?' Well, at this point in his life Melville didn't feel the need for someone to declare him valorous. He'd done his best to engage the enemy, and he could find satisfaction in the fact that his crew and passengers had come out of danger without harm.

Even his passengers weren't a significant problem. The Stolsh refugees were painfully appreciative, and only too happy to oblige any request. In fact, the female members were a bit *too* eager to please, and Melville kept his marine guards busy keeping the crew and the refugees separated. On a long voyage this would have been awkward, but on a short trip such as this it was little more than a pleasant diversion filled with relatively harmless flirtation. A bit of a preview of what awaited the returning heroes when they finally were given shore leave on Osgil.

Another major source of pleasure for Melville, and for the entire ship, was the state of improved relations on the quarterdeck. Fielder had never shown open disrespect to Melville, but the newfound regard he demonstrated toward the captain since the battle of Ambergris, their walking together and their regular consultations hadn't gone unnoticed. Melville and his first officer also found a mutual delight in trim paintwork, perfectly drawing sails, squared yards, and flemished ropes. After their stay in the Stolsh shipyard, *Fang* had never in her existence looked better and the two officers took great pride in their beautiful ship. A pride that their crew shared as they sailed trimly in and out and around a vast fleet full of Stolsh and Sylvan admirers.

Of course, there was still one major area in which *Fang*'s captain and her first officer would probably never see eye-to-eye. Melville's delight in his ship's appearance was greatly surpassed by his zeal for taking the whole beautiful, fragile edifice into righteous combat with an evil and less esthetically inclined enemy, who would do far more than just mar her paint given the opportunity. Needless to say, Fielder strongly disapproved of this sentiment, but in the end Melville *was* the captain.

Yes, Melville had been content with his world. Until this little roly-poly earthworm came into his office and started "demanding" things.

He weighed his options carefully. One course of action which he considered seriously was to have Ulrich kill the little toad and have his body slipped quietly overboard. As pleasant as that prospect was, his sense of duty and his common sense both argued against it.

"Sir," he said, with careful, measured tones. "You are a diplomat, and you should understand the need to respect the cultural mores and taboos of those around you. Especially on board a ship, where men are at each other's throats for months on end, such civilities are particularly important. There are many harsh, draconian things we must do at sea, but across the centuries we've found them to be essential to survival. Do you think that you can force them, that you can *browbeat* them into agreeing with you? Believe me, you cannot. All you can do is to generate greater and greater degrees of animosity every day. Therefore it's a reasonable and cultured compromise simply to agree to leave disagreeable topics alone."

Melville was trying very hard to be reasonable, but he was getting the impression that it wasn't working. Still, he continued, "If you aren't willing to apologize, or to accept the offer of a duel, then your only option is to mess with the crew. Or with the rest of the refugees, who are eating with the men."

"I'm under no obligation to honor the superstitions of a primitive society. And if they don't want to listen to the truth, that's their problem. Civilized men should be able to discuss matters."

"Yes, but if you cannot agree, then civilized individuals respect each other's differences and avoid disagreeable topics. When told that this topic was disagreeable, insulting, and offensive to your messmates, you continued to pursue it. Which is a perfectly acceptable course of action, as long as you're willing to give satisfaction to any offended parties."

"Then be damned to you!" shouted Cuthbert Asquith XVI, as he stalked out of the captain's office.

The ship sailed on, riding herd on a convoy of military and civilian vessels, integrating their new crew members, and training. Always, ever training. Some captains would have their men grumbling at such incessant training drills, but not this crew, and not this captain. They'd learned to love their young captain, as they'd learned to hate their enemy, both emotions forged in the crucible of battle.

Every day they fired weapons great and small, or lowered boats, or conducted contests to set sail. This was just their captain's way, and they loved their captain. QED. The Stolsh and Sylvan warships around them watched, and began to realize that the combat achievements of *Fang* and her crew were not a fluke.

There was much visiting between ships. The captain's jollyboat was lowered and his coxswain, Ulrich, commanded the crew that took the *Fang*'s officers to dinners on Stolsh and Sylvan ships. These meals were a great pleasure, but most enjoyable of all was when *Fang* entertained guests. The Fangs all took great pride in their Ship and they loved showing her off to visitors. They grinned in delight when their Stolsh and Sylvan guests shuddered upon feeling the faint tingle of feral energy upon touching her Moss. The crew were particularly pleased when their visitors looked up in wonder at her royals and studdingsails.

Hans saved the spritsail-topsail, royal studdingsails and moonsails for when they needed a burst of speed. Most of the time they swept back and forth, from one end to the other of their vast array of civilian cargo and passenger ships, constantly alert for Guldur attackers. Their cutters, under the command of their young lieutenants and midshipmen, were active in cross-loading medical supplies and food to refugee ships.

Their surgeon, Lady Elphinstone, was given one of the jollyboats to be used at her discretion. She used it to move about the fleet like an angel of mercy, descending upon those who needed her the most, ably assisted by Mrs. Vodi and her two corpsmen. By the time they arrived at Osgil, she had visited every single ship, some of them several times, tending to illness and wounds.

Meanwhile their earthworm diplomat sulked and stayed out of the way. Melville worried briefly about what Asquith would say to the ambassador, then he set the matter aside. He was content to live for the moment, and the moment was good.

The young captain again had the topic of civilized behavior brought before him during a meal he was hosting for Lady Elphinstone, his two young lieutenants, the sailing master, the carpenter, the gunner, and his four midshipmen.

The purser's successful trading endeavors had generated enough discretionary cash for the wardroom and the captain to purchase food and luxury items on Ambergris. These items made it possible for the captain and the wardroom to engage in the ritual of inviting each other to meals.

In this case it was a pleasant breakfast with Melville's youngest officers, his warrant officers, and middies. Along with the always agreeable company of Lady Elphinstone, the meal made for a welcome break in the ship's routine. The middies were scrubbed pink and all the guests had their tattered, worn uniforms cleaned and pressed as neatly as possible.

Young midshipman Aquinar brought the matter up. It was pure happenstance that Fielder and Broadax were missing, which provided the opportunity for him to ask his question.

"Sir," he asked, still an innocent young boy in spite of the numerous battles he'd seen, "what is meant by the term, 'a Weber?' "

Melville sopped up the last of his egg yolk with a crust of toast, chewing it and washing it down with a drink of his tea as he thought, then he leaned back in his chair. "First I want you to understand that it's a low term, a term that's impolite to use. It denigrates one of the greatest of the classical writers. Men whose works have endured and inspired for centuries, well, such men are far greater beings than we will ever be, and you might as well use the Lord's name as an insult, as far as I am concerned."

"I meant no offense, sir," said the boy, blushing.

"I'm sure that you didn't and no offense is taken. *Some people*, and I emphasize *some*, have held that the idea of a great, giant, beautiful female warrior is an abomination. A commercial pandering to the vapid yearning of a portion of the market. A squalid bid to attract female readers. Even if this is true, and I'm not ready to concede it, to denigrate the works of a great author just because one of his most popular characters seems unrealistic, *that* my friend, is the real abomination. And besides, that's what fiction is all about, an outlet to fulfill your fantasies."

"But sir, is the idea of a great female warrior really so unrealistic?" asked the boy, sincerely confused. "After all, we have Lieutenant Broadax."

"Aye, indeed we do, and here's to her," Melville replied, raising his tea cup in a salute, "one of the greatest warriors I've ever had the privilege to know. The point is, I guess, that there *are* great female warriors out there. And they *can* make significant, unique contributions. But they're seldom beautiful, *especially* not the ones from high gravity worlds. At least they aren't beautiful in the traditional sense. Whatever youthful beauty they *might* have had fades quickly. Even a woman bears the scars of battle. And they are cumulative."

He grinned self-deprecatingly and continued. "Hell, for that matter, most of us are no blushing beauties. Look around you. Scrawny me with half an ear missing. Gnarly old salts, hulking marines, and awkward boys. With the singular exception of Lady Elphinstone here, most of *us* wouldn't win any beauty prizes." Around the table his guests grinned and raised their cups to each other in mock salutes.

He took his pistol out of his sash and carefully set it on the table, barrel pointed safely back and to his left. "Most of the great female warriors wouldn't win a beauty contest. For that matter, most warriors of either gender usually don't survive over the years just because of their looks. They're like my pistol here. This weapon has been in my family for generations, constantly at sea. It is short, squat, and deadly as hell. The uneducated eye would call this weapon ugly, but it's beautiful to me. Perhaps a little like our Broadax. She may not be a beauty in the eyes of the world, but I love her all the more for it. As the poet said, 'verily, the rose is within the thorn.'"

Chapter the 15th

Unhappy Lords, Who Dare Not Carry Their Swords

> They have given us into the hand of new
> unhappy lords,
> Lords without anger and honour, who dare not
> carry their swords.
> They fight by shuffling papers; they have bright
> dead alien eyes;
> They look at our labour and laughter as a tired man
> looks at flies.
> And the load of their loveless pity is worse than
> the ancient wrongs,
> Their doors are shut in the evenings;
> and they know no songs.
>
> "The Secret People"
> G.K. Chesterton

"Osgil," sighed little Aquinar, who was currently serving as the signal midshipman. "At last we are among friends. Finally we are safe."

"Aye," said Lieutenant Archer, who was the officer of the watch.

Then he continued, not unkindly, "Now get on with your duties, Mr. Aquinar."

"'Governor welcomes *Fang*. Should be happy to see captain, wardroom, and midshipman's berth at sixteen o'clock,'" said the little signal midshipman to the officer of the watch, who relayed the message to the captain, five feet from its source.

"Very kind of him, I'm sure," replied Melville with a voice and continence that communicated dismay. "We cannot refuse. Please reply, 'Many thanks, accept with pleasure: *Fang*.'" They were at the main Pier of Osgil, which rose out from Flatland on the upper side. He turned to his first officer who was standing beside him. "Mr. Fielder, you know the moorings here as well as anyone, so carry on."

The officers looked at each other in consternation. They were in no condition to meet with the governor, no matter how well meaning the invitation. The only uniforms they owned were the ones they were wearing when they'd come over from *Kestrel*, and these had seen multiple battles since. Their tattered uniforms weren't a source of shame in the heat of battle on Ambergris. But the humiliation that awaited them here filled them with dread.

There was one possible solution. Melville moved quickly to the upper fo'c'sle where his two rangers, his purser and his surgeon stood looking at the vast Pier. Elphinstone immediately perceived that something was amiss. "Why hast thou such a long face, Captain?" she asked.

"My lady, we've been invited to dinner. The governor has kindly invited the wardroom and the midshipmen to dinner, but while our ship is fit for an admiral's inspection, our uniforms are in tatters and we aren't fit to see any decent folk. I turn to you for succor. I couldn't refuse the invitation without giving offense, but if you went immediately to the governor and explained our situation, perhaps he'd understand?"

"My captain," she replied with a sad, kind smile and just the hint of a tear, "thou are the mightiest hero to come to Osgil in many an age. The city is thine. Thou hast but to ask, and it shall be done. By dinner tonight we shall have ye *all* in new dress uniforms of the finest quality."

The Westerness Navy's tradition of feeding its midshipmen on ship's stores (to the extent that it fed them at all, apart from their impoverished private stocks) led to a group of young men who were eternally hungry and obsessed with food. The local time and the ship's time were out of synch, and the meal was several hours later than they were accustomed to. So it was that the captain and his officers were very hungry, and their poor midshipmen were truly famished.

Thus the Fangs approached Government House slavering with greed, groomed, shaved and shined to the highest degree, after a kaleidoscopic day of fitting and primping. True to her promise, Lady Elphinstone had turned out a small army of tailors. These professionals quickly decided that the basic Westerness naval uniform was so similar to that of His Majesty's Twenty-First Sappers as to make no difference, that the hats of the Northern Militia would do quite nicely with just a little reshaping and by changing the hat bands, and that the shoes of The King's Own Outer Guard were absolutely identical to the Westerness standard. The advantage was that all of these local uniforms were ready made, and on the shelf, as were suitable shirts and stockings. By simply transferring the buttons and insignia from the old, tattered uniforms, they got the job done in a single afternoon, and had time to measure the rest of the crew for new uniforms as well, save for the twelve tailors and two cobblers who worked overtime to have Lieutenant Broadax's uniform done in time.

The end result was the very essence of perfection and of far better quality than most of Melville's men were accustomed to. Only the individuals going to the Governor's dinner had been taken care of today, but within a few days the entire ship would turn out in uniforms of the same quality.

Throughout that first triumphant meal, Melville tried to control his midshipmen's rapacious assault upon their food. His task was aggravated by the fact that Sylvan food wasn't completely satisfying to races whose metabolisms were designed to function in higher gravity. The midshipmen consumed great quantities of vegetables and mushrooms and whole flocks of small birds, and yet they still weren't satisfied. Melville was fearful lest their culinary covetousness should get them off on the wrong foot with their hosts, but it soon became clear that his concerns were groundless. In the eyes of the Sylvans, they could do no wrong.

The next few days were dedicated to bringing in fresh water and nonperishable stores, so that they could leave at short notice, as was expected of Her Majesty's Ships. When that was completed, Melville prepared to release his crew for shore duty. Only the barest skeleton crew would be left with the Ship. The crew lined up for a partial pay on their way down the gangplank, "So's the lads'll 'ave a li'l walkin'-around money," as Hans put it.

The crew was lining up for their pay when Melville became aware that his monkey was gone. On the few occasions that it left him it never went far, so he looked around for it. Then he realized that everyone around him was also looking for their missing monkeys. He experienced a moment of surprisingly intense fear and loss. Most of the little creatures had appeared from nowhere, and there was suddenly the fear that they could disappear just as easily. He had a sickening sense of just how much the little creatures would be missed if they were truly gone.

"There they is!" shouted a voice. There was a period of bewilderment, followed by laughter when it became apparent that the monkeys, every single one of them, were queuing up at the end of the line, waiting patiently for their pay.

Okay, thought Melville, *I can handle this. The important thing is not to lose them, to make them full-fledged members of the crew and give them an obligation to stay with us.*

Melville jogged up the steps to the quarterdeck, turned and addressed his crew. "Shipmates," he began, "We've been through some hard times, and some remarkable adventures. You are *all* professionals. You have proven it over and over again. You have made us proud. Now isn't the time to let that professionalism lapse. Now is not the time to bring shame upon your Ship. Take your pay, go out, and have a good time. You'll find that the people of Osgil are grateful and generous. Your pay will go far. *All of you*," and here he made a point of pointing to the entire mass, and especially the monkeys, trying to make eye contact with them, "will be required to report for formation, here at dockside, every morning at eleven o'clock. Most of you should be able to stagger out to the ship by then." This drew appreciative laughs. "If you do not report for formation, you'll be reported AWOL. Again, you have all served us honorably and well. Do not let your Ship down now. As you take the King's coin, you accept your responsibility as servants of the crown."

Then he turned specifically to the monkeys, pointing at them as he continued, "The monkeys will be paid as ship's boys, third class. You'll be on shore leave like everyone else, and you'll be required to report for formation like everyone else. *Do you understand?*"

There was a brief, pregnant pause, then all the monkeys hopped up and down, screeching joyfully. This was immediately echoed by the crew's cheers. Melville stood with his hands on the quarterdeck rail and watched as his men were paid, then the boys. Finally the monkeys, with comic dignity, each took their pay as they strode down the gangplank and were unleashed upon the good citizens of Osgil.

From this point on, their experiences were a whirlwind of grand balls and parties in flets perched high up in the vast trees of Osgil. Even the three-quarters Earth gravity of the planet added to their sense of lighthearted joy.

Osgil was faced with a vast war, unlike any they'd experienced before. It was being called the Two-Space War, and it had begun with a series of unparalleled disasters and defeats for the Sylvan and Stolsh. The Sylvans had every cause to fear the future. But while they dreaded the path before them, they also found joy in the one great victory that they'd enjoyed, and the heroes who bought that victory for them.

The Sylvans knew how to greet returning heroes. It was in their heritage. It was their tradition to reward deeds of great valor. It was even in their new philosophy inspired by classic Earth science fiction. "TANSTAAFL," the Fangs were told repeatedly. "'There ain't no such thing as a free lunch.' Aye? Well this be no free lunch, young sailor. Thou hast *earned* it."

A Fang's money wasn't accepted here. Night after night, every member of the crew was wined and dined somewhere. Down to the lowliest seaman, they told the tale of their battles over and over again, with bread crusts and wine stains on tabletops. They never grew weary of the tale, or the open hearts and open arms that awaited them afterwards.

Even the monkeys were accepted with open arms. Osgil was a sophisticated galactic port. Over the centuries a wide assortment of alien creatures had arrived at her docks, and Osgil took "*Fang*'s Monkeys," as they quickly became known, in stride.

During the whirl of balls and parties that he was invited to, Melville found himself being repeatedly paired with Princess Glaive Newra. Slender and barely five foot tall, she was strawberry blond, with the most remarkable peaches and cream complexion, and an impish sense of humor that charmed and delighted him. She was actually the granddaughter of the King of Osgil. One of many, many granddaughters, barely fitting under an extended definition of the title of princess. But she was the very personification of a princess to him. He tried hard to keep his defenses up, yet whenever he was with her he truly felt like a knight, as though he were *her* paladin, dedicated to protecting and serving her kingdom and her civilization.

The Westerness embassy, on the other hand, had no experience with knights or paladins, no tradition of rewarding heroes. For a week, every message to the Westerness ambassador went unanswered. The ambassador would be obligated to be present when Melville went before the king. But that was one audience that hadn't occurred yet, even though it seemed like he'd met every other member of the royalty.

His lack of contact with the embassy troubled him. There was a sense of unseen wheels spinning. Decisions were being made in hidden chambers. Battles were being fought all around him, but for once Melville had no idea what to do, how to fight, how to make a difference in this struggle. So he was resolved to make as many friends as he could, to be as polite as he could to as many people as he could, and to live for the moment. And the moment was good.

Then a marine courier arrived at his inn with a message directing him to report to the Westerness ambassador at thirteen o'clock the next day.

It was 12:30 in the afternoon when he turned off of a wide boulevard and entered into the gateway to the embassy grounds. Large portions of the planet didn't support the vast root structure for the towering forests that the Sylvan race preferred to live in. In Osgil the embassies, the Pier, the inns for visitors, many shops, taverns and the extensive "disreputable" district, were all mixed together in such an area. Off in the distance Melville could see the giant trees, rising like a wall of green skyscrapers marking the downtown district of some high-tech world. Last night he'd been dancing at a ball held high in a flet in one of those trees.

Melville missed the comforting, companionable weight of his monkey on his shoulder, but found some solace in his impeccable uniform. A marine guard stood at the open iron gate, his red uniform contrasting splendidly with the white wall and the green grass. Melville noted that he was apparently unarmed. The guard saluted him with obvious recognition and pleasure, and directed him to the main entrance of the large stone building that housed the embassy. It was most gratifying to be known, to have a good reputation among the troops.

He was striding along in the three-quarters gravity, crossing the grassy, tree covered grounds in the uniform of a lieutenant in the Westerness Navy. Black shoes with silver buckles, white pants, sword and belt chased in gold, and a blue jacket with gold plated buttons and a gold washed, brass epaulet on his left shoulder. After all the time spent barefoot aboard ship, on Broadax's World, on Pearl, and on Ambergris, his shoes still felt strange.

At the building's entrance there were two more unarmed marine guards. The sight of unarmed individuals on guard duty made him sad and uneasy. Whoever was in authority here was the kind of wretched, pathetic individual who didn't trust, respect, or appreciate the young warriors who were trained and willing to fight and die for them. Again he was saluted with apparent pleasure, then the embarrassed guards asked him to leave his sword with them. This was unusual. Armed individuals were commonplace on Westerness, at all military bases, and everywhere he'd traveled on Osgil. Yet here, in the one piece of Osgil that was actually a part of Westerness, he was immediately disarmed. The guards assured him that it was nothing personal, no one was permitted into the embassy with weapons.

He was escorted through wood-paneled hallways that were weakly illuminated by gas lights. Then he was led into a waiting room where he . . . waited. It seemed to him that he'd waited for over an hour. There was no clock or window in the waiting room and he didn't have a watch. No sailor would ever spend money on an object that would instantly become a piece of junk upon entering two-space.

Finally, a nondescript, wizened old clerk took him into the ambassador's office. No coffee, no seat offered. Just a darkened room, a wide desk, and the glowering, scowling presence of the ambassador, who possessed the unlikely appellation of Sir Percival Incessant.

If I had a name like that, thought Melville, *I might be pissed off at the world, too.*

Melville stood quietly before the desk and the ambassador shuffled papers. Everything about the diplomat communicated the fact that he was obviously a very busy man, far too busy to be troubled by this trivial occurrence. Then he looked up, and cut directly to the point.

"Lieutenant, you have caused us an enormous amount of trouble. Do you see this stack of paper? It represents the mass of complaints and charges brought against you. First we have a complaint from the Guldur embassy. They were, er, sent packing by the King of Osgil several weeks ago, but not before they had the chance to communicate to us their dismay at your unprovoked attack and seizure of one of their ships. They demand the return of the ship and all their captured sailors."

He was an odd little man. Almost as though he were trying to play some archetypal role. He was wearing a dark suit, with a pair of reading glasses perched halfway down a large nose that might have been inherited from an unhappy eagle, or perhaps a vulture, somewhere in his family lineage.

"Then we have a complaint, also from the Guldur embassy, delivered shortly before their, er, departure, demanding that you be delivered to them for the unprovoked sinking of several of their ships off of Ambergris."

He looked at each piece of paper as though it were a worm in his salad.

"Then, through diplomatic channels, we have a complaint from the King of Guldur himself, stating that you participated in hostilities on Ambergris. Apparently they hold you, and members of your crew, accountable for the deaths of what is, I must admit, an improbable number of their military leaders."

His eyes grew slightly wide and he held the next piece of paper at arm's length, as though it were going to bite him.

"And then, most remarkable of all, through diplomatic channels, we have a complaint from the Eman of Orak. It seems that they hold you and your crew accountable for the deaths of many of their soldiers during the, er, recent, unpleasant occurrences on Ambergris.

We do not even have diplomatic relations with them. Their vast empire is an immeasurable distance away, and yet somehow you seem to have contrived to have personally killed one of their senior officers, a distant member of their royal family. The details are remarkably precise. Apparently you dispatched him with . . . er, two bullets in the forehead and a bullet in the mouth. They state that the precise placement of the bullets could have happened only as a result of what was clearly an execution-style slaying. Ahm."

He looked up at Melville with horror and amazement, holding another piece of paper as he continued.

"And during your return trip you seem to have threatened and gravely offended the senior surviving member of the Westerness consulate on Ambergris, who *just happens to be a citizen of Earth!*" The exertion of this last statement apparently left him winded, and he drew several deep breaths before he could continue.

"Lieutenant, we have spent hundreds of years building a star kingdom based on trade, and studiously *avoiding* any involvement in the affairs of the Elder Races. Where disharmony rules, commerce flags! Now you have created *more* disharmony, you have done *more* harm to our relations, you have caused *more* diplomatic emergencies *in one voyage*, than the rest of the history of Westerness *put together*! The vast empires of Guldur and Orak, and the diplomatic representatives of Earth are all very, very angry. In one . . . brief . . . period of time, you have managed to get a sizable portion of the galaxy very, *very pissed off at you*!"

Again he had to draw several deep breaths before he could continue, using a handkerchief to mop his brow and to wipe the fine spray of spittle from his lips and chin.

"Here is what you are going to do, *Lieutenant*. You will recant. You will write a personal apology in response to every single one of these letters. You will state that these were unprovoked attacks, conducted by you, without authority. You will beg for their mercy. If you do that, then we will not turn you over to them, and we will not punish your crew. Instead we will ship you to Westerness, where you will face trial and punishment by your own people. Do you understand?"

There was a roaring in Melville's ears. The dark little room seemed to close in upon him. His crew. They would punish his crew. He could save his crew, all the brave men and women who suffered and served so nobly. He could save them if he cooperated.

All he had to do was to tell this little man's lies. Sacrifice himself, and his crew was safe.

It was his duty. It would be so easy to accept failure, to simply die and let it end. Here was his lawful authority telling him to surrender, and he was a good sailor, an obedient officer, a *disciplined* warrior. It would be so easy, but something in him couldn't give up. Something made him struggle against the fate that this little man had decreed for him. His duty was all he had. Obedience was his duty. What could be more important than duty.

But wait. The enemy was obedient. The Guldur commander who murdered his captain, he was just doing *his* duty. The enemy was just obeying orders. And still the enemy was evil. So what was the difference? The difference was Honor. A code of honor. Decency, nobility, gentleness . . . all of that was in the warrior's code of honor.

There *was* something more important than duty. It was honor. How did Shakespeare put it? "Mine honor is my life; both grow in one; Take honor from me, and my life is done."

> Once to ev'ry man and nation
>   Comes the moment to decide,
> In the strife of truth with falsehood,
>   For the good or evil side;

"No sir. I won't do that. You've read my report. I see them there before you. They're confirmed by all my officers, and by the two Sylvan members of my ship. Lady Elphinstone isn't a liar. Neither am I, or any of the others who signed that report."

This was easy. It was like combat. You knew you were probably going to die, but you did it anyway without a second thought. Because it needed to be done.

"A vast war is brewing. The enemy is evil. They murdered my captain, murdered our Ship, all under a flag of truce. They attacked the Stolsh without provocation, dropping onto their worlds without warning, inflicting unimaginable horrors upon innocent civilians. No one is asking you to make the decision. Just tell the truth to Westerness. Let them decide, based on the facts as sworn to by my officers, not your lies."

> Some great cause, some great decision,
>   Off'ring each the bloom or blight,

And the choice goes by forever,
'Twixt that darkness and that light.

He looked into the eyes of the ambassador, and knew what he was seeing. He knew of senior officers who were capable of great bravery in combat, but when it came to their precious careers, they compromised and prostituted themselves and their sacred honor. They sold their souls a nickel at a time, and in the end they had nothing left. They became very small men. In the end they'd become that most wretched of creatures, politicians.

Then to side with truth is noble,
When we share her wretched crust,
Ere her cause bring fame and profit,
And 'tis prosp'rous to be just;

His voice dropped to a whisper. "Darkness falls. The shadows call. Shadow and flame. But our fight is true. Our enemy is moving. They're coming for us, Guldur and Orak. In the years to come we will have no choice but to fight them. Right now we have a chance to join in the fight for the very right to *exist*, for they bring genocide with them. We are on the brink of destruction. We must unite, or we will fall. While we dither, their power grows. We can fight them now, while we have allies, or we can fight them later and die alone."

Then Melville's voice grew strong and he stood tall, with a faint smile. "You can turn me over to them. And in so doing you will have handed me undying fame, glory and honor. While you will have brought eternal shame upon yourself . . . and Westerness. Our allies know the truth. It *will* come out. On every Sylvan and Stolsh world across the galaxy, they will know what you have done. You fear losing trade? You fear bad diplomatic relations? Doing *this* to me will destroy your relations with every Sylvan and Stolsh world in the galaxy. You would sacrifice me to prevent war, yet war is inevitable. It *will* happen, and throughout history you'll be remembered as the man, the appeaser, the Quisling, who turned me over to our enemies."

Then it is the brave man chooses
While the coward stands aside,

Till the multitude make virtue
Of the faith they had denied.

Sir Percival Incessant sat breathing deeply through his nose. Then he picked up a small bell and rang it ("tinkle-tinkle-tink") and two marines came in. Melville noted that they, too, were unarmed. Here, indeed, was an unhappy lord who dared not carry his sword, nor trust anyone else to do so.

Incessant sat back and steepled his fingers. Always a bad sign in politicians, lawyers, diplomats and their ilk. "This man is under arrest. Place him in your jail or brig or whatever. Get him away from me." He turned to Melville and made one last parting shot, "Lieutenant, you *will* hang for this."

Tho' the cause of evil prosper,
Yet 'tis truth alone is strong:
Tho' her portion be the scaffold,
And upon the throne be wrong;

The young marine corporal looked at Melville with tears welling up in his eyes. "I'm sorry, sir . . ."

"Don't apologize, son. You're just doing your job." Then, looking at the ambassador he added, "Hell, someone has to."

Yet that scaffold sways the future,
And, behind the dim unknown,
Standeth God within the shadow
Keeping watch above his own.

Melville had only been in his cell for a few hours. But they'd been some of the worst hours of his life. Doubts about what he had done ate at him. He worried about his family and the shame that he was bringing upon them. Perhaps it meant more than shame for his family, perhaps they too would be punished to appease his enemies. He couldn't help but think that the ambassador, far older and wiser in the ways of the world, might be right. He was gambling it all: his life, his fortune, and his sacred honor.

He kept telling himself that it was no different from the risk of combat. That in the end, they could *not* take his honor away. They could take his life. They could take his fortune. (Such as it was! Small loss there.) But they couldn't take his sacred honor. Only *he* could do that, and if he agreed to tell their lies then *that* was what he would have done. But how could he be sure?

He lay back on his cot, his mind spinning like a wheel trying to gain traction, when there was a knocking at his door. In spite of everything he smiled to himself. You don't *knock* at a prisoner's door. "Come in!" he said, sitting up in the light gravity. Gunny Von Rito walked in.

"Well, sir," said the gunny, a grin splitting his scarred face, "you've got yourself in a hell of a fix. But not to worry, we've come to spring you."

Melville shook his head with a sad smile as he looked up at the big NCO in his red jacket. The full magnitude of what had happened was just beginning to set in. "Don't get yourself in trouble, Gunny."

"Sir," the gunny answered, his friendly grin suddenly becoming feral, "It's not *me* that has trouble. *Or you*. The marine guards let us know what happened. Just scuttlebutt among jarheads, you know? We just happened to let Lady Elphinstone and Valandil know what was up. The King of Osgil, and the King-in-Exile of Stolsh, along with the Dwarrowdelf League ambassador, have summoned you to an audience. Tonight. The Westerness ambassador has informed them that you won't be available. *Now* it is the Westerness ambassador who has trouble. And now you, sir, are about to disappear, escaping from durance vile, adding yet another chapter to your legend."

"Things do move fast around here," said Melville, standing up. "But I get a sense that it has been building up to this for quite a while."

The situation was clear. His allies had made a massive flanking maneuver upon the enemy, and now he had to make his move. Melville wasn't very good at the whole angst business. He didn't need hope when despair could be delayed. He lived for the moment. And once again, the moment was good.

On his way out the gunny reverently handed him a .45 auto in a hand-tooled leather paddle holster, designed to fit snugly into his waistband in the small of his back, where it would be concealed by his uniform jacket. Another small paddle holster held two magazines on his left hip.

"The embassy's emergency supplies," said the gunny smugly. "They seem to have suddenly become available to most of our officers. Oh, and Lieutenant Broadax asked me to tell you that as the senior marine she would have come . . . but we decided I might be slightly less conspicuous."

As they left the cell the young marine guard had Melville's sword in his hand. He handed the sword to Melville, came to a rigid position of attention, saluted smartly, and conducted an "about face" that would have made his drill sergeant proud.

"You ready, son?" asked Von Rito.

"Aye, Gunny."

"Sorry, 'bout this, but you know you'll be in big trouble without this souvenir. And we can't be having that!"

Then, "Thunk!" and Von Rito gave him a precisely measured punch to the back of the head, guaranteed to leave a good lump. The guard crumpled quietly to the floor.

"Aye, you're a wily devil, sir," said the gunny as he led them out. "No cell can hold *you* by God!"

High upon the loftiest flet in the tallest tree in Osgil, the King of Osgil sat upon his throne in a flowing robe of green. Emeralds, rubies, and vivid, glowing, sunshine-yellow gems flashed from his crown and gown. Upon the dais, standing on each side of the king, were the King-in-Exile of Stolsh, garbed in elaborate robes made of all the swirling colors of a living world as seen from space, and the bearded ambassador of the Dwarrowdelf League, in glistening scale mail, steel helmet and battle-ax.

There was nothing above them but the two radiant moons of Osgil and a vast sea of stars. The two moons made the immense platform as bright as lamplight. The scene was surrounded, virtually *framed*, by elegant Sylvan landscape, architecture, and design, consisting of sweeping, flowing, naturalistic lines—*and* naturist lines, which is quite different, incorporating the elegant beauty of the nude form. It was art nouveau long, long before nouveau was new on Old Earth.

Behind the dais, an orchestra played a noble tune that sounded faintly regal to the visitors.

Arrayed to the left and right of the dais were the ambassadors of all the worlds with embassies on Osgil. Notably absent was the Guldur ambassador, who had been sent home several weeks prior. Notably present was Sir Percival Incessant, his face red with anger, the nostrils of his oversized nose flaring. Standing sullenly beside him, as the senior representative of Earth, was the Honorable Cuthbert Asquith XVI.

In formation before the king was the crew of *H.M.S. Fang*. Each crew member had their monkey perched proudly upon their shoulder. Melville stood in front, with Lady Elphinstone and Valandil, the two Sylvan members of his crew, immediately to his left.

The Sylvan and Stolsh nobility were gathered around the Fangs' square formation, chatting among themselves with drinks in their hands.

To the rear of the formation, servers stood beside tables groaning under the load of a Sylvan banquet. Not a *fully* satisfying meal to human appetites, but definitely a bounty of tasty snacks. All around them were the lovingly tended trees and flower beds of the Royal Gardens, perched high above the earth.

The orchestra played a final, stately chord and fell silent, which was the signal for all conversation to cease as the king began to address the crowd.

"Be it known to one and all, that we here gathered: the King of Osgil, representing the Sylvan peoples across the galaxy . . ." The Sylvan were one of the most diverse and widespread races in the galaxy. Osgil was their Prime World, and he was only the king of this one world. But if anyone could speak for all the myriad Sylvan worlds, he was the one to do it.

" . . . the King-in-Exile of Stolsh," here the tall Stolsh king bowed to the crowd in a swirl of colors, "representing the Kingdom of Stolsh which is currently besieged and occupied by vile attackers . . .

" . . . and the ambassador to the Dwarrowdelf League . . ." and here the ambassador raised his battle ax and slammed the hilt into the ground three times. He was of royal lineage, and was the rightful king of the large Dwarrowdelf population on Osgil. The word "king" more rightfully translated as "mine boss."

" . . . do hereby decree and declare the following . . ."

It was interesting to watch the Westerness ambassador's eyes begin to shift back and forth, like rodents trying to escape, as the magnitude of the political forces aligned against him became clear.

"We decree that the *joint* expedition aboard the ship *Kestrel*, representing the Kingdom of Westerness and the King of Osgil, and containing a citizen of the Dwarrowdelf League, was unjustly and murderously attacked, under the flag of truce, by the forces of Guldur. This was a premeditated act of war against the Kingdoms which dispatched this expedition, and the rulers here assembled do decree that all actions taken by the acting captain and by the crew were under the full authority of ourselves, and the joint agreement under which the expedition was dispatched. We do advise our Sister, Victoria the Fifth, the queen of Westerness, to accept this as a premeditated assault upon the nation of Westerness, and to join us in the mutual defense of our realms."

That, thought Melville, *is stretching the terms of the joint agreement for our expedition significantly, but who is going to disagree with the King of Osgil's interpretation of his own agreement?*

"We do further decree, to those assembled here, and to the galaxy at large, that the Ship *Fang* belongs to the Queen of Westerness, rightfully captured in an act of lawful self defense. We grant prize rights for the Ship to Captain Thomas Melville, which Ship is now bonded and bound to him and him alone, by right of blood and battle. And we grant prize money, as determined by the Osgil Prize Court, to Captain Melville and the current crew of *H.M.S. Fang.*"

This drew a great cheer from the Fangs. Patriotism, promotion and prize-money had been described as the three masts of the old British Royal Navy. Now this crew, which so prized tradition and the rich heritage of Aubrey and Hornblower, was delighted to be the first Westerness crew to ever receive prize money from a Sylvan Prize Court.

As a part of their recent treaty, Westerness and Osgil had agreed to respect each other's Prize Courts. This treaty was signed by Westerness as a measure to foster trade by supporting mutual counterpiracy operations. It's doubtful that any Westerness diplomat had ever foreseen the current situation, but Melville was beginning to wonder if the long-lived and far-sighted Sylvans hadn't anticipated this possibility.

This had all been briefly presented to Melville ahead of time. He didn't understand exactly why, but the only thing the Sylvans asked of him was two of *Fang*'s 24-pounder cannons. They'd promised two 12-pounders in return, and they'd promised to reimburse them handsomely in prize money for these two guns. It hurt to let go of *any* of his guns, but this was a small price to pay in return for such generosity.

"We do further decree," continued the king, his deep, powerful voice rolling across the assemblage, "that Captain Thomas Melville, commanding the Westerness ship *Kestrel*, and later the

Westerness ship *Fang,* acted in keeping with all civilized traditions and behavior in all aspects of his conduct."

Well, thought Melville, *nothing like getting a total pardon for all actions from three of the greatest empires in the Galaxy. Piss off powerful enemies, and I suppose it's only fair that you get powerful friends.* Looking at Sir Percival Incessant, now white with rage, Melville began to wonder just where he stood with one *other* major star kingdom: his own.

"We do further decree, that Captain Melville's actions in capturing *H.M.S. Fang,* breaking through the blockade of Ambergris, resisting the unprovoked invasion of Ambergris, and assisting in the evacuation of Ambergris, were acts of valor and military prowess unprecedented in the long histories of our peoples. Actions deserving of the highest honors our kingdoms are empowered to bestow."

There was an appreciative rumbling from the formation of Fangs, and applause from the audience standing beside them, applause which built to a thundering crescendo, echoed by one and all. Except for the Fangs who were standing at rigid attention, the three leaders upon the dais who were nodding regally, and the Westerness ambassador. Even Asquith, standing beside Incessant, gave a few puzzled, limp claps.

Then the awards were given. First Melville was called forward and made a Member of the Order of Knights Companion of the King of Osgil, and a member of the Royal Host of Glory by the King of Stolsh. The Dwarrowdelf ambassador declared him a Friend of the Dwarrowdelf League, apologizing in a deep gravelly voice that while he deserved more, that was the best that a lowly ambassador was authorized to do. The two kings each hung a very impressive medal around his neck, while the Dwarrowdelf ambassador settled for reaching up and giving a hearty handshake. In his enthusiasm the ambassador's huge, calloused hands nearly crushed Melville's hand.

Melville's monkey sat proudly and serenely through it all, its eyes sparkling as it took everything in. Then the King of Osgil declared that the tiny monkey was now a Squire to the King. The little creature seemed to be deeply affected, cooing slightly and stretching its head out timidly to let a ribbon be placed around it. With one hand it grasped the medal that hung from the ribbon, peering at it studiously while stroking the ribbon with several other hands.

Then each of his officers were called up to become Knights of the Realm of Osgil and Members of the Royal Order of Honor in Stolsh. And to receive a bone crushing handshake and the Friendship of the Dwarrowdelf League from their ambassador. Their monkeys also calmly accepted their masters' honors, but they too appeared deeply touched when they were declared Royal Squires and given beribboned medals.

A particularly poignant moment occurred when Broadax stood before her people's ambassador. The burly, bearded old Dwarrowdelf paused and looked her over carefully. It was known that she'd left her own people in some sort of rebellion, if not outright disgrace. The Fangs held their breath and waited to see if their beloved lieutenant would be snubbed.

Tears began to flood from the Dwarrowdelf ambassador's eyes, flowing freely down into his beard. He reached out his hand and Broadax took it slowly. The old Dwarrowdelf pulled her to him and wrapped his other arm around her. His voice was loud and sounded like grinding gravel as he said, for all to hear, "You have made us proud, good sister warrior. A Dwarrowdelf ax has struck a *mighty* blow in this first great battle against an evil foe. This is *good*. This is *very good*!"

At this the Fangs all cheered spontaneously, and a red flush rose upwards from Broadax's neck like a barbarian horde, burning everything in its way.

Then the three rulers walked the ranks of the Fangs, with Melville leading them and introducing each man, woman, and boy. These were truly *noble* representatives of their three races, noble in speech and noble in deed, each of them shaking every hand and personally thanking each crew member as they bestowed a medal upon him. And in every case his monkey was duly declared and bedecked as a Royal Orderly. A group of aides followed them as they made their rounds, carrying a seemingly inexhaustible supply of medals to go with the handshakes.

Even the Guldur members of the crew, standing timidly, feeling unworthy of recognition, were encouraged, thanked, and rewarded. They may have fought with the Guldur initially, but they fought for the right side in the battles that mattered, and they were living proof that the Guldur were an oppressed people. All three rulers made it clear to *Fang*'s Guldur crew members that they blamed their rulers, and not them; and would welcome any of their race who rallied to their cause in the years to come.

After the last crew member was duly bemedaled and beshook,

the King of Osgil turned to Melville. "But, some of thy crew who came with thee to our fair planet are not here!"

"Sire," said Melville, "Your navy was kind enough to provide caretakers for our ship during our absence. All of my crew members are here."

The old king's eyes sparkled and he grinned a grin that looked a lot like his granddaughter's mischievous smile. "Nay, good captain, what of the dogs and cats who have served ye so well? Would ye forget them? I have not. We are not, as a rule, partakers of red meat, but an imported beefsteak has been purchased and sent to your ship. Even as we speak, the four-legged members of your crew are being rewarded in the manner that they prefer best."

Finally, after every individual was recognized, the King of Osgil returned to his throne and concluded with these Words. "A valiant paladin of thy home world once said, '*Where* do we get such warriors? What loving God hath provided, that each generation, *afresh*, there should arise new giants in the land to answer the summons of the trumpet. Were we to go but a single generation without such *heroes,* then within the span of that generation we should surely be both damned and doomed.' So now let us partake of the meal that awaits us, and let us give thanks in every way for these worthy warriors who have answered the summons of the trumpet in our hour of need."

Melville saluted the dais. This was not a prescribed military action but it felt appropriate to do so, as a pure and simple act of recognition and greeting between warriors. Then he executed an about-face, looked out on his crew, and with a smile of sheer joy he commanded, "Fall out!"

"Do you understand the full magnitude of what you have done? You are leading our nation down the path of war. Nothing is worse than war! . . ."

It didn't take long for Sir Percival Incessant to corner Melville. They hadn't even sat down yet. Out of respect, the others backed away and discreetly watched as the Westerness Ambassador to Osgil publicly self-destructed.

"Nothing is worse than war . . ." Aye, thought Melville. Aye, he knew the horrors of war far, far better than the man standing in front of him. Visions raced through his mind. AiEe burning. Her brave people, ravaged, raped, tormented, and dying. A little body

crumpled on his quarterdeck. Had he really brought that upon Westerness? For a brief moment his moral compass spun and the world reeled. *Dear God, I'd do anything to avoid this. But it* cannot *be avoided. It has been brought to us, inflicted upon us, and our only choice is to fight or die.*

Aye, there is *something worse than war,* Melville thought to himself. *How did John Stuart Mill put it? "War is an ugly thing, but not the ugliest of things; the decayed and degraded state of moral and patriotic feeling which thinks nothing worth a war is worse . . . A man who has nothing he cares more about than he does his personal safety is a miserable creature who has no chance of being free, unless made and kept so by the exertions of better men than himself."*

Melville tuned out the ambassador's words as he studied the individual standing before him.

No matter how this turned out, Incessant's career as a diplomat was finished. Here was a man who could rise to positions of rank and recognition that most people would never dream of, and then spend his every effort scheming to gain even more. Melville looked into the heart of the man standing in front of him and felt only contempt and pity. In the end, however high he rose, whatever he achieved, he would never be happy. A lifelong diet of festering resentment and spite would leave him old and bitter, with a belly full of bile.

Here was a man with great reservoirs of vindictiveness and spite, dammed up behind fragile walls of paranoia and ineptitude. Now his actions, his policies, and he himself had been publicly repudiated by three major galactic powers. Now the dam had burst, and the flood of hate was so great that the ambassador lost all sense of propriety. He was going mad before Melville's eyes.

Melville tuned back into Incessant's rant for a moment. " . . . Do you really think you have the *right* to command a frigate?" he demanded, spraying spittle and shaking a finger in Melville's face.

Did he have a *right* to command a frigate? Not much. Hundreds of men were senior to him. No, he didn't have a *right* to command *Fang*, no more than he had a *right* to capture her, or to break through the blockade of Ambergris, or to blow countless Guldur frigates out of the water, or to woo a Sylvan princess.

Yet he had done so.

All of a sudden it dawned on Melville that the little man in front of him had no power over him. Whatever harm the man could do, he would. There was nothing Melville could do that would change this man. No words, no concession, no act could ever satisfy him.

And there was freedom in that.

So Melville simply turned and walked away as Incessant shouted, "You might have your ship, but you will be sent to the other side of the galaxy, and you will never do anything but deliver mail and worthless cargoes to frontier outposts for the rest of your miserable, insolent life. I can see what has happened here. I know that I am finished, but I still have authority. I have given that order, written and sealed, and it will not be rescinded!"

As Melville strode toward the tables he was joined by Princess Glaive in a gown that was like a swirl of translucent, gauzy green grass, with patches of dandelions artfully sited in strategic locations. She studiously ignored the whole incident with Incessant and immediately, impishly brought him back into the joy of the moment. "Shouldst I be whispering in thine ear, 'Remember, O Caesar, all glory is fleeting,' hmmm?"

Melville smiled and wrapped his arm around her, causing her gown to ripple delightfully, as though a mischievous breeze was blowing across her meadow. "I think it was a slave who was assigned to that duty, not a princess."

"Mmmm," she purred, standing up on tiptoes to kiss his cheek, "wouldst thou have me for thy slave girl?"

The rest of the dinner was a perfect, flawless gem of purest joy. Melville had a habit of taking the good times and identifying them to himself. *This, this is something special, something wonderful,* he said to himself. *I will take this day, this joy, and I will save it away. I will invest it in a mental, emotional "bank account." Some day when the years turn bad, when pain and sorrow fill my life, I will make a withdrawal from that account, and it will sustain me in my dark hours. I've known joy such as many people will never know. If the world should turn on me, as it did earlier today, may I have the decency* not *to moan and wail, and bear my fate with dignity and grace.*

A swirling rainbow of well-wishers came past his table. Most of them were only a colorful blur in his memory, but one in particular stuck with him. A Westerness Marine officer came up to him, escorted by Lieutenant Broadax. Broadax had lit a cigar, and was beaming in a cloud of smoke as she introduced him.

"Sir, this here's Lieutenant Colonel Hayl. Ye needs ta know 'at he was o' some service to us today. The colonel's the head o' the embassy's marine detail, an' aye, he *was* o' service, if'n ye takes my meanin'." This last was said with a broad wink that was about as subtle as a musket volley.

Melville stood and held out his hand to the tall marine, noting from his ribbons that he'd done service as a ranger, which was impressive.

"May I introduce you to Princess Glaive Newra, and may I say that I'm obliged for any assistance that you have given to me and my ship in this hour."

Hayl bowed and kissed the princess' hand, murmuring, "Charmed, Your Highness, I'm truly charmed." Then he looked at Melville, smiled and replied, "Truly it was nothing. I did absolutely nothing."

"Well, sir," said Melville, taking his meaning and returning the smile, "then I'm sincerely obliged to you for nothing, and if there is any way I can ever repay you, please don't hesitate to let me know."

"Aye, well, there is a boon that I would beg of you."

"If it's within my power, it shall be done."

"Well, Captain, my son is twelve years old. I've taught him everything that I can across the years. He has been well schooled, and I'd be honored if you would consider interviewing him for service with you as a midshipman. I've already provided him with a sea chest, all regulation requirements, and a yearly stipend. He's followed your exploits and is an enormous fan of yours, as am I, and if you'd accept him it would be the highest honor."

"Indeed, Colonel, I do have some openings in my midshipman's berth, and I'd be honored to meet the boy. But you do understand how these openings occurred?" A flicker of anguish flashed across Melville's face, a glint of black pain amidst the rainbow joy of this evening. Beside him, Princess Glaive squeezed his hand.

"Aye. I understand, Captain, and these are the risks we take and accept as warriors. Actually, I've taken the liberty of bringing the boy with me," at which he gestured and Melville became aware of a young boy standing a few feet away.

"Come here, son," said Melville kindly.

The boy strode forward, his chin held high but quivering ever so slightly.

"Do you want to serve on my ship?"

"Aye, sir."

"You know that it's dangerous, and it may be years before you'll be back with your family?"

"Aye, sir."

"You're certain?"

"*Aye,* sir."

"Very well, then. You aren't committed yet, I want you to be able to spend a few days on board ship before you make a final decision. But if, after seeing the ship and spending a few days with us, you *still* think you want the position, then you may have it."

Melville turned to the senior Hayl and continued, "Colonel, you can have his gear sent to the ship as soon as is convenient. I understand that we are under orders to sail soon. I don't know how soon it will be, but I'd like for young Mister Hayl to get a chance to look over the ship and make a final decision."

"Aye, Captain. If we can send him off tonight I think that may be best. Heads are rolling at the embassy, and my options may be somewhat more limited in the very near future. My son is prepared to depart; he has said his goodbyes."

"Indeed. As you can see, I do have some allies. And I, too, can ask boons. If you need my help please let me know. Mister Hayl, you can wait for me outside the cloakroom. You will accompany me back to my inn tonight. I can't guarantee that any of my men will be functional tonight, but you can come over to the ship with me, first thing in the morning."

"Aye, sir," said young Hayl.

"I thank you sir," added his father.

"It's nothing, sir, truly nothing," said Melville with a smile.

Chapter the 16th
Was a Lady Such a Lady . . .

You common people of the skies;
What are you, when the Moon shall rise?
"Elizabeth of Bohemia"
Sir Henry Wotton

"Well, looky there mates," muttered Broadax through her cigar stub as they walked into their inn. "They killed the little piggy afore 'e even 'ad a chance t' finish 'is apple. Damn I'm hungry fer *real* food," she went on, licking her lips, "I could eat the whole piggy m'self."

Melville, his first officer, and his marine officer were just returning from the king's award banquet. Their "gongs" were still hanging from ribbons around their necks. But, as always, they'd found the Sylvan food unsatisfying.

They'd walked confidently through the dangerous late night streets of Osgil, in the certain knowledge that the darkness held nothing more terrible than themselves. Melville was keeping young Midshipman Hayl with him until he could be safely stored aboard ship. The other members of their crew were all at other inns, or had other engagements, other opportunities tonight.

To their front was the dimly lit, broad stairs up to their rooms. To their left was an alcove for coats and boots, and to the right was the entrance to a long, brightly lit banquet hall with a table full of revelers reaching down its length. The table was dominated by a whole roasted pig. One moon had set, but bright moonlight from Osgil's remaining satellite still flowed in from skylights in the steep roof far overhead.

Standing in the doorway to their right were two other customers, both of them human. The inn was on the ground, rather than up in a flet, and was commonly frequented by humans. About half the customers that could be seen sitting at the table were descendants of Old Earth, the rest were mostly Sylvan.

"Aye," responded Fielder looking to his right at the huge roasted pig that Broadax was lusting after, sitting indignantly astride the table. He and Broadax were developing a fragile truce based on mutual cynicism, distrust of the Sylvans, and dislike of their refined food, a truce that had been cultivated across countless boring banquets. "And he looks quite angry about it. That Sylvan food. You eat and eat, and an hour later you're still hungry. I wish they'd saved us some of the beefsteaks that they sent to the dogs. I'd kill for some red meat." Then the door to the inn swung shut behind them, and Fielder heard the door being braced shut from the *outside.*

Broadax's hearing was poor, a natural trait of her race, aggravated by too many stints in front of the firing line. Hayl was too young to know danger and Melville was enthralled by the lingering effects of some feminine Sylvan magic, temporarily oblivious to the world around him. Only Fielder realized their danger.

Melville had sat beside Princess Glaive during the dinner and his mind was still adrift in a warm buzz of love and yearning. Under the table they had held hands and he kept his calf and foot woven against her dainty leg throughout much of the dinner. He didn't remember much about the meal, it was all a dim haze to him, but later they stepped out into the gardens, the princess limping slightly, and they had a few minutes of privacy to whisper to each other.

Was a lady such a lady,
    cheeks so round and lips so red,—
On her neck the small face buoyant,
    like a bell flower on its bed,

O'er the breast's superb abundance
where a man might base his head?

There is a fifth sense of touch, besides pressure, pain, heat, and cold, and that's the light, warm, stroking, comforting touch of another human being. A baby will die without it. In adults it's a key ingredient in courtship, flirting and making love. That, along with a lingering sense of smell, is probably responsible for the "afterglow" feeling that lovers have after leaving their love. His palm still felt warm and smelled faintly of her subtle perfume, and his mind wandered. Her touch and smell still echoed through his mind and body.

"Danger, mates," Fielder hissed as he heard the door being braced shut behind them. He immediately understood that someone wanted to bar their exit from this room. His blue uniform jacket was already unbuttoned and he placed both hands on his hips, under the jacket, ready to draw his .45 auto from the small of his back. Then he leaned gently back against the door. If the door were opened behind them he would know the instant it moved and would be in position to respond.

That night their lives were saved by two things: Fielder's constant paranoia, and their enemy's arrogance. All three of their monkeys hunched down and pulled out short, hardwood belaying pins from where they were kept tucked under their bodies. Melville snapped out of his fog, quickly unbuttoning his jacket and placing his right hand casually back on his hip while pulling Hayl behind him with his left hand. Broadax spit out her cigar stub and disappeared into the alcove to their left. Fielder took a shuffle step in that direction, his right shoulder still in contact with the door.

"What's so dangerous here?" asked young Hayl with a squeak, looking around the moonlit room bewilderedly.

"Us!" snarled Melville.

Then, appearing legs-first down the darkened stairs in front of them, came a group of large, ugly Sylvan males dressed in some household livery of khaki pants and maroon jackets, with semi-automatic pistols held casually in their hands. Melville had heard of interbreeding between Sylvans and Ogres, and this looked like living proof to him. They looked as if they could be written off their owner's taxes as a business expense, under "misc. heavy equipment." One of them was far-and-away the biggest, ugliest Sylvan Melville had ever seen. He must have had mostly Ogre blood in him. *Good,* thought Melville, *big guys, hopefully picked for their brawn, not their pistol skill.*

They came down and spread to the left and right, four on each side. Then two Sylvan females descended down to the bottom step. The first was tall and slender in an elegant, dark maroon gown, chased in gold and cut low across her ample bosom. Long dark hair framed her face in what Melville thought of as a Cleopatra style. The elegant, long-barrelled pistol in her hand coordinated perfectly with her ensemble. She was ravishingly beautiful, but it was the kind of deliberate, calculated beauty that came from a team of expert hair stylists, make-up artists, and dressmakers. And religious attention to vigorous daily workouts. You knew immediately that she took her beauty, and herself, very seriously.

Beside her was a dour, gray-haired old Sylvan lady dressed in layers of black and dark gray clothing, with slim maroon piping around the hems. Her plain, modest dress fit her matronly appearance perfectly.

When Fielder saw them his eyes grew wide and began to dart around like trapped animals.

"They always remind me of ballerinas," whispered Melville as he watched them come down the moonlit steps. "So elegant and graceful."

"Yeah," muttered Fielder, "the nutcracker suite."

The two customers in the door to the banquet room turned to watch what was happening, and several of the goons pointed their guns at them and motioned them into the middle of the room. The revelers in the banquet room couldn't see the stairs and had no indication that there was trouble.

"Baronet Daniello Sans-Fielder. The nobleman without a 'field.' " said the elegant Sylvan lady with a nod and a pleasant smile. "And Captain Thomas Melville," she continued with a nod in his direction. "You must come with us. You are in great danger."

"Why?" said Melville, leaving the revelation of Fielder's full name and title to be considered later.

"Because we will kill you if you don't," she said, her smile suddenly turning feral. "Actually, you will die anyway, but this way you will live just a little while longer. In fact," she continued, licking her lips and picking up momentum, "I intend to kill you myself, and I intend to enjoy it. Perhaps I will toy with the boy a little first, but you are all, already, dead men. You should resign yourselves to that fact." You could tell that she was getting pleasure from this. Her eyes were sparkling and her lips began to glisten.

Fielder smiled. Threats made him feel at home. Appeals to his better nature, his duty, and his country always made him uncomfortable. But threats now, threats he could handle. She had arrogantly and foolishly stated her intent and blocked off his escape route, leaving no option but to fight and kill them. First he needed to buy time. He could hear that lunatic Broadax up to something in the cloakroom to his left, and time would only work in their favor. If *he* were in Broadax's position, odds were good he'd never come back out, but that demented dwarf would *never* run from a battle.

"Lady Madelia," Fielder replied with something between a grimace and a smile.

"You know her?" Melville asked.

"Oh, yes sir. Careful! Don't look her in the eyes. She'll steal your soul. How very good to see you again, Maddy. But, you know, that gown *just* isn't *you*. Last time I saw you, you were wearing considerably less, *and* you were blindfolded and tied to the bed with an assortment of vegetables to keep you company. I liked you a lot better that way. Too bad you have adult supervision now," he added with a waggle of his eyebrows. "Lose them and we could still have a lot of fun, just like last time."

Her face went slightly red and the elderly Sylvan's face went beet red. The huge guard to her right began to raise his pistol with a growl, but Fielder was betting that she couldn't let an insult go unanswered. The Sylvans' one besetting weakness was their arrogance, and he intended to work it for all he could.

She reached out and put a restraining hand on her goon's arm and replied in a syrupy voice, "Why Daniel, is that the way to talk to the only woman who ever slept with you sober? Sex is only for revenge or making babies. In your case I was getting exquisite revenge on my father by having an affair with a hairy, underevolved *human*. It was delightfully wicked. For me you were a pet, like a dog or a horse, only you could be publicly flaunted. But then," she went on with a pout, "my point was made and it was time to put the beast down, and you were nowhere to be found. But you couldn't stay out at sea forever, could you? Now I have you *and* the dog who is panting after my niece."

The matron beside her was clearly stunned by these revelations. Her face went from red to bloodless white. You could tell that she was the kind of woman who might be aware that, somewhere beneath the complex strata of her petticoats and undergarments, there was some flesh and other female accouterments, but that didn't necessarily mean she approved of it. Madelia's last comment had ensured that, whatever the old lady might have contributed to the coming battle, it wasn't going to happen now.

"Maddy," said Fielder, dragging out the "y" with an infuriating grin and a knowing cant to his head. Infuriating grins were his specialty and this was a prize winner. "'Sex is only for babies or revenge?' You'd only eat your babies, and everyone knows all about your penchant for revenge, so how *do* you ever have fun? Have you considered the advantages of autocopulation?"

"Oh, Daniel, that is so *low*. Next you'll be making scatological culinary recommendations. How tiresome." She was back to the pout. This was a bad sign and Broadax was finished making noise to his left. That meant the demented dwarf was up to something, and Fielder had to buy her time. At least Broadax had sense enough to spit out that damned cigar first.

"A quick death is the best you could have expected, Daniel, but now perhaps something more is called for. After all, my lover, only the brave deserve the fair, and we *know* that you are not brave. Now don't we? You put up *such* a good front now, but oh my *how* you will whimper and beg under my knife."

At one level his guts were turning to water and a whimper was striving to escape from his lips, but his finely tuned survival instinct knew that groveling would lead straight to death. The good news was that he'd pissed her off so bad that she wasn't going to kill them out of hand. The old, "Let's torture them in some creative way," really meant "Let's be stupid and not kill them right now while we have the chance." Truly dangerous people didn't threaten, they just killed. Quickly and efficiently. Melville, Broadax and Fielder were as different as three people could be from each other, but they had this in common: they were *profoundly* dangerous people.

Melville chimed in at just the right time, naive as a puppy but a master of tactics once the situation was clear to him. Now he was playing the same game as Fielder, maneuvering to give Broadax time. "Madam," he said calmly, "do I understand that Princess

Glaive Newra is your niece, and that the family disapproves of my attentions? I assure you that we've been quite honorable in our relations, and thus far none of her relatives have communicated any disapproval."

Now she was back to angry. "You pathetic little *man.* Your superiors most certainly do *not* approve. Your own ambassador has turned you over to us."

She gestured with her left hand to the elderly lady standing beside her. "Furthermore, this is my aunt Ondelesa, Princess Glaive's great-aunt. *She* is the family matriarch and she most assuredly does *not* approve."

"Actually, sir," said Fielder, "she controls the *money* in the family, and money and morals are rarely on speaking terms. Are they, Maddy?"

"Daniel," asked Melville with mock innocence as Aunt Madelia's knuckles grew white from gripping the pistol in her right hand, "Whatever did you do to make this lady so angry?"

Angry is good, thought Fielder. Keep her talking. "You know how it is, sir. Put me next to a beautiful woman and one of two things happens. She either surrenders or screams. Sometimes both. You did a lot of surrendering and *then* screaming, didn't you, my little Maddy? My back still has the scars. But in the end, it didn't work out." Cocking his head slightly toward Melville, he confided, "I dumped her when she started to get mean and fat."

"Fat!" she screamed. Then she took control of herself and went icy cold. "Why Daniel," she said, "don't you find me attractive any more? Your discipline might have to take a very special form. Perhaps I will make you beg for me when I'm done. But when I'm done *no woman will want you,* and you will *beg* for death." It was obvious that her pleasure was becoming intense now. The moonlight was beginning to highlight two shadows emerging across the front of her sheer maroon gown, like two thumbs protruding, as she licked her lips.

"Captain," she said, licking her lips and turning the full power of her megawatt gaze upon Melville, "Daniel finds me unattractive. What do *you* think?"

Sylvan females seemed to have some kind of physical impact that was incredibly powerful. Perhaps a kind of pheromonal control. Melville found his knees growing weak. His stomach and regions further south seemed to ignite and twist into knots. Then he found his salvation, *and* a tactical diversion, in poetry. He gestured up at the moonlight flowing in from the skylights, intentionally pointing them away from where Broadax seemed to be moving, and said,

> "You meaner beauties of the night,
> That poorly satisfy our eyes
> More by your number than your light,
> You common people of the skies;
> What are you, when the Moon shall rise?"

Their tormentor's eyes crossed slightly as she absorbed this. It was like a fuse being lit as they waited for the reaction when she finally comprehended what Melville had said.

At the top of their peripheral vision, up in the high, vaulted, smoky dark ceiling, Fielder and Melville both saw movement in the shadows of the rafters, and they had to concentrate to avoid looking.

"Captain," continued Fielder, maintaining the momentum, "I think we should both forget about women, and stick to handguns. Handguns are infinitely superior to women. For example, a handgun won't ask, 'Do these new grips make me look fat?'" There, that was a good hint to get ready for a gunfight!

"You monkey scum! I've had about all the 'fat' I'm going to take off of you!"

"You know another way that a pistol is better than a woman?" Fielder continued relentlessly. "You can buy a silencer for a pistol."

On that note, Broadax dropped like a red bolt of lightning from the sky. Or from the ceiling, as the case may be. She'd crawled from the alcove up into the rafters, creeping slowly, avoiding the moonlight flowing through the skylights, and moving quietly through the shadows. As soon as she was in position she dropped onto the shoulders of the big goon. She held a *very* short, sawed-off, double-barreled, 10-gauge shotgun pistol in her left hand, and a short hand-ax in her right. She must have kept them concealed on her body, which was ample in width and depth, if not height, and had plenty of concealment space.

Melville mentally numbered the goons, from his left to right, as one through four. Huge-goon was number four. Then came the two hags, first Aunt Madelia and then Great Aunt Ondelesa, back and up on the step, followed by goons five through eight.

As she dropped down to goon four's shoulders, Broadax fired both barrels in the direction of goon five. For the unsuspecting Sylvans it was a deafening "BLA-BLOOM!" from out of nowhere. As always, she was a terrible shot, and even with a sawed-off shotgun, with barrels little longer than the shells, she only succeeded in spraying a few buckshot rounds into goon five's feet. The really amazing thing was that goon four was *not* knocked to the floor by the impact of 250-plus pounds of compact marine. At least his knees buckled. Meanwhile Broadax swung her ax to the right, cleanly cutting a cleft halfway through goon three's skull, her ax coming out in a vivid arc of blood and brains that sprayed across Aunt Madelia's décolletage.

Melville and Fielder took completely different approaches to life, but there was one rule they both could firmly agree upon: "Be polite. Be professional. And have a plan to kill everyone you meet." Thus they were both completely, mentally and physically prepared for Broadax's signal. They saw the feet emerge before her body fell, giving them a split second's warning, and they began to move as soon as her body began to drop. Already the effects of auditory exclusion had kicked in, so they barely heard Broadax's shotgun blast.

Melville crouched and cut to his left, since the right was blocked by the two dumbfounded innocent bystanders. He drew his .45 with his right hand as he pulled young Hayl along with his left. He raised the pistol up before his eyes. Thousands of practice reps made it smooth, like a martial art. Weapon up, thumb safety down with a comforting "snick."

He brought the front sight into focus, *pressing* the trigger as the sight covered goon six's face and . . . "_____!" You never "pull" a trigger. There are many things in life that are good to pull, but not triggers, not if you want to hit your target. The recoil pulled his pistol up. He forced it rapidly down and to the right, covering goon seven's face with the front sight and, "_____!" A very satisfying fountain of blood and brains erupted from the backs of both goons' skulls, spewing an interesting pattern of red and gray across Great Aunt Ondelesa's ashen face.

Fielder also cut to his left and drew his weapon. He didn't try for fancy head shots. Not bothering to get a good sight picture, he simply shot goons three, two and one as quickly as he could in the gut, turning the weapon sideways and letting the recoil carry the pistol to the left, covering each target in turn, "_____!", _____!", _____!"

He wanted *very* badly to shoot Madelia. She scared him profoundly and he derived great personal satisfaction from shooting people who frightened him, but she cut back behind the massive bulk of goon four and there was no clear shot at her.

The Sylvan goons foolishly subscribed to the belief that just pointing guns at your enemy rendered them helpless. After all, that's the way it worked in countless plays and stories, and in every movie and video on the high-tech worlds they'd visited. In reality, a good opponent can almost always draw a weapon and fire before a man with a gun pointed at him could shoot. The process was first outlined by Colonel John Boyd, an early warrior science pioneer in the mid-twentieth century. He called it the OODA loop: Observe, Orient, Decide, Act.

Thus, the OODA loop for the early stage of this battle went something like this:

Melville and Fielder "Observed" and "Oriented" when Broadax began to lower herself. They "Decided" to draw and shoot, and began to "Act" when she dropped.

The goons began *their* OODA loop when their opponents began to draw their weapons.

> —Observe: "Dey's doin' sumfin. Watar dey doin? Dey's drawin' guns!"
>
> —Orient: "Dat's dangerous! Sumbuddy could get hurt!"
>
> —Decide: "I'm gonna hafta shoot 'em!"

Then, just as they got this far, before they could Act, a new data point came into play when Broadax fired her shotgun and landed on goon four's shoulders, and the goons began a *new* OODA loop.

> —Observe: " . . ." (Pause a beat here to be stunned by the sensory overload caused by the noise, concussion, smell, and flash of the shotgun blast.) "Wot da hale wus *thaat*!"
>
> —Orient: "It came from ober ter!"
>
> —Decide: "Bedda look!"
>
> —Act: "Looky der!"

Then a *new* OODA loop began as they processed this new data.

—Observe: "They's a giant red monkey on 'is back!
—Orient: "Where da *hale* did dat come frum! Now we's got two problims! Do I kill da one up der, or the ones out der? Wottel I dew? Wottel I dew?!" (Note that the more options you have to consider, the longer it will take to complete the Orient and Decide phases.)
—Decide: "Bedda kill da ones out der!"

Again, just as they were getting about this far, and before they could Act, several of the goons' OODA loops were interrupted by .45 caliber chunks of lead going into their brains or guts. Even those who *weren't* hit were distracted, and they had to begin a *new* OODA loop, initiated by the gunshots. "Dey's shootin' *us*! Dey can't dodat!" And, if they happened to be looking in the direction of their falling comrades, there was a further distraction and yet *another* OODA loop, "Oops, der goes Og. An' he owed me money!"

Sometimes this whole process was referred to as an "action-reaction drill" and the person on the "reaction" side of the equation almost always lost. Additionally, the effects of tunnel vision meant the goons were figuratively "looking through a toilet-paper tube." A target making a rapid lateral movement, as Melville and Fielder were doing, could quickly cut out of the field of view and literally disappear off their narrow "radar screen."

Goons one and two were busy cogitating upon the bullets in their guts. However, much to Fielder's disgust, they had body armor on. Even with good body armor, a .45 will still knock the wind out of a man, but they were only temporarily distracted and even managed to get off a few wild shots.

Goon three was suffering from a massive, ax-induced, prefrontal lobotomy.

Broadax was sitting on goon four's shoulders. She'd punched the hot, empty shotgun barrel in her left hand through his lips and teeth ("*Crunch!*") and ground it deeply into his mouth, muttering, "Suk on *dis*, big boy!" Then she yanked the shotgun to the side and was having a fair degree of success at unscrewing his head with it, while flailing unsuccessfully at Aunt Madelia with the ax in her right hand.

Great Aunt Ondelesa was in deep shock, and she didn't have a weapon anyway. Goon five was understandably distracted by a spray of buckshot going into his feet, but he managed to get off a few wild shots. Goons six and seven thought whatever final thoughts a brain thinks as a bullet goes through it. Then they died without getting off a shot.

Goon eight was the only one capable of accurate fire, since he was the only one without any major distractions. Unfortunately for the goon team, he chose to fire at the two bystanders, since they were the targets directly in front of him. In an ideal world, *all* of the goons would have killed the targets directly in front of them. This was their "assigned sector of fire." But the sudden, violent action taken by the Westerness officers threw an eight-legged monkey wrench into their plans.

The feeble fire from the stunned Sylvans failed to hit the two Westerness officers as they dodged into the alcove to their left. Melville pulled Hayl with him, while the profoundly frightened Hayl left a trail of unnecessary body mass behind him. Both Melville and Fielder fired a few more wild shots as they ducked around the corner, and like all wild shots they accomplished little. The monkeys on their shoulders didn't have to deflect a single bullet, satisfying themselves with a defiant "Eeek!"

The two innocent customers to their right, fellow humans whose only crime was to witness what was occurring, were both hit. One took a bullet through the heart and the other received a blast to the gonads that made the officers' eyes water in sympathy. Both of these individuals tried to stagger mindlessly after them into the alcove. The man shot in the groin didn't make it far before he was debilitated by the pain of his wound and fell to the ground, coiled around his private pain. But the luckless customer shot through the heart had five to seven seconds before his body would lose hydraulics. He used that time to stumble into the alcove. Crouching on the floor beside the dying human, Melville and Fielder edged around the corner of the alcove to cover Broadax's retreat.

Goons one and two, shot in the gut but saved by their bulletproof vests, were ready for them. "They're wearing body armor," grunted Fielder in disgust. Melville and Fielder each picked one off with a bullet in the head, their monkeys blocking incoming bullets with an "Eeek!" of protest and terror. Meanwhile Broadax used her legs, one apelike arm, and the leverage from the shotgun shoved in goon four's mouth to finish unscrewing his head with one vicious jerk, "snAAP!crack-krunch." Then with a kick of her legs she spun to his front and dropped to the floor as her victim toppled backwards. She broke her fall by plunging her ax into her victim, ripping him open from sternum to crotch as she fell, spilling his innards out onto his feet as he fell back.

Melville noticed that the big goon didn't look any better on the inside than on the outside. Yep, he hated his guts.

Aunt Madelia and goons five and eight fired at Broadax as she made her exit. Her monkey stood backwards on her shoulders, shaking its fists and screaming its outrage as it blocked the shots. Then it mooned the goons as the marine officer scampered into the alcove.

Hayl lay looking at the face of the dead bystander. "He's awful still," the boy said cautiously. "Is something bad happening to him?"

"Could be," answered Fielder distractedly. "He's dead."

By this time Broadax had joined them, her monkey still sitting backwards to cover the retreat.

"Gosh," said Hayl, still fixated on his first dead man. "I'm sorry that happened."

"Now *that* is a view which I'm sure he shares," said Fielder. "It could be worse," he added. "It could be me."

"But this is all wrong," whimpered Hayl. "We were taught that the Sylvans were a noble race. Wise and fair, with fluid laughter and a wonderful, subtle sense of humor."

Broadax and Fielder's belt buckle exchanged quick glances. "I think ye must be thinkin' about diff'r'nt Sylvans," Broadax said slowly. "We jist seem ta have the udder sort here," she added, as she broke open the shotgun, ejecting two smoking 12-gauge shells ("Click, tiiing!, thum-thump"), and inserted two more and slammed the breech shut ("thuun-thuung, Chung!").

These sound effects made Hayl jump and twitch, as his recently expelled body fluids continued to stain the leg of his trousers. Then he apologized with an abject, embarrassed, " . . . sorry."

"'S okay, lad," said Broadax kindly. "We're all a bit jumpy."

"Except him," added Fielder, nodding at their dead, unknown companion. He used the momentary lull to conduct a tactical reload, ejecting and saving a mostly empty magazine while slamming home a full one, all with his left hand in a smooth, fluid motion, while keeping the gun up and ready in his right hand.

"Mr. Hayl," began Melville, conducting his own tac reload. "You need to know that the Sylvans engage in some very dirty dynastic infighting. Knives, subtle poisons, and arranged accidents are common. You're correct about the laughter and subtle sense of humor though. They have been known to use quite hilarious booby traps involving numerous needle-sharp spears in the nether regions. Direct confrontations like this are rare, but not unheard of."

"Aye," muttered Fielder. "A very 'pointed' sense of humor, generally applied to family feuds. Heir today, gone tomorrow."

Then they heard someone outside the entrance to the inn. It had been braced shut behind them after they entered it. "Madam!" shouted a voice. "Is everything all right? Do you need us?"

Madelia screamed, "Yes you idiots, come in and kill them!"

"Okay," Melville continued quickly. "We're going across this room, into the dining room, *across* the table, and out the back door. Broadax and Hayl go low, we'll go high." Glancing down at the reproachful eyes of the dead customer, and then at his still-writhing associate, Melville added, "Shoot to kill as we go. It's only fair."

Hayl nodded. Broadax growled, hand-ax held ready in one hand and shotgun in the other. Fielder pulled a two-shot derringer from an ankle holster and said with a nod, holding a weapon in each hand, "Here's another reason why a handgun is better than a woman. Your primary handgun doesn't mind if you have a backup."

With a flurry of accurate .45 rounds Melville led, "_____!-_____!-_____!-_____!," followed a split second later by Fielder's deadly pistol fire, "_____!-_____!-_____!" and the "_____!!-_____!!" of Broadax's blind, double-barreled fusillade of double-ought buckshot. The Sylvans responded with a satisfying spray of blood and groans, and a feeble rattle of return fire punctuated by Aunt Madelia's curses. Fielder took several shots at her, but she was retreating quickly up the stairs and her vitals were above the field of view and unavailable. As she turned to the left at the top of the landing, Fielder got a side view of her most massy visible target centered in his front sight and pressed off a round. He got a brief and very satisfying glimpse of the bullet creasing both cheeks as she screamed and ran out of view with a bloody line etched across her hams.

The four officers raced across the room, their monkeys again blocking bullets with a feeble, futile, half-hearted "eek," of protest.

Then they moved into the long, narrow banquet hall, dominated by the fully laden banquet table, whose occupants were arching their necks to observe the dinner show next door.

"Where are we running to?" asked young Hayl.

"Where isn't important," answered Fielder, "*from* is what matters."

They entered the dining room just as the inn's entrance door opened up and Aunt Madelia's reinforcements finally arrived.

Their monkeys sat backwards on their shoulders, ready to block incoming fire. Fielder and Melville jumped onto the table and ran along it, stepping on hands and plates, and trailing apologies and a few cautionary gunshots to their rear, "_____!-_____!" Broadax and Hayl ran straight underneath the table, barely ducking as Broadax's monkey dismounted and scampered along beside her, stepping on toes and not bothering at all to apologize. The captain and his first mate jumped down at the other end, joined by their midshipman, marine officer, and her monkey. They raced through the kitchen and out into the alley.

"Now there's something I thought I'd never see," said one old retired Westerness navy officer, putting down his silverware and turning to his dinner companion as Fielder and Melville thundered past.

"Wot's 'at?" replied his friend, a crusty old retired marine NCO, as he set his tipped wine glass back up and reached for the bottle.

"Those new .45 autos. I thought they'd never get them into service," the old navy officer replied, handing his wine glass over to be filled. "I'm happy to see that they seem to be working well."

As they raced down the alley Fielder asked, "Anyone know where this alley goes?"

"It goes away from all them people wats chasin' us!" answered Broadax. "An' away from yer crazy gurlfriend!"

"Good, good! In that case, I *like* this alley."

They cut around a corner, and ducked into the alley's alley. Then they froze, motionless and panting. Their wool dress uniform jackets looked good, but that was about all you could say for them on a warm night like this. After all the excitement and exertion they were now wearing several pints of cold, clammy water. Hayl felt an additional discomfort and humiliation as the contents of his bowel and bladder sloshed around in his boots.

"Oh man. Ohmanohman," gasped Fielder, starting to slide into a funk now that the impetus of danger was over. Glossing over the fact that it was *his* ex-girlfriend who had tried to kill them, he began to vent. "He takes us halfway across the galaxy, desperate battles at every turn, then, when we are finally safe, he gets us into one more battle, *with our allies!*"

"Yeah!" whispered Broadax, with fond admiration. "Excitin' stuff *does* happen around our cap'n, eh?"

"One of my favorite writers put it something like this," Fielder muttered in reply. " 'If complete and utter chaos were lightning, then he'd be the sort to stand on a hilltop in a thunderstorm wearing wet copper armor and shouting "All gods are bastards.' " Find anything to eat?"

"Aye, I grabbed a nice bit o' meat, ripe off the bone, wot seemed ta dropped down inta a feller's lap," she said, holding out her handax with a large chunk of ham firmly impaled on it. "And ye?"

"Leg of . . . beef I think. The owner seemed to have lost his appetite. Bit heavy-handed on the sauce though."

"Mmeephk," contributed Broadax's monkey, holding sausages in its mouth and three hands, and a bullet-riddled belaying pin in another, as it used its four remaining legs to scamper back up on Broadax's back. Once there, it kindly handed a sausage over to the bewildered, reeking Hayl.

Young Hayl looked at them in wonder. He didn't think it was natural to worry about food when you're being shot at. Certainly *his* reaction, and the response of many individuals in similar circumstances, took place at the other end of the digestive tract. But these were veterans of many battles. They were warriors who could take a larger view of things. He even understood that they were doing these things to impress each other. Certainly *he* was impressed. The one acted like he was timid, but it was timid like a timber wolf. The other tried to make people think she was crazy, but it was crazy like a fox. And the captain tried to be calm, but he was calm like the sea.

"Here," said Melville absently, handing a lit cigar to Broadax, "only slightly used I think."

"Hot damn!" she said, taking the pilfered stogie lovingly.

"Daniel," said Melville, "I fired most of one full magazine in the initial barrage, another in the retreat. I'm pretty much down to one mag. How about you?"

"Yesh shir," Fielder replied through a mouthful of beef, "shame here, and my back-up gun is empty. Damn," he added, swallowing his mouthful and continuing in a reflective, muttered monologue, "I knew two extra mags wasn't enough. If you carry a gun, people call you paranoid. That's ridiculous. If I have a gun, what in the hell do I have to be paranoid about? If I carry more than two extra magazines, now *then* you know I'm worried. Grandma BenGurata always told me, 'There are three things in life you can never have too much of. Money, good looks, and ammunition.' But then, that's *another* reason why a handgun is better than a woman. Your handgun will stick with you, even if you're out of ammo."

Melville turned to Broadax and commented, "Speaking of someone sticking with you, nice job tonight. I didn't even know you had that little ax."

"It's like Mr. Fielder an' 'is handguns, sir," she replied with a smile and a blissful puff of cigar smoke. "A girl can't *have* too much cutlery."

They jumped as two figures silently materialized from the darkness beside them. "It's Westminster and Valandil," came a low voice. A voice they were *very* happy to hear.

"Lady Elphinstone sent us," continued Valandil quietly. "She said it looked as though a run-in with thy future in-laws was in the offing."

"In-laws? Dear Lord, that's right. If I were to marry Princess Glaive, those two demented aunts *would* be my in-laws! After tonight I'm having second thoughts about having anything to do with *that* crazy family."

"Aye," said Fielder quietly, "well said, sir. The better part of valor and all that. Stick with your pistol. After all, a handgun will function normally every day of the month."

"Aye," said Melville as they began to move quietly down the alley and away from the recent battle. "Perhaps it's all for the best. Damn I'm tired." It had truly been a roller coaster of a day.

"Yes, sir," drawled Westminster with a flash of white teeth. "Ah must agree completely with Mister Fielder. Women are far more trouble than they're worth, and your handgun won't mind if you go right to sleep after you've used it."

~ ~ ~

As they approached the Ship—their only real refuge, if even that was truly safe—Fielder conducted a quiet monologue. "In truth, we're all a little bit 'Hoka.' That's the genius of that genre. In our own minds, we are *all* playing little roles based on our favorite mythos, with ourselves as the heroes. You guys are trying to convince yourselves that you're living in the Tolkien mythos, but after tonight I'm not sure that's the right one."

"Aw, damn ye, don' say it," snarled Broadax through her cigar. "I wus jist gettin' ta like ye a little."

"Face it, you're a character in an entirely different kind of story. One word: Pratchett!"

"Nooo!"

"Leave her alone, Daniel," said Melville absently. "And see if we can get someone to tend to young Hayl here."

Hayl stumbled along beside them, bewildered and confused, still holding a sausage in one hand, and clutching at his slimy trousers with the other.

As they stood at the gangplank, Melville knelt in front of little Hayl and looked him in the eye, "You did well, boy. I'm proud of you, you kept alert, you didn't panic. The things that happened to you, and the way you responded are normal. We've all been there."

"Welcome ta the service of Her Royal Majesty, the Queen of Westerness," said Broadax kindly, turning her back on Fielder and pointedly ignoring him. "How's it feel ta be a sailor, lad?"

"Kinda crappy, ma'am," sniffed little Hayl, tears running down his face.

"You get used to it," said Fielder, always pleased to find *someone* more miserable and frightened than himself. . . .

Chapter the 17th
True Thomas

True Thomas lay on Huntlie bank;
    A ferlie he spied wi' his e'e;
And there he saw a ladye bright
    Come riding down by the Eildon Tree.

Anon.

Lieutenant Thomas Melville waited in the Royal Glen. It was a kind of park beneath the trees where the royalty had their flets. He was seated on a patch of moss, with his back against the broad brown bole of an immense tree. There were no medium sized trees here, nor small trees. Just ancient forest giants arching far overhead, and moss and ferns below.

It was hard to relax after the activities of the previous day. He'd come with Ulrich and a few marines, all of them armed, in case Aunt Madelia decided to come back for a second helping. The invitation that Princess Glaive sent him got him into the park, but Ulrich and his guards had to wait outside with the Royal Sylvan Guards. So he was alone, if you didn't count his monkey and his .45, both of which felt comforting.

He contemplated the worth of his many victories. Analyzing the cost. The scars. The deaths. The loss of innocence.

What a price he had paid. Mostly lonely, seldom alone. Always alert, ever vigilant. Because if he wasn't vigilant, if he wasn't ready, then his Ship, his men, all that he loved, could die in an instant.

He had traveled far since that landing on Broadax's World. So very far. War changes people. Sometimes it changes them into dead people. For those who live, war can fill the holes in men's hearts. Sometimes the pieces were good, sometimes bad. One way or another, some of the gaps in his soul were filled. But he knew the puzzle was yet to be completed. He lacked the final piece. Was she the piece that would fill the void in his soul? He was cynical, suspicious. Above all, he would not be manipulated.

He waited for a princess, but was she *his* princess? He surveyed his outer perimeter. *How had she entered? Smiles and warmth. Not with me you don't.* He had no patience with triviality.

He heard her coming. First a breath, then a whisper. Tinkling. No, chiming. A mellifluous *ringing* of many, tiny, perfect bells.

Then she came into view, riding down the forest trail. Princess Glaive.

She was riding sidesaddle atop her horse, a great hairy creature bedecked with bells that called to the forest like a chorus of angels. Her strawberry blond hair, strands of copper and gold, flashed in a brief flicker of sunlight. She was garbed in her traditional green, with black velvet trim and a yellow sash.

Her skirt was o' the grass-green silk,
Her mantle o' the velvet fyne;
At ilka tett o' her horse's mane,
Hung fifty siller bells and nine.

The forest was a verdant cathedral overhead. Lit like emerald stained glass, with speckles of sky blue and vivid rainbow flecks where birds fluttered. Their throats echoed the call of her horse's bells.

No. Not a horse. As she grew near, close inspection revealed that she was mounted atop a dog. A great, hairy, lap-tongued beast that proceeded to stride up and baptize Melville into the universal church of the happy dog.

"Eemph?" said his monkey as the dog dedicated the full

attentions of its vast, pink, sopping salute to the monkey. The little creature would have been lifted from Melville's back except that it gripped tight to his wool uniform jacket with all eight hands.

Melville stood, shoving aside the dog's massive head, looking up at the princess.

Eyes aglow, she looked down at him. So diminutive, yet she knew no fear.

Their eyes locked. He raised the alarm. Defenses manned.

She stormed his defenses like the hosts of heaven. As a smitten man is wont to do, it seemed to him that she was sent from above.

He dropped to his knee with a self mocking smile and reached up to take her hand. "My lady, you are surely heaven sent."

True Thomas he pu'd aff his cap,
And louted low down on his knee:
"Hail to thee, Mary, Queen of Heaven!
For thy peer on earth could never be."

But was he truly in love? Or was he being beguiled, manipulated?

"Nay, True Thomas. I am but a Sylvan princess, come as my grandfather's herald."

There was a thrill of eldritch wonder when he heard her call him "True Thomas." *Wait a minute*, he asked himself. *How'd she get inside my poem?*

"O no, O no, Thomas," she said,
"That name does not belang to me;
I'm but the Queen o' fair Elfland,
That am hither come to visit thee."

His poetry had always provided him with a frame of reference. For some people there was background music or a theme song playing in their minds. For him it was poetry that provided his theme. Now it seemed as though she'd joined him in "his" poem. As if she'd tuned in to his mind and started speaking to him at that level. Was it empathy or was he being manipulated?

It was as though a lonely man played solitaire in an empty room for his entire life, then suddenly someone sat down and played the game against him. Against him? Or with him? A partner, or an opponent? *That* was the question.

"What word from the king, fair herald?" he asked, standing up shakily, still holding her hand.

"Lift me down from my steed, Thomas, and I shall apprise thee of deeds done and offers made." Then she slid down to dismount. He reached up and caught her by the hips, setting her down on the ground, light as the frothy swirl of silk that enveloped her.

Her mount turned its head to her and she pushed it away. "Be off with ye, Daisy."

"*Daisy?*"

"Aye," she said, watching fondly as the dog circled twice and lay down, scratching behind one huge, floppy ear, "she is a great hairy beaste, but I do love her. And now," she continued, looking up into Melville's face as she stood before him, "Thou must know that the Westerness ambassador encountered an accident on his way home last night. A distinctly Sylvan style of accident. Alas, he died of terminal stupidity. 'Tis the only universal capital crime. As always, the judgment was immediate, and final. There was no appeal."

Melville was suddenly gripped with amazement and horror. She looked so beautiful and innocent standing here in the peaceful forest. It was disconcerting to hear this seemingly gentle creature tell him so lightly, so blithely, of the diplomatic dispatch of an ambassador.

"'Tis truly fortunate that the sad little man refused to allow his guards to be armed. It would have been a shame to have to kill them. They tried manfully to defend him, even though they despised him. What magnificent warriors you do craft in that vast star kingdom of yours, my Thomas."

He could read between the lines. Incessant could well have tried to confront the Sylvan king. In his madness and self-righteous indignation the little mouse might have tried to beard the lion. And he'd been crushed without hesitation. Truly these were *alien* peoples. He reaffirmed his determination to maintain his distance, to resist her wiles, as she continued.

"O Thomas," she said as she reached out and took his hand. Perhaps she understood some of what was going on in his mind. "My grandfather would not have had it happen thus. But the ambassador's manner was intolerable! In their anger, I fear that some of the King's Own Bodyguards took offense and killed him out of hand. Needless to say, their lives will be forfeit should Westerness demand it."

"Aye," he replied, for what more could you say. The Sylvan king killed the Westerness ambassador, and now he offers the lives of his bodyguards as repayment. Well, no one would miss Sir Percival Incessant, who, in the end, didn't live up to his name. And sometimes there was something to be said for the Sylvans' straightforward approach to life. "I'd guess that Westerness response depends on who writes the reports."

"Aye, indeed, Thomas," she said, nodding her pretty head soberly as she stood looking up at him, now pressing his hand with both of hers. "The ambassador's report had not yet been written. *Thou* art the senior naval officer, and as the military attaché Colonel Hayl is the senior member of the embassy. 'Tis *thy* report, and *his* report that shall be sent to Westerness. However, Sir Percival did write orders dispatching you to duty on the far side of the Westerness star kingdom. The fool. The only Westerness Navy Ship on this side of the Grey Rift, and he would send thee to the far side of the galaxy for ignominious duty. But, Thomas, 'twas written, 'twas seen and known by all, and it cannot be changed. Colonel Hayl believes that to change the order would be to exceed his current mandate and he cannot help us there. He says that *if* thou art to remain under Westerness authority, thou must go."

If *I remain under authority. Is that where this is headed? Maybe Hayl can't change it, but maybe the king wants it to stay that way so that I'm faced with this dilemma and will rebel. Will I?*

"Aye, my lady. Thus were deeds done, and they cannot be undone. You spoke also of offers made?"

"Sit next to me upon yon mossy bower, and I shall tell thee, Thomas."

He unbuttoned his jacket and spread it across the moss for her to sit upon. She watched with her head canted quizzically, and then laughed a clear, ringing laugh as she sat upon it. "Dear Thomas, we wear green to be one with our forest, to recline and repose without care. Now thou wouldst interpose thy jacket betwixt the Sylvan princess and her forest. Thou art *truly* dear and charming."

Then she took his hand and continued. "Now, Thomas, the first part of the offer is from me, not my grandfather. I offer thee my kiss. For if thou wouldst kiss me, I know that thou shalt be mine.

I will not require it of ye, thou shalt not be bound, but I know that thou shalt desire to be mine."

Melville looked at her with wordless confusion.

She smiled and stroked his hair. "Thou knowest not our ways, my Thomas, so I shall spell it out. First ye *must* know that we are sorry for what my Aunt Madelia did last night. She is an eccentric woman."

Eccentric! he thought, *So* that's *what they call it.*

"She is twisted and alien even to us, and she must seem powerful strange to thee. We were beginning to fear her. Her minions were fell and skillful, but thou hast well and truly pulled her teeth."

Aye, we killed *her teeth, but I fear that we didn't get them all.*

"Enough of her. Just know that she is an aberration. Know also that in our lands, Thomas, when a lady gives a man her kiss, she is offering a challenge. She is wagering that she shall beguile the man. 'Tis a weird to us. Perhaps 'tis magic, perhaps 'tis pheromones, *perhaps* 'tis true love. A high-tech world would dissect it, and they would kill it in their effort to find out what it is. Whate'er it is, I offer thee this challenge. Kiss me, Thomas. After thou hast tasted, thou shalt be mine."

> *"Harp and carp, Thomas," she said;*
> *"Harp and carp along wi' me;*
> *And if ye dare to kiss my lips,*
> *Sure of your bodie I will be."*

Alien. Unexpected, unheralded, yet consistently and inevitably, the reminders come. They are alien.

No, this is no creature of heaven. What she desires is to be kissed, worshipped, and adored . . . on earth. But what man of mettle could turn down such a challenge and still respect himself?

"What if I am undaunted? What if I accept this challenge from a charming lady, as any gallant gentleman would? What, O Princess, if I choose to taste the fruit of your lips and am *not* bewitched? If I'm *not* beguiled, what then?"

She reached out and stroked his face again, tenderly, with the tips of her fingers, with a tear in her eye as she replied, "Then ye wouldst gain even more honor amongst us, for few can summon the willpower, the resolve to do so. And I should *still* be, and ever *shall* be, a true friend to ye. My love is mine to give to whom I will. But if love is offered and rejected, 'tis still love.

Otherwise 'twould be some selfish, twisted thing that surely is *not* love."

"Then for good or ill, for well or woe, I accept your challenge, and 'your weird' shall not daunt me."

"Betide me weal, betide me woe,
That weird shall never daunten me,"
Syne he has kiss'd her rosy lips,
All underneath the Eildon Tree.

Melville took his monkey from off his shoulder, and gently placed it upon Daisy's head where it scampered about, delightedly probing and exploring the huge, patient beaste. Then he wrapped his arms around his princess, and leaned her back onto his jacket, spread across the deep, soft moss.

The monkey had a *very* good time. . . .

"Now I am thine," she said, "and thou art mine. Ever and always mine. . . ."

"Now ye must go wi' me," she said,
"True Thomas, ye must go wi' me;
And ye must serve me seven years,
Thro' weal or woe as may chance to be."

"Now rest thy head, and I will tell thee what it is that I offer to thee, my True Thomas. . . ."

"Light down, light down now, true Thomas,
And lean your head upon my knee;
Abide ye there a little space,
And I will show you ferlies three."

"On the one hand, thou canst follow the path of duty to thy Queen and Kingdom . . ."

"O see ye not yon narrow road,
So thick beset wi' thorns and briers?
That is the Path of Righteousness,
Though after it but few inquires."

"Ah! 'The road less traveled,'" he said with a smile. "That's the one for me."

"Nay, Thomas," she said, placing a finger on his lips, "hear me out, I pray thee. For on the other hand thou canst go the way of the world, and chose selfishness, and greed."

"And see ye not yon broad, broad road,
That lies across the lily leven?
That is the Path of Wickedness,
Though some call it the Road to Heaven."

"Or, on the gripping hand, ye can chose fealty to my grandfather. *That* is my grandfather's offer. And dost thou see, Thomas, that *is* thy duty! Wouldst thou take that magnificent Ship and crew so far away when righteous battle calls? Nay! *This* is thy duty, thy destiny! I have studied thy history. 'Tis an honorable choice. Thou wouldst be like Chenault and his Flying Tigers in China. Like the American fliers who served the RAF early in Earth's World War Two! And thou wouldst receive wealth, appreciation, and honor."

"And see ye not yon bonny road
That winds about the fernie brae?
That is the Road to fair Elfland,
Where thou and I this night must gae."

Aye, though Melville, looking at her wonderingly, *she's not from Heaven or from Hell. She's not the least concerned with wickedness or righteousness. She's interested only in the road that leads to the country where she is queen. Conquest in the country of men's hearts. Of* my *heart. That's what is most important to her.* And yet it was all so beautiful, so pure. There was no pretense. No deception. She had made her bid, offered her challenge, thrown down her gauntlet. She had given it her best shot, her best *kiss*. And what a kiss it was . . . Now the choice was his, to be enchanted and beguiled . . . or not.

Still, he didn't fully understand. "Why do you want me? What makes me worthy to be wooed by a princess?"

"O Thomas. 'Tis thee that I love. Were thee but a lowly foot soldier I think that I shouldst love thee still. But as a princess royal I may not give myself and my love to just anyone. But thou! Thou, my Thomas, hast earned it. 'Tis thy martial glories that make thee respected and revered. Our men would follow thee." She smiled wickedly and added, "And thou hast neatly depleted Auntie's carefully chosen household retainers. The survivors are scared to death of thee." Then she added with a slight shudder, "And it takes a *lot* to frighten them. So Aunt Madelia cannot stand in thy way. Great Aunt Ondelesa has been quite distressed by how the whole matter turned out. *She* will not stand in thy way. At every turn thou hast earned thy way into our family and our navy by right of battle and blood!"

It was mirk, mirk night, there was nae starlight,
They waded thro' red blude to the knee;
For a' the blude that's shed on the earth
Runs through the springs o' that countrie.

Aye, a trail of blood brought him here, and made him desired by kings and princesses. A river of blood. How much blood ran upon the decks of his Ship? Other Ships? Frozen in space? Soaked into the soil of Broadax's World? How much blood?

"Blood," he said, thoughtfully. "It's always about blood and battle. Even you, my princess, are named after a sword. That's what 'Glaive' means in our tongue. Did you know that?"

"Aye, as 'Bilbo' in thy mythos is named after an obscure word meaning a sword, a well-tempered blade. We chose the English translations of our names very carefully. Your language is so powerful, so beautiful. Like your literature, it has conquered us."

Melville smiled. "Churchill called it, 'the all-conquering English language.' By the end of the twentieth century it was the common language spoken by every pilot coming into every international airport in the world, and over ninety percent of everything on the old Internet was in English. By the end of the twenty-first century it was the first or second language of almost every person on Earth, and all the other languages were well on their way to virtually disappearing. Even in Churchill's time it was evident that English would conquer the Earth, but I wonder what he would have made of this."

Melville was determined not to be distracted, so he brought the subject around to its original intent, to understand about her. "Princess Glaive Newra. That has subtle meaning to us. I understand the Newra part, but why Glaive, why a *sword*?"

"My father said that only two women had ev'r been faithful and true in his hour of need. His wife—mine mother—and his sword. When I was born he named me after his blade, and bade me to be straight and true."

"Aye, he has named you well. And straight and true you have cut to my soul and pierced my heart. You are my glaive, and I am your warrior. But I cannot grant your request, I cannot obey your command. Not now, much as I may desire it."

She looked bewildered as he continued. As if she couldn't believe that he was denying her.

"I cannot explain it, but only the concept of duty, the fulfillment of my oath to Constitution and Queen, only they can make all the blood right. If I'm not under authority, then I'm just another criminal, and the vilest of mass murderers at that. But I follow an oath. Would you really want a man who could lightly set aside his oath? Would your father really want such a man? I would not."

"Oh, Thomas," she said, tears beginning to well up in her eyes, "our nation is at war and we need thee. Just pledge thy sword! Pledge thy sword, and pledge that silver tongue of thine. Pledge it to my grandfather. And . . . to me," she added coyly through her tears. "And we shall take thee away from a lifetime of tramping across the galaxy, buying and selling, and give thee pride of place in a nation that honors its mighty warriors."

He held her hand tightly and felt his traitor voice quaver, as he took a deep breath and said, "Send my love and my friendship to your grandfather, and you *have* my love and my heart. But my tongue is my own, and my sword is pledged to *my* Queen. Your grandfather couldn't truly respect me if I broke my oath. I wouldn't be the man you want, I wouldn't be the man you love, if I were to do as you ask."

"My toungue is my ain," true Thomas he said;
"A goodly gift ye would give to me!"
"Now hold thy peace, Thomas," she said,
"For as I say, so must it be."

She smiled softly. O such a smile. It made his heart melt. "It is not over, dear Thomas. Thou shalt remember me, and thou shalt come back to me. I will call thee from across the galaxy, and thou shalt come. I have woven mine magic, the simple magic of a sincere woman's true love, and now thou art mine. *For as I say, so must it be.*"

"Aye," he said, and now it was his turn to reach out and stroke her face, striving to echo her gentleness with his rough hands, so calloused by sword, pistol and his Ship's rigging. "If it is within my power, I shall return. I'm not sure of the ending, but it will never be boring. I promise."

Chapter the 18th
Conclusion: The Dreamer

> Sentry pass him through!
> Drawbridge let fall, 'tis the Lord of us all,
> The Dreamer whose dreams come true!
>
> "The Fairies' Siege"
> Rudyard Kipling

After meeting with Princess Glaive in the Royal Glen, Melville went to the embassy to confer with Colonel Hayl. Now it was late in the day as he finally walked home. His guards were behind him. Ulrich was scowling along beside him.

His coxswain seemed to have been offended (perhaps mortified or humiliated would be a better word) at missing out on the gunfight against Aunt Madelia's goons. He seemed to be determined to make up for it, right *now,* by starting a fight with every individual who came down the street. If looks could incite a battle, then Ulrich would have completed an entire war by the time they got halfway back to the Ship.

The Ship. His Ship. *He* was going to take *his Ship* to the far side of the galaxy. Distant ports. Exotic lands. *Adventure!* And his princess waited for him.

Adventure before him, great deeds behind him, and love waiting patiently for him. What more could any man ask?

As he walked along through the Sylvan streets an overwhelming fit of random, senseless happiness came over him. There was a song in his heart and a bounce in his step. Far more of a bounce than could be explained by the light gravity. He was walking on air with the disgusted, scowling Ulrich serving as his anchor.

As they headed down the streets toward the Pier, Melville saw something strange in front of him. Later he felt guilty for thinking it, but in truth the very first thing he thought was that a skinny man was leading an ape by the hand.

Then he realized that it was Hans and Broadax, in civilian clothing, walking hand-in-hand down the street. The two crusty ex-NCOs—his sailing master and his marine lieutenant—were walking down the street holding hands, headed toward him. Again he was ashamed of himself, but he couldn't help a panicky initial inclination to duck down a side street and avoid the meeting. But it was too late; they saw him and waved.

He gulped, breathed, and tried not to change his pace as he walked toward them. Funny, when someone was watching you closely and you consciously *tried* to walk nonchalantly, it was almost impossible to do. "Conscious nonchalance" was probably an oxymoron, or at least damned difficult, and he suddenly felt very young and awkward as he approached them.

Their civilian clothing was in subtle disarray. Broadax was in a blue gingham dress (a *dress* by God!) and Hans wore denim pants and a red plaid shirt. Broadax was absent her helmet with her wiry hair in wild disorder, but she had her cigar in her mouth, puffing happily, and various lumps in her dress indicated that she was carrying her "cutlery" with her. There was also the distinct tinkle of her chainmail lingerie. Hans had a chaw of tobacco in his lip and a bulge that could only be a .45 ("*. . . or are you just happy to see me?*" said some uncontrollable, mischievous inner voice). Their monkeys lounged comfortably on their shoulders.

They also were obviously well lubricated by alcohol and . . . yes, apparently . . . love. Or a reasonable facsimile thereof . . .

My mistress' eyes are nothing like the sun;
Coral is far more red than her lips' red:

If snow be white, why then her breasts are dun;
If hairs be wires, black wires grow on her head.

As they drew to speaking distance, Hans wrapped his arm around Broadax (or kind of *down* and around) and caressed her. At least . . . that's what it might have been, Melville tried hard not to look. They were both grinning like fools, but this last action by Hans caused Broadax to giggle, exhaling a cloud of noxious cigar smoke.

I have seen roses damasked, red and white,
But no such roses see I in her cheeks;
And in some perfumes is there more delight
Than in the breath that from my mistress reeks.

Broadax.

Giggle.

Those two words didn't belong in the same sentence. Hell, they didn't belong in the same paragraph. Then Melville's stunned mind realized that Broadax had little blue gingham bows in her sparse, stringy beard.

"Evenin', Cap'n," said Hans pleasantly.

"Lieutenant Broadax, Mister Hans, good evening to you both." Then, taking the bull, or bulls, by the . . . horns, or whatever, Melville continued. "I see that you two have taken this opportunity to become friends . . . ?"

"Aye Cap'n," said Broadax jovially, in her gravelly voice. "Ye might say that." She laughed again, sounding like a foghorn, and Hans joined in with a hooting chuckle.

I love to hear her speak,—yet well I know
That music hath far more pleasing sound;
I grant I never saw a goddess go,—
My mistress when she walks, treads on the ground;

Thank God she didn't giggle again, thought Melville. He didn't think he could handle another giggle from her. He looked her up and down, or at least down and further down, and wondered what Hans saw.

"Aye, well I know you're both professionals, so . . . hopefully you'll keep it on shore."

"Oh, aye, Cap'n," Broadax said and they both seemed to sober up a little, "but we's both ossifers, so's it's okay, eh?"

Melville nodded. Fraternization between superiors and subordinate was forbidden, but it was permitted within the same ranks, off ship.

Hans continued, "Aye, so's we'll be gittin' while the gittin's gud! Heh heh. Good day to ya sur, an' God bless ya fer a hell of a damn fine cap'n, if'n I may say so."

"Aye," echoed Broadax, "Aye, by God ta that!"

Then with mutual nods they went their way. Melville looked over his shoulder and watched wonderingly as they walked away, holding each other tightly, finding a little bit of love in the midst of war and madness.

And yet, by heavens, I think my love as rare
As any she belied with false compare.

On his way up to his ship Melville saw the Honorable Cuthbert Asquith XVI pacing the pier next to *Fang*'s berth. He looked haggard and worn, and appeared as though he was going to approach Melville. Then he appeared to change his mind, and he spun away. Melville shook his head in bewilderment. The whole world was acting crazy today.

When Melville came aboard he had many things to deal with, and little time to dwell on his officers' antics ashore, or the bizarre behavior of an earthworm diplomat. A good portion of the crew was on shore leave, but his first officer was standing by. Melville grinned to himself as he realized that Fielder was unlikely to leave the ship again in this port. Melville called him into his cabin.

"Daniel, the Sylvans will come tomorrow to take two of the 24-pounders. Apparently they want to conduct research on them so they can start manufacturing their own 24-pounders. Do you suppose you 'manufacture' Keel charges?"

"Damned if I know, sir," Fielder replied pleasantly. "How the Keels are made is a deep dark secret of the Celebrimbor shipwrights. Whatever their reason, I guess this is the Sylvan's price for all the support they have given us."

"Aye. I do hate to give up the guns, but they promise to replace them with their finest 12-pounders. And, as you say, it's really a small price to pay for all that they have done for us. After that they'll give us the prize money. I want us to get underway after the crew has had one day on the town with their prize money. Hopefully they won't be able to fritter it all away in just one day. Also, coordinate for a Sylvan bank representative to be here when we pass out the prize money. We'll pressure the men to save some of their money in the bank."

"Aye, sir. Prize money," Fielder said with wonder and amazement. "Now *that* is a civilized way of saying 'thank you.' "

"For me the money's just a way of keeping score."

"Huh!" grunted Fielder in surprise, looking carefully at his young captain. He could actually say things like that with a straight face, and seemed to be truly sincere about it. Fielder realized that for Melville the glory was all that mattered, and prize money was a way to put numbers on glory. "Then the 'score' is, 'Us: a whole bunch. Every other ship in the whole damned Westerness and Sylvan Navies: zero.' Any way you cut it, it's damned good of them, and we're winning the game."

Then Melville dropped his bomb. "They also say that we can keep the Sylvan topmen, and that Lady Elphinstone and Ranger Valandil will continue to stay with us, as part of their exchange program."

"Well, I *will* be damned," replied Fielder, leaning forward and looking at Melville with a touch of wonder and suspicion. "I'd have thought that with the war coming on they could have found a better use for crack topmen, an elite ranger and a master surgeon. Sir, this is not a good sign if you ask me. It means that they still have plans for us, and if it's all the same to you I'd just as soon never again get involved in this crazy Two-Space War of theirs."

Melville smiled confidently as he said, "Well, Daniel, I'm not about to turn them down. And whether or not we see any more action depends on whether anyone attacks us, and on what Westerness decides to do about the war. Frankly, I don't see Westerness getting involved. Yet."

"Aye," Fielder agreed cautiously.

"Another matter we need to discuss," Melville continued, intentionally changing the subject, "is why the Honorable Cuthbert Asquith is pacing the docks below. What do you know about it?"

"Well, sir," said Fielder with an evil grin, "I got the inside intel on that. It seems that old Cuthbert has got himself in trouble with the Sylvan secret police."

"*Secret* police?"

"Aye, sir. The name doesn't translate all that well. You might call them the 'thought police,' or maybe the 'culture cops,' or the 'technology cops.' Whatever you want to call them, they're the tool the Sylvans have developed across the centuries to deal with agitators, innovators, and technological trouble makers. It appears that Asquith shot his mouth off, as he did with us, and was turned over to the tender mercies of the secret police. He has been released, but only under the condition that he leave on the next ship headed west. There is a high risk that the Guldur will attack any unescorted ships, so the Sylvan admiralty is organizing a convoy system, but it will be a week or so until the first convoy is escorted out. So it appears that *we* are the next ship out and he has a choice. He can come groveling back to us, eating dirt every step of the way. Or he can be picked up by the culture cops again."

They both smiled rather unpleasant smiles, as Melville reflected on Asquith's dilemma. Then he said, "Daniel, sooner or later, no matter what we do, Asquith *will* probably get back to Earth and give his report."

"Aye, sir," agreed Fielder. "Even the Sylvans appear to be reluctant to murder a citizen of Earth in cold blood, no matter how bad the provocation, or how terminal his stupidity. They might like to, but they'd never get away with it. I think that they honestly didn't *want* the king's guards to kill the Westerness ambassador. He just provoked some young hothead bodyguard too badly, and now the whole kingdom has to be on their best behavior."

"Yes," said Melville. "Like us, the Sylvans need all the goodwill they can get. Hopefully the Earth authorities know that Asquith is a fool and a twit, and releasing him will probably do *less* harm than killing him would. You know, maybe this is an opportunity for us to be his 'saviors.' People *do* grow, they do learn, and perhaps he has already been taught an important lesson by the Sylvans."

"I see where you're headed, sir. On the long voyage across the Grey Rift, perhaps the legendary 'Stockholm Syndrome' will set in, and we can win him over."

"Daniel, I know that you can be most genteel when you want to. I'd like for you to go talk to Asquith, tell him that just a simple apology will be accepted and all will be forgiven if he'll respect our culture and values. At best we might win him over a little, and at worst . . . well, at worst he can't say anything worse about us than he's probably already going to say."

"Aye," Fielder replied with an evil grin, "and without a shipload of passengers who might witness it, there is always the possibility that he might have an 'accident' this time."

"No, Daniel, I want to make it very clear that we don't want any of that. Earth will hire countless private investigators, bounty hunters and mercenaries to scour the galaxy and seek justice if one of their citizens disappears. We don't want any of that. Just talk to him. Turn on the charm and see if you can work it out."

"Aye, sir," his first officer replied with a wry grin. "While I'm gone, perhaps you can talk to Private Jarvis. His enlistment is up this week and he seems determined not to re-up. Everybody in his chain of command has talked to him. Perhaps you can change his mind."

"Okay, I'll give it a try. Send him in."

On his way out Fielder noticed that McAndrews, the captain's steward, had Melville's uniform jacket in his hand. He was shaking his head and muttering peevishly, "Don' know how I'm ever gonna get those grass stains out . . ." Melville just blushed slightly and tried to ignore him, as Fielder grinned evilly.

"I didn't become a marine for this. Not to go around killing people!"

"Perhaps you should have been a sailor instead." Melville chuckled, but it was clear that Private Harold Jarvis didn't see the humor in the situation.

"Sir, it's different for people like you and Lieutenant Broadax. You *like* combat, but I was scared to death every single time. I was *so* scared. And it hasn't gotten any better."

"Son, I can't speak for Broadax, but I hope you'll believe me if I tell you that I was scared to death every time. Only my training and my conditioning carried me through. Then, afterwards, when we had to bury shipmates . . ."

"Aye, sir."

"Jarvis, I know you want to go back to the farm. I understand. Your family comes from a planet with what, just a few dozen families?"

"Aye, sir. Fairhome. There's just a Pier and a couple of dozen homesteads. A Ship comes a couple of times a year. Other than that it's just us. It's a beautiful world, sir," and here the young, broad-shouldered farmboy's voice began to choke up a little. "Lord I miss it. The cry of the pixies at night, the sun coming up over the dewdab trees. It's a simple, quiet life. Everyone goes to bed with the chickens and gets up with the cows. . . ."

Melville paused briefly to dwell upon the dangers associated with a literal interpretation of a loosely worded saying. "Aye . . . Jarvis, you saw what the Guldur did to Ambergris. Would you say that they are evil? What they did there, in your opinion, was that evil?"

"Aye, sir. They were powerful bad. If ever the word evil ever deserved to be used, I reckon it deserves to be used on them."

"A very wise man once wrote that 'the only scientific definition of evil is that you can't ignore it.' We can't ignore them. We can't ignore the fact that there is evil in the universe, and *someone* has to man the ramparts of civilization so that our families can sleep safely in their beds."

"Aye, sir."

"What you saw happen in Ambergris, is that what you want for your homeworld? Most of the thousand worlds in the Westerness Kingdom are like that. We are a young kingdom, full of homestead worlds who are completely unable to defend themselves. If the Guldur come West across the Rift, then worlds like Earth can use their high technology to blast anything foolish enough to come down their Pier. And Westerness has a population base that could hold off the enemy for generations. But the only way we can keep *your* homeworld safe, the only way Fairhome and hundreds of other worlds like it can be truly safe, is to have professional warriors manning our frontiers. If there weren't men like you in our armed forces, if there weren't people willing to suffer and endure, then we would be doomed. It will be easier for you next time. But someone else, starting fresh, might die in a situation where you could survive."

"I understand that. I accept it. That's not the hard part. But sir, the part that bothers me is the lies. It's all a lie. The poetry and the glory and the honor, it's a lie. I've seen war, and it's not like that."

"No, my friend, it's not a lie," said Melville gently. "It's men making the best of a dirty, nasty job that *has* to be done. There are times when evil comes, when darkness falls, and good men must fight. Then we make a virtue of necessity. Pain shared is pain divided. Joy shared is joy multiplied. Every night around the campfire, or with our messmates over dinner, we talk about the battle. Each time we divide our pain and we multiply our joy. Until in the end we've turned combat into something we can live with, something we can keep on doing. It would be a lie if we completely forgot the pain, the suffering and the loss. But it's not a lie to recognize that there is good to be found in battle. And it's not a lie to focus on the good parts, to magnify the joy and divide the pain so that we can live with it. There is glory, if we give it to them. There is honor, if we honor those who do it. Sometimes wars have to be fought. It destroys enough, it harms enough *during* the war. It is foolishness, it is madness to let it destroy us *after* the war. So we turn it into something we can live with. And we turn ourselves into creatures who can do this dirty, desperate job, do it well, and live with ourselves afterward."

Jarvis nodded. He was a good troop; there was real potential here. He wasn't stupid, and he sincerely wanted to learn. He respected his captain, so he listened, truly *listened* as Melville continued.

"Very few of us can be Heinleiners all the time, although we strive for it and maybe we can have moments of courage, confidence and competence. And most of us won't be Cherryh's most of the time, living in a constant miasma of fear and tension. Most of us just get on with life, one day at a time."

Jarvis nodded again, still listening. He wasn't trying to think about what to say next, which is how most people spend a conversation. He just listened.

"You remember that Earthling, Asquith?"

"Aye, sir."

"He was giving our officers a hard time about our veneration of *The Lord of the Rings.* He asked, 'where are the Hobbits?' He didn't understand that *we* are the Hobbits. Few of us will be noble Striders, or magnificent Gandalfs. Those are goals to strive for, almost like angels. But most of us are less than the angels. We fall short, and are Hobbits.

"For me the Shire is the *real* world, full of soft, sleepy, unassuming souls who are capable of great deeds if pressed. And we are the Hobbits. We are Bilbos doing a desperate, dirty job out of a sense of responsibility, because if we didn't, then the job may not get done. Or we are a Samwise, bearing an unimaginably horrible burden out of love for our fellow warriors. Or we're Merrys and Pippins, silly fools who don't have a clue what they're getting into, but who grow into something noble and larger than life in the end."

Jarvis nodded thoughtfully. Melville put a hand on the young marine's shoulder as he concluded. "Just think about it. That's all I ask. No one will blame you if you leave; you have served honorably and well. But the 'Fellowship' calls to you," he said with a little, faintly self-mocking grin.

"Asquith apologized. He seemed relieved to do it. And he seemed sincerely surprised that that was all there was to it. That we honestly would accept him after that. I think he's beginning to understand that we don't expect him to change his opinions, just not force them on us. Maybe it will work out."

Melville was sitting in his cabin engaging in one of his hobbies when Fielder came in to report on his conversation with the earthworm. They were docked out at the end of the Pier, away from most of the other ships. Out the big stern window of his cabin there was nothing but the vast panorama of two-space. A target hung from a spar coming off the mizzenmast, dangling just outside the open window. Melville was sitting in his chair, with his back to the bulkhead and the window to his right. He was plinking out the window with his old double-barreled .45 pistol.

Melville had a steaming cup of tea in his left hand, and his pistol in the other. He was rocked back in his chair with his feet propped up on the table. "Well done, Daniel. Thank you for handling that."

"No problem."

"Would you like a cup of tea? Coffee perhaps?"

"Coffee would be good, thank you."

"McAndrews! Coffee for the first officer. You know how he likes it."

"Aye, sir," said his steward, who had been listening outside the door.

"You know, sir," said Fielder, "I've always wanted to try a few shots from that pistol of yours. May I?"

"Certainly," said Melville, pleased at his first mate's interest. "It's an old Colt. It's been in my family for centuries," he said as he handed it over, "and the Keel charge seems to be extra smart, like a wise old hound dog, except this dog never really grows old, he just gets better. The two of us have bonded pretty nicely."

Fielder squeezed off both barrels, <<Grrrr!>> "Crack!" <<Grrrr!>> "Crack!" making the target flip and spin.

"Sweet. Truly a sweet little pistol. Pretty *intense* little fellow too. I think I'll pick out one of the ship's pistols and make it my own, maybe pass it down through the generations."

"That's an excellent idea. Some of the ship's pistols are over a hundred years old, but they have never really bonded with anyone for long. It would be good to have a weapon that you're really comfortable with to use in two-space, just like you're comfortable with a .45 auto in three-space."

"Aye," Fielder replied with a grin, sitting down at the table and taking a cup of coffee from the steward as he bustled in. "There's *another* way that a handgun is better than a woman. You can have one handgun at home and another for the road," he said, grinning. "Mind if I try it again?"

"Certainly, be my guest," Melville replied as he passed a small pouch of bullets to the first officer.

"And there's one more advantage to a handgun," said Fielder as he loaded the pistol. "If you admire a friend's handgun and tell him so, he'll be pleased and let you try a few rounds with it."

Melville added, "*And*, a handgun doesn't take up a lot of closet space."

"That's the spirit, sir. I just wish I could convince old Hans of that," he said with what appeared to be a very sincere shudder.

"Oh. You heard about Hans' . . . girlfriend?"

"Aye. Oh, *aye*, sir. As Grandma BenGurata told me,

> "Don't sweat the petty things,
> and don't pet the sweaty things."

"Well," said Melville, searching for something appropriate to say, "what would we be without love?"

"Rare? Perhaps extinct?"

There was an awkward moment of silence as they considered each other. They were two very different men who had been tempered in battle and made old beyond their years. Yet in some ways they were strangely immature for men of their experience and position in life. If they weren't, they wouldn't be here. The truly mature man, the prudent man wouldn't be found sailing the galaxy in a fragile wooden vessel. Some men will remain forever young in their dreams and ambitions.

Melville decided to cut to the chase, and put it clearly and bluntly to Fielder as the first officer loaded the pistol. "Daniel, you have a choice. You can leave right now and possibly have a normal career, with hope of a command. Although just being associated with this ship may be an undying blot on your record. Or, you can continue to serve as first mate with me. They have officially blessed me as captain of this Ship, and I have the authority to offer you a permanent position as first mate, locked into this Ship, damned and cursed by the Admiralty for all eternity. Or until they change their minds."

Fielder scowled, sighted the pistol, and fired two shots, <<Grrrr!>> "Crack!" <<Grrrr!>> "Crack!"

Then he replied, setting the pistol on the table as the target spun, "Frankly . . . if I may speak frankly, sir?" Melville nodded and Fielder continued, "Frankly, sir, I think you're one wave short of a shipwreck. The contact you've had with these alien minds—the Ship and the 24-pounders—it's changed you. I'm not at all sure how it's going to turn out. And," he added cautiously, "—again, no offense intended—you were never wrapped too tight in the first place. The end result appears to be a weird mix of brilliance, paranoia, and murderous ferocity all in the same person. But your brilliance and paranoia has kept us alive, and your ferocity is focused solely on the enemy."

His scowl disappeared, and he continued, thoughtfully, "So I think I'll follow you. Perhaps out of self interest. Perhaps out of idle curiosity," he added with a microscopic, sardonic grin that took some of the bitterness out. "For whatever reason, I'll stay *if you'll have me.* My question is, though, why would you want me? Why not be rid of me while you have the chance?"

"I guess you're my anchor, Daniel. I feel myself slipping . . . away, sometimes, a little. You, Broadax, Hans, Elphinstone, and all the rest are my anchors, my link to humanity. We may not always like each other, but we do balance each other out. We have become bonded in battle, and only that forge is hot enough to do such work."

"I look at it like this," Fielder said, looking off into the distance reflectively as he loaded the pistol. "*Every* man is the 'hero' in his own 'novel.' In war there are a thousand 'novels,' no, ten thousand, a hundred thousand, that all turn into sad little unpublished short stories. Many end with the early, obscure, pointless death of the 'hero.' That's the reality of life. I was lucky enough to play a part in a story where the hero overcame long odds. If I were the senior officer we'd all have died. But you were in command, and we lived. And so I choose to finish the book. I choose to follow you. You're good with poetry, sir. But two can play that game, and I think I found one that applies here." Then he continued, with his usual sardonic smile,

"I have been given my charge to keep—
Well have I kept the same!
Playing with strife for the most of my life,
But this is a different game.
I'll not fight against swords unseen,
Or spears that I cannot view—
Hand him the keys of the place on your knees—
'Tis the Dreamer whose dreams come true!

"Ask him his terms and accept them at once.
Quick, ere we anger him, go!
Never before have I flinched from the guns,
But this is a different show.
I'll not fight with the Herald of God.
(I know what his Master can do!)
Open the gate, he must enter in state,
'Tis the Dreamer whose dreams come true!

"I'd not give way for an Emperor,
I'd hold my road for a King—
To the Triple Crown I would not bow down—
But this is a different thing.
I'll not fight with the Powers of Air,
Sentry pass him through!
Drawbridge let fall, 'tis the Lord of us all,
The Dreamer whose dreams come true!"

Melville laughed in sheer delight to hear Fielder wield poetry on *him*. The first officer was, as usual, half mocking and half flattering, and always clever.

"We are destined to the back of beyond," Fielder continued, "where there is no possible duty but mail delivery and a lifetime of carrying borderline cargos. But I will follow. We may have a long dull life in front of us, but at least we have a life, and the story will continue. I've always hated short stories, and I've always had a soft spot for a good series."

And it will get you away from that crazy Sylvan ex-girlfriend of yours, thought Melville with a knowing smile. "Daniel, we are headed out to the frontier," he said, leaning forward intently. "The *frontier*. The wildest, most unknown, exotic part of the galaxy. We *will* find adventure and glory there!"

"Damn. I was afraid of that."

There, there was that grin again.

After Fielder left, Melville sat in his cabin, looking out the stern windows at the wonder of Flatland spreading out before him and the brilliant, vivid stars strewn above him. He had one hand on his dog, scratching behind its ear, and one hand on the white, Moss-coated bulkhead, faintly in commo with his ship. His monkey and his dog's monkey were in the corner chittering to each other and assiduously hunting down some poor, tormented vermin.

He shook his head in wonder, still thinking about Hans and Broadax. *To each his own*, he thought. The contented panting of his dog blended into his mind, echoing in perfect harmony with the contentment he felt coming from his ship. *To each his own. As for me . . .*

I must down to the seas again, to the lonely sea
and the sky,
And all I ask is a tall ship and a star to steer her by,
And the wheel's kick and the wind's song
and the white sail's shaking,
And a gray mist on the sea's face and a
gray dawn breaking.

I must down to the sea again, for the call of the
running tide

Is a wild call and a clear call that must not
be denied;
And all I ask is a merry yarn from a laughing
fellow-rover,
And quiet sleep and a sweet dream when the
long trick's over.

Poetry References

Chapter 1:
An orphan's curse would drag to hell . . .
"The Rime of the Ancient Mariner," Samuel Taylor Coleridge

Chapter 2:
The fighting man shall take from the sun . . .
(and following stanzas)
"Into Battle," Julian Grenfell
I never shall forget the way . . .
"The Modern Traveler," Hilaire Belloc

Chapter 3:
. . . The burning sun no more shall heat . . .
"As Weary Pilgrim," Anne Bradstreet

Chapter 4:
Here dead lie we because we did not chose . . .
"Here Dead Lie We," A.E. Housman
There's a land that is fairer than day . . .
"Sweet By and By," S.F. Bennett and J.P. Webster
High in the wreck I held the cup . . .
"The Deluge," G.K. Chesterton
. . . Kilmeny had been where the cock never crew . . .
"Kilmeny," James Hogg
Read here the moral roundly writ . . .
"Boxing," from "Verses on Games," Rudyard Kipling
We are the Dead. Short days ago . . .
"In Flanders Field," John McCrae

I've lived a life of sturt and strife . . .
"MacPherson's Farewell," Robert Burns

Soft as the voice of an angel . . .
"Whispering Hope," Septimus Winner

Oh yesterday our little troop was ridden through and through . . .
"To-morrow," John Masefield

Chapter 5:

Biding God's pleasure and their chief's command . . .
"The Birkenhead," Sir Henry Yule

But now ye wait at Hell-Mouth Gate and not in Berkely Square . . .
"Tomlinson," Rudyard Kipling

Chapter 6:

Quoth he, "The she-wolf's litter . . ."
"Horatius," Lord Macaulay

And out the red blood spouted . . .
"The Battle of Lake Regillus," Lord Macaulay

I shall not die alone, alone, but kin to all the powers . . .
(and following couplets)
"The Last Hero," G.K. Chesterton

Through teeth, and skull, and helmet . . .
"Horatius," Lord Macaulay

Chapter 7:

A child said *What is the grass?* . . .
"Song of Myself," Walt Whitman

Too delicate is flesh to be . . .
"The Debt," E.V. Lucas

Was there love once? I have forgotten her . . .
(and following four stanzas)
"Fulfillment," Robert Nichols

For, alas, alas, with me . . .
"To One in Paradise," E.A. Poe

Chapter 8:

Around no fire the soldiers sleep to-night . . .
(and following stanza)
"The Battlefield," Sydney Oswald

When first I saw you in the curious street . . .
"German Prisoners," Joseph Lee

The recipe for "Thrice Cooked Javalina Brains," and the story about "Major" are from the wonderful (and highly recommended) book, *The Contented Poacher's Epicurean Odyssey*, by Elantu Viovodi, with the author's gracious permission.

Bind her, grind her, burn her with fire . . .

"A Chant of Love for England," Helen Gray Cone

Chapter 9:

Big bugs have little bugs . . .

Originally by Jonathan Swift, then modified by Ogden Nash and anon.

Burned from the ore's rejected dross . . .

"The Anvil," Laurence Binyon

All that is gold does not glitter . . .

From *The Fellowship of the Ring*, J.R.R. Tolkien,

The fewer men, the greater share of honour . . .

From *Henry V*, Shakespeare

A thousand shapes of death surround us . . .

The Iliad, Book 12, Homer

Chapter 10:

Shall I retreat from him, from clash of combat . . .

The Iliad, Book 18, Homer

She reached our range. Our broadside rang . . .

(and following stanzas)

"On Board the *Cumberland*" George H. Boker

Then the dead men fouled the scuppers and the wounded filled the chains . . .

"The Ballad of John Silver," John Masefield

No heed he gave to the flying ball . . .

"The Sword-Bearer," George H. Boker

Victory! Victory! . . .

"Boy Brittan," Forceythe Willson

Chapter 11:

He said: "Thou petty people, let me pass . . .

"The Kaiser and Belgium," Stephen Phillips

Efficient, thorough, strong, and brave—his vision is to kill . . .

"The Superman," Robert Grant

Hark, hark, the dogs do bark . . .

"Mother Goose", anon.

All other stanzas are from Service's "The Call"

Chapter 12:
A hundred thousand fighting men . . .
(and following stanzas)
"The Battle of Liège," Dana Burnet
Three hundred thousand men, but not enough . . .
(and following stanza)
"Verdun," Eden Phillpotts

Chapter 13:
All drawn from "A Consecration," John Masefield

Chapter 14:
All drawn from "Once to Every Man and Nation," James Russell Lowell

Chapter 16:
Was a lady such a lady, cheeks so round and lips so red . . .
"A Toccatta of Galuppi's," Robert Browning
You meaner beauties of the night . . .
"Elizabeth of Bohemia," Sir Henry Wotton

Chapter 17:
True Thomas lay on Huntlie bank . . .
(and following stanzas)
"True Thomas," anon.
Some text has been derived from a poem entitled, "The Warrior and the Lady," by Billy Martin, copyright 2001, with the author's gracious permission.

Chapter 18:
My mistress' eyes are nothing like the sun . . .
"Sonnet CXXX," Shakespeare
I have been given my charge to keep . . .
"The Fairies' Siege," Rudyard Kipling
I must down to the seas again, to the lonely sea and the sky . . .
"Sea Fever," John Masefield